FALLEN

LAUREN KATE

CORGI BOOKS

FALLEN
A CORGI BOOK 978 0 552 56749 7

First published in Great Britain by Doubleday Books,
an imprint of Random House Children's Publishers UK
A Random House Group Company

Doubleday edition published 2009
Corgi edition published 2010

This edition exclusive to WHSmith 2012

1 3 5 7 9 10 8 6 4 2

The Random House Group Limited supports the Forest Stewardship Council (FSC®),
the leading international forest certification organization. Our books carrying the
FSC label are printed on FSC®-certified paper. FSC is the only forest certification
scheme endorsed by the leading environmental organizations, including
Greenpeace. Our paper procurement policy can be found at
www.randomhouse.co.uk/environment.

Corgi Books are published by Random House Children's Publishers UK,
61–63 Uxbridge Road, London W5 5SA

www.randomhousechildrens.co.uk
www.totallyrandombooks.co.uk
www.randomhouse.co.uk

Addresses for companies within The Random House Group Limited
can be found at: www.randomhouse.co.uk/offices.htm

THE RANDOM HOUSE GROUP Limited Reg. No. 954009

A CIP catalogue record for this book is available from the British Library.

Printed and bound by CPI Group (UK) Ltd, Croydon, CR0 4YY

PRAISE FOR FALLEN
BY LAUREN KATE

'dark and romantic, an absolute
blinder of a book' *Sun*

'Sexy, fascinating and scary'
P.C. Cast, author of the *House of Night* series

'...ully gripping love story'
Bliss

'a gothic love story featuring fallen angels and forbidden
love (a winning formula) that will thrill and delight
in equal measure' *Fantasy Book Review*

'a seriously excellent book'
The Bookbag

'a compelling dark and sexy page turner'
Chicklish

AND FROM HER FANS…

'a piece of genius' *Hayley*

'these books are going to bury vampires
six feet under' *Abbigale*

'this book is just as good as Twilight,
if not better' *Taunya*

'An amazingly beautiful book that I felt
privileged just to read' *Jennifer*

www.fallenbooks.co.uk

Also by Lauren Kate:

FALLEN

TORMENT

PASSION

RAPTURE

FALLEN IN LOVE

THE BETRAYAL OF
NATALIE HARGROVE

FOR MY FAMILY,

WITH GRATITUDE AND LOVE

ACKNOWLEDGMENTS

Enormous thanks to everyone at Random House and Delacorte Press for doing so much so quickly and so well. To Wendy Loggia, whose easy generosity and enthusiasm have spurred me on from the beginning. To Krista Vitola, for a hugely helpful behind-the-scenes job. To Brenda Schildgen at UC Davis, for the background and inspiration. To Nadia Cornier, for helping get this whole thing off the ground. To Ted Malawer, for his sharp, graceful, and funny editorial guidance. To Michael Stearns, former boss-man, now trusted colleague and friend. You are, simply, a genius.

To my parents; my grandparents; Robby, Kim, and Jordan; and my new family in Arkansas. Words fail when I think of your unwavering support. I love you all.

And to Jason, who talks to me about characters as if they are real people until I can figure them out. You inspire me, you challenge me, you make me laugh every day. You have my heart.

But paradise is locked and bolted. . . .

We must make a journey around the world

to see if a back door has perhaps been left open.

—HEINRICH VON KLEIST, *"On the Puppet Theater"*

IN THE BEGINNING

HELSTON, ENGLAND

SEPTEMBER 1854

Around midnight, her eyes at last took shape. The look in them was feline, half determined and half tentative—all trouble. Yes, they were just right, those eyes. Rising up to her fine, elegant brow, inches from the dark cascade of her hair.

He held the paper at arm's length to assess his progress. It was hard, working without her in front of him, but then, he never could sketch in her presence. Since he had arrived from London—no, since he had first seen her—he'd had to be careful always to keep her at a distance.

Every day now she approached him, and every day was more difficult than the one before. It was why he was leaving in the morning—for India, for the Americas, he didn't know or care. Wherever he ended up, it would be easier than being here.

He leaned over the drawing again, sighing as he used his thumb to perfect the smudged charcoal pout of her full bottom lip. This lifeless paper, cruel imposter, was the only way to take her with him.

Then, straightening up in the leather library chair, he felt it. That brush of warmth on the back of his neck.

Her.

Her mere proximity gave him the most peculiar sensation, like the kind of heat sent out when a log shatters to ash in a fire. He knew without turning around: She was there. He covered her likeness on the bound papers in his lap, but he could not escape her.

His eyes fell on the ivory-upholstered settee across the parlor, where only hours earlier she'd turned up unexpectedly, later than the rest of her party, in a rose silk gown, to applaud the eldest daughter of their host after a fine turn at the harpsichord. He glanced across the room, out the window to the veranda, where the day before she'd crept up on him, a fistful of wild white peonies in her hand. She still thought the pull she felt toward him was innocent, that their frequent rendezvous in the gazebo were merely . . . happy coincidences. To be so naïve! He would never tell her otherwise—the secret was his to bear.

He stood and turned, the sketches left behind on the leather chair. And there she was, pressed against the ruby velvet curtain in her plain white dressing gown. Her black hair had fallen from its braid. The look on her face was the same as the one he'd sketched so many times. There was the fire, rising in her cheeks. Was she angry? Embarrassed? He longed to know, but could not allow himself to ask.

"What are you doing here?" He could hear the snarl in his voice, and regretted its sharpness, knowing she would never understand.

"I—I couldn't sleep," she stammered, moving toward the fire and his chair. "I saw the light in your room and then"—she paused, looking down at her hands—"your trunk outside the door. Are you going somewhere?"

"I was going to tell you—" He broke off. He shouldn't lie. He had never intended to let her know his plans. Telling her would only make things worse. Already, he had let things go too far, hoping this time would be different.

She drew nearer, and her eyes fell on his sketchbook. "You were drawing me?"

Her startled tone reminded him how great the gap was in their understanding. Even after all the time they'd spent together these past few weeks, she had not yet begun to glimpse the truth that lay behind their attraction.

This was good—or at least, it was for the better. For the past several days, since he'd made the choice to leave, he'd been struggling to pull away from her. The effort took so much out of him that, as soon as he was alone, he had to give in to his pent-up desire to draw her. He had filled up his book with pages of her arched neck, her marble collarbone, the black abyss of her hair.

Now, he looked back at the sketch, not ashamed at being caught drawing her, but worse. A cold chill spread through him as he realized that her discovery—the exposure of his feelings—would destroy her. He should have been more careful. It always began like this.

"Warm milk with a spoonful of treacle," he murmured, his back still to her. Then he added sadly, "It helps you sleep."

"How did you know? Why, that's exactly what my mother used to—"

"I know," he said, turning to face her. The astonishment in her voice did not surprise him, yet he could not explain to her how he knew, or tell her how many times he had administered this very drink to her in the past when the shadows came, how he had held her until she fell asleep.

He felt her touch as though it were burning through his shirt, her hand laid gently on his shoulder, causing him to gasp. They had not yet touched in this life, and the first contact always left him breathless.

"Answer me," she whispered. "Are you leaving?"

"Yes."

"Then take me with you," she blurted out. Right on cue, he watched her suck in her breath, wishing to take back her plea. He could see the progression of her emotions settle in the crease between her eyes: She would feel impetuous, then bewildered, then ashamed by her own forwardness. She always did this, and too many times before, he had made the mistake of comforting her at this exact moment.

"No," he whispered, remembering . . . always remembering. . . . "I sail tomorrow. If you care for me at all, you won't say another word."

"*If* I care for you," she repeated, almost as if she were speaking to herself. "I—I *love*—"

"Don't."

"I have to say it. I—I love you, I'm quite sure, and if you leave—"

"If I leave, I save your life." He spoke slowly, trying to reach a part of her that might remember. Was it there at all, buried somewhere? "Some things are more important than love. You won't understand, but you have to trust me."

Her eyes drilled into him. She stepped back and crossed her arms over her chest. This was his fault, too—he always brought out her contemptuous side when he spoke down to her.

"You mean to say there are things more important than this?" she challenged, taking his hands and drawing them to her heart.

Oh, to be her and not know what was coming! Or at least to be stronger than he was and be able to stop her. If he didn't stop her, she would never learn, and the past would only repeat itself, torturing them both again and again.

The familiar warmth of her skin under his hands made him tilt his head back and moan. He was trying to ignore how close she was, how well he knew the feel of her lips on his, how bitter he felt that all of this had to end. But her fingers traced his so lightly. He could feel her heart racing through her thin cotton gown.

She was right. There was nothing more than this. There never was. He was about to give in and take her in his arms when he caught the look in her eyes. As if she'd seen a ghost.

She was the one to pull away, a hand to her forehead.

"I'm having the strangest sensation," she whispered.

No—was it already too late?

Her eyes narrowed into the shape in his sketch and she came back to him, her hands on his chest, her lips parted expectantly. "Tell me I'm mad, but I swear I've been right here before. . . ."

So it *was* too late. He looked up, shivering, and could feel the dark descending. He took one last chance to seize her, to hold her as tightly as he'd been yearning to for weeks.

As soon as her lips melted into his, both of them were powerless. The honeysuckle taste of her mouth made him dizzy. The closer she pressed against him, the more his stomach churned with the thrill and the agony of it all. Her tongue traced his, and the fire between them burned brighter, hotter, more powerful with every new touch, every new exploration. Yet none of it was new.

The room quaked. An aura around them started to glow.

She noticed nothing, was aware of nothing, understood nothing besides their kiss.

He alone knew what was about to happen, what dark companions were prepared to fall on their reunion. Even though he was unable to alter the course of their lives yet again, he knew.

The shadows swirled directly overhead. So close, he might have touched them. So close, he wondered whether she could hear what they were whispering. He watched as the cloud passed over her face. For a moment he saw a spark of recognition growing in her eyes.

Then there was nothing, nothing at all.

ONE

PERFECT STRANGERS

Luce barged into the fluorescent-lit lobby of the Sword &
Cross School ten minutes later than she should have. A
barrel-chested attendant with ruddy cheeks and a clipboard
clamped under an iron bicep was already giving orders—
which meant Luce was already behind.

"So remember, it's meds, beds, and reds," the attendant barked at a cluster of three other students all standing with their backs to Luce. "Remember the basics and
no one gets hurt."

Luce hurried to slip in behind the group. She was still trying to figure out whether she'd filled out the giant stack of paperwork correctly, whether this shaven-headed guide standing before them was a man or a woman, whether there was anyone to help her with this enormous duffel bag, whether her parents were going to get rid of her beloved Plymouth Fury the minute they arrived home from dropping her off here. They'd been threatening to sell the car all summer, and now they had a reason even Luce couldn't argue with: No one was allowed to have a car at Luce's new school. Her new *reform* school, to be precise.

She was still getting used to the term.

"Could you, uh, could you repeat that?" she asked the attendant. "What was it, meds—?"

"Well, look what the storm blew in," the attendant said loudly, then continued, enunciating slowly: "*Meds.* If you're one of the medicated students, this is where you go to keep yourself doped up, sane, breathing, whatever." *Woman,* Luce decided, studying the attendant. No man would be catty enough to say all that in such a saccharine tone of voice.

"Got it." Luce felt her stomach heave. "Meds."

She'd been off meds for years now. After the accident this past summer, Dr. Sanford, her specialist in Hopkinton—and the reason her parents had sent her to boarding school all the way in New Hampshire—had wanted to consider medicating her again. Though she'd finally convinced him of her quasi-stability, it had taken an extra month of analysis on her part just to stay off those awful antipsychotics.

Which was why she was enrolling in her senior year at Sword & Cross a full month after the academic year had begun. Being a new student was bad enough, and Luce had been really nervous about having to jump into classes where everyone else was already settled. But from the looks of this tour, she wasn't the only new kid arriving today.

She sneaked a peek at the three other students standing in a half circle around her. At her last school, Dover Prep, the campus tour on the first day was where she'd met her best friend, Callie. On a campus where all the other students had practically been weaned together, it would have been enough that Luce and Callie were the only non-legacy kids. But it didn't take long for the two girls to realize they also had the exact same obsession with the exact same old movies—especially where Albert Finney was concerned. After their discovery freshman year while watching *Two for the Road* that neither one of them could make a bag of popcorn without setting off the fire alarm, Callie and Luce hadn't left each other's sides. Until . . . until they'd had to.

At Luce's sides today were two boys and a girl. The girl seemed easy enough to figure out, blond and

Neutrogena-commercial pretty, with pastel pink mani-cured nails that matched her plastic binder.

"I'm Gabbe," she drawled, flashing Luce a big smile that disappeared as quickly as it had surfaced, before Luce could even offer her own name. The girl's waning interest reminded her more of a southern version of the girls at Dover than someone she'd expect at Sword & Cross. Luce couldn't decide whether this was comforting or not, any more than she could imagine what a girl who looked like this would be doing at reform school.

To Luce's right was a guy with short brown hair, brown eyes, and a smattering of freckles across his nose. But the way he wouldn't even meet her eyes, just kept picking at a hangnail on his thumb, gave Luce the im-pression that, like her, he was probably still stunned and embarrassed to find himself here.

The guy to her left, on the other hand, fit Luce's im-age of this place a little bit too perfectly. He was tall and thin, with a DJ bag slung over his shoulder, shaggy black hair, and large, deep-set green eyes. His lips were full and a natural rose color most girls would kill for. At the back of his neck, a black tattoo in the shape of a sunburst seemed almost to glow on his light skin, rising up from the edge of his black T-shirt.

Unlike the other two, when this guy turned to meet her gaze, he held it and didn't let go. His mouth was set in a straight line, but his eyes were warm and alive. He gazed at her, standing as still as a sculpture, which made Luce feel rooted to her spot, too. She sucked in her breath. Those eyes were intense, and alluring, and, well, a little bit disarming.

With some loud throat-clearing noises, the attendant interrupted the boy's trancelike stare. Luce blushed and pretended to be very busy scratching her head.

"Those of you who've learned the ropes are free to go after you dump your hazards." The attendant gestured at a large cardboard box under a sign that said in big black letters PROHIBITED MATERIALS. "And when I say *free*, Todd"—she clamped a hand down on the freckled kid's shoulder, making him jump—"I mean gymnasium-bound to meet your preassigned student guides. You"—she pointed at Luce—"dump your hazards and stay with me."

The four of them shuffled toward the box and Luce watched, baffled, as the other students began to empty their pockets. The girl pulled out a three-inch pink Swiss Army knife. The green-eyed guy reluctantly dumped a can of spray paint and a box cutter. Even the hapless Todd let loose several books of matches and a small container of lighter fluid. Luce felt almost stupid that she wasn't concealing a hazard of her own—but when she saw the other kids reach into their pockets and chuck their cell phones into the box, she gulped.

Leaning forward to read the PROHIBITED MATERIALS

sign a little more closely, she saw that cell phones, pagers, and all two-way radio devices were strictly forbidden. It was bad enough that she couldn't have her car! Luce clamped a sweaty hand around the cell phone in her pocket, her only connection to the outside world. When the attendant saw the look on her face, Luce received a few quick slaps on the cheek. "Don't swoon on me, kid, they don't pay me enough to resuscitate. Besides, you get one phone call once a week in the main lobby."

One phone call . . . once a week? But—

She looked down at her phone one last time and saw that she'd received two new text messages. It didn't seem possible that these would be her two *last* text messages. The first one was from Callie.

Call immediately! Will be waiting by the phone all nite so be ready to dish. And remember the mantra I assigned you. You'll survive! BTW, for what it's worth, I think everyone's totally forgotten about . . .

In typical Callie fashion, she'd gone on so long that Luce's crap cell phone cut the message off four lines in. In a way, Luce was almost relieved. She didn't want to read about how everyone from her old school had already forgotten what had happened to her, what she'd done to land herself in *this* place.

She sighed and scrolled down to her second message. It was from her mom, who'd only just gotten the hang of texting a few weeks ago, and who surely had not known about this one-call-once-a-week thing or she would never have abandoned her daughter here. Right?

Kiddo, we are always thinking of you. Be good and try to eat enough protein. We'll talk when we can. Love, M&D

With a sigh, Luce realized her parents must have known. How else to explain their drawn faces when she'd waved goodbye at the school gates this morning, duffel bag in hand? At breakfast, she'd tried to joke about finally losing that appalling New England accent she'd picked up at Dover, but her parents hadn't even cracked a smile. She'd thought they were still mad at her. They never did the whole raising-their-voice thing, which meant that when Luce really messed up, they just gave her the old silent treatment. Now she understood this morning's strange demeanor: Her parents were already mourning the loss of contact with their only daughter.

"We're still waiting on one person," the attendant sang. "I wonder who it is." Luce's attention snapped back to the Hazard Box, which was now brimming with contraband she didn't even recognize. She could feel the dark-haired boy's green eyes staring at her. She looked up and noticed that *everyone* was staring. Her turn. She closed her eyes and slowly opened her fingers, letting her phone slip from her grasp and land with a sad *thunk* on top of the heap. The sound of being all alone.

Todd and the fembot Gabbe headed for the door without so much as a look in Luce's direction, but the third boy turned to the attendant.

"I can fill her in," he said, nodding at Luce.

"Not part of our deal," the attendant replied automatically, as if she'd been expecting this dialogue. "You're a new student again—that means new-student restrictions. Back to square one. You don't like it, you should have thought twice before breaking parole."

The boy stood motionless, expressionless, as the attendant tugged Luce—who'd stiffened at the word "parole"—toward the end of a yellowed hall.

"Moving on," she said, as if nothing had just happened. "Beds." She pointed out the west-facing window to a distant cinder-block building. Luce could see Gabbe and Todd shuffling slowly toward them, with the third boy walking slowly, as if catching up to them were the last thing on his list of things to do.

The dorm was formidable and square, a solid gray block of a building whose thick double doors gave away nothing about the possibility of life inside them. A large stone plaque stood planted in the middle of the dead lawn, and Luce remembered from the Web site the words PAULINE DORMITORY chiseled into it. It looked even uglier in the hazy morning sun than it had looked in the flat black-and-white photograph.

Even from this distance, Luce could see black mold covering the face of the dorm. All the windows were obstructed by rows of thick steel bars. She squinted. Was that barbed wire topping the fence around the building?

The attendant looked down at a chart, flipping through Luce's file. "Room sixty-three. Throw your bag in my office with the rest of them for now. You can unpack this afternoon."

Luce dragged her red duffel bag toward three other nondescript black trunks. Then she reached reflexively for her cell phone, where she usually keyed in things she needed to remember. But as her hand searched her empty pocket, she sighed and committed the room number to memory instead.

She still didn't see why she couldn't just stay with her parents; their house in Thunderbolt was less than a half hour from Sword & Cross. It had felt so good to be back home in Savannah, where, as her mom always said, even the wind blew lazily. Georgia's softer, slower pace suited Luce way more than New England ever had.

But Sword & Cross didn't feel like Savannah. It hardly felt like anywhere at all, except the lifeless, colorless place where the court had mandated she board.

She'd overheard her dad on the phone with the headmaster the other day, nodding in his befuddled biology-professor way and saying, "Yes, yes, maybe it would be best for her to be supervised all the time. No, no, we wouldn't want to interfere with your system."

Clearly her father had not seen the conditions of his only daughter's supervision. This place looked like a maximum-security prison.

"And what about, what did you say—the reds?" Luce asked the attendant, ready to be released from the tour.

"Reds," the attendant said, pointing toward a small wired device hanging from the ceiling: a lens with a flashing red light. Luce hadn't seen it before, but as soon as the attendant pointed the first one out, she realized they were everywhere.

"Cameras?"

"Very good," the attendant said, voice dripping condescension. "We make them obvious in order to remind you. All the time, everywhere, we're watching you. So don't screw up—that is, if you can help yourself."

Every time someone talked to Luce like she was a total psychopath, she came that much closer to believing it was true.

All summer, the memories had haunted her, in her dreams and in the rare moments her parents left her alone. *Something* had happened in that cabin, and everyone (including Luce) was dying to know exactly what.

The police, the judge, the social worker had all tried to pry the truth out of her, but she was as clueless about it all as they were. She and Trevor had been joking around the whole evening, chasing each other down to the row of cabins on the lake, away from the rest of the party. She'd tried to explain that it had been one of the best nights of her life, until it turned into the worst.

She'd spent so much time replaying that night in her head, hearing Trevor's laugh, feeling his hands close around her waist, and trying to reconcile her gut instinct that she really was innocent.

But now, every rule and regulation at Sword & Cross seemed to work against that notion, seemed to suggest that she was, in fact, dangerous and needed to be controlled.

Luce felt a firm hand on her shoulder.

"Look," the attendant said. "If it makes you feel any better, you're far from the worst case here."

It was the first humane gesture the attendant had made toward Luce, and she believed that it *was* intended to make her feel better. But. She'd been sent here because of the suspicious death of the guy she'd been crazy about, and *still* she was "far from the worst case here"? Luce wondered what else exactly they were dealing with at Sword & Cross.

"Okay, orientation's over," the attendant said. "You're on your own now. Here's a map if you need to find anything else." She gave Luce a photocopy of a crude hand-drawn map, then glanced at her watch. "You've got an hour before your first class, but my soaps come on in five, so"—she waved her hand at Luce— "make yourself scarce. And don't forget," she said, pointing up at the cameras one last time. "The reds are watching you."

Before Luce could reply, a skinny, dark-haired girl appeared in front of her, wagging her long fingers in Luce's face.

"Ooooooh," the girl taunted in a ghost-story-telling voice, dancing around Luce in a circle. "The reds are watching youuuu."

"Get out of here, Arriane, before I have you lobotomized," the attendant said, though it was clear from her first brief but genuine smile that she had some coarse affection for the crazy girl.

It was also clear that Arriane did not reciprocate the love. She mimed a jerking-off motion at the attendant, then stared at Luce, daring her to be offended.

"And just for that," the attendant said, jotting a furious note in her book, "you've earned yourself the task of showing Little Miss Sunshine around today."

She pointed at Luce, who looked anything but sunny in her black jeans, black boots, and black top. Under the "Dress Code" section, the Sword & Cross Web site had cheerily maintained that as long as the students were on good behavior, they were free to dress as they pleased, with just two small stipulations: style must be modest and color must be black. Some freedom.

The too-big mock turtleneck Luce's mom had forced on her this morning did nothing for her curves, and even her best feature was gone: Her thick black hair, which used to hang down to her waist, had been almost completely shorn off. The cabin fire had left her scalp singed and her hairline patchy, so after the long, silent ride home from Dover, Mom had planted Luce in the bathtub, brought out Dad's electric razor, and wordlessly shaved her head. Over the summer, her hair had grown out a little, just enough so that her once-enviable waves now hovered in awkward twists just below her ears.

Arriane sized her up, tapping one finger against her pale lips. "Perfect," she said, stepping forward to loop her arm through Luce's. "I was just thinking I could really use a new slave."

The door to the lobby swung open and in walked the tall kid with green eyes. He shook his head and said to Luce, "This place isn't afraid to do a strip search. So if you're packing any other *hazards*"—he raised an eyebrow and dumped a handful of unrecognizables in the box—"save yourself the trouble."

Behind Luce, Arriane laughed under her breath. The boy's head shot up, and when his eyes registered Arriane, he opened his mouth, then closed it, like he was unsure how to proceed.

"Arriane," he said evenly.

"Cam," she returned.

"You know him?" Luce whispered, wondering whether there were the same kinds of cliques in reform schools as there were in prep schools like Dover.

"Don't remind me," Arriane said, dragging Luce out the door into the gray and swampy morning.

The back of the main building let out onto a chipped sidewalk bordering a messy field. The grass was so overgrown, it looked more like a vacant lot than a school commons, but a faded scoreboard and a small stack of wooden bleachers argued otherwise.

Beyond the commons lay four severe-looking buildings: the cinder-block dormitory on the far left, a huge old ugly church on the far right, and two other expansive structures in between that Luce imagined were the classrooms.

This was it. Her whole world was reduced to the sorry sight before her eyes.

Arriane immediately veered right off the path and led Luce to the field, sitting her down on top of one of the waterlogged wooden bleachers.

The corresponding setup at Dover had screamed Ivy League jock-in-training, so Luce had always avoided hanging out there. But this empty field, with its rusted, warped goals, told a very different story. One that wasn't as easy for Luce to figure out. Three turkey vultures swooped overhead, and a dismal wind whipped through the bare branches of the oak trees. Luce ducked her chin down into her mock turtleneck.

"Soooo," Arriane said. "Now you've met Randy."

"I thought his name was Cam."

"We're not talking about him," Arriane said quickly. "I mean she-man in there." Arriane jerked her head toward the office where they'd left the attendant in front of the TV. "Whaddya think—dude or chick?"

"Uh, chick?" Luce said tentatively. "Is this a test?"

Arriane cracked a smile. "The first of many. And you passed. At least, I think you passed. The gender of most of the faculty here is an ongoing, schoolwide debate. Don't worry, you'll get into it."

Luce thought Arriane was making a joke—in which case, cool. But this was all such a huge change from Dover. At her old school, the green-tie-wearing, pomaded future senators had practically oozed through the halls in the genteel hush that money seemed to lay over everything.

More often than not, the other Dover kids gave Luce a don't-smudge-the-white-walls-with-*your*-fingerprints sideways glance. She tried to imagine Arriane there: lazing on the bleachers, making a loud, crude joke in her peppery voice. Luce tried to imagine what Callie might think of Arriane. There'd been no one like her at Dover.

"Okay, spill it," Arriane ordered. Plopping down on

the top bleacher and motioning for Luce to join her, she said, "What'd ya do to get in here?"

Arriane's tone was playful, but suddenly Luce had to sit down. It was ridiculous, but she'd half expected to get through her first day of school without the past creeping up and robbing her of her thin façade of calm. Of course people here were going to want to know.

She could feel the blood thrumming at her temples. It happened whenever she tried to think back—really think back—to that night. She'd never stop feeling guilty about what had happened to Trevor, but she also tried really hard not to get mired down in the shadows, which by now were the only things she could remember about the accident. Those dark, indefinable things that she could never tell anyone about.

Scratch that—she'd *started* to tell Trevor about the peculiar presence she'd felt that night, about the twisting shapes hanging over their heads, threatening to mar their perfect evening. Of course, by then it was already too late. Trevor was gone, his body burned beyond recognition, and Luce was . . . was she . . . guilty?

No one knew about the murky shapes she sometimes saw in the darkness. They'd always come to her. They'd come and gone for so long that Luce couldn't even remember the first time she'd seen them. But she could remember the first time she realized that the shadows didn't come for everyone—or actually, *anyone* but her.

When she was seven, her family had been on vacation in Hilton Head and her parents had taken her on a boat trip. It was just about sunset when the shadows started rolling in over the water, and she'd turned to her father and said, "What do you do when they come, Dad? Why aren't you afraid of the monsters?"

There were no monsters, her parents assured her, but Luce's repeated insistence on the presence of *something* wobbly and dark had gotten her several appointments with the family eye doctor, and then glasses, and then appointments with the ear doctor after she made the mistake of describing the hoarse whooshing noise that the shadows sometimes made—and then therapy, and then more therapy, and finally the prescription for anti-psychotic medication.

But nothing ever made them go away.

By the time she was fourteen, Luce refused to take her meds. That was when they found Dr. Sanford, and the Dover School nearby. They flew to New Hampshire, and her father drove their rental car up a long, curved driveway to a hilltop mansion called Shady Hollows. They planted Luce in front of a man in a lab coat and asked her if she still saw her "visions." Her parents' palms were sweating as they gripped her hands, brows furrowed with the fear that there was something terribly wrong with their daughter.

No one came out and said that if she didn't tell Dr.

Sanford what they all wanted her to say, she might be seeing a whole lot more of Shady Hollows. When she lied and acted normal, she was allowed to enroll at Dover, and only had to visit Dr. Sanford twice a month.

Luce had been permitted to stop taking the horrible pills as soon as she started pretending she didn't see the shadows anymore. But she still had no control over when they might appear. All she knew was that the mental catalog of places where they'd come for her in the past—dense forests, murky waters—became the places she avoided at all costs. All she knew was that when the shadows came, they were usually accompanied by a cold chill under her skin, a sickening feeling unlike anything else.

Luce straddled one of the bleachers and gripped her temples between her thumbs and middle fingers. If she was going to make it through today, she had to push her past to the recesses of her mind. She couldn't stand probing the memory of that night by herself, so there was no way she could air all the gruesome details to some weird, maniacal stranger.

Instead of answering, she watched Arriane, who was lying back on the bleachers, sporting a pair of enormous black sunglasses that covered the better part of her face. It was hard to tell, but she must have been staring at Luce, too, because after a second, she shot up from the bleachers and grinned.

"Cut my hair like yours," she said.

"What?" Luce gasped. "Your hair is beautiful."

It was true: Arriane had the long, thick locks that Luce so desperately missed. Her loose black curls sparkled in the sunlight, giving off just a tinge of red. Luce tucked her hair behind her ears, even though it still wasn't long enough to do anything but flop back down in front of them.

"Beautiful schmootiful," Arriane said. "Yours is sexy, edgy. And I want it."

"Oh, um, okay," Luce said. Was that a compliment? She didn't know if she was supposed to be flattered or unnerved by the way Arriane assumed she could have whatever she wanted, even if what she wanted belonged to someone else. "Where are we going to get—"

"Ta-da!" Arriane reached into her bag and pulled out the pink Swiss Army knife Gabbe had tossed into the Hazard Box. "What?" she said, seeing Luce's reaction. "I always bring my sticky fingers on new-student drop-off days. The idea alone gets me through the dog days of Sword & Cross internment . . . er . . . summer camp."

"You spent the whole summer . . . here?" Luce winced.

"Ha! Spoken like a true newbie. You're probably expecting a spring break." She tossed Luce the Swiss Army knife. "We don't get to leave this hellhole. Ever. Now cut."

"What about the reds?" Luce asked, glancing around with the knife in her hand. There were bound to be cameras somewhere out here.

Arriane shook her head. "I refuse to associate with pansies. Can you handle it or not?"

Luce nodded.

"And *don't* tell me you've never cut hair before." Arriane grabbed the Swiss Army knife back from Luce, pulled out the scissor tool, and handed it back. "Not another word until you tell me how fantastic I look."

In the "salon" of her parents' bathtub, Luce's mother had tugged the remains of her long hair into a messy ponytail before lopping the whole thing off. Luce was sure there had to be a more strategic method of cutting hair, but as a lifelong haircut avoider, the chopped-off pony was about all she knew. She gathered Arriane's hair in her hands, wrapped an elastic band from her wrist around it, held the small scissors firmly, and began to hack.

The ponytail fell to her feet and Arriane gasped and whipped around. She picked it up and held it to the sun. Luce's heart constricted at the sight. She still agonized over her own lost hair, and all the other losses it symbolized. But Arriane just let a thin smile spread across her lips. She ran her fingers through the ponytail once, then dropped it into her bag.

"Awesome," she said. "Keep going."

"Arriane," Luce whispered before she could stop herself. "Your neck. It's all—"

"Scarred?" Arriane finished. "You can say it."

The skin on Arriane's neck, from the back of her left ear all the way down to her collarbone, was jagged and marbled and shiny. Luce's mind went to Trevor—to those awful pictures. Even her own parents wouldn't look at her after they saw them. She was having a hard time looking at Arriane now.

Arriane grabbed Luce's hand and pressed it to the skin. It was hot and cold at the same time. It was smooth and rough.

"I'm not afraid of it," Arriane said. "Are you?"

"No," Luce said, though she wished Arriane would take her hand away so Luce could take hers away, too. Her stomach churned as she wondered whether this was how Trevor's skin would have felt.

"Are you afraid of who you really are, Luce?"

"No," Luce said again quickly. It must be so obvious that she was lying. She closed her eyes. All she wanted from Sword & Cross was a fresh start, a place where people didn't look at her the way Arriane was looking at her right now. At the school's gates that morning, when her father had whispered the Price family motto in her ear— "Prices never crash"—it had felt possible, but already Luce felt so run down and exposed. She tugged her hand away. "So how'd it happen?" she asked, looking down.

"Remember how I didn't press you when you clammed up about what you did to get here?" Arriane asked, raising her eyebrows.

Luce nodded.

Arriane gestured to the scissors. "Touch it up in the back, okay? Make me look real pretty. Make me look like you."

Even with the same exact cut, Arriane would still only look like a very undernourished version of Luce. While Luce attempted to even out the first haircut she'd ever given, Arriane delved into the complexities of life at Sword & Cross.

"That cell block over there is Augustine. It's where we have our so-called Social events on Wednesday nights. And all of our classes," she said, pointing at a building the color of yellowed teeth, two buildings to the right of the dorm. It looked like it had been designed by the same sadist who'd done Pauline. It was dismally square, dismally fortresslike, fortified by the same barbed wire and barred windows. An unnatural-looking gray mist cloaked the walls like moss, making it impossible to see whether anyone was over there.

"Fair warning," Arriane continued. "You're going to hate the classes here. You wouldn't be human if you didn't."

"Why? What's so bad about them?" Luce asked. Maybe Arriane just didn't like school in general. With her black nail polish, black eyeliner, and the black bag that only seemed big enough to hold her new Swiss Army knife, she didn't exactly look bookish.

"The classes here are soulless," Arriane said. "Worse,

they'll strip you of your soul. Of the eighty kids in this place, I'd say we've only got about three remaining souls." She glanced up. "Unspoken for, anyway . . ."

That didn't sound promising, but Luce was hung up on another part of Arriane's answer. "Wait, there are only eighty kids in this whole school?" The summer before she went to Dover, Luce had pored over the thick Prospective Students handbook, memorizing all the statistics. But everything she'd learned so far about Sword & Cross had surprised her, making her realize that she was coming into reform school completely unprepared.

Arriane nodded, making Luce accidentally snip off a chunk of hair she'd meant to leave. Whoops. Hopefully Arriane wouldn't notice—or maybe she'd just think it was edgy.

"Eight classes, ten kids a pop. You get to know everybody's crap pret-ty quickly," Arriane said. "And vice versa."

"I guess so," Luce agreed, biting her lip. Arriane was joking, but Luce wondered whether she'd be sitting here with that cool smirk in her pastel blue eyes if she knew the exact nature of Luce's backstory. The longer Luce could keep her past under wraps, the better off she'd be.

"And you'll want to steer clear of the hard cases."

"Hard cases?"

"The kids with the wristband tracking devices," Arriane said. "About a third of the student body."

"And they're the ones who—"

"You don't want to mess with. Trust me."

"Well, what'd they do?" Luce asked.

As much as Luce wanted to keep her own story a secret, she didn't like the way Arriane was treating her like some sort of ingénue. Whatever those kids had done couldn't be much worse than what everyone told her she had done. Or could it? After all, she knew next to nothing about these people and this place. The possibilities stirred up a cold gray fear in the pit of her stomach.

"Oh, you know," Arriane drawled. "Aided and abetted terrorist acts. Chopped up their parents and roasted them on a spit." She turned around to wink at Luce.

"Shut up," Luce said.

"I'm serious. Those psychos are under much tighter restrictions than the rest of the screwups here. We call them *the shackled*."

Luce laughed at Arriane's dramatic tone.

"Your haircut's done," she said, running her hands through Arriane's hair to fluff it up a little. It actually looked really cool.

"Sweet," Arriane said. She turned to face Luce. When she ran her fingers through her hair, the sleeves of her black sweater fell back on her forearms and Luce caught a glimpse of a black wristband, dotted with rows of silver studs, and, on the other wrist, another band that looked more . . . mechanical. Arriane caught her looking and raised her eyebrows devilishly.

"Told ya," she said. "Total effing psychos." She grinned. "Come on, I'll give you the rest of the tour."

Luce didn't have much choice. She scrambled down the bleachers after Arriane, ducking when one of the turkey vultures swooped dangerously low. Arriane, who didn't seem to notice, pointed at a lichen-swathed church at the far right of the commons.

"Over here, you'll find our state-of-the-art gymnasium," she said, assuming a nasal tour guide tone of voice. "Yes, yes, to the untrained eye it looks like a church. It used to be. We're kind of in an architectural hand-me-down Hell here at Sword & Cross. A few years ago, some calisthenic-crazed shrink showed up ranting about overmedicated teens ruining society. He donated a shit-ton of money so they'd convert it into a gym. Now the powers that be think we can work out our 'frustrations' in a 'more natural and productive way.'"

Luce groaned. She had always loathed gym class.

"Girl after my very own heart," Arriane commiserated. "Coach Diante is ee-vil."

As Luce jogged to keep up, she took in the rest of the grounds. The Dover quad had been so well kept, all manicured and dotted with evenly spaced, carefully pruned trees. Sword & Cross looked like it had been plopped down and abandoned in the middle of a swamp. Weeping willows dangled to the ground, kudzu grew along the walls in sheets, and every third step they took squished.

And it wasn't just the way the place looked. Every humid breath Luce took stuck in her lungs. Just breathing at Sword & Cross made her feel like she was sinking into quicksand.

"Apparently the architects got in a huge standoff over how to retrofit the style of the old military academy buildings. The upshot is we ended up with half penitentiary, half medieval torture zone. And no gardener," Arriane said, kicking some slime off her combat boots. "Gross. Oh, and there's the cemetery."

Luce followed Arriane's pointing finger to the far left side of the quad, just past the dormitory. An even thicker cloak of mist hung over the walled-off portion of land. It was bordered on three sides by a thick forest of oaks. She couldn't see into the cemetery, which seemed almost to sink below the surface of the ground, but she could smell the rot and hear the chorus of cicadas buzzing in the trees. For a second, she thought she saw the dark swish of the shadows—but she blinked and they were gone.

"That's a *cemetery*?"

"Yep. This used to be a military academy, way back in the Civil War days. So that's where they buried all their dead. It's creepy as all get-out. And *lawd,*" Arriane said, piling on a fake southern accent, "it stinks to *high Heaven.*" Then she winked at Luce. "We hang out there a lot."

Luce looked at Arriane to see if she was kidding. Arriane just shrugged.

"Okay, it was only once. And it was only after a really big pharmapalooza."

Now, that was a word Luce recognized.

"Aha!" Arriane laughed. "I just saw a light go on up there. So somebody *is* home. Well, Luce, my dear, you may have gone to boarding school parties, but you've never seen a throw-down like reform school kids do it."

"What's the difference?" Luce asked, trying to skirt the fact that she'd never actually been to a big party at Dover.

"You'll see." Arriane paused and turned to Luce. "You'll come over tonight and hang out, okay?" She surprised Luce by taking her hand. "Promise?"

"But I thought you said I should stay away from the hard cases," Luce joked.

"Rule number two—don't listen to me!" Arriane laughed, shaking her head. "I'm certifiably insane!"

She started jogging again and Luce trailed after her.

"Wait, what was rule number one?"

"Keep up!"

❈

As they came around the corner of the cinder-block classrooms, Arriane skidded to a halt. "Affect cool," she said.

"Cool," Luce repeated.

All the other students seemed to be clustered around the kudzu-strangled trees outside Augustine. No one looked exactly happy to be hanging out, but no one looked ready to go inside yet, either.

There hadn't been much of a dress code at Dover, so Luce wasn't used to the uniformity it gave a student body. Then again, even though every kid here was wearing the same black jeans, black mock-turtleneck T-shirt, and black sweater tied over the shoulders or around the waist, there were still substantial differences in the way they pulled it off.

A group of tattooed girls standing in a crossed-armed circle wore bangle bracelets up to their elbows. The black bandanas in their hair reminded Luce of a film she'd once seen about motorcycle-gang girls. She'd rented it because she'd thought: *What could be cooler than an all-girls motorcycle gang?* Now Luce's eyes locked with those of one of the girls across the lawn. The sideways squint of the girl's darkly lined cat-eyes made Luce quickly shift the direction of her gaze.

A guy and a girl who were holding hands had sewn sequins in the shape of skulls and crossbones on the back of their black sweaters. Every few seconds, one of them would pull the other in for a kiss on the temple, on the earlobe, on the eye. When they looped their arms around each other, Luce could see that each wore the blinking wristband tracking device. They looked a little rough, but it was obvious how much in love they were. Every time she saw their tongue rings flashing, Luce felt a lonely pinch inside her chest.

Behind the lovers, a cluster of blond boys stood pressed against the wall. Each of them wore his sweater, despite the heat. And they all had on white oxford shirts underneath, the collars starched straight up. Their black pants hit the vamps of their polished dress shoes perfectly. Of all the students on the quad, these boys seemed to Luce to be the closest thing to Doverites. But a closer look quickly set them apart from boys she used to know. Boys like Trevor.

Just standing in a group, these guys radiated a specific kind of toughness. It was right there in the look in their eyes. It was hard to explain, but it suddenly struck Luce that just like her, everyone at this school had a past. Everyone here probably had secrets they wouldn't want to share. But she couldn't figure out whether this realization made her feel more or less isolated.

Arriane noticed Luce's eyes running over the rest of the kids.

"We all do what we can to make it through the day," she said, shrugging. "But in case you hadn't observed the low-hanging vultures, this place pretty much reeks of death." She took a seat on a bench under a weeping willow and patted the spot next to her for Luce.

Luce wiped away a mound of wet, decaying leaves, but just before she sat down, she noticed another dress code violation.

A very attractive dress code violation.

He wore a bright red scarf around his neck. It was far

from cold outside, but he had on a black leather motor-cycle jacket over his black sweater, too. Maybe it was because his was the only spot of color on the quad, but he was all that Luce could look at. In fact, everything else so paled in comparison that, for one long moment, Luce forgot where she was.

She took in his deep golden hair and matching tan. His high cheekbones, the dark sunglasses that covered his eyes, the soft shape of his lips. In all the movies Luce had seen, and in all the books she'd read, the love interest was mind-blowingly good-looking—except for that one little flaw. The chipped tooth, the charming cowlick, the beauty mark on his left cheek. She knew why—if the hero was *too* unblemished, he'd risk being unapproach-able. But approachable or not, Luce had always had a weakness for the sublimely gorgeous. Like this guy.

He leaned up against the building with his arms crossed lightly over his chest. And for a split second, Luce saw a flashing image of herself folded into those arms. She shook her head, but the vision stayed so clear that she almost took off toward him.

No. That was crazy. Right? Even at a school full of crazies, Luce was well aware that this instinct was insane. She didn't even *know* him.

He was talking to a shorter kid with dreads and a toothy smile. Both of them were laughing hard and genuinely—in a way that made Luce strangely jealous.

She tried to think back and remember how long it had been since she'd laughed, really laughed, like that.

"That's Daniel Grigori," Arriane said, leaning in and reading her mind. "I can tell he's attracted *somebody's* attention."

"Understatement," Luce agreed, embarrassed when she realized how she must have looked to Arriane.

"Yeah, well, if you like that sort of thing."

"What's not to like?" Luce said, unable to stop the words from tumbling out.

"His friend there is Roland," Arriane said, nodding in the dreadlocked kid's direction. "He's cool. The kind of guy who can get his hands on things, ya know?"

Not really, Luce thought, biting her lip. "What kinds of things?"

Arriane shrugged, using her poached Swiss Army knife to saw off a fraying strand from a rip in her black jeans. "Just things. Ask-and-you-shall-receive kind of stuff."

"What about Daniel?" Luce asked. "What's his story?"

"Oh, she doesn't give up." Arriane laughed, then cleared her throat. "No one really knows," she said. "He holds pretty tight to his mystery man persona. Could just be your typical reform school asshole."

"I'm no stranger to assholes," Luce said, though as soon as the words came out, she wished she could take them back. After what had happened to Trevor— whatever *had* happened—she was the last person who should be making character judgments. But more than that, the rare time she made even the smallest reference to that night, the shifting black canopy of the shadows came back to her, almost like she was right back at the lake.

She glanced again at Daniel. He took his glasses off and slid them inside his jacket, then turned to look at her.

His gaze caught hers, and Luce watched as his eyes widened and then quickly narrowed in what looked like surprise. But no—it was more than that. When Daniel's eyes held hers, her breath caught in her throat. She recognized him from somewhere.

But she would have remembered meeting someone like him. She would have remembered feeling as absolutely shaken up as she did right now.

She realized they were still locking eyes when Daniel flashed her a smile. A jet of warmth shot through her and she had to grip the bench for support. She felt her lips pull up in a smile back at him, but then he raised his hand in the air.

And flipped her off.

Luce gasped and dropped her eyes.

"What?" Arriane asked, oblivious to what had just gone down. "Never mind," she said. "We don't have time. I sense the bell."

The bell rang as if on cue, and the whole student body started the slow shuffle into the building. Arriane was tugging on Luce's hand and spouting off directions about where to meet her next and when. But Luce was still reeling from being flipped the bird by such a perfect stranger. Her momentary delirium over Daniel had vanished, and now the only thing she wanted to know was: What was that guy's problem?

Just before she ducked into her first class, she dared to glance back. His face was blank, but there was no mistaking it—he was watching her go.

TWO

FIT TO BE TIED

Luce had a piece of paper with her schedule printed on it, a half-empty notebook she'd started to fill at Dover in her Advanced European History class last year, two number two pencils, her favorite eraser, and the sudden bad feeling that Arriane might have been right about the classes at Sword & Cross.

The teacher had yet to materialize, the flimsy desks were arranged in haphazard rows, and the supply closet was barricaded with stacks of dusty boxes piled in front of it.

What was worse, none of the other kids seemed to notice the disarray. In fact, none of the other kids seemed to notice that they were in a classroom at all. They all stood clustered near the windows, taking one last drag of a cigarette here, repositioning the extra-large safety pins on their T-shirts there. Only Todd was seated at an actual desk, carving something intricate onto its surface with his pen. But the other new students seemed to have already found their places among the crowd. Cam had the preppy Dover-looking guys in a tight cluster around him. They must have been friends when he was enrolled at Sword & Cross the first time. Gabbe was shaking hands with the tongue-pierced girl who'd been making out with the tongue-pierced guy outside. Luce felt stupidly envious that she wasn't daring enough to do anything but take a seat closer to the unthreatening Todd.

Arriane flitted about the others, whispering things Luce couldn't make out, like some sort of goth princess. When she passed Cam, he tousled her newly chopped hair.

"Nice mop, Arriane." He smirked, tugging on a strand at the back of her neck. "My compliments to your stylist."

Arriane swatted him away. "Hands off, Cam. Which is to say: In your dreams." She jerked her head in Luce's direction. "And you can give your compliments to my new pet, right over there."

Cam's emerald eyes sparkled at Luce, who stiffened. "I believe I will," he said, and started walking toward her.

He smiled at Luce, who was sitting with her ankles crossed under her chair and her hands folded neatly on her heavily graffitied desk.

"Us new kids have to stick together," he said. "Know what I mean?"

"But I thought you'd been here before."

"Don't believe everything Arriane says." He glanced back at Arriane, who was standing at the window, eyeing them suspiciously.

"Oh no, she didn't say anything about you," Luce said quickly, trying to remember whether or not that was actually true. It was clear Cam and Arriane didn't like each other, and even though Luce was grateful to Arriane for taking her around this morning, she wasn't ready to pick any sides yet.

"I remember when I was a new kid here . . . the first time." He laughed to himself. "My band had just broken up and I was lost. I didn't know anyone. I could have used someone without"—he glanced at Arriane—"an *agenda* to show me the ropes."

"What, and you have no agenda?" Luce said, surprised to hear a flirting lilt in her voice.

An easy smile spread across Cam's face. He raised one eyebrow at her. "And to think I didn't want to come back here."

Luce blushed. She didn't usually get involved with rocker guys—but then again, none of them had ever pulled the desk next to her even closer, plopped down beside her, and stared at her with eyes quite so green. Cam reached into his pocket and pulled out a green guitar pick with the number 44 printed on it.

"This is my room number. Come by anytime."

The guitar pick wasn't far from the color of Cam's eyes, and Luce wondered how and when he'd had these printed up, but before she could answer—and who knew *what* she would have answered—Arriane clamped a hard hand down on Cam's shoulder. "I'm sorry, did I not make myself clear? I've already called dibs on this one."

Cam snorted. He looked straight at Luce as he said, "See, I thought there was still such a thing as free will. Maybe your *pet* has a path of her own in mind."

Luce opened her mouth to claim that of course she had a path, it was just her first day here and she was still figuring out the ropes. But by the time she was able to get the words straight in her head, the minute-warning bell rang, and the little gathering over Luce's desk dissolved.

The other kids filed into desks around her, and soon it stopped being so noteworthy that Luce was sitting prim and proper at her desk, keeping her eye on the door. Keeping a lookout for Daniel.

Out of the corner of her eye, she could feel Cam sneaking peeks at her. She felt flattered—and nervous, then frustrated with herself. Daniel? Cam? She'd been at this school for what, forty-five minutes?—and her mind was already juggling two different guys. The whole reason she was at this school at all was because the last time she'd been interested in a guy, things had gone horribly, horribly wrong. She should *not* be allowing herself to get all smitten (twice!) on her very first day of school.

She looked over at Cam, who winked at her again, then brushed his dark hair away from his eyes. Staggering good looks aside—yeah, right—he really did seem like a useful person to know. Like her, he was still adjusting to the setting, but had clearly been around the Sword & Cross block a few times before. And he was nice to her. She thought about the green guitar pick with his room number, hoping he didn't give those out freely. They could be . . . friends. Maybe that was all she needed. Maybe then she would stop feeling quite so obviously out of place at Sword & Cross.

Maybe then she'd be able to forgive the fact that the only window in the classroom was the size of a business envelope, caked with lime, and looked out on a massive mausoleum in the cemetery.

Maybe then she'd be able to forget the nose-tickling odor of peroxide emanating from the bleached-blond punk chick sitting in front of her.

Maybe then she could actually pay attention to the stern, mustached teacher who marched into the room, commanded the class to *shapeupandsitdown,* and firmly closed the door.

The smallest tweak of disappointment tugged at her heart. It took her a moment to trace where it had come from. Until the teacher shut the door, she'd been holding out a little hope that Daniel would be in her first class, too.

What did she have next hour, French? She looked down at her schedule to check what room it was in. Just then, a paper airplane skidded across her schedule, overshot her desk, and landed on the floor by her bag. She checked to see who'd noticed, but the teacher was busy tearing through a piece of chalk as he wrote something on the board.

Luce glanced nervously to her left. When Cam looked over at her, he gave her a wink and a flirty little wave that caused her whole body to tense up. But he didn't seem to have seen or been responsible for the paper airplane.

"Psssst," came the quiet whisper behind him. It was Arriane, who motioned with her chin for Luce to pick up the paper plane. Luce bent down to reach for it and saw her name written in small black letters on the wing. Her first note!

Already looking for the exit?
Not a good sign.
We're in this hellhole until lunch.

That *had* to be a joke. Luce double-checked her schedule and realized with horror that all three of her morning classes were in this very same room 1—and all three would be taught by the very same Mr. Cole.

He'd detached himself from the blackboard and was sleepily threading his way through the room. There was no introduction for the new kids—and Luce couldn't decide whether she was glad about that or not. Mr. Cole merely slapped syllabi down on each of the four new students' desks. When the stapled packet landed in front of Luce, she leaned forward eagerly to take a look. *History of the World,* it read. *Circumventing the Doom of Mankind.* Hmmm, history *had* always been her strongest subject, but circumventing doom?

A closer look at the syllabus was all it took for Luce to see that Arriane had been right about being in a hell-hole: an impossible reading load, TEST in big, bold letters every third class period, and a thirty-page paper on— seriously?—the failed tyrant of your choice. Thick black parentheses had been drawn in black Sharpie around the assignments Luce had missed during the first few weeks. In the margins, Mr. Cole had written *See me for Makeup Research Assignment.* If there was a more effective way of soul-sucking, Luce would be scared to find out.

At least she had Arriane sitting back there in the next row. Luce was glad the precedent had already been set for SOS note-passing. She and Callie used to text each other on the sly, but to make it here, Luce was definitely going to need to learn to fold a paper airplane. She tore a sheet from her notebook and tried to use Arriane's as a model.

After a few origami-challenged minutes, another

plane landed on her desk. She glanced back at Arriane, who shook her head and gave her a you-have-so-much-to-learn roll of the eyes.

Luce shrugged an apology and swiveled back around to open the second note:

> *Oh, and until you're confident about your aim, you might not want to fly any Daniel-related messages my way. Dude behind you is famous on the football field for his interceptions.*

Good to know. She hadn't even seen Daniel's friend Roland come in behind her. Now she turned very slightly in her seat until she glimpsed his dreadlocks out of the corner of her eye. She dared a glance down at the open notebook on his desk and caught his full name. Roland Sparks.

"No note-passing," Mr. Cole said sternly, causing Luce to whip her head back to attention. "No plagiarizing, and no looking at one another's papers. I didn't put myself through graduate school only to receive your divided attention."

Luce nodded in unison with the other dazed kids just as a third paper plane glided to a stop in the middle of her desk.

Only 172 minutes to go!

A hundred and seventy-three torturous minutes later, Arriane was leading Luce to the cafeteria. "What'd ya think?" she asked.

"You were right," Luce said numbly, still recovering from how painfully bleak her first three hours of class had been. "Why would anyone teach such a depressing subject?"

"Aw, Cole'll ease up soon. He puts on his no-guff face every time there's a new student. Anyway," Arriane said, poking Luce, "it could be worse. You could have gotten stuck with Ms. Tross."

Luce glanced down at her schedule. "I have her for biology in the afternoon block," she said with a sinking feeling in her gut.

As Arriane sputtered out a laugh, Luce felt a bump on her shoulder. It was Cam, passing them in the hall on his way to lunch. Luce would have gone sprawling if not for his hand reaching back to steady her.

"Easy there." He shot her a quick smile, and she wondered if he had bumped her intentionally. But he didn't seem that juvenile. Luce glanced at Arriane to see whether she'd noticed anything. Arriane raised her eyebrows, almost inviting Luce to speak, but neither one of them said a thing.

When they crossed the dusty interior windows

separating bleak hall from bleaker cafeteria, Arriane took hold of Luce's elbow.

"Avoid the chicken-fried steak at all costs," she coached as they followed the crowd into the din of the lunchroom. "The pizza's fine, the chili's okay, and actually the borscht ain't bad. Do you like meat loaf?"

"I'm a vegetarian," Luce said. She was glancing around the tables, looking for two people in particular. Daniel and Cam. She'd just feel more at ease if she knew where they were so she could go about having her lunch pretending that she didn't see either one of them. But so far, no sightings . . .

"Vegetarian, huh?" Arriane pursed her lips. "Hippie parents or your own meager attempt at rebellion?"

"Uh, neither, I just don't—"

"Like meat?" Arriane steered Luce's shoulders ninety degrees so that she was looking directly at Daniel, sitting at a table across the room. Luce let out a long exhale. There he was. "Now, does that go for *all* meat?" Arriane sang loudly. "Like you wouldn't sink your teeth into *him*?"

Luce slugged Arriane and dragged her toward the lunch line. Arriane was cracking up, but Luce knew she was blushing badly, which would be excruciatingly obvious in this fluorescent lighting.

"Shut up, he totally heard you," she whispered.

Part of Luce felt glad to be joking about boys with a friend. Assuming Arriane was her friend.

She still felt unglued by what had happened this morning when she'd seen Daniel. That pull toward him—she still didn't understand where it came from, and yet here it was again. She made herself tear her eyes away from his blond hair, from the smooth line of his jaw. She refused to be caught staring. She did *not* want to give him any reason to flip her off a second time.

"Whatever," Arriane scoffed. "He's so focused on that hamburger, he wouldn't hear the call of Satan." She gestured at Daniel, who did look intensely focused on chewing his burger. Scratch that, he looked like someone *pretending* to be intensely focused on chewing his hamburger.

Luce glanced across the table at Daniel's friend Roland. He was looking straight at her. When he caught her eye, he waggled his eyebrows in a way that Luce couldn't make sense of but that still creeped her out a little.

Luce turned back to Arriane. "Why is everyone at this school so weird?"

"I'm going to choose not to take offense at that," Arriane said, picking up a plastic tray and handing one to Luce. "And I'm going to move on to explaining the fine art of selecting a cafeteria seat. You see, you never want to sit anywhere near the—Luce, look out!"

All Luce did was take one step backward, but as soon as she did, she felt the rough shove of two hands on her shoulders. Immediately, she knew she was going down.

She reached out in front of her for support, but all her hands found was someone else's full lunch tray. The whole thing tumbled down right along with her. She landed with a thud on the cafeteria floor, a full cup of borscht in her face.

When she'd wiped enough mushy beets out of her eyes to see, Luce looked up. The angriest pixie she'd ever seen was standing over her. The girl had spiky bleached hair, at least ten piercings on her face, and a death glare. She bared her teeth at Luce and hissed, "If the sight of you hadn't just ruined my appetite, I'd make you buy me another lunch."

Luce stammered an apology. She tried to get up, but the girl clamped the heel of her black stiletto boot down on Luce's foot. Pain shot up her leg, and she had to bite her lip so she wouldn't cry out.

"Why don't I just take a rain check," the girl said.

"That's enough, Molly," Arriane said coolly. She reached down to help Luce to her feet.

Luce winced. The stiletto was definitely going to leave a bruise.

Molly squared her hips to face Arriane, and Luce got the feeling this was not the first time they'd locked horns.

"Fast friends with the newbie, I see," Molly growled. "This is very bad behavior, A. Aren't you supposed to be on probation?"

Luce swallowed. Arriane hadn't mentioned anything

about probation, and it didn't make sense that that would prohibit her from making new friends. But the word was enough to make Arriane clench her fist and throw a fat punch that landed on Molly's right eye.

Molly reeled backward, but it was Arriane who caught Luce's attention. She'd begun convulsing, her arms thrown up and jerking in the air.

It was the wristband, Luce realized with horror. It was sending some sort of shock through Arriane's body. Unbelievable. This was cruel and unusual punishment, for sure. Luce's stomach churned as she watched her friend's entire body quake. She reached out to catch Arriane just as she sank to the floor.

"Arriane," Luce whispered. "Are you okay?"

"Terrific." Arriane's dark eyes flickered open, then shut.

Luce gasped. Then one of Arriane's eyes popped back open. "Scared ya, did I? Aw, that's sweet. Don't worry, the shocks won't kill me," she whispered. "They only make me stronger. Anyway, it was worth it to give that cow a black eye, ya know?"

"All right, break it up. Break it up," a husky voice boomed behind them.

Randy stood in the doorway, red-faced and breathing hard. It was a little too late to break anything up, Luce thought, but then Molly was lurching toward them, her stiletto heels clicking on the linoleum. This girl was shameless. Was she really going to kick the crap out of Arriane with Randy standing right there?

Luckily, Randy's burly arms closed around her first. Molly tried to kick her way out and started screaming.

"Somebody better start talking," Randy barked, squeezing Molly until she went limp. "On second thought, all three of you report for detention tomorrow morning. Cemetery. Crack of dawn!" Randy looked at Molly. "Have you *chilled* yet?"

Molly nodded stiffly, and Randy released her. She crouched down to where Arriane still lay in Luce's lap, her arms crossed over her chest. At first Luce thought Arriane was sulking, like an angry dog with a shock collar, but then Luce felt a small jolt from Arriane's body and realized that the girl was still at the mercy of the wristband.

"Come on," Randy said, more softly. "Let's go turn you off."

She extended her hand to Arriane and helped heave up her tiny, shaking body, turning back only once at the doorway to repeat her orders for Luce and Molly.

"Crack of dawn!"

"Looking forward to it," Molly said sweetly, reaching down to pick up the plate of meat loaf that had slipped from her tray.

She dangled it over Luce's head for a second, then turned the plate upside down and mashed the food into her hair. Luce could hear the squish of her own mortification as all of Sword & Cross got its viewing of the meat-loaf-coated new girl.

"Priceless," Molly said, pulling out the tiniest silver camera from the back pocket of her black jeans. "Say . . . meat loaf," she sang, snapping a few close-up shots. "These will be *great* on my blog."

"Nice hat," someone jeered from the other side of the cafeteria. Then, with trepidation, Luce turned her eyes to Daniel, praying that somehow he had missed this whole scene. But no. He was shaking his head. He looked annoyed.

Until that moment, Luce had thought she had a chance at standing up and just shaking off the incident—literally. But seeing Daniel's reaction—well, it finally made her crack.

She would *not* cry in front of any of these horrible people. She swallowed hard, got to her feet, and took off. She rushed toward the nearest door, eager to feel some cool air on her face.

Instead, the southern September humidity cloaked her, choking her, as soon as she got outside. The sky was that no-color color, a grayish brown so oppressively bland it was difficult even to find the sun. Luce slowed down, but got as far as the edge of the parking lot before she came to a complete stop.

She longed to see her battered old car there, to sink into the fraying cloth seat, rev the engine, crank up the stereo, and peel the hell out of this place. But as she stood on the hot black pavement, reality set in: She was stuck here, and a pair of towering metal gates separated her from the world outside Sword & Cross. Besides, even if she'd had a way out . . . where was she going to go?

The sick feeling in her gut told her all she needed to know. She was already at the last stop, and things were looking pretty grim.

It was as depressing as it was true: Sword & Cross was all she had.

She dropped her face into her hands, knowing she had to go back. But when she lifted her head, the residue on her palm reminded her that she was still coated in Molly's meat loaf. Ugh. First stop, the nearest bathroom.

Back inside, Luce ducked into the girls' room just as the door was swinging open. Gabbe, who appeared even more blond and flawless now that Luce looked like she'd just gone Dumpster diving, squeezed past.

"Whoops, 'scuse me, honey," she said. Her southern-accented voice was sweet, but her face crumpled up at the sight of Luce. "Oh God, you look terrible. What happened?"

What happened? As if the whole school didn't already know. This girl was probably playing dumb so Luce would relive the whole mortifying scene.

"Wait five minutes," Luce replied, with more of an edge in her voice than she meant. "I'm sure gossip spreads like the plague around here."

"You want to borrow my foundation?" Gabbe asked, holding up a pastel blue cosmetics case. "You haven't seen yourself yet, but you're going to—"

"Thanks, but no." Luce cut her off, pushing into the bathroom. Without looking at herself in the mirror, she turned on the faucet. She splashed cold water on her face and finally let it all out. Tears streaming, she pumped the soap dispenser and tried to use some of the cheap pink powdered hand soap to scrub off the meat loaf. But there was still the matter of her hair. And her clothes had definitely looked and smelled better. Not that she needed to worry about making a good first impression anymore.

The bathroom door cracked open and Luce scrambled against the wall like a trapped animal. When a stranger walked in, Luce stiffened and waited for the worst.

The girl had a squat build, accentuated by an abnormal amount of layered clothing. Her wide face was surrounded by curly brown hair, and her bright purple glasses wobbled when she sniffed. She looked fairly unassuming, but then, looks could be deceiving. Both her hands were tucked behind her back in a way that, after the day Luce had had, she just couldn't trust.

"You know, you're not supposed to be in here without a pass," the girl said. Her even tone seemed to mean business.

"I know." The look in the girl's eyes confirmed Luce's suspicion that it was absolutely impossible to catch a break at this place. She started to sigh in surrender. "I just—"

"I'm kidding." The girl laughed, rolling her eyes and relaxing her posture. "I snagged some shampoo from the locker room for you," she said, bringing her hands around to display two innocent-looking plastic bottles of shampoo and conditioner. "Come on," she said, pulling over a beat-up folding chair. "Let's get you cleaned up. Sit here."

A half-whimpering, half-laughing noise she'd never made before escaped from Luce's lips. It sounded, she guessed, like relief. The girl was actually being nice to her—not just reform school nice, but regular-person nice! For no apparent reason. The shock of it was almost too great for Luce to stand. "Thanks?" Luce managed to say, still feeling a little bit guarded.

"Oh, and you probably need a change of clothes," the girl said, looking down at her black sweater and pulling it over her head to expose an identical black sweater underneath.

When she saw the surprised look on Luce's face, she said, "What? I have a hostile immune system. I have to wear a lot of layers."

"Oh, well, will you be okay without this one?" Luce made herself ask, even though she would have done just about anything right then to get out of the meat cloak she was wearing.

"Of course," the girl said, waving her off. "I've got

three more on under this. And a couple more in my locker. Be my guest. It pains me to see a vegetarian covered in meat. I'm very empathetic."

Luce wondered how this stranger knew about her dietary preferences, but more than that, she had to ask: "Um, why are you being so nice?"

The girl laughed, sighed, then shook her head. "Not everyone at Sword & Cross is a whore or a jock."

"Huh?" Luce said.

"Sword & Cross . . . Whores and Jocks. Lame nickname in town for this school. Obviously there aren't really any jocks here. I won't oppress your ears with some of the cruder nicknames they've come up with."

Luce laughed.

"All I meant was, not everyone here is a complete jerk."

"Just the majority?" Luce asked, hating it that she already sounded so negative. But it had been such a long morning, and she'd already been through so much, and maybe this girl wouldn't judge her for being a little bit gruff.

To her surprise, the girl smiled. "Exactly. And they sure give the rest of us a bad name." She stuck out her hand. "I'm Pennyweather Van Syckle-Lockwood. You can call me Penn."

"Got it," Luce said, still too frazzled to realize that, in a former life, she might have stifled a laugh at this girl's moniker. It sounded like she'd hopped straight off the pages of a Dickens novel. Then again, there was something trustworthy about a girl with a name like that who could manage to introduce herself with a straight face. "I'm Lucinda Price."

"And everybody calls you Luce," Penn said. "And you transferred from Dover Prep in New Hampshire."

"How'd you know that?" Luce asked slowly.

"Lucky guess?" Penn shrugged. "I'm kidding, I read your file, duh. It's a hobby."

Luce stared at her blankly. Maybe she'd been too hasty with that trustworthy judgment. How could Penn have access to her file?

Penn took over running the water. When it got warm, she motioned for Luce to lower her head into the sink.

"See, the thing is," she explained, "I'm not actually crazy." She pulled Luce up by her wet head. "No offense." Then lowered her back down. "I'm the only kid at this school without a court mandate. And you might not think it, but being legally sane has its advantages. For example, I'm also the only kid they trust to be an office aide. Which is dumb on their part. I have access to a lot of confidential shit."

"But if you don't *have* to be here—"

"When your father's the groundskeeper of the school, they kind of have to let you go for free. So . . ." Penn trailed off.

Penn's father was the groundskeeper? From the looks

of the place, it hadn't crossed Luce's mind that they even *had* a groundskeeper.

"I know what you're thinking," Penn said, helping Luce shampoo the last of the gravy from her hair. "That the grounds aren't exactly well kept?"

"No," Luce lied. She was eager to stay on this girl's good side and wanted to put out the be-my-friend vibe way more than she wanted to seem like she actually cared about how often someone mowed the lawn at Sword & Cross. "It's, um, really nice."

"Dad died two years ago," Penn said quietly. "They got as far as sticking me with decaying old Headmaster Udell as my legal guardian, but, uh, they never really got around to hiring a replacement for Dad."

"I'm sorry," Luce said, lowering her voice, too. So someone else here knew what it was like to go through a major loss.

"It's okay," Penn said, squirting conditioner into her palm. "It's actually a really good school. I like it here a lot."

Now Luce's head shot up, sending a spray of water across the bathroom. "You sure you're not crazy?" she teased.

"I'm kidding. I hate it here. It totally sucks."

"But you can't bring yourself to leave," Luce said, tilting her head, curious.

Penn bit her lip. "I know it's morbid, but even if I weren't stuck with Udell, I couldn't. My dad's here." She gestured toward the cemetery, invisible from here. "He's all I've got."

"Then I guess you've got more than some other people at this school," Luce said, thinking of Arriane. Her mind rolled back to the way Arriane had gripped her hand on the quad today, the eager look in her blue eyes when she made Luce promise she'd swing by her dorm room tonight.

"She's gonna be okay," Penn said. "It wouldn't be Monday if Arriane didn't get carted off to the nurse after a fit."

"But it wasn't a fit," Luce said. "It was that wristband. I saw it. It was shocking her."

"We have a very broad definition of what makes for a 'fit' here at Sword & Cross. Your new enemy, Molly? She's thrown some legendary fits. They keep saying they're going to change her meds. Hopefully you'll have the pleasure of witnessing at least one good freak-out before they do."

Penn's intel was pretty remarkable. It crossed Luce's mind to ask her what the story was with Daniel, but the complicated intensity of her interest in him was probably best kept to a need-to-know basis. At least until she figured it out herself.

She felt Penn's hands wringing the water from her hair.

"That's the last of it," Penn said. "I think you're finally meat-free."

Luce looked in the mirror and ran her hands through her hair. Penn was right. Except for the emotional scarring and the pain in her right foot, there was no evidence of her cafeteria brawl with Molly.

"I'm just glad you have short hair," Penn said. "If it were still as long as it was in the picture in your file, this would have been a much lengthier operation."

Luce gawked at her. "I'm going to have to keep an eye on you, aren't I?"

Penn looped her arm through Luce's and steered her out of the bathroom. "Just stay on my good side and no one gets hurt."

Luce shot Penn a worried look, but Penn's face gave nothing away. "You're kidding, right?" Luce asked.

Penn smiled, suddenly cheery. "Come on, we gotta get to class. Aren't you glad we're in the same afternoon block?"

Luce laughed. "When are you going to stop knowing everything about me?"

"Not in the foreseeable future," Penn said, tugging her down the hall and back toward the cinder-block classrooms. "You'll learn to love it soon, I promise. I'm a very powerful friend to have."

THREE

DRAWING DARK

Luce meandered down the dank dormitory hallway toward her room, dragging her red Camp Gurid duffel bag with the broken strap in her wake. The walls here were the color of a dusty blackboard—and the whole place was strangely quiet, save for the dull hum of the yellow fluorescent lamps hanging from the water-stained drop-panel ceilings.

Mostly, Luce was surprised to see so many shut doors. Back at Dover, she'd always wished for more privacy, a break from the hallwide dorm parties that sprang up at all hours. You couldn't walk to your room without tripping over a powwow of girls sitting cross-legged in matching jeans, or a lip-locked couple pressed against the wall.

But at Sword & Cross . . . well, either everyone was already getting started on their thirty-page term papers . . . or else the socializing here was of a much more behind-closed-doors variety.

Speaking of which, the closed doors themselves were a sight to be seen. If the students at Sword & Cross got resourceful with their dress code violations, they were downright ingenious when it came to personalizing their spaces. Already Luce had walked by one door frame with a beaded curtain, and another with a motion-detecting welcome mat that encouraged her to "move the hell on" when she passed it.

She came to a stop in front of the only blank door in the building. Room 63. Home bitter home. She fumbled for her key in the front pocket of her backpack, took a deep breath, and opened the door to her cell.

Except it wasn't *terrible*. Or maybe it wasn't as terrible as she'd been expecting. There was a decent-sized window that slid open to let in some less stifling night air. And past the steel bars, the view of the moonlit commons was actually sort of interesting, if she didn't think too hard about the graveyard that lay beyond it. She had a closet and a little sink, a desk to do her work at—come to think of it, the saddest-looking thing in the room was the glimpse Luce caught of herself in the full-length mirror behind the door.

She quickly looked away, knowing all too well what she'd find in the reflection. Her face looking pinched and tired. Her hazel eyes flecked with stress. Her hair like her family's hysterical toy poodle's fur after a rainstorm. Penn's sweater fit her like a burlap sack. She was shivering. Her afternoon classes had been no better than the morning's, due mainly to the fact that her biggest fear had come to fruition: The whole school had already started calling her Meat Loaf. And unfortunately, much like its namesake, the moniker seemed like it was going to stick.

She wanted to unpack, to turn generic room 63 into her own place, where she could go when she needed to escape and feel okay. But she only got as far as unzipping her bag before she collapsed on the bare bed in defeat. She felt so far away from home. It only took twenty-two minutes by car to get from the loose-hinged whitewashed back door of her house to the rusty wrought iron entrance gates of Sword & Cross, but it might as well have been twenty-two years.

For the first half of the silent drive with her parents this morning, the neighborhoods had all looked pretty much the same: sleepy southern middle-class suburbia.

But then the road had gone over the causeway toward the shore, and the terrain had grown more and more marshy. A swell of mangrove trees marked the entrance into the wetlands, but soon even those dwindled out. The last ten miles of road to Sword & Cross were dismal. Grayish brown, featureless, forsaken. Back home in Thunderbolt, people around town always joked about the strangely memorable moldering stench out here: You knew you were in the marshes when your car started to reek of pluff mud.

Even though Luce had grown up in Thunderbolt, she really wasn't that familiar with the far eastern part of the county. As a kid, she'd always just assumed that was because there wasn't any reason to come over here—all the stores, schools, and everyone her family knew were on the west side. The east side was just less developed. That was all.

She missed her parents, who'd stuck a Post-it on the T-shirt at the top of her bag—*We love you! Prices never crash!* She missed her bedroom, which looked out on her dad's tomato vines. She missed Callie, who most certainly had sent her at least ten never-to-be-seen text messages already. She missed Trevor . . .

Or, well, that wasn't exactly it. What she missed was the way life had felt when she'd first started talking to Trevor. When she had someone to think about if she couldn't sleep at night, someone's name to doodle dorkily inside her notebooks. The truth was, Luce and Trevor never really had the chance to get to know each other all that well. The only memento she had was the picture Callie had snapped covertly, from across the football field between two of his squat sets, when he and Luce had talked for fifteen seconds about . . . his squat sets. And the only date she'd ever gone on with him hadn't even been a real date—just a stolen hour when he'd pulled her away from the rest of the party. An hour she'd regret for the rest of her life.

It had started out innocently enough, just two people going for a walk down by the lake, but it wasn't long before Luce started to feel the shadows lurking overhead. Then Trevor's lips touched hers, and the heat coursed through her body, and his eyes turned white with terror . . . and seconds later, life as she'd known it had gone up in a blaze.

Luce rolled over and buried her face in the crook of an arm. She'd spent months mourning Trevor's death, and now, lying in this strange room, with the metal bars digging into her skin through the thin mattress, she felt the selfish futility of it all. She hadn't known Trevor any more than she knew . . . well, Cam.

A knock on her door made Luce shoot up from the bed. How would anyone know to find her here? She tiptoed to the door and pulled it open. Then she stuck her head into the very empty hallway. She hadn't even heard footsteps outside, and there was no sign of anyone having just knocked.

Except the paper airplane pinned with a brass tack to the center of the corkboard next to her door. Luce smiled to see her name written in black marker along the wing, but when she unfolded the note, all that was written inside was a black arrow pointing straight down the hall.

Arriane *had* invited her over tonight, but that was before the incident with Molly in the cafeteria. Looking down the empty hallway, Luce wondered about following the cryptic arrow. Then she glanced back at her giant duffel bag, her pity party waiting to be unpacked. She shrugged, pulled her door shut, put her room key in her pocket, and started walking.

She stopped in front of a door on the other side of the hall to check out an oversized poster of Sonny Terry, a blind musician who she knew from her father's scratchy record collection was an incredible blues harmonica player. She leaned forward to read the name on the corkboard and realized with a start that she was standing in front of Roland Sparks's room. Immediately, annoyingly, there was that little part of her brain that started calculating the odds that Roland might be hanging out with Daniel, with only a thin door separating them from Luce.

A mechanical buzzing sound made Luce jump. She looked straight into a surveillance camera drilled into the wall over Roland's door. The reds. Zooming in on her every move. She shrank away, embarrassed for reasons no camera would be able to discern. Anyway, she'd come here to see Arriane—whose room, she realized, just happened to be directly across the hall from Roland.

In front of Arriane's room, Luce felt a little stab of tenderness. The entire door was covered with bumper stickers—some printed, others obviously homemade. There were so many that they overlapped, each slogan half covering and often contradicting the one before it. Luce laughed under her breath as she imagined Arriane collecting the bumper stickers indiscriminately (MEAN PEOPLE RULE . . . MY DAUGHTER IS AN F STUDENT AT SWORD & CROSS . . . VOTE NO ON PROP 666), then slapping them with a haphazard—but committed—focus onto her turf.

Luce could have kept herself entertained for an hour reading Arriane's door, but soon she started to feel self-conscious about standing in front of a dorm room she was only half certain she'd actually been invited to. Then she saw the second paper airplane. She pulled it down from the corkboard and unfolded the message:

My Darling Luce,

If you actually showed up to hang out tonight, props! We'll get along juuust fine.

If you bailed on me, then . . . get your claws off my private note, ROLAND! How many times do I have to tell you? Jeez.

Anyhow: I know I said to swing by tonight, but I had to dash straight from R&R in the nurse's station (the silver lining of my Taser treatment today) to a makeup biology review with the Albatross. Which is to say—rain check?

Yours psychotically,

A

Luce stood with the note in her hands, unsure about what to do next. She was relieved to read that Arriane was being taken care of, but she still wished she could see the girl in person. She wanted to hear the nonchalance in Arriane's voice for herself, so that she'd know how to feel about what had happened in the cafeteria today. But standing there in the hallway, Luce was ever more uncertain how to process the day's events. A quiet panic filled her when it finally registered that she was alone, after dark, at Sword & Cross.

Behind her, a door cracked open. A sliver of white light opened up on the floor beneath her feet. Luce heard music being played inside a room.

"Whatcha doin'?" It was Roland, standing in his doorway in a torn white T-shirt and jeans. His dreads were gathered in a yellow rubber band on top of his head and he held a harmonica up next to his lips.

"I came to see Arriane," Luce said, trying to keep herself from looking past him to see if anyone else was in the room. "We were supposed to—"

"Nobody's home," he said, cryptically. Luce didn't

know if he meant Arriane, or the rest of the kids in the dorm, or what. He played a few bars on the harmonica, keeping his eyes on her the whole time. Then he held open the door a little bit wider and raised his eyebrows. She couldn't tell whether or not he was inviting her to come in.

"Well, I was just swinging by on my way to the library," she lied quickly, turning back the way she'd come. "There's a book I need to check out."

"Luce," Roland called.

She turned around. They hadn't officially met yet, and she hadn't expected him to know her name. His eyes flashed a smile at her and he used the harmonica to point in the opposite direction. "Library's that way," he said. He crossed his arms over his chest. "Be sure to check out the special collections in the east wing. They're really something."

"Thanks," Luce said, feeling truly grateful as she changed course. Roland seemed so real right then, waving and playing a few parting slides on the harmonica as she left. Maybe he'd only made her nervous earlier because she thought of him as Daniel's friend. For all she knew, Roland could be a really nice person. Her mood lifted as she walked down the hallway. First Arriane's note had been snappy and sarcastic, then she'd had a non-awkward encounter with Roland Sparks; plus she really *did* want to check out the library. Things were looking up.

Near the end of the hall, where the dorm elbowed off toward the library wing, Luce passed the only cracked-open door on the floor. There was no decorative flair on this door, but someone had painted it all black. As she got closer, Luce could hear angry heavy metal music playing inside. She didn't even have to pause to read the name on the door. It was Molly's.

Luce quickened her steps, suddenly aware of every clop of her black riding boots on the linoleum. She didn't realize she'd been holding her breath until she pushed through the wood-grained library doors and exhaled.

A warm feeling came over Luce as she looked around the library. She'd always loved the faintly sweet musty way that only a roomful of books smelled. She took comfort in the soft occasional sound of turning pages. The library at Dover had always been her escape, and Luce felt almost overwhelmed with relief as she realized that this one might offer her the same sense of sanctuary. She could hardly believe that this place belonged to Sword & Cross. It was almost . . . it was actually . . . inviting.

The walls were a deep mahogany and the ceilings were high. A fireplace with a brick hearth lay along one wall. There were long wooden tables lit by old-fashioned green lamps, and aisles of books that went on farther than she could see. The sound of her boots was hushed by a thick Persian carpet as Luce wandered past the entryway.

A few students were studying, none that Luce knew by name, but even the more punky-looking kids seemed less threatening with their heads bent over books. She neared the main circulation desk, which was a great round station at the center of the room. It was strewn with stacks of papers and books and had a homey academic messiness that reminded Luce of her parents' house. The books were piled so high that Luce almost didn't see the librarian seated behind them. She was rooting through some paperwork with the energy of someone panning for gold. Her head popped up as Luce approached.

"Hello!" The woman smiled—she actually *smiled*—at Luce. Her hair was not gray but silver, with a kind of brilliance that sparkled even in the soft library light. Her face looked old and young at the same time. She had pale, almost incandescent skin, bright black eyes, and a tiny, pointed nose. When she spoke to Luce, she pushed up the sleeves of her white cashmere sweater, exposing stacks and stacks of pearl bracelets decorating both of her wrists. "Can I help you find something?" she asked in a happy whisper.

Luce felt instantly at ease with this woman, and glanced down at the nameplate on her desk. Sophia Bliss. She wished she did have a library request. This woman was the first authority figure she'd seen all day whose help she would actually have wanted to seek out. But she was just here wandering around . . . and then she remembered what Roland Sparks had said.

"I'm new here," she explained. "Lucinda Price. Could you tell me where the east wing is?"

The woman gave Luce a you-look-like-the-reading-sort smile that Luce had been getting from librarians all her life. "Right that way," she said, pointing toward a row of tall windows on the other side of the room. "I'm Miss Sophia, and if my roster's correct, you're in my religion seminar on Tuesdays and Thursdays. Oh, we're going to have some fun!" She winked. "In the meantime, if you need anything else, I'm here. A pleasure to meet you, Luce."

Luce smiled her thanks, told Miss Sophia happily that she'd see her tomorrow in class, and started toward the windows. It was only after she'd left the librarian that she wondered about the strange, intimate way the woman had called her by her nickname.

She'd just cleared the main study area and was passing through the tall, elegant book stacks when something dark and macabre passed over her head. She glanced up.

No. Not here. Please. Let me just have this one place.

When the shadows came and went, Luce was never sure exactly where they ended up—or how long they would be gone.

She couldn't figure out what was happening now. Something was different. She was terrified, yes, but she didn't feel cold. In fact, she felt a little bit flushed. The library was warm, but it wasn't *that* warm. And then her eyes fell on Daniel.

He was facing the window, his back to her, leaning

over a podium that said SPECIAL COLLECTIONS in white letters. The sleeves of his worn leather jacket were pushed up around his elbows, and his blond hair glowed under the lights. His shoulders were hunched over, and yet again, Luce had an instinct to fold herself into them. She shook it from her head and stood on tiptoe to get a better look at him. From here, she couldn't be certain, but he looked like he was drawing something.

As she watched the slight movement of his body as he sketched, Luce's insides felt like they were burning, like she'd swallowed something hot. She couldn't figure out why, against all reason, she had this wild premonition that Daniel was drawing her.

She *shouldn't* go to him. After all, she didn't even know him, had never actually spoken to him. Their only communication so far had included one middle finger and a couple of dirty looks. Yet for some reason, it felt very important to her that she find out what was on that sketchpad.

Then it hit her. The dream she'd had the night before. The briefest flash of it came back to her all of a sudden. In the dream, it had been late at night—damp and chilly, and she'd been dressed in something long and flowing. She leaned up against a curtained window in an unfamiliar room. The only other person there was a man . . . or a boy—she never got to see his face. He was sketching her likeness on a thick pad of paper. Her hair.

Her neck. The precise outline of her profile. She stood behind him, too afraid to let him know she was watching, too intrigued to turn away.

Luce jerked forward as she felt something pinch the back of her shoulder, then float over her head. The shadow had resurfaced. It was black and as thick as a curtain.

The pounding of her heart grew so loud that it filled her ears, blocking out the dark rustle of the shadow, blocking out the sound of her footsteps. Daniel glanced up from his work and seemed to raise his eyes to exactly where the shadow hovered, but he didn't start the way she had.

Of course, he couldn't see them. His focus settled calmly outside the window.

The heat inside her grew stronger. She was close enough now that she felt like he must be able to feel it coming off her skin.

As quietly as she could, Luce tried to peer over his shoulder at his sketchpad. For just a second, her mind saw the curve of her own bare neck sketched in pencil on the page. But then she blinked, and when her eyes settled back on the paper, she had to swallow hard.

It was a landscape. Daniel was drawing the view of the cemetery out the window in almost perfect detail. Luce had never seen anything that made her quite so sad.

She didn't know why. It was crazy—even for her—to have expected her bizarre intuition to come true. There was no reason for Daniel to draw her. She knew that. Just like she knew he'd had no reason to flip her off this morning. But he had.

"What are you doing over here?" he asked. He'd closed his sketchbook and was looking at her solemnly. His full lips were set in a straight line and his gray eyes looked dull. He didn't look angry, for a change; he looked exhausted.

"I came to check out a book from Special Collections," she said in a wobbly voice. But as she looked around, she quickly realized her mistake. Special Collections wasn't a section of books—it was an open area in the library for an art display about the Civil War. She and Daniel were standing in a tiny gallery of bronze busts of war heroes, glass cases filled with old promissory notes and Confederate maps. It was the only section of the library where there wasn't a single book to check out.

"Good luck with that," Daniel said, opening up his sketchbook again, as if to say, preemptively, *goodbye*.

Luce was tongue-tied and embarrassed and what she would have liked to do was escape. But then, there were the shadows, still lurking nearby, and for some reason Luce felt better about them when she was next to Daniel. It made no sense—like there was anything he could do to protect her from them.

She was stuck, rooted to her spot. He glanced up at her and sighed.

"Let me ask you, do you like being sneaked up on?"

Luce thought about the shadows and what they were doing to her right now. Without thinking, she shook her head roughly.

"Okay, that makes two of us." He cleared his throat and stared at her, driving home the point that she was the intruder.

Maybe she could explain that she was feeling a little light-headed and just needed to sit down for a minute. She started to say, "Look, can I—"

But Daniel picked up his sketchbook and got to his feet. "I came here to get away," he said, cutting her off. "If you're not going to leave, I will."

He shoved his sketchbook into his backpack. When he pushed past, his shoulder brushed hers. Even as brief as the touch was, even through their layers of clothes, Luce felt a shock of static.

For a second, Daniel stood still, too. They turned their heads to look back at each other, and Luce opened her mouth. But before she could speak, Daniel had turned on his heel and was walking quickly toward the door. Luce watched as the shadows crept over his head, swirled in a circle, then rushed out the window into the night.

She shivered in the chill of their wake, and for a long time after that, stood in the special collections area, touching her shoulder where Daniel had, feeling the heat cool down.

FOUR

GRAVEYARD SHIFT

Ahhh, Tuesday. *Waffle day.* For as long as Luce could remember, summer Tuesdays meant fresh coffee, brimming bowls of raspberries and whipped cream, and an unending stack of crispy golden brown waffles. Even this summer, when her parents started acting a little scared of her, waffle day was one thing she could count on. She could roll over in bed on a Tuesday morning, and before she was aware of anything else, she knew instinctively what day it was.

Luce sniffed, slowly coming to her senses, then sniffed again with a little more gusto. No, there was no buttermilk batter, nothing but the vinegary smell of peeling paint. She rubbed the sleep away and took in her cramped dorm room. It looked like the "before" shot on a home renovation show. The long nightmare that had been Monday came back to her: the surrender of her cell phone, the meat loaf incident and Molly's flashing eyes in the lunchroom, Daniel brushing her off in the library. What it was that made him so spiteful, Luce didn't have a clue.

She sat up to look out the window. It was still dark; the sun hadn't even peeked over the horizon yet. She never woke up this early. If pressed, she didn't actually think she could remember ever having seen the sunrise. Truthfully, something about sunrise-watching as an activity had always made her nervous. It was the waiting moments, the just-before-the-sun-snapped-over-the-horizon moments, sitting in the darkness looking out across a tree line. Prime shadow time.

Luce sighed an audibly homesick, lonely sigh, which made her even more homesick and lonely. What was she going to do with herself for the three hours between the crack of dawn and her first class? *Crack of dawn*—why did the words ring in her ears? Oh. Crap. She was supposed to be at detention.

She scrambled out of bed, tripping over her still-packed

duffel bag, and yanked another boring black sweater from the top of a stack of boring black sweaters. She tugged on yesterday's black jeans, winced as she caught a glimpse of her disastrous bed head, and tried to run her fingers through her hair as she dashed out the door.

She was out of breath when she reached the waist-high, intricately sculpted wrought iron gates of the cemetery. She was choking on the overwhelming smell of skunk cabbage and feeling far too alone with her thoughts. Where was everyone else? Was their definition of "crack of dawn" different from hers? She glanced down at her watch. It was already six-fifteen.

All they'd told her was to meet at the cemetery, and Luce was pretty sure this was the only entrance. She stood at the threshold, where the gritty asphalt of the parking lot gave way to a mangled lot full of weeds. She spotted a lone dandelion, and it crossed her mind that a younger Luce would have pounced on it and then made a wish and blown. But this Luce's wishes felt too heavy for something so light.

The delicate gates were all that divided the cemetery from the parking lot. Pretty remarkable for a school with so much barbed wire everywhere else. Luce ran her hand along the gates, tracing the ornate floral pattern with her fingers. The gates must have dated back to the Civil War days Arriane was talking about, back when the cemetery was used to bury fallen soldiers. When the school attached to it was not a home for wayward psychos. When the whole place was a lot less overgrown and shadowy.

It was strange—the rest of the campus was as flat as a sheet of paper, but somehow, the cemetery had a concave, bowl-like shape. From here, she could see the slope of the whole vast thing before her. Row after row of simple headstones lined the slopes like spectators at an arena.

But toward the middle, at the lowest point of the cemetery, the path through the grounds twisted into a maze of larger carved tombs, marble statues, and mausoleums. Probably for Confederate officers, or just the soldiers who came from money. They looked like they'd be beautiful up close. But from here, the sheer weight of them seemed to drag the cemetery down, almost like the whole place was being swallowed into a drain.

Footsteps behind her. Luce whirled around to see a stumpy, black-clad figure emerge from behind a tree. Penn! She had to resist the urge to throw her arms around the girl. Luce had never been so glad to see anyone—though it was hard to believe Penn ever got detentions.

"Aren't you late?" Penn asked, stopping a few feet in front of Luce and giving her an amused you-poor-newbie shake of the head.

"I've been here for ten minutes," Luce said. "Aren't *you* the one who's late?"

Penn smirked. "No way, I'm just an early riser. I

never get detention." She shrugged and pushed her purple glasses up on her nose. "But you do, along with five other unfortunate souls, who are probably getting angrier by the minute waiting for you down at the monolith." She stood on tiptoe and pointed behind Luce, toward the largest stone structure, which rose up from the middle of the deepest part of the cemetery. If Luce squinted, she could just make out a group of black figures clustered around its base.

"They just said meet at the cemetery," Luce said, already feeling defeated. "No one told me where to go."

"Well, I'm telling you: monolith. Now get down there," Penn said. "You're not going to make many friends by cutting into their morning any more than you already have."

Luce gulped. Part of her wanted to ask Penn to show her the way. From up here, it looked like a labyrinth, and Luce did not want to get lost in the cemetery. Suddenly, she got that nervous, far-away-from-home feeling, and she knew it was only going to get worse in there. She cracked her knuckles, stalling.

"Luce?" Penn said, giving her shoulders a bit of a shove. "You're still standing here."

Luce tried to give Penn a brave thank-you smile, but had to settle for an awkward facial twitch. Then she hurried down the slope into the heart of the cemetery.

The sun still hadn't risen, but it was getting closer, and these last few predawn moments were always the ones that creeped her out the most. She tore past the rows of plain headstones. At one point they must have been upright, but by now they were so old that most of them tipped over to one side or the other, giving the whole place the look of a set of morbid dominoes.

She slopped in her black Converse sneakers through puddles of mud, crunched over dead leaves. By the time she cleared the section of simple plots and made it to the more ornate tombs, the ground had more or less flattened out, and she was totally lost. She stopped running, tried to catch her breath. Voices. If she calmed down, she could hear voices.

"Five more minutes, then I'm out," a guy said.

"Too bad your opinion has no value, Mr. Sparks." An ornery voice, one Luce recognized from her classes yesterday. Ms. Tross—the Albatross. After the meat loaf incident, Luce had shown up late to her class and hadn't exactly made the most favorable impression on the dour, spherical science teacher.

"Unless anyone wants to lose his or her social privileges this week"—groans from among the tombs—"we will all wait patiently, as if we had nothing better to do, until Miss Price decides to grace us with her presence."

"I'm here," Luce gasped, finally rounding a giant statue of a cherub.

Ms. Tross stood with her hands on her hips, wearing a variation of yesterday's loose black muumuu. Her thin mouse-brown hair was plastered to her scalp and her dull brown eyes showed only annoyance at Luce's arrival. Biology had always been tough for Luce, and so far, she wasn't doing her grade in Ms. Tross's class any favors.

Behind the Albatross were Arriane, Molly, and Roland, scattered around a circle of plinths that all faced a large central statue of an angel. Compared to the rest of the statues, this one seemed newer, whiter, grander. And leaning up against the angel's sculpted thigh—she almost hadn't noticed—was Daniel.

He was wearing the busted black leather jacket and the bright red scarf she'd fixated on yesterday. Luce took in his messy blond hair, which looked like it hadn't yet been smoothed down after sleep . . . which made her think about what Daniel might look like when he was sleeping . . . which made her blush so intensely that by the time her eyes made their way down from his hairline to his eyes, she was thoroughly humiliated.

By then he was glaring at her.

"I'm sorry," she blurted out. "I didn't know where we were supposed to meet. I swear—"

"Save it," Ms. Tross said, dragging a finger across her throat. "You've wasted enough of everyone's time. Now, I'm sure you all remember whatever despicable indiscretion you committed to find yourself here. You can think about that for the next two hours while you work. Pair up. You know the drill." She glanced at Luce and let out her breath. "Okay, who wants a protégée?"

To Luce's horror, all of the other students looked at

their feet. But then, after a torturous minute, a fifth student stepped into view around the corner of the mausoleum.

"I do."

Cam. His black V-neck T-shirt fit close around his broad shoulders. He stood almost a foot taller than Roland, who moved aside as Cam pushed past and walked toward Luce. His eyes were glued to her as he strode forward, moving smoothly and confidently, as at ease in his reform school garb as Luce was ill at ease. Part of her wanted to avert her eyes, because it was embarrassing the way Cam was staring at her in front of everyone. But for some reason, she was mesmerized. She couldn't break his gaze—until Arriane stepped between them.

"Dibs," she said. "I called dibs."

"No you didn't," Cam said.

"Yes I did, you just didn't hear me from your weird perch back there." The words rushed out of Arriane. "I want her."

"I—" Cam started to respond.

Arriane cocked her head expectantly. Luce swallowed. Was he going to come out and say *he* wanted her, too? Couldn't they just forget about it? Serve detention in a group of three?

Cam patted Luce's arm. "I'll catch up with you after, okay?" he said to her, like it was a promise she'd asked him to keep.

The other kids hopped off tombs they'd been sitting

on and trooped toward a shed. Luce followed, clinging to Arriane, who wordlessly handed her a rake.

"So. Do you want the avenging angel, or the fleshy embracing lovers?"

There was no mention of yesterday's events, or of Arriane's note, and Luce somehow didn't feel she should bring anything up with Arriane now. Instead, she glanced overhead to find herself flanked by two giant statues. The one closer to her looked like a Rodin. A nude man and woman stood tangled in an embrace. She'd studied French sculpture back at Dover, and always thought Rodins were the most romantic pieces. But now it was hard to look at the embracing lovers without thinking of Daniel. *Daniel.* Who hated her. If she needed any further proof of that after he'd basically bolted from the library last night, all she had to do was think back to the fresh glare she'd gotten from him this morning.

"Where's the avenging angel?" she asked Arriane with a sigh.

"Good choice. Over here." Arriane led Luce to a massive marble sculpture of an angel saving the ground from the strike of a thunderbolt. It might have been an interesting piece, back in the day when it was first carved. But now it just looked old and dirty, covered in mud and green moss.

"I don't get it," Luce said. "What do we do?"

"Scrub-a-dub-dub," Arriane said, almost singing. "I

like to pretend I'm giving them a little bath." With that, she scrambled up the giant angel, swinging her legs over the statue's thunderbolt-thwarting arm, as if the whole thing were a sturdy old oak tree for her to climb.

Terrified of looking like she was asking for more trouble from Ms. Tross, Luce starting working her rake across the base of the statue. She tried to clear away what seemed like an endless pile of damp leaves.

Three minutes later, her arms were *killing* her. She definitely hadn't dressed for this kind of muddy manual labor. Luce had never been sent to detention at Dover, but from what she'd overheard, it consisted of filling a piece of paper with "I will not plagiarize off the Internet" a few hundred times.

This was brutal. Especially when all she'd really done was accidentally bump into Molly in the lunchroom. She was trying not to make snap judgments here, but clearing mud from the graves of people who'd been dead over a century? Luce totally hated her life right now.

Then a tease of sunlight finally filtered through the trees, and suddenly there was color in the graveyard. Luce felt instantly lighter. She could see more than ten feet in front of her. She could see Daniel . . . working side by side with Molly.

Luce's heart sank. The airy feeling disappeared.

She looked at Arriane, who shot her a this-blows sympathy glance but kept working.

"Hey," Luce whispered loudly.

Arriane put a finger to her lips but motioned for Luce to climb up next to her.

With much less grace and agility, Luce grabbed the statue's arm and swung herself up onto the plinth. Once she was fairly certain that she wasn't going to tumble to the ground, she whispered, "So . . . Daniel's friends with Molly?"

Arriane snorted. "No way, they totally hate each other," she said quickly, then paused. "Why d'you ask?"

Luce pointed at the two of them, doing no work whatsoever to clear brush from their tomb. They were standing close to each other, leaning on their rakes and having a conversation that Luce desperately wished she could hear. "They look like friends to me."

"It's detention," Arriane said flatly. "You have to pair up. Do you think Roland and Chester the Molester are friends?" She pointed at Roland and Cam. They seemed to be arguing about the best way to divvy up their work on the lovers' statue. "Detention buddies does *not* equal real-life buddies."

Arriane looked back at Luce, who could feel her face falling, despite her best efforts to appear unfazed.

"Look, Luce, I didn't mean . . ." She trailed off. "Okay, aside from the fact that you made me waste a good twenty minutes of my morning, I have no problem with you. In fact, I think you're sort of interesting. Kinda fresh. That said, I don't know what you were expecting in terms of mushy-gushy friendship here at Sword & Cross. But let me be the first to tell you, it just ain't that easy. People are here because they've got baggage. I'm talking curbside-check-in, pay-the-fine-'cause-it's-over-fifty-pounds kind of baggage. Get it?"

Luce shrugged, feeling embarrassed. "It was just a question."

Arriane snickered. "Are you always so defensive? What the hell did you do to get in here, anyway?"

Luce didn't feel like talking about it. Maybe Arriane was right, she'd be better off not trying to make friends. She hopped down and went back to attacking the moss at the base of the statue.

Unfortunately, Arriane was intrigued. She hopped down, too, and brought her rake down on top of Luce's to pin it in place.

"Ooh, tell me tell me tell me," she taunted.

Arriane's face was so close to Luce's. It reminded Luce of yesterday, crouching over Arriane after she'd convulsed. They'd had a moment, hadn't they? And part of Luce badly wanted to be able to talk to someone. It had been such a long, stifling summer with her parents. She sighed, resting her forehead on the handle of her rake.

A salty, nervous taste filled her mouth, but she couldn't swallow it away. The last time she'd gone into these details, it had been because of a court order. She would just as soon have forgotten them, but the longer Arriane stared her down, the clearer the words grew, and the closer they came to the tip of her tongue.

"I was with a friend one night," she started to explain, taking a long, deep breath. "And something terrible happened." She closed her eyes, praying that the scene wouldn't play out in a burst under the red-black of her eyelids. "There was a fire. I made it out . . . and he didn't."

Arriane yawned, much less horrified by the story than Luce was.

"Anyway," Luce went on, "afterwards, I couldn't remember the details, how it happened. What I could remember—what I told the judge, anyway—I guess they thought I was crazy." She tried to smile, but it felt forced.

To Luce's surprise, Arriane squeezed her shoulder. And for a second, her face looked really sincere. Then it changed back into its smirk.

"We're all *so* misunderstood, aren't we?" She poked Luce in the gut with her finger. "You know, Roland and I were just talking about how we don't have any pyromaniac friends. And everyone knows you need a good pyro to pull off any reform school prank worth the effort." She was scheming already. "Roland thought maybe that other new kid, Todd, but I'd rather cast my lot with you. We should all collaborate sometime."

Luce swallowed hard. She wasn't a pyro. But she was

done talking about her past; she didn't even feel like defending herself.

"Ooh, wait until Roland hears," Arriane said, throwing down her rake. "You're like our dream come true."

Luce opened her mouth to protest, but Arriane had already taken off. *Perfect,* Luce thought, listening to the sound of Arriane's shoes squishing through the mud. Now it was only a matter of minutes before word traveled around the cemetery to Daniel.

Alone again, she looked up at the statue. Even though she'd already cleared a huge pile of moss and mulch, the angel looked dirtier than ever. The whole project felt so pointless. She doubted anyone ever came to visit this place anyway. She also doubted that any of the other detainees were still working.

Her eye just happened to fall on Daniel, who *was* working. He was very diligently using a wire brush to scrub some mold off the bronze inscription on a tomb. He'd even pushed up the sleeves of his sweater, and Luce could see his muscles straining as he went at it. She sighed, and—she couldn't help it—leaned her elbow against the stone angel to watch him.

He's always been such a hard worker.

Luce quickly shook her head. Where had that come from? She had no idea what it meant. And yet, she'd been the one who'd thought it. It was the kind of phrase that sometimes formed in her mind just before she drifted into sleep. Senseless babble she could never assign to anything outside her dreams. But here she was, wide-awake.

She needed to get a handle on this Daniel thing. She'd known him for one day, and already, she could feel herself slipping into a very strange and unfamiliar place.

"Probably best to stay away from him," a cold voice behind her said.

Luce whipped around to find Molly, in the same pose she'd found her in yesterday: hands on her hips, pierced nostrils flaring. Penn had told her that Sword & Cross's surprising ruling that allowed facial piercings came from the headmaster's own reluctance to remove the diamond stud in his ear.

"Who?" she asked Molly, knowing she sounded stupid.

Molly rolled her eyes. "Just trust me when I tell you that falling for Daniel would be a very, very bad idea."

Before Luce could answer, Molly was gone. But Daniel—it was almost as if he'd heard his name—was looking straight at her. Then *walking* straight at her.

She knew the sun had gone behind a cloud. If she could break his stare, she could look up and see it for herself. But she couldn't look up, she couldn't look away, and for some reason, she had to squint to see him. Almost like Daniel was creating his own light, like he was blinding her. A hollow ringing noise filled up her ears, and her knees began to tremble.

She wanted to pick up her rake and pretend she didn't see him coming. But it was too late to play it cool.

"What'd she say to you?" he asked.

"Um," she hedged, racking her brain for a sensible lie. Finding nothing. She cracked her knuckles.

Daniel cupped his hand over hers. "I hate it when you do that."

Luce jerked away instinctively. His hand on hers had been so fleeting, yet she felt her face flush. He meant it was a pet peeve of his, that knuckle cracking from *anyone* would bother him, right? Because to say that he hated it when *she* did that implied that he'd seen her do it before. And he couldn't have. He barely knew her.

Then why did this feel like a fight they'd had before?

"Molly told me to stay away from you," she said finally.

Daniel tilted his head from side to side, seeming to consider this. "She's probably right."

Luce shivered. A shadow drifted over them, darkening the angel's face just long enough for Luce to worry. She closed her eyes and tried to breathe, praying Daniel couldn't tell anything was strange.

But the panic was rising inside her. She wanted to run. She couldn't run. What if she got lost in the cemetery?

Daniel followed her gaze toward the sky. "What is it?"

"Nothing."

"So are you going to do it?" he asked, crossing his arms over his chest, a dare.

"What?" she said. *Run?*

Daniel took a step toward her. He was now less than a foot away. She held her breath. She kept her body completely still. She waited.

"Are you going to stay away from me?"

It almost sounded like he was flirting.

But Luce was completely out of sorts. Her brow was damp with sweat, and she squeezed her temples between two fingers, trying to regain possession of her body, trying to take it back from his control. She was totally unprepared to flirt back. That was, if what he was doing was actually flirting.

She took a step back. "I guess so."

"Didn't hear you," he whispered, cocking an eyebrow and taking another step closer.

Luce backed up again, farther this time. She practically slammed into the base of the statue, and could feel the gritty stone foot of the angel scraping her back. A second, darker, colder shadow whooshed over them. She could have sworn Daniel shivered along with her.

And then the deep groan of something heavy startled them both. Luce gasped as the top of the marble statue teetered over them, like a tree branch swaying in the breeze. For a second, it seemed to hover in the air.

Luce and Daniel stood staring at the angel. Both of

them knew it was on its way down. The angel's head bowed slowly toward them, like it was praying—and then the whole statue picked up speed as it started hurtling down. Luce felt Daniel's hand wrap around her waist instantly, tightly, like he knew exactly where she began and where she ended. His other hand covered her head and forced her down just as the statue toppled over them. Right where they'd been standing. It landed with a massive crash—headfirst in the mud, with its feet still resting on the plinth, leaving a little triangle underneath, where Daniel and Luce crouched.

They were panting, nose to nose, Daniel's eyes scared. Between their bodies and the statue, there were only a few inches of space.

"Luce?" he whispered.

All she could do was nod.

His eyes narrowed. "What did you see?"

Then a hand appeared and Luce felt herself being pulled out of the space under the statue. There was a scraping against her back and then a waft of air. She saw the flicker of daylight again. The detention crew stood gaping, except for Ms. Tross, who was glaring, and Cam, who helped Luce to her feet.

"Are you okay?" Cam asked, running his eyes over her for scrapes and bruises and brushing some dirt from her shoulder. "I saw the statue coming down and I ran over to try and stop it, but it was already . . . You must have been so terrified."

Luce didn't respond. Terrified was only part of how she'd felt.

Daniel, already on his feet, didn't even turn around to see whether she was okay or not. He just walked away.

Luce's jaw dropped as she watched him go, as she watched everyone else seem not to care that he had bailed.

"What did you do?" Ms. Tross asked.

"I don't know. One minute, we were standing there"—Luce glanced at Ms. Tross—"um, working. The next thing I knew, the statue just fell over."

The Albatross bent down to examine the shattered angel. Its head had cracked straight down the middle. She started muttering something about forces of nature and old stones.

But it was the voice at Luce's ear that stayed with her, even after everyone else had gone back to work. It was Molly, just inches behind her shoulder, who whispered, "Looks like someone should start listening when I give advice."

FIVE

THE INNER CIRCLE

"Don't ever scare me like that again!" Callie reprimanded Luce on Wednesday evening.

It was just before sundown and Luce was folded into the Sword & Cross phone cubby, a tiny beige confine in the middle of the front office area. It was far from private, but at least no one else was loafing around. Her arms were still sore from the graveyard shift at yesterday's detention, her pride still wounded from Daniel's fleeing the second they'd been pulled out from under the statue. But for fifteen minutes, Luce was trying hard to push all that out of her mind, to soak up every blissfully frantic word her best friend could spit out in the allotted time. It felt so good to hear Callie's high-pitched voice, Luce almost didn't care that she was being yelled at.

"We promised we wouldn't go an *hour* without speaking," Callie continued accusingly. "I thought someone had eaten you alive! Or that maybe they stuck you in solitary in one of those straitjackets where you have to chew through your sleeve to scratch your face. For all I knew, you could have descended into the ninth circle of—"

"Okay, *Mom*," Luce said, laughing and settling into her role as Callie's breathing instructor. "Relax." For a split second, she felt guilty that she hadn't used her one phone call to dial up her real mom. But she knew Callie would wig out if she ever discovered Luce hadn't seized her very first opportunity to get in touch. And in a weird way, it was always soothing to hear Callie's hysterical voice. It was one of the many reasons the two were such a good fit: Her best friend's over-the-top paranoia actually had a calming effect on Luce. She could just picture Callie in her dorm room at Dover, pacing her bright orange area rug, with Oxy smeared over her t-zone and pedicure foam separating her still-wet fuchsia toenails.

"Don't *Mom* me!" Callie huffed. "Start talking. What are the other kids like? Are they all scary and popping diuretics like in the movies? What about your classes? How's the food?"

Through the phone, Luce could hear *Roman Holiday*

playing in the background on Callie's tiny TV. Luce's favorite scene had always been the one where Audrey Hepburn woke in Gregory Peck's room, still convinced the night before had all been a dream. Luce closed her eyes and tried to picture the shot in her mind. Mimicking Audrey's drowsy whisper, she quoted the line she knew Callie would recognize: "There was a man, he was so *mean* to me. It was *wonderful*."

"Okay, Princess, it's *your* life I want to hear about," Callie teased.

Unfortunately, there was nothing about Sword & Cross that Luce would even consider describing as wonderful. Thinking about Daniel for, oh, the eightieth time that day, she realized that the only parallel between her life and *Roman Holiday* was that she and Audrey both had a guy who was aggressively rude and uninterested in them. Luce rested her head against the beige linoleum of the cubby walls. Someone had carved the words BIDING MY TIME. Under normal circumstances, this would be when Luce would spill everything about Daniel to Callie.

Except, for some reason, she didn't.

Whatever she might want to say about Daniel wouldn't be based on anything that had actually happened between them. And Callie was big on guys making an effort to show they were worthy of you. She'd want to hear things like how many times he'd held open a door for Luce, or whether he'd noticed how good her

French accent was. Callie didn't think there was anything wrong with guys writing the kind of sappy love poems Luce could *never* take seriously. Luce would come up severely short on things to say about Daniel. In fact, Callie'd be much more interested in hearing about someone like Cam.

"Well, there *is* this guy here," Luce whispered into the phone.

"I knew it!" Callie squealed. "Name."

Daniel. *Daniel.* Luce cleared her throat. "Cam."

"Direct, uncomplicated. I can dig it. Start from the beginning."

"Well, nothing's really happened yet."

"He thinks you're gorgeous, blah blah blah. I told you the cropped cut made you look like Audrey. Get to the good stuff."

"Well—" Luce broke off. The sound of footsteps in the lobby silenced her. She leaned out the side of the cubby and craned her neck to see who was interrupting the best fifteen minutes she'd had in three whole days.

Cam was walking toward her.

Speak of the devil. She swallowed the horrifically lame words on the tip of her tongue: *He gave me his guitar pick.* She still had it tucked in her pocket.

Cam's demeanor was casual, as if by some stroke of luck he hadn't heard what she'd been saying. He seemed to be the only kid at Sword & Cross who didn't change out of his school uniform the minute classes were over. But the black-on-black look worked for him, just as much as it worked to make Luce look like a grocery store checkout girl.

Cam was twirling a golden pocket watch that swung from a long chain looped around his index finger. Luce followed its bright arc for a moment, almost mesmerized, until Cam clapped the face of the watch to a stop in his fist. He looked down at it, then up at her.

"Sorry." His lips pursed in confusion. "I thought I signed up for the seven o'clock phone call." He shrugged. "But I must have written it down wrong."

Luce's heart sank when she glanced at her own watch. She and Callie had barely said fifteen words to each other—how could her fifteen minutes already be up?

"Luce? Hello?" Callie sounded impatient on the other end of the phone. "You're being weird. Is there something you're not telling me? Have you replaced me already with some reform school cutter? What about the boy?"

"Shhh," Luce hissed into the phone. "Cam, wait," she called, holding the phone away from her mouth. He was already halfway out the door. "Just a second, I was"—she swallowed—"I was just getting off."

Cam slipped the pocket watch into the front of his black blazer and doubled back toward Luce. He raised his eyebrows and laughed when he heard Callie's voice growing louder from the earpiece. "Don't you dare hang up on me," Callie protested. "You've told me nothing. *Nothing!*"

"I don't want to piss anyone off," Cam joked, gesturing at the barking telephone. "Take my slot, you can get me back another time."

"No," Luce said quickly. As badly as she wanted to keep talking to Callie, she imagined Cam probably felt the same way about whomever he'd come here to call. And unlike a lot of the people at this school, Cam had been nothing but nice to her. She didn't want to make him give up his turn at the telephone, especially now, when she'd be way too nervous to gossip with Callie about him.

"Callie," she said, sighing into the phone. "I gotta go. I'll call again as soon as—" But by then there was just the vague buzz of a dial tone in her ear. The phone itself had been rigged to cap each call at fifteen minutes. Now she saw the tiny timer blinking 0:00 on its base. They hadn't even gotten to say goodbye and now she'd have to wait another whole week to call. Time stretched out in Luce's mind like an endless gulf.

"BFF?" Cam asked, leaning up against the cubby next to Luce. His dark eyebrows were still arched. "I've got three younger sisters, I can practically smell the best-friend vibe through the phone." He bent forward as if he was going to sniff Luce, which made her chuckle . . . and then freeze. His unexpected closeness had made her heart pick up.

"Let me guess." Cam straightened back up and lifted his chin. "She wanted to know *all* about the reform school bad boys?"

"No!" Luce shook her head to deny vehemently that guys were on her mind at all . . . until she realized Cam was only kidding. She blushed and took a stab at joking back. "I mean, I told her there's not a single good one here."

Cam blinked. "Precisely what makes it so exciting. Don't you think?" He had a way of standing very still, which made Luce stand very still, which made the ticking sound of the pocket watch inside his blazer seem louder than it possibly could have been.

Frozen next to Cam, Luce suddenly shivered as something black swooped into the hall. The shadow seemed to hopscotch across the panels in the ceiling in a very deliberate way, blacking out one and then the next and then the next. Damn. It was never good to be alone with someone—especially someone as focused on her as Cam was at the moment—when the shadows arrived. She could feel herself twitching, trying to appear calm as the darkness swirled around the ceiling fan in a dance. That alone she could have endured. Maybe. But the shadow was also making the worst of its terrible noises, a sound like the one Luce had heard when she'd watched a baby owl fall from its palmetto tree and choke to death. She wished Cam would just stop looking at her. She wished something would happen to divert his attention. She wished—

Daniel Grigori would walk in.

And then he did. Saved by the gorgeous boy wearing holey jeans and a holier white T-shirt. He didn't look much like salvation—slouched over his heavy stack of library books, gray bags under his gray eyes. Daniel actually looked kind of wrecked. His blond hair drooped over his eyes, and when they settled on Luce and Cam, Luce watched them narrow. She was so busy fretting over what she'd done to annoy Daniel this time, she almost didn't realize the momentous thing that happened: The second before the lobby door closed behind him, the shadow slipped through it and into the night. It was like someone had taken a vacuum and cleared out all the grit from the hall.

Daniel just nodded in their direction and didn't slow down as he passed.

When Luce looked at Cam, he was watching Daniel. He turned to Luce and said, more loudly than he needed to, "I almost forgot to tell you. Having a little party in my room tonight after Social. I'd love for you to come."

Daniel was still within earshot. Luce had no idea what this Social thing was, but she was supposed to meet Penn beforehand. They were supposed to walk over together.

Her eyes were fixed on the back of Daniel's head, and she knew she needed to answer Cam about his party, and it really shouldn't be so hard, but when Daniel turned around and looked back at her with eyes she swore were mournful, the phone behind her started ringing, and Cam reached for it and said, "I've got to take this, Luce. You'll be there?"

Almost imperceptibly, Daniel nodded.

"Yes," Luce told Cam. "Yes."

❊

"I still don't see why we have to run," Luce was panting twenty minutes later. She was trying to keep up with Penn as they scrambled back across the commons toward the auditorium for the mysterious Wednesday Night Social, which Penn still hadn't explained. Luce had barely enough time to make it upstairs to her room, to slick on lip gloss and her better jeans just in case it was *that* kind of social. She was still trying to slow her breath down from her run-in with Cam *and* Daniel when Penn barged into her room to drag her back out the door.

"People who are chronically tardy never understand the many ways in which they screw up the schedules of people who are punctual and *normal*," Penn told Luce as they splashed through a particularly soggy portion of the lawn.

"Ha!" A laugh erupted behind them.

Luce looked back and felt her face light up when she saw Arriane's pale, skinny frame jogging to catch up with them. "Which quack said you were normal, Penn?" Arriane nudged Luce and pointed down. "Watch out for the quicksand!"

Luce sloshed to a halt just before she'd have landed in a scarily muddy patch on the lawn. "Somebody please tell me where we're going!"

"Wednesday night," Penn said flatly. "Social Night."

"Like . . . a dance or something?" Luce asked, visions of Daniel and Cam already moving across the dance floor of her mind.

Arriane hooted. "A dance with death by boredom. The term 'social' is typical Sword & Cross doublespeak. See, they're required to schedule social events for us, but they are also terrified of scheduling social events for us. Sticky predicky."

"So instead," Penn added, "they have these really awful events like movie nights followed by lectures about the movie, or—God, do you remember last semester?"

"There was that whole symposium on taxidermy?"

"So, so creepy." Penn shook her head.

"Tonight, my dear," Arriane drawled, "we get off easy. All we have to do is snore through one of the three movies on rotation in the Sword & Cross video library. Which one do you think it'll be tonight, Pennyloafer? *Starman? Joe Versus the Volcano?* Or *Weekend at Bernie's?*"

"It's *Starman*." Penn groaned.

Arriane shot Luce a baffled look. "She knows *everything*."

"Hold on," Luce said, tiptoeing around the quicksand and lowering her voice to a whisper as they approached the front office of the school. "If you've all seen these movies so many times, why the rush to get here?"

Penn pulled open the heavy metal doors to the "auditorium," which, Luce realized, was a euphemism for a regular old room with low, drop-paneled ceilings and chairs arranged to face a blank white wall.

"Don't want to get stuck in the hot seat next to Mr. Cole," Arriane explained, pointing at the teacher. His nose was buried deep inside a thick book, and he was surrounded by the few remaining empty chairs in the room.

As the three girls stepped through the metal detector at the door, Penn said, "Whoever sits there has to help pass out his weekly 'mental health' surveys."

"Which wouldn't be so bad—" Arriane chimed in.

"—if you didn't have to stay late to analyze the findings," Penn finished.

"Thereby missing," Arriane said with a grin, steering Luce toward the second row as she whispered, "the *after-party*."

Finally they'd gotten down to the heart of the matter. Luce chuckled.

"I heard about that," she said, feeling slightly with it for a change. "It's in Cam's room, right?"

Arriane looked at Luce for a second and ran her tongue across her teeth. Then she looked past, almost through, Luce. "Hey, Todd," she called, waving with just the tips of her fingers. She pushed Luce into one seat, claimed the safe spot next to her (still two seats down from Mr. Cole), and patted the hot seat. "Come sit with us, T-man!"

Todd, who'd been shifting his weight in the doorway, looked immensely relieved to be given the directive, any directive. He started toward them, swallowing. No sooner had he fumbled into the seat than Mr. Cole looked up from his book, cleaned his glasses on his handkerchief, and said, "Todd, I'm glad you're here. I'm wondering if you can help me with a small favor after the film. You see, the Venn diagram is a very useful tool for . . ."

"Mean!" Penn popped her face up between Arriane and Luce.

Arriane shrugged and produced a giant bag of popcorn from her carpetbag. "I can only look after so many new students," she said, tossing a buttery kernel at Luce. "Lucky you."

As the lights in the room dimmed, Luce looked around until her eyes landed on Cam. She thought about her abbreviated dish session on the phone with Callie, and how her friend always said that watching a movie with a guy was the best way to get to know things about him, things that might not come out in a conversation. Looking at Cam, Luce thought she knew what Callie meant: There would be something sort of thrilling about glancing out of the corner of her eye to see what jokes Cam thought were funny, to join his laughter with her own.

When his eyes met hers, Luce felt an embarrassed

instinct to look away. But then, before she could, Cam's face lit up in a broad smile. It made her feel remarkably unabashed about being caught staring. When he put his hand up in a wave, Luce couldn't help thinking about how the exact opposite had happened the few times Daniel had caught her looking at him.

Daniel rolled in with Roland, late enough that Randy had already taken a head count, late enough that the only remaining seats were on the floor at the front of the room. He passed through the beam of light from the projector and Luce noticed for the first time a silver chain around his neck, and some sort of medallion tucked inside his T-shirt. Then he dipped completely out of her view. She couldn't even see his profile.

As it turned out, *Starman* wasn't very funny, but the other students' constant Jeff Bridges impersonations were. It was hard for Luce to stay focused on the plot. Plus, she was getting that uncomfortable icy feeling at the back of her neck. Something was about to happen.

When the shadows came this time, Luce was expecting them. Then she started to think about it and counted a tally on her fingers. The shadows had been popping up at an increasingly alarming rate, and Luce couldn't figure out whether she was just nervous at Sword & Cross . . . or whether it meant something else. They'd never been this bad before. . . .

They oozed overhead in the auditorium, then slithered

along the sides of the movie screen, and finally traced the lines of the floorboards like spilled ink. Luce gripped the bottom of her chair and felt an ache of fear swell through her legs and arms. She tightened all the muscles in her body, but she couldn't keep from trembling. A squeeze on her left knee made her look over at Arriane.

"You okay?" Arriane mouthed.

Luce nodded and hugged her shoulders, pretending she was merely cold. She wished she was, but this particular chill had nothing to do with Sword & Cross's overzealous air conditioner.

She could feel the shadows tugging at her feet under her chair. They stayed like that, deadweight for the whole movie, and every minute dragged on like an eternity.

❄❄

An hour later, Arriane pressed her eye up against the peephole of Cam's bronze-painted dorm room door. "Yoo-hoo," she sang, giggling. "The festivities are here!"

She produced a hot-pink feather boa from the same magic carpetbag the bag of popcorn had come from. "Give me a boost," she said to Luce, dangling her foot in the air.

Luce hooked her fingers together and positioned them under Arriane's black boot. She watched as Arriane pushed off the ground and used the boa to cover the face of the hallway surveillance camera while she reached around the back of the device and switched it off.

"That's not suspicious or anything," Penn said.

"Does your allegiance lie with the after-party?" Arriane shot back. "Or the red party?"

"I'm just saying there are smarter ways." Penn snorted as Arriane hopped down. Arriane slung the boa over Luce's shoulders, and Luce laughed and started to shimmy to the Motown song they could hear through the door. But when Luce offered the boa to Penn for a turn, she was surprised to see her still looking nervous. Penn was biting her nails and sweating at the brow. Penn wore six sweaters in the swampy southern September heat—she was never hot.

"What's wrong?" Luce whispered, leaning in.

Penn picked at the hem of her sleeve and shrugged. She looked like she was just about to answer when the door behind them opened up. A whoosh of cigarette smoke, blasting music, and suddenly Cam's open arms greeted them.

"You made it," he said, smiling at Luce. Even in the dim light, his lips had a berry-stained glow. When he folded her in for a hug, she felt tiny and safe. It lasted only a second; then he turned to nod hello at the other two girls, and Luce felt a little proud to have been the one who got the hug.

Behind Cam, the small, dark room was crammed with people. Roland was in one corner, at the turntable, holding up records to a black light. The couple Luce had seen on the quad a few days before cozied up against the window. The preppy boys with the white oxford shirts were all huddled up together, occasionally checking out the girls. Arriane wasted no time shooting across the room toward Cam's desk, which looked like it was doubling as a bar. Almost immediately, she had a champagne bottle between her legs and was laughing as she tried to pry off the cork.

Luce was baffled. She hadn't even known how to get booze at Dover, where the outside world had been a lot less off-limits. Cam had been back at Sword & Cross for only a few days, but already, he seemed to know how to smuggle everything he needed to throw a Dionysian soirée the entire school showed up to. And somehow everyone else inside thought this was normal.

Still standing at the threshold, she heard the pop, then the cheers from the rest of the crowd, then Arriane's voice calling out: "Lucindaaa, get in here. I'm about to make a toast."

Luce could feel the party's magnetism, but Penn looked much less ready to budge.

"You go ahead," she said, waving a hand at Luce.

"What's wrong? You don't want to go in?" The truth was, Luce was a little nervous herself. She had no idea what might go down at these things, and since she still wasn't sure how reliable Arriane was, it would definitely make her feel better to have Penn at her side.

But Penn frowned. "I'm . . . I'm out of my element. I

do libraries . . . workshops on how to use PowerPoint. You want a file hacked into, I'm your girl. But this—" She stood on tiptoes and peered into the room. "I don't know. People in there just think I'm some kind of know-it-all."

Luce attempted her best give-me-a-break frown. "And they think *I'm* a slab of meat loaf, and *we* think *they're* all totally bananas." She laughed. "Can't we all just get along?"

Slowly Penn curled her lip, then took the feather boa and draped it around her shoulders. "Oh, all right," she said, clomping inside ahead of Luce.

Luce blinked as her eyes adjusted. A cacophony filled the room, but she could hear Arriane's laughing voice. Cam shut the door behind her and tugged Luce's hand so she'd hang back, away from the heart of the party.

"I'm really glad you came," he said, putting his hand on the small of her back and bending his head so she could hear him in the loud room. Those lips looked almost tasty, especially when they said things like "I jumped up every time someone knocked, hoping it'd be you."

Whatever had drawn Cam to her so quickly, Luce didn't want to do anything to mess it up. He was popular and unexpectedly thoughtful, and his attention made her feel more than flattered. It made her feel more comfortable in this strange new place. She knew if she tried to respond to his compliment, she'd stumble over the words. So she just laughed, which made him laugh, and then he pulled her in for another hug.

Suddenly there was no place to put her own hands but around his neck. She felt a little light-headed as Cam squeezed her, lifting her feet slightly off the ground.

When he put her back down, Luce turned to the rest of the party, and the first thing she saw was Daniel. But she didn't think he liked Cam. Still, he was sitting cross-legged on the bed, his white T-shirt glowing violet in the black light. As soon as her eyes found him, it was hard to look anywhere else. Which didn't make sense, because a gorgeous and friendly guy was standing right behind her, asking her what she'd like to drink. The other gorgeous, infinitely less friendly guy sitting across from her should not be the one she couldn't stop looking at. And he was staring at her. *So* intently, with a cryptic, squinting look in his eyes that Luce thought she'd never decode, even if she saw it a thousand times.

All she knew was the effect it had on her. Everyone else in the room went out of focus and she melted. She could have stared back all night if it hadn't been for Arriane, who had climbed on top of the desk and called out to Luce, her glass raised in the air.

"To Luce," she toasted, giving Luce a saintly smile. "Who was obviously zoning and missed my entire welcome speech and who will *never* know how utterly fabulous it was—wasn't it fabulous, Ro?" she leaned down to ask Roland, who patted her ankle affirmatively.

Cam slipped a plastic cup of champagne into Luce's

hand. She blushed and tried to laugh it off as the whole rest of the party echoed, "To Luce! To Meat Loaf!"

At her side, Molly slithered up and whispered a shorter version in her ear: "To Luce, who will *never* know."

A few days before, Luce would have flinched away. Tonight, she simply rolled her eyes, then turned her back on Molly. The girl had never said a word that didn't leave Luce feeling bitten, but showing it seemed only to egg her on. So Luce just hunkered down to share the desk chair with Penn, who handed her a rope of black licorice.

"Can you believe it? I think I'm actually having fun," Penn said, chewing happily.

Luce bit down on the licorice and took a tiny sip of the fizzy champagne. Not a very palatable combination. Kind of like her and Molly. "So is Molly that evil to everyone, or am I a special case?"

For a second Penn looked like she was going to give a different answer, but then she patted Luce on the back. "Just her usual charming demeanor, my dear."

Luce looked around the room at all the free-flowing champagne, at Cam's fancy vintage turntable, at the disco ball spinning over their heads, casting stars on everyone's faces.

"Where do they get all this stuff?" she wondered aloud.

"People say Roland can smuggle anything into Sword & Cross," Penn said matter-of-factly. "Not that I've ever asked him."

Maybe this was what Arriane meant when she said Roland knew how to get things. The only off-limits item Luce could imagine wanting badly enough to ask about was a cell phone. But then . . . Cam had said not to listen to Arriane about the inner workings of the school. Which would have been fine, except so much of his party seemed to be courtesy of Roland. The more she tried to untangle her questions, the less things added up. She should probably stick to being just "in" enough to get invited to the parties.

"Okay, all you rejects," Roland said loudly to get everyone's attention. The record player had quieted down to the static between songs. "We're going to start the open-mike portion of the night, and I'm taking requests for karaoke."

"Daniel Grigori!" Arriane hooted through her hands.

"No!" Daniel hooted back without missing a beat.

"Aww, the silent Grigori sits another one out," Roland said into the microphone. "You sure you don't want to do your version of 'Hellhound on My Trail'?"

"I believe that's *your* song, Roland," Daniel said. A faint smile spread across his lips, but Luce got the feeling it was an embarrassed smile, a someone-else-take-the-spotlight-please smile.

"He's got a point, folks." Roland laughed. "Though karaoke-ing Robert Johnson has been known to clear out a room." He plucked an R. L. Burnside album from the stack and cued the record player in the corner. "Let's go down south instead."

As the bass notes of an electric guitar picked up, Roland took center stage, which was really just a few square feet of moonlit empty space in the middle of the room. Everyone else was clapping or stomping their feet in time, but Daniel was looking down at his watch. She kept seeing the image of him nodding at her in the lobby earlier that night, when Cam invited her to the party. Like Daniel wanted her there for some reason. Of course, now that she'd shown up, he made no move to acknowledge her existence.

If only she could get him alone . . .

Roland so monopolized the attention of the guests that only Luce noticed when, midway through the song, Daniel stood up, edged himself around Molly and Cam, and slipped silently out the door.

This was her chance. While everyone around her was applauding, Luce slowly got to her feet.

"Encore!" Arriane called out. Then, noticing Luce rising from her chair, she said, "Oh, snap, is that my girl stepping up to sing?"

"No!" Luce did not want to sing in front of this roomful of people any more than she wanted to admit the real reason why she was standing up. But there she was, standing right in the middle of her first party at Sword & Cross, with Roland thrusting the mike under her chin. Now what?

"I—I just feel bad for, uh, Todd. That he's missing out." Luce's voiced echoed back to her over the speakers. She was already regretting her bad lie, and the fact that there was no turning back now. "I thought I'd run down and see if he's done with Mr. Cole."

None of the other kids seemed to know quite what to do with this. Only Penn called out timidly, "Hurry back!"

Molly was smirking down her nose at Luce. "Geek love," she said, fake-swooning. "So romantic."

Wait, did they think she liked Todd? Oh, who cared—the one person Luce would really not want thinking that was the one person she'd been trying to follow outside.

Ignoring Molly, Luce scooted toward the door, where Cam met her with crossed arms. "Want company?" he asked hopefully.

She shook her head. On any other errand, she probably would have wanted Cam's company. But not right now.

"I'll be right back," she said brightly. Before she could register the disappointment on his face, she slinked out into the hall. After the roar of the party, the quiet rang in her ears. It took a second before she could make out hushed voices just around the corner.

Daniel. She'd recognize his voice anywhere. But she was less certain who he was talking to. A girl.

"Ah'm sorrrry," whoever she was said . . . with a distinctive southern twang.

Gabbe? Daniel had been sneaking out to see blond and airbrushed *Gabbe*?

"It won't happen again," Gabbe continued, "I swear to—"

"It *can't* happen again," Daniel whispered, but his tone practically screamed *lovers' quarrel.* "You promised you'd be there, and you weren't."

Where? When? Luce was in agony. She inched along the hallway, trying not to make a sound.

But the two of them had fallen silent. Luce could picture Daniel taking Gabbe's hands in his. Could picture him leaning in to her for a long, deep kiss. A sheet of all-consuming envy spread across Luce's chest. Around the corner, one of them sighed.

"You're going to have to trust me, honey," she heard Gabbe say, in a saccharine voice that made Luce decide once and for all that she hated her. "I'm the only one you've got."

SIX

NO SALVATION

Bright and early Thursday morning, a loudspeaker crackled to life in the hallway outside Luce's room:

"Attention, Sword & Crosstians!"

Luce rolled over with a groan, but as hard as she crammed the pillow around her ears, it did little to block out Randy's bark over the PA.

"You have exactly nine minutes to report to the gymnasium for your annual fitness examination. As you know, we take a dim view of stragglers, so be prompt and be ready for bodily assessment."

Fitness examination? Bodily assessment? At six-thirty in the morning? Luce had already been regretting staying out so late last night . . . and staying up so much later lying in bed, stressing.

Right around the time she started imagining Daniel and Gabbe kissing, Luce had begun to feel queasy—that specific kind of queasiness that came from knowing she'd made a fool of herself. There was no going back to the party. There was only prying herself off the wall and slinking back to her dorm room to second-guess that strange feeling she got around Daniel, the one she'd foolishly taken as some sort of connection. She'd woken up with the bad taste of the party's aftermath still in her mouth. The last thing she wanted to think about now was fitness.

She swung her feet off the bed and onto the cold vinyl floor. Brushing her teeth, she tried to picture what Sword & Cross might mean by "bodily assessment." Intimidating images of her fellow students—Molly doing dozens of mean-faced chin-ups, Gabbe effortlessly ascending a thirty-foot rope toward the sky—flooded her mind. Her only shot at not making a fool of herself—again—was to try to put Daniel and Gabbe out of her mind.

She crossed the south side of campus to the gymnasium. It was a large Gothic structure with flying buttresses and fieldstone turrets that made it look more like a church than a place where one would go to break a sweat. As Luce approached the building, the layer of kudzu coating its façade rustled in the morning breeze.

"Penn," Luce called out, spotting her tracksuit-clad friend lacing up her sneakers on a bench. Luce looked down at her regulation black clothes and black boots and suddenly panicked that she'd missed some memo about dress code. But then, some of the other students were loitering outside the building and none of them looked much different than she did.

Penn's eyes were groggy. "So beat," she moaned. "I karaoke'd *way* too hard last night. Thought I'd compensate by trying to at least *look* athletic."

Luce laughed as Penn fumbled with the double knot on her shoe.

"What happened to you last night, anyway?" Penn asked. "You never came back to the party."

"Oh," Luce said, stalling. "I decided to—"

"Gaaahh." Penn covered her ears. "Every sound is like a jackhammer in my brain. Tell me later?"

"Yeah," Luce said. "Sure." The double doors to the gym were thrust open. Randy stepped out in heavy rubber clogs, holding her ever-present clipboard. She waved the students forward, and one by one they filed past to be assigned their fitness station.

"Todd Hammond," Randy called as the wobbly-kneed kid approached. Todd's shoulders caved forward like parentheses, and Luce could see remnants of a serious farmer's tan on the back of his neck.

"Weights," Randy commanded, chucking Todd inside.

"Pennyweather Van Syckle-Lockwood," she bellowed

next, causing Penn to cower and press her palms against her ears again. "Pool," Randy instructed, reaching into a cardboard box behind her and tossing Penn a red one-piece Speedo racer-back.

"Lucinda Price," Randy continued, after consulting her list. Luce stepped forward and was relieved when Randy said, "Also pool." Luce reached up to catch the one-piece bathing suit in the air. It was stretched out and thin as a piece of parchment between her fingers. At least it smelled clean. Sort of.

"Gabrielle Givens," Randy said next, and Luce whipped around to see her new least-favorite person sashay up in short black shorts and a thin black tank top. She'd been at this school for three days . . . how had she already gotten Daniel?

"Hiii, Randy," Gabbe said, drawing out the words with a twang that made Luce want to pull a Penn and cover her own ears.

Anything but pool, Luce willed. *Anything but pool.*

"Pool," Randy said.

Walking next to Penn toward the girls' locker room, Luce tried to avoid looking back at Gabbe, who twirled what seemed to be the only fashionable bathing suit in the stack around her French-manicured index finger. Instead, Luce focused on the gray stone walls and the old religious paraphernalia covering them. She walked past ornately carved wooden crosses with their bas-relief depictions of the Passion. A series of faded triptychs hung at eye level, with only the orbs of the figures' halos still aglow. Luce leaned forward to get a better look at a large scroll written in Latin, encased in glass.

"Uplifting décor, isn't it?" Penn asked, throwing back a couple of aspirin with a swig of water from her bag.

"What is all this stuff?" Luce asked.

"Ancient history. The only surviving relics from when this place was still the site of Sunday Mass, back in Civil War days."

"That explains why it looks so much like a church," Luce said, pausing in front of a marble reproduction of Michelangelo's pietà.

"Like everything else in this hellhole, they did a totally half-assed job of updating it. I mean, who builds a pool in the middle of an old church?"

"You're joking," Luce said.

"I wish." Penn rolled her eyes. "Every summer, the headmaster gets it in his little mind to try and stick me with the task of redecorating this place. He won't admit it, but all the God stuff really freaks him out," she said. "Problem is, even if I did feel like pitching in, I'd have no idea what to do with all this junk, or even how to clear it out without offending, like, everyone and God."

Luce thought back to the immaculate white walls inside Dover's gymnasium, row after row of professionally shot varsity championship pictures, each matted with the same navy card stock, each showcased in a matching golden frame. The only hallway more hallowed at Dover was its entryway, which was where all the alumni-turned-state-senators and Guggenheim fellowship winners and run-of-the-mill billionaires displayed their head shots.

"You could hang all the current alumni's mug shots," Gabbe offered from behind them.

Luce started to laugh—it *was* funny . . . and strange, almost like Gabbe had just read her mind—but then she remembered the girl's voice the night before, telling Daniel *she* was the only one he had. Luce quickly swallowed any notion of a connection with her.

"You're straggling!" yelled an unknown gym coach, appearing from nowhere. She—at least Luce *thought* she was a she—had a frizzy wad of brown hair pulled back in a ponytail, calves like ham hocks, and yellowing "invisible" braces covering her top teeth. She hustled the girls angrily into a locker room, where each was given a padlock with a key and directed toward an empty locker with a shove. "Nobody straggles on Coach Diante's watch."

Luce and Penn scrambled into their faded, baggy bathing suits. Luce shuddered at her reflection in the mirror, then covered as much of herself as she could with her towel.

Inside the humid natatorium, she instantly understood what Penn was talking about. The pool itself was giant, Olympic-sized, one of the few state-of-the-art features she'd encountered so far on this campus. But that wasn't what made it remarkable, Luce realized in awe. This pool had been set down right in the middle of what used to be a massive church.

There was a row of pretty stained-glass windows, with only a few broken panels, spanning the walls near the high, arched ceiling. There were candlelit stone niches along the wall. A diving board had been installed where the altar probably used to be. If Luce had not been raised agnostic, but rather as a God-fearing churchgoer, like the rest of her friends in elementary school, she might have thought this place was sacrilegious.

Some of the other students were already in the water, gasping for air as they completed their laps. But it was the students who weren't in the water who held Luce's attention. Molly, Roland, and Arriane were all spread out on the bleachers along the wall. They were cracking up about something. Roland was practically doubled over, and Arriane was wiping away tears. They were in much more attractive bathing suits than Luce, but not one of them looked like they had any intention of making a move toward the pool.

Luce picked at her saggy one-piece. She wanted to go join Arriane—but just as she was weighing the pros (possible entrance into an elite world) and cons (Coach

Diante berating her as a conscientious objector to exercise), Gabbe sauntered over to the group. Like she was already best friends with all of them. She took a seat right next to Arriane and immediately started laughing, too, like whatever the joke was, she already got it.

"They always have notes to sit out," Penn explained, glaring at the popular crowd on the bleachers. "Don't ask me how they get away with it."

Luce hemmed and hawed at the side of the pool, unable to tune in to Coach Diante's instructions. Seeing Gabbe et al. clustered on the bleachers cool-kids-style made Luce wish that Cam were there. She could picture him looking buff in a sleek black bathing suit, waving her over to the crew with his big smile, making her feel immediately welcome, even important.

Luce felt a gnawing need to apologize for ducking out of his party early. Which was strange—they weren't together, so it wasn't like Luce was obligated to explain her comings and goings to Cam. But at the same time, she liked it when he paid attention to her. She liked the way he smelled—kind of free and open, like driving with the windows down at night. She liked the way he tuned in to her completely when she talked, holding still like he couldn't see or hear anyone but her. She'd even liked being lifted off her feet at the party, in plain view of Daniel. She didn't want to do anything to make Cam reconsider the way he treated her.

When the coach's whistle blew, a very startled Luce stood straight up, then looked down regretfully as Penn and the other students near her all jumped forward, into the pool. She looked to Coach Diante for guidance.

"You must be Lucinda Price—always late and never listens?" Coach sighed. "Randy told me about you. It's eight laps, pick your best stroke."

Luce nodded and stood with her toes curled over the edge. She used to love to swim. When her dad taught her how at the Thunderbolt community pool, she'd even been given an award as youngest kid ever to brave the deep end without floaties. But that was years ago. Luce couldn't even remember the last time she'd swum. The heated outdoor Dover pool had always sparkled, tempting her—but it was closed to anyone who wasn't on the swim team.

Coach Diante cleared her throat. "Maybe you didn't catch that this is a race . . . and you're already losing."

This was the most pathetic and ridiculous "race" that Luce had ever seen, but it didn't stop her competitive edge from coming out.

"And . . . you're *still* losing," Coach said, chewing on her whistle.

"Not for long," Luce said.

She checked out the competition. The guy to her left was sputtering water out of his mouth and doing a clumsy freestyle. On her right, a nose-plugged Penn was leisurely gliding along, her stomach resting on a pink foam kickboard. For a split second, Luce glanced at the crowd on the bleachers. Molly and Roland were watching; Arriane and Gabbe were collapsed on each other in an annoying fit of giggles.

But she didn't care what they were laughing at. Sort of. She was off.

With her arms bowed over her head, Luce dove in, feeling her back arch as she glided into the crisp water. Few people could do it really well, her dad once explained to an eight-year-old Luce at the pool. But once you perfected the butterfly stroke, there was no way to move faster in the water.

Letting her aggravation propel her forward, Luce lifted her upper body out of the water. The movement came right back to her and she started to beat her arms like wings. She swam harder than she'd done anything in a long, long time. Feeling vindicated, she lapped the other swimmers once, then again.

She was nearing the end of her eighth lap when her head popped above water just long enough to hear Gabbe's slow voice say, "Daniel."

Like a snuffed-out candle, Luce's momentum disappeared. She put her feet down and waited to see what else Gabbe had to say. Unfortunately, she couldn't hear anything other than a raucous splashing and, a moment later, the whistle.

"And the winner is," Coach Diante said with a

stunned expression, "Joel Bland." The skinny kid with braces from the next lane over hopped out of the pool and started raising the roof to celebrate his victory.

In the next lane, Penn kicked to a stop. "What happened?" she asked Luce. "You were totally killing him."

Luce shrugged. *Gabbe* was what had happened, but when she looked over at the bleachers, Gabbe was gone, and Arriane and Molly were gone with her. Roland alone remained where the crowd had been, and he was immersed in a book.

Luce's adrenaline had been building while she swam, but now she'd crashed so hard, Penn had to help her out of the pool.

Luce watched Roland hop down from the bleachers. "You were pretty good out there," he said, tossing her a towel and the locker room key she'd lost track of. "For a little while."

Luce caught the key in midair and wrapped the towel around her. But before she could say something normal, like "Thanks for the towel," or "Guess I'm just out of shape," this weird new hotheaded side of her instead blurted out, "Are Daniel and Gabbe together or what?"

Big mistake. Huge. She could tell from the look in his eye that her question was headed right to Daniel.

"Oh, I see," Roland said, and laughed. "Well, I couldn't really . . ." He looked down at her and scratched his nose and gave her what seemed like a sympathetic smile. Then he pointed toward the open hallway door, and when Luce followed his finger she saw Daniel's trim, blond silhouette pass by. "Why don't you just ask him yourself?"

❄❄

Luce's hair was still dripping wet and her feet were still bare when she found herself hovering at the door to a large weight room. She'd intended to go straight into the locker room to change and dry off. She didn't know why this Gabbe thing was shaking her up so much. Daniel could be with whomever he wanted, right? Maybe Gabbe liked guys who flipped her off.

Or, more likely, that kind of thing didn't happen to Gabbe.

But Luce's body got the better of her mind when she caught another glimpse of Daniel. His back was to her and he was standing in a corner picking out a jump rope from a tangled pile. She watched as he selected a thin navy rope with wooden handles, then moved to an open space in the center of the room. His golden skin was almost radiant, and every movement he made, whether he was rolling out his long neck in a stretch or bending over to scratch his sculpted knee, had Luce completely rapt. She stood pressed against the doorway, unaware that her teeth were chattering and her towel was soaked.

When he brought the rope behind his ankles just

before he began to jump, Luce was slammed with a wave of déjà vu. It wasn't exactly that she felt like she'd seen Daniel jump rope before, but more that the stance he took seemed entirely familiar. He stood with his feet hip-width apart, unlocked his knees, and pressed his shoulders down as he filled his chest with air. Luce could almost have drawn it.

It was only when Daniel began twirling the rope that Luce snapped out of that trance . . . and right into another. Never in her life had she seen anyone move like him. It was almost like Daniel was flying. The rope whipped up and over his tall frame so quickly that it disappeared, and his feet—his graceful, narrow feet—were they even touching the ground? He was moving so swiftly, even he must not have been counting.

A loud grunt and a thud on the other side of the weight room tore Luce's attention away. Todd was in a heap at the base of one of those knotted climbing ropes. She felt momentarily sorry for Todd, who was looking down at his blistered hands. Before she could look back at Daniel to see whether he'd even noticed, a cold black rush at the edge of her skin made Luce shiver. The shadow swept up on her slowly at first, icy, tenebrous, its limits indiscernible. Then, suddenly rough, it crashed into her body and forced her back. The door to the weight room slammed in her face and Luce was alone in the hallway.

"Ow!" she cried, not because she was hurt exactly, but because she had never been *touched* by the shadows before. She looked down at her bare arms, where it had felt almost like hands had gripped her, shoving her out of the gym.

That was impossible—she'd just been standing in a weird place; a draft must have shot through the gymnasium. Uneasily, she approached the closed door and pressed her face up against the small glass rectangle.

Daniel was looking around, like he'd heard something. She felt certain he didn't know it was her: He wasn't scowling.

She thought about Roland's suggestion that she just ask Daniel what was up, but quickly dismissed the notion. It was impossible to ask anything of Daniel. She didn't want to bring out that scowl on his face.

Besides, any question she might pose would be useless. She'd already heard all she needed to hear last night. She'd have to be some kind of sadist to ask him to admit he was with Gabbe. She turned back toward the locker room when she realized she couldn't leave.

Her key.

It must have slipped from her hands when she stumbled out of the room. She stood on tiptoes to look down through the small glass panel on the door. There it was, a bronze blunder on the padded blue mat. How had it gotten so far across the room, so close to where he was working out? Luce sighed and pushed the door back open, thinking if she had to go in, at least she'd make it quick.

Reaching for her key, she sneaked one last look at him. His pace was slowing, slowing, but his feet still barely touched the ground. And then, with one final light-as-air bounce, he came to a stop and turned around to face her.

For a moment, he said nothing. She could feel herself blush and really wished she wasn't wearing such a horrible bathing suit.

"Hi" was all she could think to say.

"Hi," he said back, in a much calmer tone of voice. Then, gesturing at her suit, said, "Did you win?"

Luce laughed a sad, self-effacing laugh and shook her head. "Far from it."

Daniel pursed his lips. "But you were always . . ."

"I was always what?"

"I mean, you look like you might be a good swimmer." He shrugged. "That's all."

She stepped toward him. They were standing just a foot apart. Drops of water fell from her hair and pattered like rain on the gym mats. "That's not what you were going to say," she insisted. "You said I was always . . ."

Daniel busied himself coiling the jump rope around his wrist. "Yeah, I didn't mean *you* you. I meant in general. They're always supposed to let you win your first race here. Unspoken code of conduct for us old-timers."

"But Gabbe didn't win either," Luce said, crossing

her arms over her chest. "And she's new. She didn't even get in the pool."

"She's not exactly new, just coming back after some time . . . off." Daniel shrugged, giving away nothing of his feelings for Gabbe. His obvious attempt to look unconcerned made Luce even more jealous. She watched him finish looping the jump rope into a coil, the way his hands moved almost as quickly as his feet. And here she was so clumsy and lonely and cold and left out of everything by everyone. Her lip quivered.

"Oh, Lucinda," he whispered, sighing heavily.

Her whole body warmed at the sound. His voice was so intimate and familiar.

She wanted him to say her name again, but he had turned away. He hooked the jump rope over a peg on the wall. "I should go change before class."

She rested a hand on his arm. "Wait."

He wrenched away as if he had been shocked—and Luce felt it, too, but it was the kind of shock that felt *good.*

"Do you ever get the feeling . . ." She raised her eyes to his. Up close, she could see how unusual they were. They seemed gray from far away, but up close there were violet flecks in them. She knew someone else with eyes like that. . . .

"I could swear we've met before," she said. "Am I crazy?"

"Crazy? Isn't that why you're here?" he said, brushing her off.

"I'm serious."

"So am I." Daniel's face was blank. "And for the record"—he pointed up at a blinking device attached to the ceiling—"the reds do monitor for stalkers."

"I'm not *stalking* you." She stiffened, very aware of the distance between their bodies. "Can you honestly say you have no idea what I'm talking about?"

Daniel shrugged.

"I don't believe you," Luce insisted. "Look me in the eye and tell me I'm wrong. That I've never in my life seen you before this week."

Her heart raced as Daniel stepped toward her, placing both hands on her shoulders. His thumbs fit perfectly along the grooves of her collarbone, and she wanted to close her eyes at the warmth of his touch—but she didn't. She watched as Daniel bowed his head so his nose was nearly touching hers. She could feel his breath on her face. She could smell a hint of sweetness on his skin.

He did as she asked. He looked her in the eye and said, very slowly, very clearly, so that his words could not possibly be misunderstood:

"You have never in your life seen me before this week."

SEVEN

SHEDDING LIGHT

"*Now* where are you going?" Cam asked, lowering his red plastic sunglasses.

He'd appeared outside the entrance of Augustine so suddenly that Luce almost plowed right into him. Or maybe he'd been there awhile and she just hadn't noticed in her haste to get to class. Either way, her heart started beating quickly and her palms began to sweat.

"Um, class?" Luce answered, because where did it look like she was going? Her arms were full, with her two hefty calculus books and her half-completed religion assignment.

This would have been a good time to apologize for leaving so suddenly last night. But she couldn't bring herself to do it. She was already so late. There hadn't been any hot water in the locker showers, so she'd had to trek all the way back to the dorm. Somehow, what had happened after the party didn't seem important anymore. She didn't want to draw any more attention to her leaving—especially not now, after Daniel had made her feel so pathetic. She also didn't want Cam to think she was being rude. She just wanted to steer past him and be by herself so she could move on from this morning's string of embarrassments.

Except—the longer Cam gazed at her, the less important it felt to leave. And the less Luce's pride stung over Daniel's dismissal. How could one look from Cam do all that?

With his clear, pale skin and jet-black hair, Cam was different from any guy she'd ever known. He exuded confidence, and not just because he knew everyone—and how to get everything—before Luce had even figured out where her classes were. Right then, standing outside the drab, gray school building, Cam looked like an arty black-and-white photograph, his red shades Technicolored in.

"Class, eh?" Cam yawned dramatically. He was

blocking the entrance, and something about the amused way his mouth was set made Luce want to know what wild idea he had up his sleeve. There was a canvas bag slung over his shoulder, and a disposable espresso cup between his fingers. He pressed Stop on his iPod, but left the earbuds dangling around his neck. Part of her wanted to know what song he'd been listening to, and where he'd gotten that black-market espresso. The playful smile visible only in his green eyes dared her to ask.

Cam skimmed a sip off the top of his coffee. Holding up his index finger, he said, "Allow me to share my motto about Sword & Cross classes: Better never than late."

Luce laughed, and then Cam pushed his sunglasses back up on his nose. The lenses were so dark, she couldn't see even a hint of his eyes.

"Besides." He smiled, flashing her a white arch of teeth. "It's just about lunchtime, and I've got a picnic."

Lunchtime? Luce hadn't even had breakfast yet. But her stomach *was* growling—and the idea of being reamed by Mr. Cole for missing all but the last twenty minutes of morning classes seemed less and less appealing the longer she stood next to Cam.

She nodded at the bag he was holding. "Did you pack enough for two?"

Steering Luce with a broad hand on the small of her back, Cam led her across the commons, past the library and the dismal dorm. At the metal gates to the cemetery, he stopped.

"I know this is a weird place for a picnic," he explained, "but it's the best spot I know to dip out of sight for a little while. On campus, anyway. Sometimes I just can't breathe in there." He gestured toward the building.

Luce could definitely relate to that. She felt both stifled and exposed almost all the time at this place. But Cam seemed like the last person who would share that new-student syndrome. He was so . . . collected. After that party last night, and now the forbidden espresso in his hand, she would never have guessed he'd feel suffocated, too. Or that he'd pick her to share the feeling with.

Past his head, she could see the rest of the run-down campus. From here, there wasn't much of a difference between one side of the cemetery gates and the other.

Luce decided to go with it. "Just promise to save me if any statues topple over."

"No," Cam said with a seriousness that effectively erased her joke. "That won't happen again."

Her eyes fell on the spot where only days earlier, she and Daniel had come close to ending up in the cemetery themselves. But the marble angel that had toppled over them was gone, its pedestal bare.

"Come on," Cam said, tugging her along with him. They sidestepped overgrown patches of weeds, and Cam kept turning to help her over mounds of dirt burrowed out by who-knew-what.

At one point, Luce nearly lost her balance and grabbed on to one of the headstones to steady herself. It was a large, polished slab with one rough, unfinished side.

"I've always liked that one," Cam said, gesturing at the pinkish headstone under her fingers. Luce crossed around to the front of the plot to read the inscription.

"'Joseph Miley,'" she read aloud. "'1821 to 1865. Bravely served in the War of Northern Aggression. Survived three bullets and five horses felled from under him before meeting his final peace.'"

Luce cracked her knuckles. Maybe Cam only liked it because its polished pinkish stone stood out among the mostly gray ones? Or because of the intricate whorls in the crest along the top? She raised an eyebrow at him.

"Yeah." Cam shrugged. "I just like how the headstone explains the way he died. It's honest, you know? Usually, people don't want to go there."

Luce looked away. She knew that all too well from the inscrutable epitaph on Trevor's tombstone.

"Think how much more interesting this place would be if everyone's cause of death was chiseled in." He pointed to a small grave a few plots down from Joseph Miley's. "How do you think she died?"

"Um, scarlet fever?" Luce guessed, wandering over.

She traced the dates with her fingers. The girl buried here had been younger than Luce when she died. Luce didn't really want to think too hard about how it might have happened.

Cam tilted his head, considering. "Maybe," he said. "Either that or a mysterious barn fire while young Betsy was taking an innocent 'nap' with the neighbor boy."

Luce started to pretend to act offended, but instead Cam's expectant face made her laugh. It had been a long time since she'd just goofed off with a guy. Sure, this scene was a bit more morbid than the typical movie theater parking lot flirtations she was used to, but so were the students at Sword & Cross. For better or worse, Luce was one of them now.

She followed Cam to the bottom of the bowl-like graveyard and the more ornate tombs and mausoleums. On the slope above, the headstones seemed to be looking down at them, like Luce and Cam were performers in an amphitheater. The midday sun glowed orange through the leaves of a giant live oak tree in the cemetery, and Luce shaded her eyes with her hands. It was the hottest day they'd had all week.

"Now, this guy," Cam said, pointing to a huge tomb framed by Corinthian columns. "Total draft dodger. He suffocated when a beam collapsed in his basement. Which just goes to show you, never hide out from a Confederate roundup."

"Is that so?" Luce asked. "Remind me what makes you the expert on all of this?" Even as she teased him, Luce felt strangely privileged to be there with Cam. He kept glancing at her to make sure she was smiling.

"It's just a sixth sense." He flashed her a big, innocent grin. "If you like it, there's a seventh sense, and an eight sense, and a ninth sense where that came from."

"Impressive." She smiled. "I'll settle for the sense of taste right now. I'm starving."

"At your service." Cam pulled a blanket from his tote bag and spread it out in a scrap of shade under the live oak tree. He unscrewed a thermos and Luce could smell the strong espresso. She didn't usually drink her coffee black, but she watched as he filled a tumbler with ice, poured the espresso over it, and added just the right amount of milk to the top. "I forgot to bring sugar," he said.

"I don't take sugar." She took a sip from the bone-dry iced latte, her first delicious sip of Sword & Cross–prohibited caffeine all week.

"That's lucky," Cam said, spreading out the rest of the picnic. Luce's eyes grew wide as she watched him arrange the food: a dark brown baguette, a small round of oozy cheese, a terra-cotta tub of olives, a bowl of deviled eggs, and two bright green apples. It didn't seem possible that Cam had fit all that in his bag—or that he'd been planning on eating all this food by himself.

"Where did you get this?" Luce asked. Pretending to

focus on tearing off a hunk of bread, she asked, "And who else were you planning on picnicking with before I came along?"

"Before you came along?" Cam laughed. "I can hardly remember my bleak life before you."

Luce gave him the slightest of snide looks so he'd know that she found the remark incredibly cheesy . . . and just a little bit charming. She leaned back on her elbows on the blanket, her legs crossed at the ankles. Cam was sitting cross-legged facing her, and when he reached over her for the cheese knife, his arm brushed, then rested on, the knee of her black jeans. He looked up at her, as if to ask, *Is this okay?*

When she didn't flinch, he stayed there, taking the hunk of baguette from her hand and using her leg like a tabletop while he spread a triangle of cheese onto the bread. She liked the feeling of his weight on her, and in this heat, that was saying something.

"I'll start with the easier question first," he said, finally sitting back up. "I help out in the kitchen a couple of days a week. Part of my readmittance agreement at Sword & Cross. I'm supposed to be 'giving back.'" He rolled his eyes. "But I don't mind it in there. I guess I like the heat. That is, if you don't count the grease burns." He held out his upturned wrists to expose dozens of tiny scars on his forearms. "Occupational hazard," he said casually. "But I do get the run of the pantry."

Luce couldn't resist running her fingers along them, the infinitesimal pale swells fading back into his paler skin. Before she could feel embarrassed by her forwardness and pull away, Cam grabbed her hand and squeezed.

Luce stared at his fingers wrapped around hers. She hadn't realized before how closely the shades of their skin matched. In a landscape of southern sunbathers, Luce's paleness had always made her feel self-conscious. But Cam's skin was so striking, so noticeable, almost metallic—and now she realized she might look the same to him. Her shoulders shivered and she felt a little dizzy.

"Are you cold?" he asked quietly.

When she met his eyes, she knew he knew she wasn't cold.

He scooted closer on the blanket and dropped his voice to a whisper. "Now I guess you're going to want me to admit that I saw you crossing the quad through the kitchen window and packed all this up in the hopes of convincing you to skip class with me?"

This was when she would have fished in her drink for ice, if it hadn't already melted in the stale September heat.

"And you had this whole scheme of a romantic picnic," she finished. "In the scenic cemetery?"

"Hey." He ran a finger along her bottom lip. "You're the one bringing up romance."

Luce pulled back. He was right—she'd been the

presumptuous one . . . for the second time that day. She could feel her cheeks burn as she tried *not* to think about Daniel.

"I'm kidding," he said, shaking his head at the stricken look on her face. "As if that weren't obvious." He gazed up at a turkey vulture circling a great white statue shaped like a cannon. "I know it's no Eden here," he said, tossing Luce an apple, "but just pretend we're in a Smiths song. And to my credit, it's not like there's much to work with at this school."

That was putting it mildly.

"The way I see it," Cam said, leaning back on the blanket, "location is negligible."

Luce shot him a doubtful look. She also wished he hadn't leaned away, but she was too shy to approach when he was reclining on his side.

"Where I grew up"—he paused—"things weren't so different from the penitentiary-style living at Sword & Cross. The upshot is I'm officially immune to my surroundings."

"No way." Luce shook her head. "If I handed you a plane ticket to California right now, you wouldn't be totally thrilled to break out of here?"

"Mmm . . . mildly indifferent," Cam said, popping a deviled egg into his mouth.

"I don't believe you." Luce gave him a shove.

"Then you must have had a happy childhood."

Luce bit into the chewy green skin of the apple and licked the juice running down her fingers. She ran through a mental catalog of all the parental frowns, doctors' visits, and school changes of her childhood, the black shadows hanging like a shroud over everything. No, she wouldn't say she'd had a *happy* childhood. But if Cam couldn't even see a way out of Sword & Cross, something more hopeful on the horizon, then maybe his had been worse.

There was a rustling at their feet and Luce snapped into a ball when a thick green-and-yellow snake slithered past. Trying not to get too close, she rolled to her knees and peered down at it. Not just a snake, but a snake in the middle of shedding its skin. A translucent case was coming off its tail. There were snakes all over Georgia, but she'd never seen one molt.

"Don't scream," Cam said, resting a hand on Luce's knee. His touch did make Luce feel safer. "He'll move on if we just leave him alone."

It couldn't happen quickly enough. Luce wanted very badly to scream. She had always hated and feared snakes. They were just so slithery and scaly and . . . "Eugh." She shivered, but she couldn't take her eyes off the snake until it had disappeared in the long grass.

Cam smirked as he picked up the shed skin and placed it in her hand. It still felt alive, like the dewy skin on a bulb of garlic her father had pulled fresh from his garden. But it had just come off a snake. Gross. She tossed it back on the ground and wiped her hands on her jeans.

"Come on, you didn't think it was cute?"

"Did my trembling give it away?" Luce was already feeling a bit embarrassed by how childish she must have looked.

"What about your faith in the power of transformation?" Cam asked, fingering the shed skin. "That's what we're here for, after all."

Cam had taken off his sunglasses. His emerald eyes were so confident. He was holding that inhumanly still pose again, waiting for her to answer.

"I'm starting to think you're a little bit strange," she said finally, cracking the tiniest smile.

"Oh, and just think how much more there is to know about me," he replied, leaning in closer. Closer than he had when the snake came. Closer than she'd been expecting him to. He reached out and slowly ran his fingers through her hair. Luce tensed up.

Cam was gorgeous and intriguing. What she couldn't figure out was how, when she should have been a bundle of nerves—like right then—she still somehow felt comfortable. She wanted to be right where she was. She couldn't take her eyes off his lips, which were full and pink and moving closer, making her feel even dizzier. His shoulder brushed hers and she felt a strange shiver deep inside her chest. She watched as Cam parted his lips. Then she closed her eyes.

"There y'all are!" A breathless voice pulled Luce right out of the moment.

Luce let out an exasperated sigh and shifted her attention to Gabbe, who was standing before them with a high side ponytail, and an oblivious grin on her face.

"I've been looking *everywhere*."

"Why on earth would you be doing such a thing?" Cam glowered at her, scoring him a few more points with Luce.

"Cemetery was the last place I thought of," Gabbe rattled on, counting on her fingers. "I checked your dorm rooms, then under the bleachers, then—"

"What do you *want*, Gabbe?" Cam cut her off, like a sibling, like they'd known each other a long time.

Gabbe blinked, then bit her lip. "It was Miss Sophia," she said finally, snapping her fingers. "That's right. She got frantic when Luce didn't show up for class. Kept saying how you were such a promising student and all that."

Luce couldn't read this girl. Was she for real and just following orders? Was she mocking Luce for making a good impression on a teacher? Was it not enough for her to have Daniel wrapped around her finger—she had to move in on Cam now, too?

Gabbe must have sensed that she was interrupting something, but she just stood there blinking her big doe eyes and twirling a strand of blond hair around her finger. "Well, come on," she said finally, sticking out both hands to help Luce and Cam up. "Let's get you back to class."

❊

"Lucinda, you can have station three," Miss Sophia said, looking down at a sheet of paper when Luce, Cam, and Gabbe entered the library. No *Where have you been?* No points off for tardiness. Just Miss Sophia, absently placing Luce next to Penn in the computer lab section of the library. Like she hadn't even noticed that Luce had been gone.

Luce shot Gabbe an accusatory look, but she just shrugged at Luce and mouthed, "What?"

"Wherehaveyoubeen?" Penn demanded as soon as she sat down. The only person who seemed to notice she'd been gone at all.

Luce's eyes found Daniel, who was practically burrowed into his computer at station seven. From her seat, all Luce could see of him was the blond halo of his hair, but it was enough to bring a flush to her cheeks. She sank lower in her chair, mortified all over again by their conversation in the gym.

Even after all the laughs and smiles and that one potential near kiss she'd just shared with Cam, she couldn't shut out what she felt when she saw Daniel.

And they were never going to be together.

That was the gist of what he had told her in the gym. After she'd basically thrown herself at him.

The rejection cut her so deeply, so close to her heart, she felt certain everyone around her could take one look at her and know exactly what had happened.

Penn was tapping her pencil impatiently on Luce's desk. But Luce didn't know how to explain. Her picnic with Cam had been interrupted by Gabbe before Luce had even been able to really make sense of what was happening. Or about to happen. But what was weird, and what she couldn't figure out, was why all of that felt so much less important than what had happened in the gym with Daniel.

Miss Sophia stood in the middle of the computer lab, snapping her fingers in the air like a preschool teacher to get the students' attention. Her stacks of silver bangle bracelets chimed like bells.

"If any of you have ever traced your own family tree," she called over the din of the crowd, "then you'll know what sorts of treasures lie buried in the roots."

"Oh, jeez, please kill that metaphor," Penn whispered. "Or kill me. One or the other."

"You'll have twenty minutes' access to the Internet to begin researching your own family tree," Miss Sophia said, tapping a stopwatch. "A generation is roughly twenty to twenty-five years, so aim to go back at least six generations."

Groan.

An audible sigh erupted from station seven—Daniel.

Miss Sophia turned to him. "Daniel? Do you have a problem with this assignment?"

He sighed again and shrugged. "No, not at all. That's fine. My family tree. Should be interesting."

Miss Sophia tilted her head quizzically. "I'll take that statement for an enthusiastic endorsement." Addressing the class again, she said, "I trust you'll find a line worth pursuing in a ten- to fifteen-page research paper."

Luce could not possibly focus on this right now. Not when there was so much else to process. She and Cam in the cemetery. Maybe it hadn't been the standard definition of romantic, but Luce almost preferred it that way. It was like nothing she'd ever done before. Skipping class to mosey through all those graves. Sharing that picnic, while he refilled her perfectly made latte. Making fun of her fear of snakes. Well, she could have done without that whole snake development, but at least Cam had been sweet about it. Sweeter than Daniel had been all week.

She hated to admit that, but it was true. Daniel wasn't interested.

Cam, on the other hand . . .

She studied him, a few stations away. He winked at her before he began pecking at his keyboard. So he liked her. Callie wasn't going to be able to shut up about how obviously into her he was.

She wanted to call Callie now, to bolt out of this library and take a rain check on the family tree assignment. Talking up another guy was the fastest—maybe the only—way to get Daniel out of her head. But there was that horrible Sword & Cross phone policy, and all the other students around her, who looked so diligent. Miss Sophia's tiny eyes panned the class for procrastinators.

Luce sighed, defeated, and opened the search engine on her computer. She was stuck here for another twenty minutes—with not one brain cell devoted to her assignment. The last thing she wanted to do was learn about her own boring family. Instead, her listless fingers began to tap out thirteen letters entirely of their own accord:

"Daniel Grigori."

Search.

EIGHT

A DIVE TOO DEEP

When Luce answered the knock on her door Saturday morning, Penn tumbled into her arms.

"You'd think it would dawn on me someday that doors open *in*," she apologized, straightening her glasses. "Must remember to stop leaning on peepholes. Nice digs, by the way," she added, looking around. She crossed to the window over Luce's bed. "Not a bad view, minus the bars and all."

Luce stood behind her, looking out at the cemetery

and, in plain view, the live oak tree where she'd had the picnic with Cam. And, invisible from here but clear in her head, the place she'd been pinned under that statue with Daniel. The avenging angel that had mysteriously disappeared after the accident.

Remembering Daniel's worried eyes when he whispered her name that day, the near touch of their noses, the way she'd felt his fingertips on her neck—all of it made her feel hot.

And pathetic. She sighed and turned away from the window, realizing Penn had moved on, too.

She was picking things up off Luce's desk, giving each of Luce's possessions careful scrutiny. The Statue of Liberty paperweight her dad had brought back from a conference at NYU, the picture of her mom with a hilariously bad perm when she was around Luce's age, the eponymous Lucinda Williams CD Callie had given her as a going-away present before Luce had ever heard the name Sword & Cross.

"Where are your books?" she asked Penn, wanting to detour around a trip down memory lane. "You said you were coming over to study."

By then, Penn had begun to riffle through her wardrobe. Luce watched as she quickly lost interest in the variations of dress code–style black T-shirts and sweaters. When Penn moved toward her dresser drawers, Luce stepped forward to intercept.

"Okay, that's enough, Snoop," she said. "Isn't there research we should be doing on family trees?"

"Speaking of snooping." Penn's eyes twinkled. "Yes, there is research we should be doing. But not the kind you're thinking."

Luce stared at her blankly. "Huh?"

"Look." Penn put her hand on Luce's shoulder. "If you really want to know about Daniel Grigori—"

"Shhh!" Luce hissed, jumping to close her door. She stuck her head into the hall and scanned the scene. The coast looked clear—but that didn't mean anything. People at this school had a suspicious way of appearing out of nowhere. Cam in particular. And Luce would die if he—or anyone—found out how enamored of Daniel she was. Or, at this point, anyone but Penn.

Satisfied, Luce closed and locked the door and turned back to her friend. Penn was sitting cross-legged at the edge of Luce's bed. She looked amused.

Luce locked her hands behind her back and dug her toe into the circular red rug near her door. "What makes you think I want to know anything about him?"

"Give me a break," Penn said, laughing. "A, it's totally obvious that you stare at Daniel Grigori *all* the time."

"Shhh!" Luce said again.

"B," Penn said, not dropping her voice, "I watched you stalk him online for an entire class the other day. Sue me—but you were being totally shameless. And C, don't get all paranoid. You think I blab to anyone at this school besides you?"

Penn did have a point.

"I'm only saying," she continued, "assuming *hypothetically* you did want to know more about a certain unnamed person, you could *conceivably* bark up a more fruitful tree." Penn shrugged one shoulder. "You know, if you had help."

"I'm listening," Luce said, sinking down on the bed. Her Internet search the other day had only amounted to typing, then deleting, then retyping Daniel's name into the search field.

"I was hoping you'd say that," Penn said. "I didn't bring books with me today because I'm giving you"—she widened her eyes goofily—"a guided tour of the highly off-limits underground lair of Sword & Cross office records!"

Luce grimaced. "I don't know. Prying into Daniel's files? I'm not sure I need another reason to feel like a crazy stalker girl."

"Ha." Penn snickered. "And yes, you did just say that out loud. Come on, Luce. It'll be fun. Besides, what else are you going to do on a perfectly sunny Saturday morning?"

It was a nice day—precisely the kind of nice that made you feel lonely if you didn't have anything fun and outdoorsy planned. In the middle of the night, Luce had felt a cool front brush through her open window, and when she'd awoken this morning, the heat and humidity had all but disappeared.

She used to spend these golden early-fall days tearing up the neighborhood bike path with her friends. That was before she started avoiding the woodsy trail because of the shadows none of the other girls ever saw. Before her friends sat her down one day during recess and said their parents didn't want them inviting her over anymore, in case she had an *incident*.

Truth was, Luce had been a little panicked about how she'd spend this first weekend at Sword & Cross. No classes, no terrorizing physical fitness tests, no social events on the docket. Just forty-eight endless hours of free time. An eternity. She'd had a queasy homesick feeling all morning—until Penn showed up.

"Okay." Luce tried not to laugh when she said, "Take me to your secret lair."

⁂

Penn practically skipped as she led Luce across the trampled grass of the commons to the main lobby near the school's entrance. "You don't know how long I've been waiting for a partner in crime to bring down here with me."

Luce smiled, glad Penn was more focused on having a

friend to explore with than she was on, well, this . . . *thing* Luce had for Daniel.

At the edge of the commons, they passed a few kids lazing around on the bleachers in the clear late-morning sun. It was strange to see color on campus, on these students with whom Luce so closely identified the color black. But there was Roland in a pair of lime-green soccer shorts, dribbling a ball between his feet. And Gabbe in her purple gingham button-down shirt. Jules and Phillip—the tongue-ringed couple—were drawing on the knees of each other's faded jeans. Todd Hammond sat apart from the rest of the kids on the bleachers, reading a comic book in a camouflage T-shirt. Even Luce's own gray tank top and shorts felt more vibrant than anything she'd worn all week.

Coach Diante and the Albatross were on lawn duty and had set up two plastic lawn chairs and a sagging umbrella at the edge of the commons. Aside from when they ashed their cigarettes on the lawn, they could have been asleep behind their dark sunglasses. They looked utterly bored, as imprisoned by their jobs as the charges they were monitoring.

There were a lot of people out on the commons, but as she followed closely behind Penn, she was glad to see there wasn't anyone near the main lobby at all. No one had said anything to Luce about trespassing in restricted areas, or even which areas *were* restricted, but she was sure Randy would find an appropriate punishment.

"What about the reds?" Luce asked, remembering the omnipresent cameras.

"I just stuck some dead batteries in a few of them on my way over to your room," Penn said, in the same nonchalant tone of voice someone else might use to say "I just filled the car up with gas."

Penn took a sweeping glance around before she led Luce to the main building's back entrance and down three steep steps to an olive-colored door not visible from ground level.

"Is this basement from the Civil War era, too?" Luce asked. It looked like an entrance to the kind of place where you could stash some POWs.

Penn gave the damp air a long, dramatic sniff. "Does the malodorous rot answer your question? This here is some antebellum mildew." She grinned at Luce. "*Most* students would keel over for the chance to inhale such storied air."

Luce tried not to breathe through her nose as Penn produced a hardware store's worth of keys held together on a giant lanyard. "My life would be so much easier if they got around to making a skeleton key for this place," she said, sifting through the assortment and finally pulling forward a thin silver key.

When the key turned in the lock, Luce felt an unexpected shiver of excitement. Penn was right—this was way better than mapping out her family tree.

They walked a short distance through a warm, damp

corridor whose ceiling was only a few inches higher than their heads. The stale air smelled like something had died there, and Luce was almost glad the room was too dark to clearly see the floor. Just when she was beginning to feel claustrophobic, Penn produced another key that opened a small but much more modern door. They ducked through, then were able to stand up on the other side.

Inside, the records office reeked of mildew, but the air felt much cooler and drier. It was pitch-black except for the pale red glow of the EXIT sign over their heads.

Luce could make out Penn's sturdy silhouette, her hands groping in the air. "Where's that string?" she muttered. "There."

With a gentle tug, Penn turned on a naked lightbulb hanging from the ceiling on a linked metal chain. The room was still dim, but now Luce could see that the cement walls were also painted olive green and lined with heavy metal shelves and filing cabinets. Dozens of cardboard filing boxes had been stuffed onto the shelves, and the aisles between the cabinets seemed to stretch out forever. Everything was coated with a thick felt of dust.

The sunshine outside suddenly felt very far away. Even though Luce knew they were only a flight of stairs under the ground, it might as well have been a mile. She rubbed her bare arms. If she were a shadow, this basement was exactly where she'd be. There were no signs of them yet, but Luce knew that was never a good enough reason to feel safe.

Penn, unfazed by the gloom of the basement, dragged a step stool from the corner. "Wow," she said, pulling it behind her as she walked. "Something's different. The records used to be right here. . . . I guess they've been doing a little spring cleaning since the last time I meddled in here."

"How long ago was that?" Luce asked.

"About a week. . . ." Penn's voice trailed off as she disappeared into the darkness behind a tall file cabinet.

Luce couldn't imagine what Sword & Cross would possibly need with all of these boxes. She lifted one lid and pulled out a thick file labeled REMEDIAL MEASURES. She swallowed dryly. Maybe she was better off not knowing.

"It's alphabetical by student," Penn called. Her voice sounded muffled and far away. "E, F, G . . . here we are, Grigori."

Luce followed the sound of rustling paperwork down a narrow aisle and soon found Penn with a box propped in her arms, struggling under its weight. Daniel's file was tucked under her chin.

"It's so thin," she said, lifting her chin slightly so Luce could take it. "Normally, they're so much more, um . . ." She looked up at Luce and bit her lip. "Okay, now *I* sound like the crazy stalker girl. Let's just see what's inside."

There was only a single page in Daniel's file. A black-and-white scan of what must have been his student ID picture was pasted onto the upper right-hand corner. He was looking straight at the camera, at Luce, a faint smile on his lips. She couldn't help smiling back. He looked just the same as he had that night when—well, she couldn't quite think of when. The image of his expression was so sharp in her mind, but she couldn't pin down where she would have seen it.

"God, doesn't he look exactly the same?" Penn interrupted Luce's thoughts. "And look at the date. This picture was taken three years ago when he first came to Sword & Cross."

That must have been what Luce had been thinking . . . that Daniel looked the same then as he did now. But she felt like she'd been thinking—or been about to think—something different, only now she couldn't remember what it was.

"'Parents: unknown,'" Penn read, with Luce leaning over her shoulder. "'Guardian: Los Angeles County Orphanage.'"

"Orphanage?" Luce asked, pressing her hand to her heart.

"That's all there is. Everything else listed here is his—"

"Criminal history," Luce finished, reading along. "'Loitering on public beach after hours . . . vandalism of a shopping cart . . . jaywalking.'"

Penn widened her eyes at Luce and swallowed a laugh. "Loverboy Grigori got arrested for *jaywalking*? Admit it, that's funny."

Luce didn't like picturing Daniel getting arrested for anything. She liked it even less that, according to Sword & Cross, his whole life added up to little more than a list of petty crimes. All these boxes of paperwork down here, and this was all there was on Daniel.

"There has to be more," she said.

Footsteps overhead. Luce's and Penn's eyes shot to the ceiling.

"The main office," Penn whispered, pulling a tissue from inside her sleeve to blow her nose. "It could be anyone. But no one's going to come down here, trust me."

A second later, a door deep within the room creaked open, and light from a hall illuminated a stairway. A clopping of shoes started down. Luce felt Penn's grip on the back of her shirt, pulling her against the wall behind a bookshelf. They waited, holding their breath and clutching Daniel's poached file in their hands. They were so, so busted.

Luce had her eyes closed, expecting the worst, when a haunting, melodious hum filled the room. Someone was singing.

"Doooo da da da dooo," a female voice crooned softly. Luce craned her neck between two boxes of files and could see a thin older woman with a small flashlight strapped to her forehead like a coal miner. Miss Sophia. She was carrying two large boxes, one stacked on top of the other so the only part of her that was visible was her glowing forehead. Her airy steps made it look as if the boxes were full of feathers instead of heavy files.

Penn gripped Luce's hand as they watched Miss Sophia place the file boxes on an empty shelf. She took out a pen to write down something in her notebook.

"Just a couple more," she said, then something under her breath that Luce couldn't hear. A second later, Miss Sophia was gliding back up the stairs, gone as quickly as she'd appeared. Her hum lingered for just a moment in her wake.

When the door clicked shut, Penn let out a huge gulp of air. "She said there were more. She'll probably come back."

"What do we do?" Luce asked.

"You sneak back up the stairs," Penn said, pointing. "Hang a left at the top and you'll be right back at the main office. If anyone sees you, you can say you were looking for a bathroom."

"What about you?"

"I'll put Daniel's file away and meet you by the bleachers. Miss Sophia won't get suspicious if she sees just me. I'm down here so much it's like a second dorm room."

Luce glanced at Daniel's file with a small pang of

regret. She wasn't ready to leave yet. Right around the time she'd resigned herself to checking out Daniel's file, she'd also started thinking about Cam's. Daniel was so cryptic—and unfortunately, so was his file. Cam, on the other hand, seemed so open and easy to read that it made her curious. Luce wondered what else she might be able to find out about him that he might not otherwise share. But one look at Penn's face told Luce that they were short enough on time as it was.

"If there's more to find on Daniel, we'll find it," Penn assured her. "We'll keep looking." She gave Luce a little shove toward the door. "Now, go."

Luce moved quickly down the rank corridor, then pushed open the door to the stairs. The air at the base of the stairs was still humid, but she could feel it clear a little with each step she took. When she finally rounded the corner at the top of the stairs, she had to blink and rub her eyes to readjust to the bright sunlight flooding the hallway. She stumbled around the corner and through the whitewashed doors to the main lobby. There she froze.

Two black stiletto boots, crossed at the ankles, were propped up and sticking out of the phone booth, looking very Wicked Witch of the South. Luce was hurrying toward the front door, hoping not to be spotted, when she realized that the stiletto boots were attached to a pair of snakeskin leggings, which was attached to an unsmiling

Molly. The tiny silver camera was resting in her hand. She raised her eyes to Luce, hung up the phone at her ear, and kicked her feet to the floor.

"Why do you look so guilty, Meat Loaf?" she asked, standing up with her hands on her hips. "Let me guess. You're still planning on ignoring my suggestion to stay away from Daniel."

This whole evil monster thing had to be an act. Molly had no way of knowing where Luce had just been. She didn't know anything about Luce. She had no cause to be so nasty. Since the first day of school, Luce had never done a thing to Molly—except try to stay away from her.

"Are you forgetting what a hellish disaster it was the *last* time you tried to force yourself on a guy who wasn't interested?" Molly's voice was as sharp as a knife. "What was his name again? Taylor? Truman?"

Trevor. How could Molly know about Trevor? This was it, her deepest, darkest secret. The one thing Luce wanted—*needed*—to keep under wraps at Sword & Cross. Now, not only did Evil Incarnate know all about it, she felt no shame bringing it up, cruelly, cavalierly—in the middle of the school's main office.

Was it possible that Penn had been lying, that Luce *wasn't* the only person she shared her office secrets with? Was there any other logical explanation? Luce gripped her arms over her chest, feeling as sick and exposed . . . and inexplicably guilty as she'd felt the night of the fire.

Molly cocked her head. "Finally," she said, sounding relieved. "*Something* got through to you." She turned her back on Luce and shoved open the front door. Then, just before she sauntered outside, she twisted her neck around and looked down her nose at Luce. "So don't do to dear old Daniel what you did to what's-his-name. *Capiche?*"

Luce started after her, but only got a few steps out the door before she realized she would probably crack if she tried to take on Molly now. The girl was just too vicious. Then, rubbing salt in Luce's wound, Gabbe trotted down from the bleachers to meet Molly in the middle of the field. They were far enough away that Luce couldn't make out their expressions when they both turned back to look at her. The ponytailed blond head craned toward the black pixie cut—the vilest tête-à-tête Luce had ever seen.

She balled her sweating fists together, imagining Molly spilling everything she knew about Trevor to Gabbe, who would immediately run off to relay the news to Daniel. At the thought of this, a sick ache spread from Luce's fingertips, up her arms, and into her chest. Daniel might have been caught jaywalking, but so what? It was nothing compared to what Luce was in here for.

"Heads up!" a voice called out. That had always been Luce's least favorite thing to hear. Sporting equipment of all sorts had a funny way of careening right at her. She winced, looking up directly into the sun. She couldn't see anything and didn't even have time to cover her face before she felt a smack against the side of her head and heard a loud *thwunk* ringing in her ears. *Ouch*.

Roland's soccer ball.

"*Nice* one!" Roland called out as the ball sailed directly back to him. Like she'd intended to do that. She rubbed her forehead and took a few wobbly steps.

A hand around her wrist. A spark of heat that made her gasp. She looked down to see tan fingers around her arm, then up into Daniel's deep gray eyes.

"You okay?" he asked.

When she nodded, he raised an eyebrow. "If you wanted to play soccer, you could have said so," he said. "I'd have been happy to explain some of the finer points of the game, like how most people use less delicate body parts of their body to return a kick."

He let go of her wrist, and Luce thought he was reaching toward her, to stroke the stinging side of her face. For a second, she hung there, holding her breath. Then her chest collapsed when Daniel's hand swept back to brush his own hair from his eyes.

That was when Luce realized Daniel was making fun of her.

And why shouldn't he? There was probably an imprint of a soccer ball on the side of her face.

Molly and Gabbe were still staring—and now Daniel—with their arms crossed over their chests.

"I think your girlfriend's getting jealous," Luce said, gesturing at the pair.

"Which one?" he asked.

"I didn't realize they were both your girlfriends."

"Neither one is my girlfriend," he said simply. "I don't have a girlfriend. I meant, which one did you think was my girlfriend?"

Luce was stunned. What about that whole whispered conversation with Gabbe? What about the way the girls were looking at them right now? Was Daniel lying?

He was looking at her funny. "Maybe you hit your head harder than I thought," he said. "Come on, let's take a walk, get you some air."

Luce tried to locate the snide joke in Daniel's latest suggestion. Was he saying she was an airhead who needed more air? No, that didn't even make sense. She glanced at him. How could he look so simply sincere? And just when she was getting so used to the Grigori brush-off.

"Where?" Luce asked cautiously. Because it would be too easy to feel gleeful right now about the fact that Daniel didn't have a girlfriend, about him wanting to go somewhere with her. There had to be a catch.

Daniel merely squinted at the girls across the field. "Someplace where we won't be watched."

Luce had told Penn she'd meet her at the bleachers, but there'd be time to explain later, and of course Penn would understand. Luce let Daniel lead her past the scrutinizing gaze of the girls and the little grove of half-rotted peach trees, around the back of the old church-gym. They were coming up on a forest of gorgeously twisted live oak trees, which Luce never would have guessed were tucked away there. Daniel looked back to make sure she was keeping up. She smiled as though following him were no big deal, but as she picked her way among the gnarled old roots, she couldn't help thinking about the shadows.

Now she was going into the bosky woods, the dark under the thick foliage pierced every so often by a small shaft of sunlight from above. The stench of rich, dank mud filled the air, and Luce suddenly knew there was water nearby.

If she were the kind of person who prayed, this would be when she would pray for the shadows to stay away, just for this sliver of time she had with Daniel, so he wouldn't have to see how crazy she sometimes got. But Luce had never prayed. Didn't know how. Instead, she just crossed her fingers.

"The forest opens right up here," Daniel said. They'd reached a clearing, and Luce gasped in wonder.

Something had changed while she and Daniel had been walking through the forest, something more than just the mere distance from phlegm-colored Sword & Cross. Because when they came out of the trees and stood on this high red rock, it was like they were standing in the middle of a postcard, the kind that spun around a metal rack in a small-town drugstore, a dreamy image of an idyllic South that didn't exist anymore. Every color Luce's eyes fell on was brilliant, brighter than it had seemed just a moment before. From the crystal blue lake just below them to the dense emerald forest surrounding it. Two seagulls banked in the clear sky overhead. When she stood on her toes, she could see the beginnings of a tawny-colored salt marsh, one she knew gave way to the white foam of the ocean somewhere on the invisible horizon.

She glanced up at Daniel. He looked brilliant, too. His skin was golden in this light, his eyes almost like rain. The feel of them on her face was a heavy, remarkable thing.

"What do you think?" he asked. He seemed so much more relaxed now that they were away from everyone else.

"I've never seen anything so wonderful," she said, scanning the pristine surface of the lake, feeling the urge to dive in. About fifty feet out on the water was a large, flat, moss-covered rock. "What's that?"

"I'll show you," Daniel said, kicking off his shoes. Luce tried unsuccessfully not to stare when he tugged his T-shirt over his head, exposing his muscled torso. "Come on," he said, making her realize how rooted to the spot she must have looked. "You can swim in that," he added, pointing at her gray tank top and cutoffs. "I'll even let you win this time."

She laughed. "Versus what? All those times I let you win?"

Daniel started to nod, then stopped himself abruptly. "No. Since you lost at the pool the other day."

For a second, Luce had the urge to tell him *why* she'd lost. Maybe they could laugh about the whole Gabbe-being-his-girlfriend misunderstanding. But by then, Daniel's arms were over his head and he was in the air, arcing and then falling, diving into the lake with a perfect little splash.

It was one of the most beautiful things Luce had ever seen. He had a grace like none she'd ever witnessed before. Even the splash he'd made left a lovely ring in her ears.

She wanted to be down there with him.

She tugged off her shoes and left them under the magnolia tree next to Daniel's, then stood at the edge of the rock. The drop was about twenty feet, the kind of high dive that had always made Luce's heart skip a beat. In a good way.

A second later, his head popped up above the surface. He was grinning, treading water. "Don't make me change my mind about letting you win," he called.

Taking a deep breath, she aimed her fingers over

Daniel's head and pushed off and up into a high swan dive. The fall lasted only a split second, but it was the most delicious feeling, sailing through the sunny air, down, down, down.

Splash. The water was shockingly cold at first, then ideal a second later. Luce surfaced to catch her breath, took one look at Daniel, and started in on her butterfly stroke.

She pushed herself so hard that she lost track of him. She knew she was showing off and hoped he was watching. She drew closer and closer until she slammed her hand down on the rock—an instant before Daniel.

Both of them were panting as they hauled themselves up on the flat, sun-warmed surface. Its edges were slippery because of the moss, and Luce had a hard time finding her grip. Daniel had no problem scaling the rock, though. He reached back and gave her a hand, then pulled her up to where she could kick a leg over the side.

By the time she'd hoisted herself fully out of the water, he was lying on his back, almost dry. Only his shorts gave away any hint that he'd just been in the lake. On the other hand, Luce's wet clothes clung to her body, and her hair was dripping everywhere. Most guys would have seized the opportunity to ogle a dripping-wet girl, but Daniel lay back on the rock and closed his eyes, like he was giving her a moment to wring herself out—either out of kindness or a lack of interest.

Kindness, she decided, knowing she was being hopelessly romantic. But Daniel seemed so perceptive, he must have felt at least a little bit of what Luce felt. Not just the attraction, the need to be near him when everyone around her was telling her to stay away, but that very real sense that they knew—really knew—each other from somewhere.

Daniel snapped open his eyes and smiled—the same smile as in the picture in his file. A rush of déjà vu engulfed her so completely that Luce had to lie down herself.

"What?" he asked, sounding nervous.

"Nothing."

"Luce."

"I can't get it out of my head," she said, rolling over on her side to face him. She didn't feel steady enough to sit up yet. "This feeling that I know you. That I've known you for a while."

The water lapped against the rock, splashing on Luce's toes where they dangled over the edge. It was cold and spread goose bumps up her calves. Finally, Daniel spoke.

"Haven't we been through this already?" His tone had changed, like he was trying to laugh her off. He sounded like a Dover guy: self-satisfied, eternally bored, smug. "I'm flattered you feel like we have this connection, really. But you don't have to invent some forgotten history to get a guy to pay attention to you."

No. He thought she was lying about this weird feeling she couldn't shake as a way of coming on to him? She gritted her teeth, mortified.

"Why would I make this up?" she asked, squinting in the sunlight.

"You tell me," Daniel said. "No, actually, don't. It won't do any good." He sighed. "Look, I should have said this earlier when I started to see the signs."

Luce sat up. Her heart was racing. Daniel saw the signs, too.

"I know I brushed you off in the gym before," he said slowly, causing Luce to lean forward, as if she could draw out the words more quickly. "I should have just told you the truth."

Luce waited.

"I got burned by a girl." He swung a hand into the water, plucked out a lily pad, and crumbled it in his hands. "Someone I really loved, not too long ago. It's nothing personal, and I don't want to ignore you." He looked up at her and the sun filtered through a drop of water in his hair, making it gleam. "But I also don't want you to get your hopes up. I'm just not looking to get involved with anyone, not anytime soon."

Oh.

She looked away, out at the still, midnight-blue water where only minutes ago they'd been laughing and splashing around. The lake showed no signs of that fun anymore. Neither did Daniel's face.

Well, Luce had been burned, too. Maybe if she told him about Trevor and how horrible everything had been, Daniel would open up about his past. But then again, she already knew she couldn't stand hearing about his past with someone else. The thought of him with another girl—she pictured Gabbe, Molly, a montage of smiling faces, big eyes, long hair—was enough to make her feel nauseated.

His bad-breakup story should have justified everything. But it didn't. Daniel had been so strange to her from the start. Flipping her off one day, before they'd even been introduced, then protecting her from the statue in the cemetery the next. Now he'd brought her out here to the lake—alone. He was all over the place.

Daniel's head was lowered but his eyes were staring up at her. "Not a good enough answer?" he asked, almost like he knew what she was thinking.

"I still feel like there's something you're not telling me," she said.

All of this couldn't be explained away by one bad heartbreak, Luce knew. She had experience in that department.

His back was to her and he was looking toward the path they'd taken to the lake. After a while, he laughed bitterly. "Of course there are things I'm not telling you. I barely know you. I'm not sure why you think I owe you anything." He got to his feet.

"Where are you going?"

"I've got to get back," he said.

"Don't go," she whispered, but he didn't seem to hear.

She watched, chest heaving, as Daniel dove into the water.

He came up far away and began swimming toward shore. He glanced back at her once, about midway, and gave her a definitive wave goodbye.

Then her heart swelled as he circled his arms over his head in a perfect butterfly stroke. As empty as she felt inside, she couldn't help admiring it. So clean, so effortless, it hardly looked like swimming at all.

In no time he had reached the shore, making the distance between them seem much shorter than it looked to Luce. He'd appeared so leisurely as he swam, but there was no way he could have reached the other side that quickly unless he'd really been tearing though the water.

How urgent was it for him to get away from her?

She watched—feeling a confusing mix of deep embarrassment and even deeper temptation—as Daniel hoisted himself back up onto the shore. A shaft of sunlight bit through the trees and framed his silhouette with a glowing radiance, and Luce had to squint at the sight before her eyes.

She wondered whether the soccer ball to her head had shaken up her vision. Or whether what she thought she was seeing was a mirage. A trick of the late-afternoon sunlight.

She stood up on the rock to get a better look.

All he was doing was shaking the water from his wet head, but a glaze of droplets seemed to hover over him, outside him, defying gravity in a wide span across his arms.

The way the water shimmered in the sunlight, it almost looked like he had wings.

NINE

STATE OF INNOCENCE

On Monday evening, Miss Sophia stood behind a podium at the head of the largest classroom in Augustine, attempting to make shadow puppets with her hands. She'd called a last-minute study session for the students in her religion class before the next day's midterm, and since Luce had already missed a full month of the class, she figured she had a lot to catch up on.

Which explained why she was the only one even pretending to take notes. None of the other students even noticed that the evening sun trickling in through the narrow western windows was undermining Miss Sophia's handcrafted light-box stage. And Luce didn't want to call attention to the fact that she was paying attention by standing up to draw the dusty blinds.

When the sun brushed the back of Luce's neck, it struck her just how long she'd been sitting in this room. She'd watched the eastern sun glow like a mane around Mr. Cole's thinning hair that morning during world history. She'd suffered the sweltering midafternoon heat during biology with the Albatross. It was nearly evening now. The sun had looped the entire campus, and Luce had barely left this desk. Her body felt as stiff as the metal chair she was sitting in, her mind as dull as the pencil she'd given up using to take notes.

What was up with these shadow puppets? Were she and the other students, like, five years old?

But then she felt guilty. Of all the faculty here, Miss Sophia was by far the nicest, even gently pulling Luce aside the other day to discuss how far behind Luce was in the writing of her family tree paper. Luce had to feign astonished gratitude when Miss Sophia walked her through an hour's worth of database instructions yet again. She felt a little ashamed, but playing dumb was far superior to admitting she'd been too busy obsessing over a certain male classmate to devote any time to her research.

Now Miss Sophia stood in her long black crepe dress, elegantly interlocking her thumbs and raising her hands in the air, preparing for her next pose. Outside the window, a cloud crossed over the sun. Luce zoned back in on the lecture when she noticed there was suddenly an actual shadow visible on the wall behind Miss Sophia.

"As you all remember from your reading of *Paradise Lost* last year, when God gave his angels their own will," Miss Sophia said, breathing into the microphone clipped to her ivory lapel and flapping her thin fingers like a perfect angel's wings, "there was *one* who crossed the line." Miss Sophia's voice dropped dramatically, and Luce watched as she twisted up her index fingers so the angel's wings transformed into devil's horns.

Behind Luce, someone muttered, "Big deal, that's the oldest trick in the book."

From the moment Miss Sophia had kicked off her lecture, it seemed like at least one person in the room took issue with every word that came out of her mouth. Maybe it was because Luce hadn't had a religious upbringing like the rest of them, or maybe it was because she felt sorry for Miss Sophia, but she felt a growing urge to turn around and shush the hecklers.

She was cranky. Tired. Hungry. Instead of filing down to dinner with the rest of the school, the twenty students enrolled in Miss Sophia's religion class had been informed that if they were attending the "optional"—a sad misnomer, Penn informed her—study session, their meal would be served in the classroom where the session was being held, to save time.

The meal—not dinner, not even lunch, just a generic late-afternoon fill-up—had been a strange experience for Luce, who had a hard enough time finding anything she could eat in the meat-centric cafeteria. Randy had just wheeled in a cart of depressing sandwiches and some pitchers of lukewarm water.

The sandwiches had all been mystery cold cuts, mayo, and cheese, and Luce had watched enviously as Penn chomped through one after another, leaving tooth-marked rings of crust as she ate. Luce had been on the verge of de-bologna-ing a sandwich when Cam shouldered up next to her. He'd opened his fist to expose a small cluster of fresh figs. Their deep purple skins looked like jewels in his hand.

"What's this?" she'd asked, sucking in a smile.

"Can't live on bread alone, can you?" he'd said.

"Don't eat those." Gabbe had swooped in, lifting the figs out of Luce's fingers and tossing them in the trash. She'd interrupted yet another private conversation and replaced the empty space in Luce's palm with a handful of peanut M&M's from a vending machine sack. Gabbe wore a rainbow-colored headband. Luce imagined yanking the thing from her head and pitching it in the trash.

"She's right, Luce." Arriane had appeared, glowering at Cam. "Who knows what he drugged these with?"

Luce had laughed, because of course Arriane was joking, but when no one else smiled, she shut up and slipped the M&M's into her pocket just as Miss Sophia called for them all to take their seats.

⁂

What felt like hours later, they were all still trapped in the classroom and Miss Sophia had only gotten from the Dawn of Creation to the war in Heaven. They weren't even at Adam and Eve. Luce's stomach rumbled in protest.

"And do we all know who the wicked angel was who battled God?" Miss Sophia asked, like she was reading a picture book to a bunch of children at the library. Luce half expected the room to sing out a juvenile *Yes, Miss Sophia*.

"Anyone?" Miss Sophia asked again.

"Roland!" Arriane hooted under her breath.

"That's right," Miss Sophia said, head bobbing in a saintly nod. She was just left of hard of hearing. "We call him Satan now, but over the years he's worked under many guises—Mephistopheles, or Belial, even Lucifer to some."

Molly, who'd been sitting in front of Luce, rocking the back of her chair against Luce's desk for the past hour with the express purpose of driving Luce insane, promptly dropped a slip of paper over her shoulder onto Luce's desk.

Luce . . . Lucifer . . . any relation?

Her handwriting was dark and angry and frenetic. Luce could see her high cheekbones rise up in a sneer. In a moment of hungry weakness, Luce started furiously scribbling an answer on the back of Molly's note. That she had been named for Lucinda Williams, the greatest living female singer-songwriter whose almost-rained-out concert was the site of her parents' first encounter. That after her mom slipped on a plastic cup, tumbled down a mudslide, and landed in her father's arms, she hadn't left those arms for twenty years. That *her* name stood for something romantic and what did muckle-mouthed Molly have to show for herself? And anyway, that if there was anyone in this entire school who came close to resembling Satan, it wasn't the receiver of the note, it was the sender.

Her eyes drilled into the back of Molly's newly scarlet-dyed pixie cut. Luce was ready to pelt her with the folded-up piece of paper and take her chances with Molly's temper when Miss Sophia pulled her attention to the light box.

She had both hands raised over her head, palms up and cupping the air. As she lowered them, the shadows of her fingers on the wall looked miraculously like flailing arms and legs, like someone jumping off a bridge or out of a building. The sight was so bizarre, so dark and yet so well rendered, it unnerved Luce. She couldn't turn away.

"For nine days and nine nights," Miss Sophia said, "Satan and his angels fell, further and further from Heaven."

Her words jogged something in Luce's memory. She looked two rows over at Daniel, who met her eyes for half a second before burying his face in his notebook. But that second's glance had been enough, and all at once it came back to her: the dream she'd had the night before.

It had been a revisionist history of her and Daniel at the lake. But in the dream, when Daniel said goodbye and dove back into the water, Luce had the courage to go after him. The water was warm, so comfortable that she hadn't even felt wet, and schools of violet fish swarmed all around her. She was swimming as fast as she could, and at first she thought the fish were helping push her toward Daniel and the shore. But soon the masses of fish began to darken and cloud her vision, and she couldn't see him anymore. The fish became shadowy and vicious-looking, and drew closer and closer till she couldn't see anything, and she'd felt herself sinking, slipping away, down into the silty depths of the lake. It wasn't a question of not being able to breathe, it was a question of never being able to rise back up. It was a question of losing Daniel forever.

Then, from below, Daniel had appeared, his arms spread out like sails. They scattered the shadow fish and enveloped Luce, and together the two of them soared back to the surface. They broke through the water, higher, higher, passing the rock and the magnolia tree where they'd left their shoes. A second later, they were so high Luce couldn't even see the ground.

"And they landed," Miss Sophia said, resting her hands on the podium, "in the blazing pits of Hell."

Luce closed her eyes and exhaled. It had only been a dream. Unfortunately, this was her reality.

She sighed and rested her chin on her hands, remembering her forgotten response to Molly's note. It was folded in her hands. It seemed stupid now and rash. Better not to answer, for Molly not to know she'd even affected Luce.

A paper airplane came to rest on her left forearm. She looked to the far left corner of the class, where Arriane sat holding an exaggerated winking pose.

I take it you're not daydreaming about Satan. Where'd you and DG scurry off to Saturday afternoon?

Luce hadn't had a chance to talk to Arriane alone all day. But how would Arriane have known that Luce went off with Daniel? While Miss Sophia busied herself with a shadow-puppet-focused representation of the nine circles of Hell, Luce watched Arriane sail another perfectly aimed plane at her desk.

So did Molly.

She reached up just in time to snag the plane between her slick black-painted fingernails, but Luce was not going to let her win this one. She snatched the plane back from Molly's grip, ripping its wing loudly down the middle. Luce had exactly enough time to pocket the torn note before Miss Sophia whipped around.

"Lucinda and Molly," she said, pursing her lips and steadying her hands on the podium. "I would hope whatever you two feel the need to discuss in a disrespectful passing of notes could be said before the entire class."

Luce's mind raced. If she didn't come up with something fast, Molly would, and there was no telling how embarrassing that could be.

"M-Molly was just saying," Luce stammered, "that she disagrees with your view of how Hell is broken down. She has her own ideas."

"Well, Molly, if you have an alternate schema of the underworld, I'd certainly like to hear of it."

"What the hell," Molly muttered under her breath. She cleared her throat and stood up. "Well, you've described Lucifer's mouth as the lowest place in the inferno, which is why all the traitors end up there. But for me," she said, like she'd rehearsed the lines, "I think the most tortured place in Hell"—she took a long, sweeping look back at Luce—"should be reserved not for traitors, but for cowards. The weakest, most spineless losers. Because it seems to me that traitors? At least they made a choice. But cowards? They just run around biting their fingernails, totally afraid to do anything.

Which is totally worse." She coughed out, "Lucinda!" and cleared her throat. "But that's just my opinion." She sat down.

"Thank you, Molly," Miss Sophia said carefully, "I'm sure we all feel very enlightened."

Luce didn't. She had stopped listening in the middle of Molly's rant, when she felt an eerie, sick feeling in the pit of her stomach.

The shadows. She sensed them before she saw them, bubbling up like tar from the ground. A tentacle of darkness curled around her wrist, and Luce looked down in terror. It was trying to weasel its way into her pocket. It was going for Arriane's paper plane. She hadn't even read it yet! She stuffed her fist deep into her pocket and used two fingers and all her willpower to pinch the shadow out as hard as she could.

An amazing thing happened: The shadow recoiled, rearing back like an injured dog. It was the first time Luce had ever been able to do that.

Across the room, she met Arriane's eye. Arriane's head was cocked to the side and her mouth was hanging open.

The note—she must still be waiting for Luce to read the note.

Miss Sophia flicked off the light box. "I think my arthritis has had enough Hell for one night." She chuckled, encouraging the brain-numbed students to chuckle with her. "If you'll all reread the seven critical essays I've assigned on *Paradise Lost,* I think you'll be more than prepared for tomorrow's exam."

As the other students rushed to pack up their bags and peel out of the room, Luce unfolded Arriane's note:

Tell me he didn't give you that lame "I've been burned before" bit.

Ouch. She definitely needed to talk to Arriane and find out exactly what she knew about Daniel. But first . . .

He was standing before her. His silver belt buckle shone at eye level. She took a deep breath and looked up at his face.

Daniel's violet-flecked gray eyes looked rested. She hadn't spoken to him in two days, since he'd left her at the lake. It was as if the time he'd spent away from her had rejuvenated him.

Luce realized she still had Arriane's revealing note spread open on her desk. She swallowed hard and tucked it back into her pocket.

"I wanted to apologize for leaving so suddenly the other day," Daniel said, sounding oddly formal. Luce didn't know if she was supposed to accept his apology, but he didn't give her time to respond. "I take it you made it back to dry land okay?"

She tried a smile. It crossed her mind to tell Daniel about the dream she'd had, but luckily she realized that would be totally weird.

"What did you think of the review session?" Daniel seemed withdrawn, stiff, like they'd never spoken before. Maybe he was joking.

"It was torture," Luce answered. It had always annoyed Luce when smart girls pretended they weren't into something just because they assumed that was what a guy would want to hear. But Luce was not pretending; it really *had* been torture.

"Good," Daniel said, seeming pleased.

"You hated it, too?"

"No," he said cryptically, and Luce now wished she'd lied to sound more interested than she actually was.

"So . . . you liked it," she said, wanting to say something, anything to keep him there next to her, talking. "What did you like about it exactly?"

"Maybe 'like' isn't the right word." After a long pause, he said, "It's in my family . . . studying these things. I guess I can't help feeling a connection."

It took a moment for his words to fully register with Luce. Her mind traveled into the fusty old storage basement where she'd glimpsed Daniel's single-page file. The file that claimed that Daniel Grigori had spent most of his life in a Los Angeles County Orphanage.

"I didn't know you had any family," she said.

"Why would you?" Daniel scoffed.

"I don't know. . . . So, I mean, you do?"

"The question is why you presume you know anything about my family—or me—at all?"

Luce felt her stomach plummet. She saw the *Warning: Stalker Alert* flash in Daniel's alarmed eyes. And she knew she'd botched things with him yet again.

"D." Roland came up from behind them and put his hand on Daniel's T-shirt-clad shoulder. "You want to stick around to see if there's another yearlong lecture, or are we going to roll?"

"Yeah," Daniel said softly, giving Luce a final sideways glance. "Let's get out of here."

Of course—obviously—she should have bolted several minutes ago. Like, at the first instinct to divulge any details of Daniel's file. A smart, normal person would have dodged the conversation, or changed the subject to something much less freakish, or at the very least, kept her big mouth shut.

But. Luce was proving day after day that—especially when it came to Daniel—she was incapable of doing anything that fell under the category of "normal" or "smart."

She watched as Daniel walked away with Roland. He didn't look back, and every step he took away from her made her feel more and more freakishly alone.

TEN

WHERE THERE'S SMOKE

"What are you waiting for?" Penn asked barely a second after Daniel had left with Roland. "Let's go." She tugged on Luce's hand.

"Go where?" Luce asked. Her heart was still pounding from the conversation with Daniel—and from the view of him leaving. The shape his sculpted shoulders cut out in the hall seemed to be bigger than Daniel himself.

Penn rapped lightly on the side of Luce's head. "Hello? The library, like I said in my note . . ." She took in Luce's blank expression. "You didn't get either one of my notes?" She slapped her leg, frustrated. "But I handed them to Todd to pass to Cam to pass to you."

"Pony Express." Cam wedged his way in front of Penn and presented Luce with two folded scraps of paper held between his index and middle finger.

"Give me a break. Did your horse die of exhaustion on the road?" Penn huffed, snagging the notes. "I gave you those like an hour ago. What took so long? You didn't read them—"

"Of course not." Cam pressed a hand to his broad chest, offended. He wore a thick black ring on his middle finger. "If you remember, Luce got in trouble for passing notes with Molly—"

"I was *not* passing notes with Molly—"

"Regardless," Cam said, lifting the notes back out of Penn's hand and delivering them, finally, to Luce. "I was only looking out for your best interests. Waiting for the right opportunity."

"Well, thank you." Luce tucked the notes into her pocket and gave Penn a what-are-ya-gonna-do shrug.

"Speaking of waiting for the right time," he said, "I was out the other day and saw this." He produced a small red velvet jewelry box and held it open for Luce to see.

Penn nudged around Luce's shoulder so she could get a look.

Inside, a thin gold chain held a small circular pendant with a carved line down its middle and a small serpent's head at the tip.

Luce looked up at him. Was he making fun of her?

He touched the pendant. "I thought, after the other day . . . I wanted to help you face your fear," he said, sounding almost nervous, afraid that she might not accept. Should she accept? "Only kidding. I just liked it. It's unique, it reminded me of you."

It *was* unique. And very beautiful, and it made Luce feel strangely unworthy.

"You went shopping?" she found herself asking, because it was easier to discuss how Cam had left campus than it would have been to ask *Why me?* "I thought the point of reform school is that we're all stuck here."

Cam lifted his chin slightly and smiled with his eyes. "There are ways," he said quietly. "I'll show you sometime. I could show you—tonight?"

"Cam, honey," a voice said behind him. It was Gabbe, tapping his shoulder. A thin section at the front of her hair was French-braided and pinned behind her ear, like a perfect little headband. Luce stared at it jealously.

"I need your help setting up," Gabbe purred.

Luce looked around and realized they were the only four people left in the classroom.

"Having a little party in my room later," Gabbe said,

pressing her chin into Cam's shoulder to address Luce and Penn. "Y'all are coming, right?"

Gabbe, whose mouth always looked sticky with lip gloss, and whose blond hair never failed to swoosh right in the second a guy started talking to Luce. Even though Daniel had said there was nothing going on between them, Luce knew she was never going to be friends with this girl.

Then again, you didn't have to like someone to go to her party, especially when certain other people you did like would probably be there. . . .

Or should she take Cam up on his offer? Was he really suggesting they sneak out? Only yesterday, a rumor had flown around the classroom when Jules and Phillip, the tongue-pierced couple, didn't show up for Miss Sophia's class. Apparently, they'd tried to leave campus in the middle of the night, a secret tryst gone wrong—and now they were in some type of solitary confinement whose location even Penn didn't know about.

The weirdest part was, Miss Sophia—who usually had no tolerance for whispering—hadn't shut the madly gossiping students up during her lesson. It was almost like the faculty *wanted* the students to imagine the worst possible punishment for breaking any of their dictatorial rules.

Luce swallowed, looking up at Cam. He offered his elbow, ignoring Gabbe and Penn entirely. "How about it, kid?" he asked, sounding so charmingly classic Hollywood that Luce forgot all about what had happened to Jules and Phillip.

"Sorry." Penn butted in, answering for both of them and steering Luce away by the elbow. "But we have other plans."

Cam looked at Penn like he was trying to figure out where she'd come from all of a sudden. He had a way of making Luce feel like a better, cooler version of herself. And she had a way of crossing his path right after Daniel had made her feel exactly the opposite. But Gabbe was still hovering beside him, and Penn's tug was growing stronger, so finally Luce just waved the hand still clutching Cam's gift. "Um, maybe next time! Thanks for the necklace!"

Leaving Cam and Gabbe confused in the classroom behind them, Penn and Luce booked it out of Augustine. It felt creepy to be alone in the dark building so late, and Luce could tell from the hurried slap of Penn's sandals on the stairs in front of her that she felt it, too.

Outside, it was windy. An owl crooned in its palmetto tree. When they passed under the oaks alongside the building, straggly tendrils of Spanish moss brushed them like tangled strands of hair.

"*Maybe next time?*" Penn mimicked Luce's voice. "What was that about?"

"Nothing . . . I don't know." Luce wanted to change the subject. "You make us sound very posh, Penn," she said, laughing as they trudged along the commons. "Other plans . . . I thought you had fun at the party last week."

"If you'd ever get around to reading my recent correspondence, you'd see why we have more important things on our plate."

Luce emptied her pockets, rediscovered the five uneaten M&M's, and shared them with Penn, who expressed a very Penn-like sentiment that she hoped they had come from a sanitary place, but ate them anyway.

Luce unfolded the first of Penn's notes, which looked like a photocopied page from one of the files in the underground archive:

```
Gabrielle Givens
Cameron Briel
Lucinda Price
Todd Hammond
PREVIOUS LOCATIONS:
All in the Northeast, except for T. Hammond
    (Orlando, Florida)

Arriane Alter
Daniel Grigori
Mary Margaret Zane
PREVIOUS LOCATIONS:
Los Angeles, California
```

Lucinda's group was noted as arriving at Sword & Cross on September 15 of this year. The second group had arrived March 15, three years earlier.

"Who's Mary Margaret Zane?" Luce asked, pointing.

"Only the very virtuous Molly," Penn said.

Molly's name was Mary Margaret? "No wonder she's so pissed off at the world," Luce said. "So where'd you get all this?"

"I dug it out from one of the boxes Miss Sophia brought down the other day," Penn said. "That's Miss Sophia's handwriting."

Luce looked up at her. "What does it mean? Why would she need to record this? I thought they had all our arrival dates separately in our files."

"They do. I can't figure it out, either," Penn said. "And I mean, even though you showed up at the same time as those other kids, it's not like you have anything in common with them."

"I couldn't have *less* in common with them," Luce said, envisioning the coy look Gabbe always had glued to her face.

Penn scratched her chin. "But when Arriane, Molly, and Daniel showed up, they already knew each other. I think they came from the same halfway house in L.A."

Somewhere there was a key to Daniel's story. There had to be more to him than a halfway house in

California. But thinking back to his reaction—that washed-out horror that Luce might take an interest in knowing anything about him—well, it made her feel like everything she and Penn were doing was futile and immature.

"What's the point of all of this?" Luce asked, suddenly annoyed.

"Why Miss Sophia would be collating all that information I can't figure out. Though Miss Sophia arrived at Sword & Cross the same day as Arriane, Daniel, and Molly . . ." Penn trailed off. "Who knows? Maybe it doesn't mean anything. There's just so little mention of Daniel in the archives, I figured I'd show you everything I came up with. Hence exhibit B."

She pointed toward the second note in Luce's hand.

Luce sighed. Part of her wanted to quit the search and stop feeling embarrassed about Daniel. The pushier part of her still yearned to get to know him better . . . which, strangely, was far easier to do when he wasn't technically present to give her new reasons to feel embarrassed.

She looked down at the note, a photocopy of an old-fashioned card from a library catalog.

```
Grigori, D. The Watchers: Myth in Medieval
    Europe. Seraphim Press, Rome, 1755.
Call no: R999.318 GRI
```

"Sounds like one of Daniel's ancestors was a scholar," Penn said, reading over Luce's shoulder.

"This must have been what he meant," Luce said under her breath. She looked at Penn. "He told me studying religion was in his family. This must be what he meant."

"I thought he was an orphan—"

"Don't ask," Luce said, waving her off. "Touchy subject with him." She ran her finger over the book's title. "What's a watcher?"

"Only one way to find out," Penn said. "Though we may live to regret it. 'Cause this sounds like possibly the most boring book ever. Still," she added, dusting her knuckles on her shirt, "I took the liberty of checking the catalog. The book should be in the stacks. You can thank me later."

"You're good." Luce grinned. She was eager to get up to the library. If someone in Daniel's family had written a book, it couldn't possibly be boring. Or not to Luce, anyway. But then she looked down at the other thing still in her hand. The velvet jewelry box from Cam.

"What do you think this means?" she asked Penn as they started walking up the mosaic-tiled stairs to the library.

Penn shrugged. "Your feelings on snakes are—"

"Hatred, agony, extreme paranoia, and disgust," Luce listed.

"Maybe it's like . . . okay, I used to be scared of cactus. Couldn't go near 'em—don't laugh, have you ever pricked yourself on one of those things? They stay in your skin for days. Anyway, one year, for my birthday, my dad bought me like eleven cactus plants. At first I wanted to chuck them at him. But then, you know, I got used to them. I stopped flipping out anytime I was near one. In the end, it totally worked."

"So you're saying Cam's gift," Luce said, "is actually really sweet."

"I guess," Penn said. "But if I'd known he had the hots for you, I would *not* have trusted him with our private correspondence. Sorry about that."

"He does not have the hots for me," Luce started to say, fingering the gold chain inside the box, imagining how it would look on her skin. She hadn't told Penn anything about her picnic with Cam because—well, she didn't really know why. It had to do with Daniel, and how Luce still couldn't figure out where she stood—or wanted to stand—with either of them.

"Ha." Penn cackled. "Which means you kinda like him! Cheating on Daniel. I can't keep up with you and your men."

"As if anything is going on with *either* of them," Luce said glumly. "Do you think Cam read the notes?"

"If he did, and he still gave you that necklace," Penn said, "then he's really into you."

They stepped inside the library, and the heavy double doors thudded behind them. The sound echoed through the room. Miss Sophia looked up from the mounds of paper covering her lamplit desk.

"Oh, hello, girls," she said, beaming so broadly that Luce felt guilty all over again for zoning out during her lecture. "I hope you enjoyed my brief review session!" she practically sang.

"Very much." Luce nodded, though there had been nothing brief about it. "We came here to review a few more things before the exam."

"That's right," Penn chimed in. "You inspired us."

"How wonderful!" Miss Sophia rustled through her paperwork. "I've got a further reading list somewhere. I'd be happy to make you a copy."

"Great," Penn lied, giving Luce a small push toward the stacks. "We'll let you know if we need it!"

Beyond Miss Sophia's desk, the library was quiet. Luce and Penn eyed the call numbers as they passed shelf after shelf toward the books on religion. The energy-saving lights had motion detectors and were supposed to turn on as they crossed each aisle, but only about half of them worked. Luce realized that Penn was still holding on to her arm, then realized she didn't want her to let go.

The girls came to the usually crowded study section, where only one table lamp burned. Everyone else must have been at Gabbe's party. Everyone except for Todd.

He had his feet kicked up on the chair across from him and seemed to be reading a coffee-table-sized world atlas. When the girls walked by him, he looked up with a wan expression that was either very lonely or slightly annoyed at being disturbed.

"You guys are here late," he said flatly.

"So are you," Penn retorted, sticking out her tongue dramatically.

When they'd put a few shelves between them and Todd, Luce raised an eyebrow at Penn. "What was *that*?"

"What?" Penn sulked. "He flirts with me." She crossed her arms over her chest and blew a brown curlicue of hair out of her eyes. "As if."

"Are you in fourth grade?" Luce teased.

Penn stuck her pointer finger up at Luce with an intensity that would have made Luce jump if she hadn't been giggling so much. "Do you know anyone else who would delve into Daniel Grigori's family history with you? Didn't think so. Leave me alone."

By then, they had reached the far back corner of the library, where all the 999 books were arranged along a single pewter-colored bookshelf. Penn crouched down and traced the books' spines with her finger. Luce felt a tremor, like someone was running a finger along her neck. She craned her head around and saw a wisp of gray. Not black, like the shadows usually were, but lighter, thinner. Just as unwelcome.

She watched, wide-eyed, as the shadow stretched out in a long, curling strand directly over Penn's head. It came down slowly, like a threaded needle, and Luce didn't want to think about what might happen if it touched her friend. The other day at the gym had been the first time the shadows had touched her—and she still felt violated, almost dirty from it. She didn't know what else they could do.

Nervous, unsteady, Luce stretched her arm out like a baseball bat. She took a deep breath and swung forward. She bristled at the icy contact as she knocked the shadow away—and clocked Penn upside the head.

Penn pressed her hands against her skull and looked back at Luce in shock. "*What* is wrong with you?"

Luce sank down next to her and smoothed the top of Penn's hair. "I'm so sorry. There was . . . I thought I saw a bee . . . land on your head. I panicked. I didn't want it to sting you."

She could feel how utterly, utterly lame this excuse was and waited for her friend to tell her she was crazy— what would a bee be doing in a library? She waited for Penn to walk out.

But Penn's round face softened. She took Luce's hand in both of hers and shook it. "Bees terrify me, too," she said. "I'm deathly allergic. You basically just saved my life."

It was like they were having a huge bonding moment—only they weren't, because Luce was wholly consumed by the shadows. If only there were a way to push them from her mind, to shrug the shadow thing off, without shrugging off Penn.

Luce had a strong, uneasy feeling about this light gray shadow. The uniformity of the shadows had never been comforting, but these latest variations were a new level of disconcerting. Did it mean more kinds of shadows were finding their way to her? Or was she just getting better at distinguishing them? And what about that weird moment during Miss Sophia's lecture, when she'd actually pinched a shadow back before it could enter her pocket? She'd done it without thinking, and had had no reason to expect that her two fingers would be any match for a shadow, but they had been—she glanced around the stacks—at least temporarily.

She wondered whether she had set some kind of precedent for interacting with the shadows. Except that to call what she'd done to the shadow hovering over Penn's head "interacting"—even Luce knew that was a euphemism. A cold, sick feeling grew in her gut when she realized that what she'd started doing to the shadows was more like . . . fighting them off.

"It's the strangest thing." Penn spoke up from the floor. "It should be right here between *The Dictionary of Angels* and this god-awful Billy Graham fire-and-brimstone thing." She looked up at Luce. "But it's gone."

"I thought you said—"

"I did. The computer had it listed as on the shelves

when I looked this afternoon, but we can't get online this late to check again."

"Go ask Todd-o out there," Luce suggested. "Maybe he's using it as a cover for his *Playboys*."

"Gross." Penn whacked her on the thigh.

Luce knew she'd only made the joke to try to downplay her disappointment. It was just so frustrating. She couldn't find out anything about Daniel without running up against a wall. She didn't know what she'd find inside the pages of his great-great-whatever's book, but at least it would tell her *something* more about Daniel. Which had to be better than nothing.

"Stay here," Penn said, standing up. "I'm going to go ask Miss Sophia if anyone's checked it out today."

Luce watched her traipse back up the long aisle toward the front desk. She laughed when Penn sped up to pass the area where Todd was sitting.

Alone in the back corner, Luce fingered some of the other books on the shelves. She did a quick mental runthrough of the student body at Sword & Cross, but she couldn't think of any likely candidates for checking out an old religious book. Maybe Miss Sophia had used it as reference for her review session earlier. Luce wondered what it must have been like for Daniel to sit there, listening to the librarian talk about things that had probably been dinner-table topics of conversation when he was growing up. Luce wanted to know what his childhood had been like. What had happened to his family? Had his upbringing at the orphanage been religious? Or was his childhood anything like hers, in which the only things pursued religiously were good grades and academic honors? She wanted to know whether Daniel had ever read this book by his ancestor and what he'd thought about it, and if he liked writing himself. She wanted to know what he was doing right now at Gabbe's party and when his birthday was and what size shoe he wore and whether he ever wasted a single second of his time wondering about her.

Luce shook her head. This train of thought was heading straight for Pity City, and she wanted to get off. She pulled the first book off the shelf—the very unfascinating cloth-covered *Dictionary of Angels*—and decided to distract herself by reading until Penn came back.

She'd gotten as far as the fallen angel Abbadon, who regretted siding with Satan and constantly bemoaned his bad decision—*yawn*—when a blaring noise rang out over her head. Luce looked up to see the red flash of the fire alarm.

"Alert. Alert," a monotone robotic voice announced over a loudspeaker. "The fire alarm has been activated. Evacuate the building."

Luce slid the book back on the shelf and pulled herself to her feet. They'd done this kind of thing at Dover all the time. After a while, it had reached the point where not even the teachers had heeded the monthly fire drills, so the fire department started really setting off the alarm just to get people to respond. Luce could totally see the administrators at Sword & Cross pulling a similar stunt. But when she started walking toward the exit, she was surprised to find herself coughing. There was actual smoke inside the library.

"Penn?" she called out, hearing her voice echo in her ears. She knew she'd be drowned out by the piercing shriek of the alarm.

The acrid smell of the smoke dropped her instantly back into the blaze that night with Trevor. Images and sounds flooded her mind, things she'd stuffed so deep inside her memory they might as well have been obliterated. Until now.

The shocking whites of Trevor's eyes against the orange glow. The individual tendrils of flame as the fire spread through each one of his fingers. The shrill, unending scream that rang in her head like a siren long after Trevor had given up. And the whole time, she'd stood there watching, she couldn't stop watching, frozen in that bath of heat. She hadn't been able to move. She hadn't been able to do a thing to help him. So he'd died.

She felt a hand grip her left wrist and spun around, expecting to see Penn. It was Todd. The whites of his own eyes were huge, and he was coughing, too.

"We have to get out of here," he said, breathing fast. "I think there's an exit toward the back."

"What about Penn, and Miss Sophia?" Luce asked. She was feeling weak and dizzy. She rubbed her eyes.

"They were over there." When she pointed up the aisle toward the entrance, she could see how much thicker the smoke was in that direction.

Todd looked doubtful for a second, but then he nodded. "Okay," he said, keeping hold of her wrist as they crouched down and sprinted toward the front doors of the library. They took a right when one aisle looked particularly thick with smoke, then found themselves facing a wall of books without a clue which way to run. Both of them stopped to gasp. The smoke that only a moment earlier had hovered just above their heads now pressed low against their shoulders.

Even ducking below it, they were choking. And they couldn't see as much as a few feet in front of them. Making sure to keep a hold on Todd, Luce spun around in a circle, suddenly unsure which direction they'd come from. She reached out and felt the hot metal shelf of one of the stacks. She couldn't even make out the letters on the spines. Were they in the D section or the O's?

There were no clues to guide them toward Penn and Miss Sophia, and no clues to guide them to the exit, either. Luce felt a surge of panic course through her, making it even more difficult to breathe.

"They must have already gone out the front doors!" Todd shouted, sounding only half convinced. "We have to turn back!"

Luce bit her lip. If anything happened to Penn . . .

She could barely see Todd, who was standing right in front of her. He was right, but which way was back? Luce nodded mutely, and felt his hand tugging hers.

For a long time, she moved without knowing where they were going, but as they ran, the smoke lifted, little by little, until, eventually, she saw the red glow of an emergency exit sign. Luce breathed a sigh of relief as Todd fumbled for the door handle and finally pushed it open.

They were in a hallway Luce had never seen before. Todd slammed the door shut behind them. They gasped and filled their lungs with clean air. It tasted so good, Luce wanted to sink her teeth into it, to drink a gallon of it, bathe herself in it. She and Todd both coughed the smoke out of their lungs until they started laughing, an uneasy, only half-relieved laugh. They laughed until she was crying. But even when Luce finished crying and coughing, her eyes continued to tear.

How could she breathe in this air when she didn't even know what had happened to Penn? If Penn hadn't made it out—if she was collapsed somewhere inside— then Luce had failed someone she cared about again. Only this time it would be so much worse.

She wiped her eyes and watched a puff of smoke curl out from underneath the crack at the base of the door. They weren't safe yet. There was another door at the end of the hallway. Through the glass panel in the door, Luce could see the wobble of a tree branch in the night.

She exhaled. In a few moments, they'd be outside, away from these choking fumes.

If they were fast enough, they could go around to the front entrance and make sure Penn and Miss Sophia had made it out okay.

"Come on," Luce told Todd, who was folded over himself, wheezing. "We have to keep going."

He straightened up, but Luce could see he was really overcome. His face was red, his eyes were wild and wet. She practically had to drag him toward the door.

She was so focused on getting out that it took her too long to process the heavy, swishing noise that had fallen over them, drowning out the alarms.

She looked up into a maelstrom of shadows. A spectrum of shades of gray and deepest black. She should only be able to see as far as the ceiling overhead, but the shadows seemed somehow to extend beyond its limits. Into a strange and hidden sky. They were all tangled up in each other, and yet they were distinct.

Amid them was the lighter, grayish one she'd seen earlier. It was no longer shaped like a needle, but now looked almost like the flame of a match. It bobbed over them in the hallway. Had *she* really fended off that amorphous darkness when it threatened to graze Penn's head? The memory made her palms itch and her toes curl.

Todd started banging on the walls, as if the hallway were closing in on them. Luce knew they were nowhere near the door. She grabbed for his hand, but their sweaty palms slid off each other. She wrapped her fingers tight around his wrist. He was white as a ghost, crouched down near the floor, almost cowering. A terrified moan escaped his lips.

Because the smoke was now filling up the hallway?

Or because he could sense the shadows, too?

Impossible.

And yet his face was pinched and horrified. Much more so now that the shadows were overhead.

"Luce?" His voice shook.

Another horde of shadows rose up directly in their path. A deep black blanket of dark spread out across the walls and made it impossible for Luce to see the door. She looked at Todd—could he see it?

"Run!" she yelled.

Could he even run? His face was ashy and his eyelids drooped shut. He was on the verge of passing out. But then it suddenly seemed like he was carrying her.

Or *something* was carrying both of them.

"What the hell?" Todd cried out.

Their feet skimmed the floor for just a moment. It felt like riding a wave in the ocean, a light crest that lifted her higher, filling her body with air. Luce didn't know where she was headed—she couldn't even see the door, just a snarl of inky shadows all around. Hovering but not touching her. She should have been terrified, but she wasn't. Somehow she felt protected from the shadows, like something was shielding her—something fluid but impenetrable. Something uncannily familiar. Something strong, but also gentle. Something—

Almost too quickly, she and Todd were at the door. Her feet hit the floor again, and she shoved herself against the door's emergency exit bar.

Then she heaved. Choked. Gasped. Gagged.

Another alarm was clanging. But it sounded far away.

The wind whipped at her neck. They were outside! Standing on a small ledge. A flight of stairs led down to the commons, and even though everything in her head felt cloudy and filled with smoke, Luce thought she could hear voices somewhere nearby.

She turned back to try to figure out what had just happened. How had she and Todd made it through that thickest, blackest, impenetrable shadow? And *what* was the thing that had saved them? Luce felt its absence.

She almost wanted to go back and search for it.

But the hallway was dark, and her eyes were still watering, and she couldn't make out the twisting shadow shapes anymore. Maybe they were gone.

Then there was a jagged stroke of light, something that looked like a tree trunk with branches—no, like a torso with long, broad limbs. A pulsing, almost violet column of light hovering over them. It made Luce think, absurdly, of Daniel. She was seeing things. She took a deep breath and tried to blink the smoky tears from her eyes. But the light was still there. She sensed more than heard it call to her, calming her, a lullaby in the middle of a war zone.

So she didn't see the shadow coming.

It body-slammed into her and Todd, breaking their grip on each other and tossing Luce into the air.

She landed in a heap at the foot of the stairs. An agonized grunt escaped her lips.

For one long moment, her head throbbed. She'd never known pain as deep and searing as this. She cried out into the night, into the clash of light and shadow overhead.

But then it all became too much and Luce surrendered, closing her eyes.

ELEVEN

RUDE AWAKENING

"Are you scared?" Daniel asked. His head was tilted sideways, his blond hair disheveled by a soft breeze. He was holding her, and while his grip was firm around her waist, it was as smooth and light as a silk sash. Her own fingers were laced behind his shirtless neck.

Was she scared? Of course not. She was with Daniel. Finally. In his arms. The truer question pulling at the back of her mind was: *Should* she be scared? She couldn't be sure. She didn't even know where she was.

She could smell rain in the air, close by. But both she and Daniel were dry. She could feel a long white dress flowing down to her ankles. There was only a little light left in the day. Luce felt a stabbing regret at wasting the sunset, as if there were anything she could do to stop it. Somehow she knew these final rays of light were as precious as the last drops of honey in a jar.

"Will you stay with me?" she asked. Her voice was the thinnest whisper, almost canceled out by a low groan of thunder. A gust of wind swirled around them, brushing Luce's hair into her eyes. Daniel folded his arms more tightly around her, until she could breathe in his breath, could smell his skin on hers.

"Forever," he whispered back. The sweet sound of his voice filled her up.

There was a small scratch on the left side of his forehead, but she forgot it as Daniel cupped her cheek and brought her face nearer. She tilted her head back and felt the whole of her body go slack with expectation.

Finally, finally, his lips came down on hers with an urgency that took her breath away. He kissed her as if she belonged to him, as naturally as if she were some long-lost part of him that he could at last reclaim.

Then the rain started to fall. It soaked their hair, ran down their faces and into their mouths. The rain was warm and intoxicating, like the kisses themselves.

Luce reached around his back to draw him closer,

and her hands slid over something velvety. She ran one hand over it, then another, searching for its limits, and then peered past Daniel's glowing face.

Something was unfurling behind him.

Wings. Lustrous and iridescent, beating slowly, effortlessly, shining in the rain. She'd seen them before, maybe, or something like them somewhere.

"Daniel," she said, gasping. The wings consumed her vision and her mind. They seemed to swirl into a million colors, making her head hurt. She tried to look elsewhere, anywhere else, but on all sides, all she could see besides Daniel were the endless pinks and blues of the sunset sky. Until she looked down and took in one last thing.

The ground.

Thousands of feet below them.

❈

When she opened her eyes, it was too bright, her skin was too dry, and there was a splitting pain at the back of her head. The sky was gone and so was Daniel.

Another dream.

Only this one left her feeling almost sick with desire.

She was in a white-walled room. Lying on a hospital bed. To her left, a paper-thin curtain had been dragged halfway across the room, separating her from something bustling on the other side.

Luce gingerly touched the tender spot at the base of her neck and whimpered.

She tried to get her bearings. She didn't know where she was, but she had a distinct feeling that she wasn't at Sword & Cross any longer. Her billowy white dress was—she patted her sides—a baggy hospital gown. She could feel every part of the dream slipping away— everything but those wings. They'd been so real. The touch of them so velvety and fluid. Her stomach churned. She clenched and unclenched her fists, hyper-aware of their emptiness.

Someone grasped and squeezed her right hand. Luce turned her head quickly and winced. She'd assumed she was alone. Gabbe was perched on the edge of a faded blue rolling chair that seemed, annoyingly, to bring out the color of her eyes.

Luce wanted to pull away—or at least, she *expected* to want to pull away—but then Gabbe gave her the warmest smile, one that made Luce feel somehow safe, and she realized she was glad she wasn't alone.

"How much of it was a dream?" she murmured.

Gabbe laughed. She had a pot of cuticle cream on the table next to her, and she began rubbing the white, lemon-scented stuff into Luce's nail beds. "That all depends," she said, massaging Luce's fingers. "But never mind dreams. I know that whenever I feel my world turning upside down, nothing grounds me like a manicure."

Luce glanced down. She'd never been much for nail

polish herself, but Gabbe's words reminded her of her mother, who was always suggesting they go for manicures whenever Luce had a bad day. As Gabbe's slow hands worked over her fingers, Luce wondered whether all these years, she'd been missing out.

"Where are we?" she asked.

"Lullwater Hospital."

Her first trip off campus and she ended up in a hospital five minutes from her parents' house. The last time she'd been here was to get three stitches on her elbow when she'd fallen off her bike. Her father hadn't left her side. Now he was nowhere to be seen.

"How long have I been here?" she asked.

Gabbe looked at a white clock on the wall and said, "They found you passed out from smoke inhalation last night around eleven. It's standard operating procedure to call for EMTs when they find a reform kid unconcious, but don't worry, Randy said they're going to let you out of here pretty soon. As soon as your parents give the okay—"

"My parents are here?"

"And filled with concern for their daughter, right down to the split ends of your mama's permed hair. They're in the hallway, drowning in paperwork. I told them I'd keep an eye on you."

Luce groaned and pressed her face into the pillow, calling up the deep pain at the back of her head again.

"If you don't want to see them . . ."

But Luce wasn't groaning about her parents. She was dying to see her parents. She was remembering the library, the fire, and the new breed of shadows that grew more terrifying every time they found her. They'd always been dark and unsightly, they'd always made her nervous, but last night, it had almost seemed as if the shadows *wanted* something from her. And then there was that other thing, the levitating force that had set her free.

"What's that look?" Gabbe asked, cocking her head and waving her hand in the air in front of Luce's face. "What are you thinking about?"

Luce didn't know what to make of Gabbe's sudden kindness toward her. Nurse's assistant didn't exactly seem like the kind of gig Gabbe would volunteer for, and it wasn't like there were any guys around whose attention she could monopolize. Gabbe didn't even seem to like Luce. She wouldn't just show up here of her own accord, would she?

But even as nice as Gabbe was being, there was no way to explain what had happened last night. The grisly, unspeakable gathering in the hallway. The surreal sensation of being propelled forward through that blackness. The strange, compelling figure of light.

"Where's Todd?" Luce asked, remembering the boy's fearful eyes. She'd lost her grip on him, gone flying, and then . . .

The paper curtain was suddenly slung back, and there was Arriane, wearing in-line skates and a red-and-white candy striper uniform. Her short black hair was twisted up in a series of knots on top of her head. She rolled in, carrying a tray on which sat three coconut shells topped with neon-colored umbrella party straws.

"Now lemme get this straight," she said in a throaty, nasal voice. "You put the lime in the coconut and drink 'em both up—*whoa,* long faces. What am I interrupting?"

Arriane wheeled to a stop at the foot of Luce's bed. She extended a coconut with a bobbing pink umbrella.

Gabbe jumped up and seized the coconut first, giving its contents a sniff. "Arriane, she has just been through a *trauma,*" she scolded. "And for your information, what you interrupted was the topic of Todd."

Arriane tossed her shoulders back. "Precisely why she needs something with a kick," she argued, holding the tray possessively while she and Gabbe engaged in a stare-down.

"Fine," Arriane said, looking away from Gabbe. "I'll give her *your* boring old drink." She gave Luce the coconut with the blue straw.

Luce must have been in some kind of post-traumatic daze. Where would they have gotten any of this stuff? Coconut shells? Drink umbrellas? It was like she'd been conked out at reform school and woken up at Club Med.

"Where did you guys get all this stuff?" she asked. "I mean, thank you, but—"

"We pool our resources when we need to," Arriane said. "Roland helped."

The three of them sat slurping the frosty, sweet drinks for a moment, until Luce couldn't take it anymore. "So back to Todd . . . ?"

"Todd," Gabbe said, clearing her throat. "Thing is . . . he just inhaled a lot more of that smoke than you did, honey—"

"He did not," Arriane spat. "He broke his neck."

Luce gasped, and Gabbe hit Arriane with her drink umbrella.

"What?" Arriane said. "Luce can handle it. If she's going to find out eventually, why sugarcoat it?"

"The evidence is still inconclusive," Gabbe said, stressing the words.

Arriane shrugged. "Luce was there, she must have seen—"

"I didn't see what happened to him," Luce said. "We were together and then somehow we were thrown apart. I had a bad feeling, but I didn't know," she whispered. "So he's . . ."

"Gone from this world," Gabbe said softly.

Luce closed her eyes. A chill spread through her that had nothing to do with the drink. She remembered Todd's frenzied banging on the walls, his sweaty hand squeezing hers when the shadows roared down on them, the awful moment when the two of them had been split apart and she'd been too overcome to go to him.

He'd seen the shadows. Luce was certain of it now. And he'd died.

After Trevor died, not a week had gone by without a hate letter finding its way to Luce. Her parents started trying to vet the mail before she could read the poisonous stuff, but too much still reached her. Some letters were handwritten, some were typed, one had even been cut from magazine letters, ransom-note style. *Murderer. Witch.* They'd called her enough cruel names to fill a scrapbook, caused enough agony to keep her locked inside the house all summer.

She thought she'd done so much to move on from that nightmare: leaving her past behind when she came to Sword & Cross, focusing on her classes, making friends . . . oh God. She sucked in her breath. "What about Penn?" she asked, biting her lip.

"Penn's fine," Arriane said. "She's all front-page-story, eyewitness-to-the-fire. She and Miss Sophia both got out, smelling like an East Georgia smoke pit, but no worse for the wear."

Luce let out her breath. At least there was one piece of good news. But under the paper-thin infirmary sheets, she was trembling. Soon, surely the same types of people who'd come to her after Trevor's death would come to her again. Not just the ones who wrote the angry letters. Dr. Sanford. Her parole officer. The police.

Just like before, she'd be expected to have the whole story pieced together. To remember every single detail. But of course, just like before, she wouldn't be able to. One minute, he'd been at her side, just the two of them. The next—

"Luce!" Penn barged into the room, holding a big brown helium balloon. It was shaped like a Band-Aid and said *Stick It Out* in blue cursive letters. "What is this?" she asked, looking at the other three girls critically. "Some sort of slumber party?"

Arriane had unlaced her skates and climbed onto the tiny bed next to Luce. She was double-fisting the coconut drinks and laying her head on Luce's shoulder. Gabbe was painting clear nail polish on Luce's coconut-free hand.

"Yeah," Arriane cackled. "Join us, Pennyloafer. We were just about to play Truth or Dare. We'll let you go first."

Gabbe tried to cover up her laugh with a dainty fake sneeze.

Penn put her hands on her hips. Luce felt bad for her, and was also a little scared. Penn looked pretty fierce.

"One of our classmates *died* last night," Penn carefully enunciated. "And Luce could have been really hurt." She shook her head. "How can you two play around at a time like this?" She sniffed. "Is that alcohol?"

"Ohhh," Arriane said, looking at Penn, her face serious. "You *liked* him, didn't you?"

Penn picked up a pillow from the chair behind her and chucked it at Arriane. The thing was, Penn was right. It *was* strange that Arriane and Gabbe were taking Todd's death . . . almost lightly. Like they saw this kind of thing happen all the time. Like it didn't affect them the way it affected Luce. But they couldn't know what Luce knew about Todd's last moments. They couldn't know why she felt so sick right now. She patted the foot of the bed for Penn and handed her what was left in her frosty coconut.

"We went out the back exit, and then—" Luce couldn't even say the words. "What happened to you and Miss Sophia?"

Penn glanced doubtfully at Arriane and Gabbe, but neither made a move to be obnoxious. Penn gave in and settled on the edge of the bed.

"I just went up there to ask her about—" She glanced at the other two girls again, then gave Luce a knowing look. "This question I had. She didn't know the answer, but she wanted to show me another book."

Luce had forgotten all about her and Penn's quest last night. It seemed so far away, and so beside the point after what had happened.

"We took two steps away from Miss Sophia's desk," Penn continued, "and there was this massive burst of light out of the corner of my eye. I mean, I've read about spontaneous combustion, but this was . . ."

All three of the other girls were leaning forward by then. Penn's story *was* front-page news.

"Something must have started it," Luce said, trying to picture Miss Sophia's desk in her mind. "But I didn't think there was anyone else in the library."

Penn shook her head. "There wasn't. Miss Sophia said a wire must have shorted in a lamp. Whatever happened, that fire had a lot of fuel. All her documents went right up." She snapped her fingers.

"But she's okay?" Luce asked, fingering the papery hem of her hospital gown.

"Distraught, but okay," Penn said. "The sprinklers came on eventually, but I guess she lost a whole lot of her things. When they told her what happened to Todd, it was almost like she was too numb to even understand."

"Maybe we're all too numb to understand," Luce said. This time Gabbe and Arriane nodded on either side of her. "Do—do Todd's parents know?" she asked, wondering how on earth she would explain to her own parents what had happened.

She imagined them filling out paperwork in the lobby. Would they even want to see her? Would they connect Todd's death with Trevor's . . . and trace both awful stories back to her?

"I overheard Randy on the phone with Todd's parents," Penn said. "I think they're filing a lawsuit. His body is being sent back to Florida later today."

That was it? Luce swallowed.

"Sword & Cross is having a memorial service for him on Thursday," Gabbe said quietly. "Daniel and I are going to help organize it."

"Daniel?" Luce repeated before she could control herself. She glanced at Gabbe, and even in her grief-stricken state, she couldn't help reverting to her initial image of the girl: a pink-lipped, blond seductress.

"He was the one who found the two of you last night," Gabbe said. "He carried you from the library to Randy's office."

Daniel had carried her? As in . . . his arms around her body? The dream rushed back and the sensation of flying—no, of *floating*—overwhelmed her. She felt too tethered down to her bed. She ached for that same sky, that rain, his mouth, his teeth, his tongue melding with hers again. Her face grew hot, first with desire, then with the agonizing impossibility of any of that ever happening while she was awake. Those glorious, blinding wings weren't the only fantastical things about that dream. The real-life Daniel would only carry her to the nurse's station. He would never want her, never take her in his arms, not like that.

"Uh, Luce, are you okay?" Penn asked. She was fanning Luce's flushed cheeks with her drink umbrella.

"Fine," Luce said. It was impossible to push those wings out of her mind. To forget the sensation of his face over hers. "Just still recovering, I guess."

Gabbe patted her hand. "When we heard about what happened, we sweet-talked Randy into letting us come visit," she said, rolling her eyes. "We didn't want you to wake up alone."

There was a knock at the door. Luce waited to see her parents' nervous faces, but no one came in. Gabbe stood and looked at Arriane, who made no move to get up. "You guys stay here. I'll handle this."

Luce was still overcome by what they'd told her about Daniel. Even though it didn't make any sense at all, she wanted it to be him outside that door.

"How is she?" a voice asked in a whisper. But Luce heard it. It was him. Gabbe murmured something back.

"What is all this congregating?" Randy growled from outside the room. Luce knew with a sinking heart that this meant visiting hours were over. "Whoever talked me into letting you hooligans tag along gets a detention. And no, Grigori, I will not accept flowers as bribes. All of you, get in the minivan."

Hearing the attendant's voice, Arriane and Penn cringed, then scrambled to stash the coconut shells under the bed. Penn stuffed the drink umbrellas inside her pencil case and Arriane spritzed the air with some serious vanilla musk perfume. She slipped Luce a piece of spearmint gum.

Penn gagged on a floating cloud of perfume, then leaned quickly into Luce and whispered, "As soon as you're back on your feet, we'll find the book. I think it'd be good for us both to stay busy, keep our minds off things."

Luce squeezed Penn's hand in thanks and smiled at Arriane, who looked too busy lacing up her roller skates to have heard.

That was when Randy barged through the door. "More congregating!" she cried. "Unbelievable."

"We were just—" Penn started to say.

"Leaving," Randy finished for her. She had a bouquet of wild white peonies in her hand. Strange. They were Luce's favorites. And it was so hard to find them in bloom around here.

Randy opened a cabinet under the sink and rooted around for a minute, then pulled out a small, dusty vase. She filled it with cloudy water from the tap, stuffed the peonies roughly inside, and set them on the table next to Luce. "These are from your friends," she said, "who will all now make their departures."

The door was wide open, and Luce could see Daniel leaning against the frame. His chin was lifted and his gray eyes were shadowed with concern. He met Luce's gaze and gave her a small smile. When he brushed his hair away from his eyes, Luce could see a small, dark red gash on his forehead.

Randy steered Penn, Arriane, and Gabbe out the

door. But Luce couldn't take her eyes off Daniel. He raised a hand in the air and mouthed what she thought was *I'm sorry,* just before Randy shoved them out.

"I hope they didn't wear you out," Randy said, lurking in the doorway with an unsympathetic frown.

"Oh no!" Luce shook her head, realizing how much she'd come to rely on Penn's loyalty and Arriane's quirky way of lightening even the soberest mood. Gabbe, too, had been truly kind to her. And Daniel, though she'd barely seen him, had done more to restore her peace of mind than he could ever know. He'd come by to check on her. He'd been thinking of her.

"Good," Randy said. "Because visiting hours aren't over yet."

Again, Luce's heart picked up as she waited to see her parents. But there was just a brisk clicking on the linoleum floor, and soon Luce saw the tiny frame of Miss Sophia. A colorful autumnal pashmina was draped over her thin shoulders, and her lips were painted deep red to match. Behind her walked a short, bald man in a suit, and two police officers, one chubby and one thin, both with receding hairlines and crossed arms.

The chubby police officer was younger. He took a seat on the chair next to Luce, then—noticing that no one else had moved to sit down—stood back up and re-crossed his arms.

The bald man stepped forward and offered Luce his

hand. "I'm Mr. Schultz, Sword & Cross's attorney." Luce stiffly shook his hand. "These officers are just going to ask you a couple of questions. Nothing to be used in a court, only an effort to corroborate details from the accident—"

"And I insisted on being here during the questioning, Lucinda," Miss Sophia added, coming forward to stroke Luce's hair. "How are you, dear?" she whispered. "In a state of amnesiac shock?"

"I'm okay—"

Luce broke off as she caught sight of two more figures in the doorway. She almost burst into tears when she saw her mother's dark, curly head and her father's big tortoiseshell glasses.

"Mom," she whispered, too low for anyone else to hear. "Dad."

They rushed toward the bed, throwing their arms around her and squeezing her hands. She wanted to hug them so badly, but she felt too weak to do much more than stay still and take in the familiar comfort of their touch. Their eyes looked just as scared as she felt.

"Honey, what happened?" her mom asked.

She couldn't say a word.

"I told them you were innocent," Miss Sophia said, turning to remind the officers. "Eerie similarities be damned."

Of course they had Trevor's accident on record, and of course the cops would find it . . . remarkable in light of Todd's death. Luce had enough practice with police officers to know that she was only going to leave them frustrated and annoyed.

The thin cop had long sideburns that were going gray. Her open file in his hand seemed to require his full attention, because not once did he look up at her.

"Ms. Price," he said with a slow southern drawl. "Why were you and Mr. Hammond alone in the library at such a late hour when all the other students were at a party?"

Luce glanced at her parents. Her mom was chewing off her lipstick. Her father's face was as white as the bed-sheet.

"I wasn't with Todd," she said, not understanding the line of questioning. "I was with Penn, my friend. And Miss Sophia was there. Todd was reading on his own and when the fire started, I lost Penn, and Todd was the only one I could find."

"The only one you could find . . . to do what with?"

"Hold on a minute." Mr. Schultz stepped forward to interrupt the cop. "This was an accident, may I remind you. You're not interrogating a suspect."

"No, I want to answer," Luce said. There were so many people in this tiny room that she didn't know where to look. She eyed the cop. "What do you mean?"

"Are you an angry person, Ms. Price?" He gripped the folder. "Would you call yourself a loner?"

"That's enough," her father interrupted.

"Yes, Lucinda is a serious student," Miss Sophia added. "She had no ill will toward Todd Hammond. What happened was an accident, no more."

The officer glanced toward the open doorway, as if wishing Miss Sophia would relocate herself outside it. "Yes, ma'am. Well, with these reform school cases, giving the benefit of the doubt is not always the most responsible—"

"I'll tell you everything I know," Luce said, balling up her sheet in her fist. "I don't have anything to hide."

She took them through it as best she could, speaking slowly and clearly so she would raise no new questions for her parents, so the cops could take notes. She didn't let herself slide into emotion, which seemed like exactly what everyone was expecting. And—leaving out the appearance of the shadows—the story made a lot of sense.

They'd run for the back door. They'd found the exit at the end of a long corridor. The stairs dropped quickly, steeply off the ledge, and she and Todd had both been running with such force, they couldn't stop themselves from tumbling down the stairs. She lost track of him, hit her head hard enough to wake up here twelve hours later. That was all she remembered.

She left them very little to argue over. There was only her true memory of the night for her to grapple with— on her own.

When it was over, Mr. Schultz gave the police officers an are-you-satisfied tilt of his head, and Miss Sophia beamed at Luce, as if together they'd succeeded at something impossible. Luce's mother let out a long sigh.

"We'll mull this over at the station," the thin officer said, closing Luce's file with such resignation, he seemed to want to be thanked for his services.

Then the four of them left the room and she was alone with her parents.

She gave them her very best take-me-home look. Her mom's lip trembled, but her dad only swallowed.

"Randy's going to take you back to Sword & Cross this afternoon," he said. "Don't look so shocked, honey. The doctor said you're fine."

"More than fine," her mom added, but she sounded uncertain.

Her dad patted her arm. "We'll see you on Saturday. Just a few more days."

Saturday. She closed her eyes. Parents' Day. She'd been looking forward to it from the moment she'd arrived at Sword & Cross, but now everything was tainted by Todd's death. Her parents seemed almost eager to leave her. They had a way of not really wanting to deal with the realities of having a reform school daughter. They were so normal. She couldn't really blame them.

"Get some rest now, Luce," her dad said, bending

down to kiss her forehead. "You've had a long, hard night."

"But—"

She *was* exhausted. She briefly closed her eyes and when she opened them, her parents were already waving from the doorway.

She plucked a plump white flower from the vase and brought it slowly to her face, admiring the deeply lobed leaves and fragile petals, the still-moist drops of nectar inside its center. She breathed in the flower's soft, spicy scent.

She tried to imagine the way they would have looked in Daniel's hands. She tried to imagine where he'd gotten them, and what had been on his mind.

It was such a strange choice of flower. Wild peonies didn't grow in Georgia wetlands. They wouldn't even take to the soil in her father's garden in Thunderbolt. What was more, these didn't look like any peonies Luce had ever seen before. The blooms were as large as cupped palms, and the smell reminded her of something she couldn't quite put her finger on.

I'm sorry, Daniel had said. Only Luce couldn't figure out for what.

TWELVE

INTO DUST

In the hazy dusk over the cemetery, a vulture circled. Two days had passed since Todd's death, and Luce hadn't been able to eat or sleep. She was standing in a sleeveless black dress in the basin of the graveyard, where the whole of Sword & Cross had gathered to pay its respects to Todd. As if one unenthusiastic hourlong ceremony were enough. Especially since the campus's only chapel had been turned into the natatorium, and the ceremony had to be held in the grim swampland of the cemetery.

Since the accident, the school had been on lockdown, and the faculty had been the definition of tight-lipped. Luce had spent the past two days avoiding the stares of the other students, who all eyed her with varying degrees of suspicion. The ones she didn't know very well seemed to look at her with a faint hint of fear. Others, like Roland and Molly, ogled her in a different, much more shameless manner, as if there were something darkly fascinating about her survival. She endured the probing eyes as best she could during class, and was glad at night when Penn dropped by to bring her a steaming mug of ginger tea, or Arriane slipped a dirty Mad Libs under her door.

She was desperate for anything to take her mind off that uneasy, waiting-for-the-other-shoe-to-drop feeling. Because she knew it was coming. In the form of a second visit either from the police, or from the shadows— or both.

That morning, a PA announcement had informed them that the evening's Social would be canceled out of respect for Todd's passing, and that classes would be dismissed an hour early so the students could have time to change and arrive at the cemetery at three o'clock. As if the whole school weren't already dressed for a funeral all the time.

Luce had never seen so many people congregating in one place on the campus. Randy was parked at the center of the group in a calf-length pleated gray skirt and thick, rubber-soled black shoes. A misty-eyed Miss Sophia and a handkerchief-wielding Mr. Cole stood behind her in mourning clothes. Ms. Tross and Coach Diante stood in a black-clad cluster with a group of other faculty and administrators Luce had never seen before.

The students were seated in alphabetic rows. At the front, Luce could see Joel Bland, the kid who'd won the swimming race last week, blowing his nose into a dirty handkerchief. Luce was in the nowhere land of P's, but she could see Daniel, annoyingly positioned in the G's right next to Gabbe, two rows ahead. He was dressed impeccably in a fitted black pinstriped blazer, but his head seemed to hang lower than everyone's around him. Even from the back, Daniel managed to look devastatingly somber.

Luce thought about the white peonies he'd brought her. Randy hadn't let her take the vase with her when she left the infirmary, so Luce had carried the flowers up to her room and gotten pretty inventive, cutting off the top of a plastic water bottle with a pair of manicure scissors.

The blooms were fragrant and soothing, but the message they offered was unclear. Usually when a guy brought you flowers, you didn't have to second-guess his feelings. But with Daniel, those kinds of assumptions were always a bad idea. It was so much safer to assume he'd brought them to her because that was what you did when someone went through a trauma.

But still: He'd brought her flowers! If she leaned

forward now in her folding chair and looked up at the dorm, through the metal bars on the third window from the left, she could almost make them out.

"In the sweat of thy face shalt thou eat bread," a pay-by-the-hour minister warbled from the front of the crowd. "Till thou return unto the ground. For out of it wast thou taken, for dust thou art, and unto dust shalt thou return."

He was a thin man about seventy, lost in a big black jacket. His beat-up athletic shoes were fraying at the laces; his face was lumpy and sunburned. He spoke into a microphone attached to an old plastic boom box that looked like it was from the eighties. The sound that came out was staticky and distorted and hardly carried across the crowd.

Everything about this service was inadequate and completely wrong.

No one was paying Todd any respect by being here. The whole memorial seemed more like an attempt to teach the students how unfair life could be. That Todd's body wasn't even present said so much about the school's relationship—or utter lack thereof—with the departed boy. None of them had known him; none of them ever would. There was something false about standing here to-day in this crowd, something made worse by the few people who were crying. It made Luce feel like Todd was even more of a stranger to her than he actually had been.

Let Todd rest in peace. Let the rest of them just move on.

A white horned owl crooned in the high branch of the oak tree over their heads. Luce knew there was a nest somewhere nearby with a clan of new baby owls. She'd been hearing the mother's fearful chant each night this week, followed by the frantic beating of the father's wings on the descent from his nightly hunt.

And then it was over. Luce stood up from her chair, feeling weak with the unfairness of it all. Todd had been as innocent as she was guilty, though of what she didn't know.

As she followed the other students in single file toward the so-called reception, an arm looped around her waist and pulled her back.

Daniel?

But no, it was Cam.

His green eyes searched hers and seemed to pick up her disappointment, which only made her feel worse. She bit her lip to keep from dissolving into a sob. Seeing Cam shouldn't make her cry—she was just so emotionally drained, teetering on the brink of a collapse. She bit so hard she tasted blood, then wiped her mouth on her hand.

"Hey," Cam said, smoothing the back of her hair. She winced. She still had a bump back there from where she'd hit her head on the steps. "Do you want to go somewhere and talk?"

They'd been walking with the others across the grass toward the reception under the shade of one of the oak trees. A cluster of chairs had been set up practically one on top of the other. A nearby folding card table was strewn with stacks of stale-looking cookies, pulled from their generic boxes but still sitting in their inner plastic shells. A cheap plastic punch bowl had been filled with syrupy red liquid and had attracted several flies, the way a corpse might do. It was such a pathetic reception, few of the other students even bothered with it. Luce spotted Penn in a black skirt suit, shaking hands with the minister. Daniel was looking away from them all, whispering something to Gabbe.

When Luce turned back to Cam, his finger dragged lightly across her collarbone, then lingered in the hollow of her neck. She inhaled and felt goose bumps rise on her skin.

"If you don't like the necklace," he said, leaning into her, "I can get you something else."

His lips were so close to brushing her neck that Luce pressed a hand to his shoulder and stepped back.

"I do like it," she said, thinking of the box lying on her desk. It had ended up right next to Daniel's flowers, and she'd spent half the night before looking back and forth between them, weighing the gifts and the intentions behind them. Cam was so much clearer, easier to figure out. Like he was algebra and Daniel was calculus. And she had always loved calculus, the way it sometimes took an hour to figure out a single proof.

"I think the necklace is great," she told Cam. "I just haven't had a chance to wear it yet."

"I'm sorry," he said, pursing his lips. "I shouldn't press you."

His dark hair was slicked back and showed more of his face than usual. It made him look older, more mature. And the way he looked at her was so intense, his big green eyes probing into her, like he approved of everything she held inside.

"Miss Sophia kept saying to give you space these last couple of days. I know she's right, you've been through so much. But you should know how much I thought about you. All the time. I wanted to see you."

He stroked her cheek with the back of his hand and Luce felt tears welling up. She *had* been through so much. And she felt terrible that here she was, about to cry, not over Todd—whose death did matter, and should have mattered more—but for selfish reasons. Because the past two days brought back too much past pain about Trevor and her life before Sword & Cross, things she thought she'd dealt with and could never explain, not to anyone. More shadows to push away.

It was like Cam sensed this, or at least part of this, because he folded her into his arms, pressed her head against his strong, broad chest, and rocked her from side to side.

"It's okay," he said. "It's going to be okay."

And maybe she didn't have to explain anything to him. It was like the more deranged she felt inside, the more available Cam became. What if it was enough just to stand here in the arms of someone who cared about her, to let his simple affection steady her for a little while?

It felt so *good* just to be held.

Luce didn't know how to pull away from Cam. He had always been so nice. And she did like him, and yet, for reasons that made her feel guilty, he was kind of beginning to annoy her. He was so perfect, and helpful, and exactly what she should have needed right now. It was just . . . he wasn't Daniel.

An angel food cupcake appeared over her shoulder. Luce recognized the manicured hand holding it. "There's punch over there that needs drinking," Gabbe said, handing Cam a cupcake, too. He glared at its frosted top. "You okay?" Gabbe asked Luce.

Luce nodded. For the first time, Gabbe had popped up exactly when Luce wanted saving. They smiled at each other and Luce raised her cupcake in thanks. She took a small, sweet bite.

"Punch sounds great," Cam said through gritted teeth. "Why don't you go get us a few glasses, Gabbe?"

Gabbe rolled her eyes at Luce. "Do a man one favor and he'll start treating you like a slave."

Luce laughed. Cam was a little out of line, but it was obvious to Luce what he was trying to do.

"I'll go get the drinks," Luce said, ready for a breath

of air. She headed for the card table and the punch bowl. She was skimming a fly from the surface of the punch when someone whispered in her ear.

"You want to get out of here?"

Luce turned around, ready to invent some excuse for Cam that no, she couldn't duck out—not now, and not with him. But it wasn't Cam who reached out and touched the base of her wrist with his thumb.

It was Daniel.

She melted a little. Her Wednesday phone slot was in ten minutes and she desperately wanted to hear Callie's voice, or her parents' voices. To talk about something going on outside these wrought iron gates, other than the bleakness of her last two days.

But get out of here? With Daniel? She found herself nodding.

Cam was going to hate her if he saw her leave, and he *would* see. He would be watching her. She could almost feel his green eyes on the back of her head. But of course she had to go. She slipped her hand inside Daniel's. "Please."

All the other times they'd touched, either it had been an accident, or one of them had jerked away—usually Daniel—before the bolt of warmth Luce always felt could evolve into a rising crescendo of heat. Not this time. Luce looked down at Daniel's hand, holding fast to hers, and her whole body wanted more. More of the heat, more of the tingling, more of Daniel. It was almost—not quite—as good as she'd felt in her dream. She could hardly feel her feet moving below her, just the flow of his touch taking over.

It was as if she only blinked, and they had ascended to the gates of the cemetery. Below them, far away, the rest of the memorial service wobbled out of focus as the two of them left it all behind.

Daniel stopped suddenly and, without warning, dropped her hand. She shivered, cold again.

"You and Cam," he said, letting the words hang in the air like a question. "You spend a lot of time together?"

"Sounds like you're not very fond of that idea," she said, feeling instantly stupid for playing coy. She'd only wanted to tease him for sounding a little jealous, but his face and his tone were so serious.

"He's not—" Daniel started to say. He watched a red-tailed hawk land in an oak tree over their heads. "He's not good enough for you."

Luce had heard people say that line a thousand times before. It was what everyone always said. *Not good enough.* But when the words passed Daniel's lips, they sounded important, even somehow true and relevant, not vague and dismissive the way the phrase had always sounded to her in the past.

"Well, then," she said in a quiet voice, "who is?"

Daniel put his hands on his hips. He laughed to himself for a long time. "I don't know," he said finally. "That's a terrific question."

Not exactly the answer Luce was looking for. "It's not like it's *that* hard," she said, stuffing her hands into her pockets because she wanted to reach out to him. "To be good enough for *me*."

Daniel's eyes looked like they were falling, all the violet that had been in them a moment before turned a deep, dark gray. "Yes," he said. "Yes, it is."

He rubbed his forehead, and when he did, his hair flipped back for just a second. Long enough. Luce saw the scab on his forehead. It was healing, but Luce could tell that it was new.

"What happened to your forehead?" she asked, reaching for him.

"I don't know," he snapped, pushing her hand away, hard enough that she stumbled back. "I don't know where it came from."

He seemed more unsettled by it than Luce was, which surprised her. It was just a small scrape.

Footsteps on the gravel behind them. Both of them spun around.

"I told you, I haven't seen her," Molly was saying, shrugging off Cam's hand as they ascended the grave-yard's hill.

"Let's go," Daniel said, sensing everything she felt—she was almost certain that he could—even before she shot him a nervous look.

She knew where they were going as soon as she began to follow him. Behind the church-gymnasium and into the woods. Just like she'd expected his jump rope posture before she ever saw him working out. Just like she'd known about that cut before she saw it.

They walked at just the same pace, with steps just the same length. Their feet hit the grass at the same time, every time, until they reached the forest.

"If you come to a place more than once with the same person," Daniel said, almost to himself, "I guess it isn't yours alone anymore."

Luce smiled, honored as she realized what Daniel was saying: that he'd never been to the lake before with anyone else. Only her.

As they trekked through the woods, she felt the coolness of the shade beneath the trees on her bare shoulders. It smelled the same as ever, as most coastal Georgian forests did: an oaky mulch scent that Luce used to associate with the shadows, but that she now connected to Daniel. She shouldn't feel safe anywhere after what had just happened to Todd, but next to Daniel, Luce felt like she was breathing easy for the first time in days.

She had to believe he was bringing her back here because of the way he'd skipped out on her so suddenly the last time. Like they needed a second try to get it right. What had started out feeling like their first kind of almost-date had turned into Luce feeling pitifully stood up. Daniel must have known that and felt bad about his stormy exit.

They reached the magnolia tree that marked the lookout point on the lake. The sun left a golden trail on the water as it edged over the forest to the west. Everything looked so different in the evening. The whole world seemed to glow.

Daniel leaned up against the tree and watched her watch the water. She moved to stand beside him under the waxy leaves and the flowers, which should have been dead and gone by this time of year, but looked as pure and fresh as spring blooms. Luce breathed in the musky scent, and felt closer to Daniel than she had any reason to—and loved that the feeling seemed to come from out of nowhere.

"We're not exactly dressed for a swim this time," he said, pointing at Luce's black dress.

She fingered the delicate eyelet hem at her knees, imagining her mom's shock if she ruined a good dress because she and a boy wanted to dive into a lake. "Maybe we could just stick our feet in?"

Daniel motioned toward the steep red rock path that led down to the water. They climbed over thick, tawny reeds and lake grass and used the twisted stumps of live oak trees to keep their balance. Here, the shore of the lake turned to pebbles. The water looked so still, she felt she almost could have walked on it.

Luce kicked off her black ballet flats and skimmed the lily-padded surface with her toes. The water was cooler than it had been the other day. Daniel picked a strand of lake grass and started braiding its thick stem.

He looked at her. "You ever think about getting out of here—"

"All the time," she said with a groan, assuming he meant that he did, too. Of course, she wanted to get as far away from Sword & Cross as possible. Anyone would. But she tried at least to keep her mind from whirling out of control, toward fantasies of her and Daniel plotting an escape.

"No," Daniel said, "I mean, have you really considered going somewhere else? Asking your parents for a transfer? It's just . . . Sword & Cross doesn't seem like the best fit for you."

Luce took a seat on a rock opposite Daniel and hugged her knees. If he was suggesting that she was a reject among a student body full of rejects, she couldn't help feeling a little insulted.

She cleared her throat. "I can't afford the luxury of seriously considering someplace else. Sword & Cross is"—she paused—"pretty much a last-ditch effort for me."

"Come on," Daniel said.

"You wouldn't know—"

"I would." He sighed. "There's always another stop, Luce."

"That's very prophetic, Daniel," she said. She could

feel her voice rising. "But if you're so interested in getting rid of me, what are we doing? No one asked you to drag me out here with you."

"No," he said. "You're right. I meant that you're not like people here. There's got to be a better place for you."

Luce's heart was beating quickly, which it usually did around Daniel. But this was different. This whole scene was making her sweat.

"When I came here," she said, "I made a promise to myself that I wouldn't tell anyone about my past, or what I'd done to land myself at this place."

Daniel dropped his head into his hands. "What I'm talking about has nothing to do with what happened with that guy—"

"You know about him?" Luce's face crumpled. No. How could Daniel know? "Whatever Molly told you . . ."

But she knew it was too late. Daniel had been the one to find her with Todd. If Molly had told him anything about how Luce had also been implicated in *another* mysterious fiery death, she couldn't begin to imagine explaining it.

"Listen," he said, gripping her hands. "What I'm saying, it has nothing to do with that part of your past."

She found that hard to believe. "Then does it have to do with Todd?"

He shook his head. "It has to do with this place. It has to do with things . . ."

Daniel's touch jostled something in her mind. She started thinking about the wild shadows she'd seen that night. The way they'd changed so much since she'd arrived at this school—from a sneaky, unsettling threat to now almost-ubiquitous, full-blown terrors.

She was crazy—that must be what Daniel sensed about her. Maybe he thought she was pretty, but he knew deep down she was seriously disturbed. That was why he wanted her to leave, so he wouldn't be tempted to get involved with someone like her. If that was what Daniel thought, he didn't know the half of it.

"Maybe it has to do with the weird black shadows I saw the night Todd died?" she said, hoping to shock him. But as soon as she'd said the words, she knew her intent was not to freak Daniel out even more . . . it was to finally tell someone. It wasn't like she had much more to lose.

"What did you say?" he asked slowly.

"Oh, you know," she said, shrugging now, trying to downplay what she'd just said. "Once a day or so, I get these *visits* from these dark things I call the shadows."

"Don't be cute," Daniel said curtly. And even though his tone stung, she knew he was right. She hated how falsely nonchalant she sounded, when really she was all wound up. But should she tell him? Could she? He was nodding for her to go on. His eyes seemed to reach out and pull the words from inside her.

"It's gone on for the last twelve years," she admitted finally, with a deep shudder. "It used to just be at night, when I was near water or trees, but now . . ." Her hands were shaking. "It's practically nonstop."

"What do they do?"

She would have thought he was just humoring her, or trying to get her to go on so he could crack a joke at her expense, except his voice had gone hoarse and his face was drained of color.

"Usually, they start out by hovering right about here." She reached around to the back of Daniel's neck and tickled him to demonstrate. For once, she wasn't just trying to get physically close to him—this really was the only way she knew how to explain. Especially since the shadows had begun to infringe on her body in such a palpable, physical way.

Daniel didn't flinch, so she continued. "Then sometimes they get really bold," she said, moving to her knees and placing her hands on his chest. "And they shove right up against me." Now she was right in his face. Her lip quivered and she couldn't believe she was actually opening up to anyone—let alone Daniel—about the horrible things she saw. Her voice dropped to a whisper and she said, "Recently, they don't seem satisfied until they've"—she swallowed—"taken someone's life and knocked me flat on my back."

She gave his shoulders the tiniest push, not intending to affect him at all, but the lightest touch of her finger-tips was enough to knock Daniel over.

His fall took her so much by surprise, she accidentally lost her own balance and landed in a tangled heap on top of him. Daniel was flat on his back, looking at her with wide eyes.

She should not have told him that. Here she was, on top of him, and she'd just divulged her deepest secret, the thing that *really* defined her as a lunatic.

How could she still want to kiss him so badly at a time like this?

Her heart was pounding impossibly fast. Then she realized: She was feeling both of their hearts, racing each other. A kind of desperate conversation, one they couldn't have with words.

"You really see them?" he whispered.

"Yes," she whispered, wanting to pick herself up and take it all back. And yet she was unable to move off Daniel's chest. She tried to read his thoughts—what any normal person would think about an admission like hers. "Let me guess," she said glumly. "Now you're certain I need a transfer. To a psychiatric ward."

He pushed himself out from under her, leaving her lying practically face-first on the rock. Her eyes moved up his feet, to his legs, to his torso, to his face. He was staring up at the forest.

"That's never happened before," he said.

Luce got to her feet. It was humiliating, lying there alone. Plus, it was like he hadn't even heard what she said.

"What's never happened? Before what?"

He turned to her and cupped her cheeks in his hands. She held her breath. He was so close. His lips were so close to hers. Luce gave her thigh a pinch to make sure this time she wasn't dreaming. She was wide awake.

Then he almost forcibly pulled himself away. He stood before her, breathing quickly, his arms stiff at his sides.

"Tell me again what you saw."

Luce turned away to face the lake. The clear blue water lapped softly at the bank, and she considered diving in. That was what Daniel had done the last time things had gotten too intense for him. Why couldn't she do it, too?

"It may surprise you to know this," she said. "But it's no thrill for me to sit here and talk about how thoroughly insane I am." *Especially to you.*

Daniel didn't answer, but she could feel his eyes on her. When she finally got the courage to glance at him, he was giving her a strange, disturbing, *mournful* look—one in which his eyes turned down at the corners and their particular gray was the saddest thing Luce had ever seen. She felt as if she'd let him down somehow. But this was *her* awful confession. Why should Daniel be the one to look so shattered?

He stepped toward her and leaned down until his eyes were gazing directly into hers. Luce almost couldn't take it. But she couldn't make herself budge, either. Whatever happened to break this trance would have to be up to Daniel—who was moving closer still, tilting his head toward hers and closing his eyes. His lips parted. Luce's breath caught in her throat.

She closed her eyes, too. She tilted her head toward his, too. She parted her lips, too.

And waited.

The kiss she had been dying for didn't come. She opened her eyes because nothing had happened, except for the rustling sound of a tree branch. Daniel was gone. She sighed, crestfallen but not surprised.

What was strange was that she could almost *see* the path he'd taken back through the forest. As if she were some kind of hunter who could pinpoint the rotation of a leaf and let it lead her back to Daniel. Except she was nothing of the sort, and the kind of trail that Daniel left in his wake was somehow bigger, clearer, and at the same time, even more elusive. It was as if a violet glow illuminated his path back through the forest.

Like the violet glow she'd seen during the library fire. She was seeing things. She steadied herself on the rock and looked away for a moment, rubbing her eyes. But when she looked back, it was just the same: In just one plane of her vision—as if she were looking through bi-focals with a wild prescription—the live oaks, and the mulch beneath them, and even the songs of the birds in the branches—all of it seemed to wobble out of focus. And it didn't just wobble, bathed in that faintest purple light, but seemed to emit a barely audible low-pitched hum.

She spun back around, terrified to face it, terrified of what it meant. Something was happening to her, and she could tell no one about it. She tried to focus on the lake, but even it was growing darker and difficult to see.

She was alone. Daniel had left her. And in his place, this path she didn't know how—or want—to navigate. When the sun sank behind the mountains and the lake became a charcoal gray, Luce dared another glance back at the forest. She sucked in her breath, not sure whether to be disappointed or relieved. It was a forest like any other, no quivering light or violet hum. No sign of Daniel's ever having been there at all.

THIRTEEN

TOUCHED AT THE ROOTS

Luce could hear her Converse sneakers beating hard against the pavement. She could feel the humid wind tugging on her black T-shirt. She could practically taste the hot tar from a freshly paved portion of the parking lot. But when she flung her arms around the two huddled creatures near the entrance to Sword & Cross on Saturday morning, all of that was forgotten.

She had never been so glad to hug her parents in her life.

For days, she'd been regretting how cold and distant things had been at the hospital, and she wasn't going to make the same mistake again.

They both stumbled as she plowed into them. Her mother started giggling and her dad thwacked her back in his tough-guy way with his palm. He had his enormous camera strapped around his neck. They straightened up and held their daughter at arm's length. They seemed to want a good look at her face, but as soon as they got it, their own faces fell. Luce was crying.

"Sweetheart, what's the matter?" her father asked, resting his hand on her head.

Her mom fished through her giant blue pocketbook for her stash of tissues. Eyes wide, she dangled one in front of Luce's nose and asked, "We're here now. Everything's fine, isn't it?"

No, everything was not fine.

"Why didn't you take me home the other day?" Luce asked, feeling angry and hurt all over again. "Why did you let them bring me back here?"

Her father blanched. "Every time we spoke to the headmaster, he said you were doing great, back in classes, like the trouper we raised. A sore throat from the smoke and a little bump on the head. We thought that was all." He licked his lips.

"Was there more?" her mom asked.

One look between her parents told that they'd had this fight already. Mom would have begged to visit again sooner. Luce's tough-love dad would have put his foot down.

There was no way to explain to them what had happened that night or what she'd been going through since then. She *had* gone straight back to classes, though not by her own choice. And physically, she *was* fine. It was just that in every other way—emotionally, psychologically, romantically—she couldn't have felt more broken.

"We're just trying to follow the rules," Luce's father explained, moving his big hand to squeeze her neck. The weight of it shifted her whole posture and made it uncomfortable to stand still, but it had been so long since she'd been this close to people she loved, she didn't dare move away. "Because we only want what's best for you," her dad added. "We have to take it on faith that these people"—he gestured at the formidable buildings around campus, as if they represented Randy and Headmaster Udell and the rest of them—"that they know what they're talking about."

"They don't," Luce said, glancing at the shoddy buildings and the empty commons. So far, nothing at this school made any sense to her.

Case in point, what they called Parents' Day. They'd made such a big deal about how lucky the students were to get the privilege of seeing their own flesh and blood. And yet it was ten minutes until lunchtime and Luce's parents' car was the only one in the parking lot.

"This place is an absolute joke," she said, sounding cynical enough that her parents shared a troubled look.

"Luce, honey," her mom said, stroking her hair. Luce could tell she wasn't used to its short length. Her fingers had a maternal instinct to follow the ghost of Luce's former hair all the way down her back. "We just want one nice day with you. Your father brought all your favorite foods."

Sheepishly, her father held up a colorful patchwork quilt and a large briefcase-style contraption made of wicker that Luce had never seen before. Usually when they picnicked, it was a much more casual affair, with paper grocery bags and an old ripped sheet thrown down on the grass by the canoe trail outside their house.

"Pickled okra?" Luce asked in a voice that sounded very much like little-kid Lucy. No one could say her parents weren't trying.

Her dad nodded. "And sweet tea, and biscuits with white gravy. Cheddar grits with extra jalapeños, just the way you like 'em. Oh," he said, "and one more thing."

Luce's mom reached into her purse for a fat, sealed red envelope and held it out to Luce. For the briefest moment, a pain gnawed at Luce's stomach when she thought back to the mail she was accustomed to receiving. *Psycho Killer. Death Girl.*

But when Luce looked at the handwriting on the envelope, her face broke into an enormous grin.

Callie.

She tore into the envelope and pulled out a card with

a black-and-white photograph on the front of two old ladies getting their hair done. Inside, every square inch of the card was filled with Callie's large, bubbly handwriting. And there were several pieces of scrawled-on loose-leaf paper because she'd run out of room on the card.

> *Dear Luce,*
>   *Since our phone time is now ridiculously in-sufficient (Can you __please__ petition for some more? It's downright unjust), I'm going to get all old-fashioned on you and take up epic letter writing. Enclosed you will find every single minuscule thing that happened to me over the past two weeks. Whether you like it or not . . .*

Luce clutched the envelope to her chest, still grinning, eager to devour the letter as soon as her parents headed home. Callie hadn't given up on her. And her parents were sitting right beside her. It had been way too long since Luce had felt this loved. She reached out and squeezed her father's hand.

A blaring whistle made both her parents jump. "It's just the dinner bell," she explained; they seemed relieved. "Come on, there's someone I want you to meet."

As they walked from the hot, hazy parking lot toward the commons where the opening events of Parents' Day were being held, Luce started to see the campus through her parents' eyes. She noticed anew the sagging roof of the main office, and the sickly, overripe odor of the rotting peach grove next to the gym. The way the wrought iron of the cemetery gates was overcome with orangey rust. She realized that in only a couple of weeks, she'd grown completely accustomed to Sword & Cross's many eyesores.

Her parents looked mostly horrified. Her father gestured at a dying grapevine winding its decrepit way around the splintering fence at the entrance to the commons.

"Those are chardonnay grapes," he said, wincing because when a plant felt pain, so did he.

Her mother was using two hands to grip her pocketbook to her chest, with both elbows sticking out—the stance she took when she found herself in a neighborhood where she thought she might be mugged. And they hadn't even seen the reds yet. Her parents, who were adamantly against little things like Luce getting a webcam, would hate the idea of constant surveillance at her school.

Luce wanted to protect them from all the atrocities of Sword & Cross, because she was figuring out how to manage—and sometimes even beat—the system here. Just the other day, Arriane had taken her through an obstacle course–like sprint across the campus to point out all the "dead reds" whose batteries had died or been slyly "replaced," effectively creating the blind spots of the school. Her parents didn't need to know about all that; they just needed to have a good day with her.

Penn was swinging her legs from the bleachers, where she and Luce had promised to meet at noon. She was holding a potted mum.

"Penn, these are my parents, Harry and Doreen Price," Luce said, gesturing. "Mom and Dad, this is—"

"Pennyweather Van Syckle-Lockwood," Penn said formally, extending the mum with both hands. "Thank you for letting me join you for lunch."

Ever polite, Luce's parents cooed and smiled, not asking any questions about Penn's own family's where-abouts, which Luce hadn't had the time to explain.

It was another warm, clear day. The acid-green willow trees in front of the library swayed gently in the breeze, and Luce steered her parents to a position where the willows obscured most of the soot stains and the windows broken by the fire. As they spread out the quilt on a dry patch of grass, Luce pulled Penn aside.

"How are you?" Luce asked, knowing that if she'd been the one who had to sit through a whole day honoring everyone's parents but hers, she would have needed a major pick-me-up.

To her surprise, Penn's head bobbed happily. "This is already so much better than last year!" she said. "And it's all because of you. I wouldn't have anyone today if you hadn't come along."

The compliment took Luce by surprise and made her look around the quad to see how everyone else was handling the event. Despite the still half-empty parking lot, Parents' Day seemed to be slowly filling up.

Molly sat on a blanket nearby, between a pug-faced man and woman, gnawing hungrily on a turkey leg. Arriane was crouched on a bleacher, whispering to an older punk girl with hypnotizing hot-pink hair. Most likely her big sister. The two of them caught Luce's eye and Arriane grinned and waved, then turned to the other girl to whisper something.

Roland had a huge party of people setting up a picnic lunch on a large bedspread. They were laughing and joking, and a few younger kids were throwing food at each other. They seemed to be having a great time until a corn-on-the-cob grenade went flying and almost blindsided Gabbe, who was walking across the commons. She scowled at Roland as she guided a man who looked old enough to be her grandfather, patting his elbow as they walked toward a row of lawn chairs set up around the open field.

Daniel and Cam were noticeably missing—and Luce couldn't picture what either of their families would look like. As angry and embarrassed as she'd been after Daniel bailed on her for the second time at the lake, she was still dying to catch a glimpse of anyone related to him. But then, thinking back to Daniel's thin file in the archive room, Luce wondered whether he even kept in touch with anyone from his family.

Luce's mother doled cheddar grits onto four plates, and her father topped the mounds with freshly chopped jalapeños. After one bite, Luce's mouth was on fire, just the way she liked it. Penn seemed unfamiliar with the typical Georgia fare Luce had grown up with. She looked particularly terrified by the pickled okra, but as soon as she took a bite, she gave Luce a surprised smile of approval.

Luce's mom and dad had brought with them every single one of Luce's favorite foods, even the pecan pralines from the family drugstore down the block. Her parents chomped happily on either side of her, seeming glad to fill their mouths with something other than talk of death.

Luce should have been enjoying her time with them, and washing it all down with her beloved Georgia sweet tea, but she felt like an imposter daughter for pretending this elysian lunch was normal for Sword & Cross. The whole day was such a sham.

At the sound of a short, feeble round of applause, Luce looked over at the bleachers, where Randy stood next to Headmaster Udell, a man whom Luce had never seen in the flesh before. She recognized him from the unusually dim portrait that hung in the main lobby of the school, but she saw now that the artist had been generous. Penn had already told her that the headmaster showed up on campus only one day of the year—Parents' Day—with no exceptions. Otherwise, he was a recluse who didn't leave his Tybee Island mansion, not even when a student at his school passed away. The man's jowls were swallowing his chin and his bovine eyes stared out into the crowd, not seeming to focus on anything.

At his side Randy stood, legs akimbo in white stockings. She had a lipless smile plastered across her face, and the headmaster was blotting his big forehead with a napkin. Both had their game faces on today, but it seemed to be taking a lot out of them.

"Welcome to Sword & Cross's one-hundred-and-fifty-ninth annual Parents' Day," Headmaster Udell said into a microphone.

"Is he kidding?" Luce whispered to Penn. It was hard to imagine Parents' Day during the antebellum period.

Penn rolled her eyes. "Surely a typo. I've told them to get him new reading glasses."

"We have a long and fun-filled day of family time scheduled for you, beginning with this leisurely picnic lunch—"

"Usually we only get nineteen minutes," Penn interrupted in an aside to Luce's parents, who stiffened.

Luce smiled over Penn's head and mouthed, "She's kidding."

"Next you'll have your choice of activities. Our very own biologist, Ms. Yolanda Tross, will deliver a fascinating lecture in the library on the local Savannah flora found on campus. Coach Diante will supervise a series of family-friendly races out here on the lawn. And Mr. Stanley Cole will offer a historical guided tour of our prized heroes' cemetery. It's going to be a very busy day. And yes," Headmaster Udell said with a cheesy, toothy grin, "you will be tested on this."

It was just the right kind of bland and hackneyed joke to earn some canned laughter out of the bunch of visiting family members. Luce rolled her eyes at Penn. This depressing attempt at good-natured chuckling made it all too clear that everyone was here in order to feel better about leaving their children in the hands of the Sword & Cross faculty. The Prices laughed, too, but kept looking at Luce for more cues on how to handle themselves.

After lunch, the other families around the commons packed up their picnics and retreated to various corners. Luce got the feeling that very few people were actually participating in the school-sanctioned events. No one had followed Ms. Tross up to the library, and so far only Gabbe and her grandfather had climbed into a potato sack at the other end of the field.

Luce didn't know where Molly or Arriane or Roland

had sneaked off to with their families, and she still hadn't seen Daniel. She did know that her own parents would be disappointed if they saw nothing of the campus and didn't participate in any planned events. Since Mr. Cole's guided tour seemed like the least of the evils, Luce suggested they pack up their leftovers and join him by the cemetery gates.

As they were on the way over, Arriane swung herself off the top bleacher like a gymnast dismounting a parallel bar. She stuck her landing right in front of Luce's parents.

"Helloooo," she crooned, doing her best crazy-girl impression.

"Mom and Dad," Luce said, squeezing their shoulders, "this is my good friend Arriane."

"And this"—Arriane pointed at the tall, hot-pink-headed girl who was slowly picking her way down the bleacher stairs, "is my sister, Annabelle."

Annabelle ignored Luce's extended hand and swept her into her open arms for an extended, intimate hug. Luce could feel their bones crunching together. The intense hug lasted long enough for Luce to wonder what was up with it, but just as she was starting to feel uncomfortable, Annabelle let her go.

"It's so good to meet you," she said, taking Luce's hand.

"Likewise," Luce said, giving Arriane a sideways glance.

"Are you two going on Mr. Cole's tour?" Luce asked Arriane, who was also looking at Annabelle as if she were crazy.

Annabelle opened her mouth, but Arriane quickly cut her off. "Hell no," she said. "These activities are for absolute lame-o's." She glanced at Luce's parents. "No offense."

Annabelle shrugged. "Maybe we'll have a chance to catch up later!" she called to Luce before Arriane tugged her away.

"They seemed nice," Luce's mother said in the probing voice she used when she wanted Luce to explain something.

"Um, why was that girl so into you?" Penn asked.

Luce looked at Penn, then at her parents. Did she really have to defend, in front of them, the fact that someone might like her?

"Lucinda!" Mr. Cole called, waving from the otherwise unoccupied meet-up point by the cemetery gates. "Over here!"

Mr. Cole clasped both of her parents' hands warmly and even gave Penn's shoulders a squeeze. Luce was trying to decide whether she should be more annoyed by Mr. Cole's participation in Parents' Day or impressed by his fake show of enthusiasm. But then he began speaking and surprised her.

"I practice for this day all year," he whispered. "A chance to take the students out in the fresh air and explain the many marvels of this place—oh, I do love it. It's the closest a reform school teacher gets to a real field trip. 'Course, no one's ever shown up for my tours in years past, which makes you my inaugural tour—"

"Well, we're honored," Luce's dad boomed, giving Mr. Cole a big smile. Immediately, Luce could tell that it wasn't just Dad's cannon-hungry Civil War buff side speaking. He clearly felt that Mr. Cole was legit. And her father was the best judge of character she knew.

Already the two men had started trooping down the steep slope at the entrance of the cemetery. Luce's mom left the picnic basket at the gates and gave Luce and Penn one of her well-worn smiles.

Mr. Cole waved a hand to get their attention. "First, a bit of trivia. What"—he raised his eyebrows—"would you guess is the oldest element of this cemetery?"

While Luce and Penn looked down at their feet—avoiding his eyes as they did during class—Luce's father stood on his toes to take a gander at some of the larger statues.

"Trick question!" Mr. Cole bellowed, patting the ornate wrought iron gates. "This front portion of the gates was built by the original proprietor in 1831. They say his wife, Ellamena, had a lovely garden, and she wanted something to keep the guinea hens out of her tomatoes." He laughed under his breath. "That was before the war. And before the sinkhole. Moving on!"

As they walked, Mr. Cole rattled off fact after fact

about the construction of the cemetery, the historical backdrop against which it was built, and the "artist"—even he used the term loosely—who'd come up with the winged beast sculpture at the top of the monolith in the center of the grounds. Luce's father peppered Mr. Cole with questions while Luce's mom ran her hands over the tops of some of the prettiest headstones, letting out a murmured "Oh my" every time she paused to read an inscription. Penn shuffled after Luce's mother, possibly wishing she'd latched on to a different family for the day. And Luce brought up the rear, considering what might happen if she were to give her parents her own personal tour of the cemetery.

Here's where I served my first detention. . . .

And here's where a falling marble angel nearly decapitated me. . . .

And here's where a reform school boy you'd never approve of took me on the strangest picnic of my life.

"Cam," Mr. Cole called as he led the tour around the monolith.

Cam was standing with a tall, dark-haired man in a tailored black business suit. Neither of them heard Mr. Cole or saw the party he was leading on the tour. They were talking quietly and gesturing in a very involved manner at the oak tree, the way Luce had seen her drama teacher gesture when the students were blocking a scene in a play.

"Are you and your father late arrivals to our tour?"

Mr. Cole asked Cam, this time more loudly. "You've missed most of it, but there's still an interesting fact or two I'm sure I could impart."

Cam slowly turned his head their way, then back at his companion, who seemed amused. Luce didn't think the man, with his classic tall, dark, and handsome good looks and huge gold watch, looked old enough to be Cam's father. But maybe he had just aged well. Cam's eyes skimmed Luce's bare neck, and he seemed briefly disappointed. She blushed, because she could feel her mother taking in the whole scene and wondering just what was going on.

Cam ignored Mr. Cole and approached Luce's mother, drawing her hand to his lips before anyone could even introduce them. "You must be Luce's older sister," he said rakishly.

To her left, Penn gagged into her elbow and whispered so only Luce could hear, "Please tell me someone else is nauseated."

But Luce's mom seemed somewhat dazzled, in a way that made Luce—and her father, clearly—uncomfortable.

"No, we can't stay for the tour," Cam announced, winking at Luce and drawing back just as Luce's father approached. "But it was so lovely"—he glanced at each of the three of them, excluding only Penn—"to encounter you here. Let's go, *Dad*."

"Who was that?" Luce's mother whispered when

Cam and his father, or whoever he had been, disappeared back up the side of the cemetery.

"Oh, just one of Luce's admirers," Penn said, trying to lighten the mood and doing exactly the opposite.

"*One* of?" Luce's father peered down at Penn.

In the late-afternoon light, Luce could see for the first time a few gray whiskers in her dad's beard. She didn't want to spend today's last moments convincing her father not to worry about the boys at her reform school.

"It's nothing, Dad. Penn's kidding."

"We want you to be careful, Lucinda," he said.

Luce thought about what Daniel had suggested— quite strongly—the other day. That maybe she shouldn't be at Sword & Cross at all. And suddenly she wanted so badly to bring it up to her parents, to beg and plead for them to take her far away from here.

But it was that same memory of Daniel that made Luce hold her tongue. The thrilling touch of his skin on hers when she'd pushed him down at the lake, the way his eyes were sometimes the saddest things she knew. It felt at once absolutely crazy and absolutely true that it might be worth all of this hell at Sword & Cross just to spend a little more time with Daniel. Just to see if anything might come of it.

"I hate goodbyes," Luce's mother breathed, interrupting her daughter's thoughts to draw her in for a brisk hug. Luce looked down at her watch and her face fell. She didn't know how the afternoon had gone by so quickly, how it could already be time for them to go.

"You'll call us on Wednesday?" her dad asked, kissing both her cheeks the way the French side of his family always did.

As they all walked back up toward the parking lot, Luce's parents gripped her hands. Each of them gave her another strong hug and series of kisses. When they shook Penn's hand and wished her well, Luce saw a video camera clamped to the brick post housing a broken call box at the exit. There must have been a motion detector attached to the reds, because the camera was panning, following their movement. This one hadn't been on Arriane's tour and was certainly not a dead red. Luce's parents noticed nothing—and maybe it was better that way.

Then they were walking away, looking back twice to wave at the two girls standing at the entrance to the main lobby. Dad cranked up his old black Chrysler New Yorker and rolled down the window.

"We love you," he called out so loudly that Luce would have been embarrassed if she hadn't been so sad to see them go.

Luce waved back. "Thank you," she whispered. *For the pralines and the okra. For spending all day here. For taking Penn under your wing, no questions asked. For still loving me despite the fact that I scare you.*

When the taillights disappeared around the bend, Penn tapped Luce's back. "I was thinking I'd go see my dad." She kicked the ground with the toe of her boot and looked bashfully up at Luce. "Any chance you'd want to come? If not, I understand, seeing as it involves another trip inside—" She jerked her thumb back toward the depths of the cemetery.

"Of course I'll come," Luce said.

They walked around the perimeter of the cemetery, staying high on the rim until they'd reached the far east corner, where Penn paused in front of a grave.

It was modest, white, and covered with a tawny layer of pine needles. Penn got down on her knees and started to wipe it clean.

STANFORD LOCKWOOD, the simple tombstone read, WORLD'S BEST FATHER.

Luce could hear Penn's poignant voice behind the inscription, and she felt tears spring to her eyes. She didn't want Penn to see—after all, Luce still had her parents. If anyone should cry right now, it should be . . . Penn *was* crying. She was trying to hide it with the mildest of sniffles and a few tears wiped on the ragged hem of her sweater. Luce got down on her knees, too, and started helping her brush the needles away. She put her arms around her friend and held on as tight as she could.

When Penn drew back and thanked Luce, she reached into her pocket and pulled out a letter.

"I usually write him something," she explained.

Luce wanted to give Penn a moment alone with her dad, so she got up, took a step back, and turned away, heading down the slope toward the heart of the cemetery. Her eyes were still a little glassy, but she thought she could see someone sitting alone on top of the monolith. Yes. A guy with his arms wrapped around his knees. She couldn't imagine how he'd gotten up there, but there he was.

He looked stiff and lonely, as if he'd been there all day. He didn't see Luce or Penn. He didn't seem to see anything. But Luce didn't have to be close enough to see those violet-gray eyes to know who it was.

All this time Luce had been searching for explanations about why Daniel's file was so sparse, what secrets his ancestor's missing book held in the library, where his mind had traveled to that day she'd asked about his family. Why he'd been so hot and cold with her . . . always.

After such an emotional day with her own parents, the thought nearly brought Luce to her knees with sadness. Daniel was alone in the world.

FOURTEEN

IDLE HANDS

It rained all day on Tuesday. Pitch-black clouds rolled in from the west and churned over the campus, doing nothing to help clear Luce's mind. The downpour came in uneven waves—drizzling, then pouring, then hailing—before it tapered off to start all over again. The students hadn't even been allowed to go outside during breaks, and by the end of her calculus class, Luce was going stir-crazy.

She realized this when her notes began to veer away

from the mean value theorem and started looking more like this:

>*September 15: Introductory flip-off from D*
>*September 16: Statue toppling, hand on head to protect me (alternately: just him groping for a way out); D's immediate exit*
>*September 17: Potential misreading of D's head bob as suggestion that I attend Cam's party. Disturbing discovery of D & G's relationship (mistake?)*

Spelled out like that, it was the beginning of a pretty embarrassing catalog. He was just so hot and cold. It was possible he felt the same way about her—though, if pressed, Luce would insist that any weirdness on *her* part was only in response to utter weirdness on *his* part.

No. This was *precisely* the kind of circular argument she did not want to engage in. Luce didn't want to play any games. She just wanted to be with him. Only, she had no idea why. Or how to go about it. Or really, what being with him would even mean. All she knew was that, despite everything, he was the one she thought about. The one she cared about.

She'd thought if she could track every time they'd connected and every time he'd pulled away, she might be able to find some reason behind Daniel's erratic behavior.

But her list so far was only making her depressed. She crumpled the page into a ball.

When the bell finally rang to dismiss them for the day, Luce hurried out of the classroom. Usually she waited to walk with either Arriane or Penn, dreading the moment they parted ways, because then Luce would be alone with her thoughts. But today, for a change, she didn't feel like seeing anyone. She was looking forward to some Luce time. She had only one sure idea about how to take her mind off Daniel: a long, hard, solitary swim.

While the other students started trucking back toward their dorm rooms, Luce pulled up the hood of her black sweater and darted into the rain, eager to get to the natatorium.

As she bounded down the steps of Augustine, she plowed straight into something tall and black. Cam. When she jostled him, a tower of books teetered in his arms, then tumbled to the wet pavement with a series of thuds. He'd had his own black hood pulled over his head and his earbuds blaring in his ears. He probably hadn't seen her coming, either. They'd both been in their own worlds.

"Are you okay?" he asked, putting a hand on her back.

"I'm fine," Luce said. She'd barely stumbled. It was Cam's books that had taken the spill.

"Well, now that we've knocked over one another's books, isn't the next step for our hands to accidentally touch while we're picking them up?"

Luce laughed. When she handed him one of the books, he held on to her hand and squeezed it. The rain had soaked his dark hair, and big drops gathered in his long, thick eyelashes. He looked really good.

"How do you say 'embarrassed' in French?" he asked.

"Um . . . *gêné*," Luce started to say, feeling suddenly a little *gênée* herself. Cam was still holding on to her hand. "Wait, aren't you the one who got an A on the French quiz yesterday?"

"You noticed?" he asked. His voice sounded strange.

"Cam," she said, "is everything okay?"

He leaned toward her and brushed a drop of water she'd felt running down the bridge of her nose. The single touch of his forefinger made her shiver, and suddenly she couldn't help thinking about how wonderful and warm it might feel if he folded her into his arms the way he'd done at Todd's memorial.

"I've been thinking about you," he said. "Wanting to see you. I waited for you at the memorial, but someone told me you left."

Luce got the feeling he knew whom she'd left with. And that he wanted her to know he knew.

"I'm sorry," she said, having to shout to be heard

over a clap of thunder. By now they were both soaked from the streaming downpour.

"Come on, let's get out of this rain." Cam tugged her back toward the covered entrance to Augustine.

Luce looked over his shoulder toward the gym and wanted to be there, not here or anywhere else with Cam. At least, not right now. Her head was brimming with too many confusing impulses, and she needed time and space away—from everyone—to sort them out.

"I can't," she said.

"How about later? How about tonight?"

"Sure, later, okay."

He beamed. "I'll come by your room."

He surprised her by pulling her in to him, just for the briefest moment, and kissing her gently on the forehead. Luce felt instantly soothed, almost like she'd been given a shot of something. And before she had a chance to feel anything more, he'd released her and was walking quickly back toward the dorm.

Luce shook her head and splashed slowly toward the gym. Clearly she had more to sort out than just Daniel.

There was a chance it might be good, fun even, to spend some time with Cam later tonight. If the rain let up, he'd probably take her to some secret part of the campus and be all charismatic and gorgeous in that un-nervingly still manner of his. He'd make her feel special. Luce smiled.

Since she'd last set foot in Our Lady of Fitness (as Arriane had christened the gym), the school's maintenance staff had begun to fight the kudzu. They had stripped the green blanket away from much of the building's façade, but they were only half finished, and green vines dangled like tentacles across the doors. Luce had to duck under a few long tendrils just so she could get inside.

The gym was empty, and pin-drop quiet compared to the thunderstorm outside. Most of the lights were off. She hadn't asked if she was allowed to use the gym after hours, but the door was unlocked, and, well, no one was there to stop her.

In the dim hallway, she passed the old Latin scrolls in the glass cases, and the miniature marble reproduction of the pietà. She paused in front of the door to the weight room, where she'd happened upon Daniel jumping rope. Sigh. That'd be a great addition to her catalog:

September 18: D accuses me of stalking him.
Followed two days later by:
September 20: Penn convinces me to really begin
    stalking him. I consent.

Ugh. She was in a black hole of self-loathing. And yet she couldn't stop herself. In the middle of the hallway, she froze. All at once she understood why this whole day she'd felt even more consumed by Daniel than usual, and also even more conflicted about Cam. She'd dreamed about them both last night.

She'd been wandering through a dusty fog, someone holding her hand. She'd turned, thinking it would be Daniel. But while the lips she pressed against were comforting and tender, they weren't his. They were Cam's. He gave her innumerable soft kisses, and every time Luce peeked at him, his stormy green eyes were open, too, boring into her, questioning her about something she couldn't answer.

Then Cam was gone, and the fog was gone, and Luce was wrapped tightly in Daniel's arms, right where she wanted to be. He dipped her low and kissed her fiercely, as if he were angry, and each time his lips left hers, even just for half a second, the most parching thirst ran through her, making her cry out. This time, she knew they were wings, and she let them wrap around her body like a blanket. She wanted to touch them, to fold them around her and Daniel completely, but soon the brush of velvet was receding, folding back on itself. He stopped kissing her, watched her face, waited for a reaction. She didn't understand the strange hot fear growing in the pit of her stomach. But there it was, making her uncomfortably warm, then blisteringly hot—until she could stand it no longer. That was when she jolted awake: In the dream's last moment, Luce herself had seared and splintered—then had been obliterated into ash.

She'd woken up soaked with sweat—her hair, her

pillow, her pajamas all wet and suddenly making her so, so cold. She'd lain there shivering and alone until the morning's first light.

Luce rubbed her rain-soaked sleeves to warm up. Of course. The dream had left her with a fire in her heart and a chill in her bones she'd been unable to reconcile all day. Which was why she'd come here for a swim, to try to work it out of her system.

This time, her black Speedo actually fit, and she'd remembered to bring a pair of goggles. She pushed open the door to the pool and stood under the high-dive platform alone, breathing in the humid air with its dull tang of chlorine. Without the distraction of the other students, or the trill of Coach Diante's whistle, Luce could feel the presence of something else in the church. Something almost holy. Maybe it was only that the natatorium was such a gorgeous room, even with the rain pelting in through the cracked stained-glass windows. Even with none of the candles lit in the red side altars. Luce tried to imagine what the place had looked like before the pool had replaced the pews, and she smiled. She liked the idea of swimming under all those praying heads.

She lowered her goggles and leaped in. The water was warm, much warmer than the rain outside, and the crash of thunder outside sounded harmless and far away when she ducked her head underwater.

She pushed off and began a slow warm-up crawl stroke.

Her body quickly loosened up, and a few laps later, Luce increased her speed and began the butterfly. She could feel the burn in her limbs, and she pushed through it. This was exactly the feeling she was after. Totally in the zone.

If she could just talk to Daniel. Really talk, without him interrupting or telling her to transfer schools or ducking out before she could get to her point. That might help. It also might require tying him up and taping his mouth shut just so he'd listen to her.

But what would she even say? All she had to go on was this *feeling* she got around him, which, if she thought about it, had nothing to do with any of their interactions.

What if she could get him back to the lake? He was the one who'd implied it had become *their* place. This time, she could lead him there, and she'd be super-careful not to bring up anything that seemed to freak him out—

It wasn't working.

Crap. She was doing it again. She was supposed to be swimming. Just swimming. She'd swim until she was too tired to think about anything else, especially Daniel. She'd swim until—

"Luce!"

Until she was interrupted. By Penn, who was standing at the side of the pool.

"What are you doing here?" Luce asked, spitting water.

"What are *you* doing here?" Penn returned. "Since

when do you exercise willingly? I don't like this new side of you."

"How did you find me?" Luce didn't realize until she'd said it that her words might have sounded rude, like she was trying to avoid Penn.

"Cam told me," Penn said. "We had a whole conversation. It was weird. He wanted to know if you were all right."

"That *is* weird," Luce agreed.

"No," Penn said, "what was weird was that he approached me and we had a whole conversation. Mr. Popularity . . . and *me*. Need I spell out my surprise any further? Thing is, he was actually really nice."

"Well, he *is* nice." Luce pulled her goggles off her head.

"To you," Penn said. "He's so nice to you that he snuck out of school to buy you that necklace—which you never wear."

"I wore it once," Luce said. Which was true. Five nights before, after the second time Daniel left her stranded at the lake, alone with his path lit up in the forest. She hadn't been able to shake the image of it and hadn't been able to sleep. So she'd tried on the necklace. She'd fallen asleep clutching it near her collarbone, and woken up with it hot in her hand.

Penn was waving three fingers at Luce, as if to say, *Hello? And your point is . . . ?*

"My point is," Luce said finally, "I'm not so superficial that all I'm looking for is a guy who buys me things."

"Not so superficial, eh?" Penn asked. "Then I dare you to make a non-superficial list of why you're so into Daniel. Which means no *He's got the loveliest little gray eyes* or *Ooh, the way his muscles ripple in the sunlight.*"

Luce had to crack up at Penn's high falsetto and the way she held her hands clasped to her heart. "He just gets me," she said, avoiding Penn's eyes. "I can't explain it."

"He gets that you deserve to be ignored?" Penn shook her head.

Luce had never told Penn about the times she'd spent alone with Daniel, the times when she'd seen a flash that he cared about her, too. So Penn couldn't really understand her feelings. And they were far too private and too complicated to explain.

Penn crouched down in front of Luce. "Look, the reason I came to find you in the first place was to drag you to the library for a Daniel-related mission."

"You found the book?"

"Not exactly," Penn said, extending a hand to help Luce out of the pool. "Mr. Grigori's masterpiece is still mysteriously missing, but I kind of sort of maybe hacked Miss Sophia's subscribers-only literary search engine, and a couple of things turned up. I thought you might find them interesting."

"Thanks," Luce said, hoisting herself out with Penn's help. "I'll try not to be too annoyingly gushy over Daniel."

"Whatever," Penn said. "Just hurry up and dry off. We're in a brief no-rain window outside and I don't have an umbrella."

❉

Mostly dry and back in her school uniform, Luce followed Penn to the library. Part of the front portion had been blocked off by yellow police tape, so the girls had to slip through the narrow space between the card catalog and the reference section. It still smelled like a bonfire, and now, thanks to the sprinklers and the rain, possessed an added mildewy quality.

Luce took her first look at where Miss Sophia's desk had sat, now a charred, nearly perfect circle on the old tile floor in the library's center. Everything in a fifteen-foot radius had been removed. Everything beyond that was strangely undamaged.

The librarian wasn't at her station, but a folding card table had been set up for her next to the burned spot. The table was depressingly bare, save for a new lamp, a pencil jar, and a gray pad of sticky notes.

Luce and Penn gave each other a that-sucks grimace before they continued to the computer stations at the back. When they passed the study section where they'd last seen Todd, Luce glanced over at her friend. Penn kept her face forward, but when Luce reached over and squeezed her hand, Penn squeezed back pretty hard.

They pulled two chairs up to one computer terminal, and Penn typed in her user name. Luce glanced around just to make sure no one else was nearby.

A red error box popped up on the screen.

Penn groaned.

"What?" Luce asked.

"After four, you need special permission to access the Web."

"*That's* why this place is always so empty at night."

Penn was rooting through her backpack. "Where did I put that encrypted password?" she mumbled.

"There's Miss Sophia," Luce said, flagging down the librarian, who was crossing the aisle in a black fitted blouse and bright green cropped pants. Her shimmery earrings dusted her shoulders, and she had a pencil poked into the side of her hair. "Over here," Luce whispered loudly.

Miss Sophia squinted at them. Her bifocals had slipped down her nose, and with a stack of books under each arm, she didn't have a free hand to push them up. "Who's that?" she called, walking over.

"Oh, Lucinda. Pennyweather," she said, sounding tired. "Hello."

"We were wondering if you could give us the password to use the computer," Luce asked, pointing at the error message on the screen.

"You're not doing social networking, are you? Those sites are the devil's work."

"No, no, this is serious research," Penn said. "You'd approve."

Miss Sophia leaned over the girls to unlock the computer. Fingers flying, she typed in the longest password Luce had ever seen. "You have twenty minutes," she said flatly, walking away.

"That should be enough," Penn whispered. "I found a critical essay on the Watchers, so until we track down the book, we can at least read up on what it's about."

Luce sensed someone standing behind her and turned around to see that Miss Sophia had returned. Luce jumped. "I'm sorry," she said. "I don't know why you scared me."

"No, I'm the one who's sorry," Miss Sophia said. Her smile practically made her eyes disappear. "It's just been so hard recently, since the fire. But there's no reason for me to take my sorrow out on two of my most promising students."

Neither Luce nor Penn really knew what to say. It was one thing to comfort each other after the fire. Reassuring the school librarian seemed a little bit out of their league.

"I've been trying to keep busy, but . . ." Miss Sophia trailed off.

Penn glanced nervously at Luce. "Well, we might be able to use some help with our research, if, that is, you—"

"I can help!" Miss Sophia tugged over a third chair. "I see you're looking into the Watchers," she said, reading over their shoulders. "The Grigoris were a very influential clan. And I just happen to know of a papal database. Let me see what I can pull up."

Luce nearly choked on the pencil she'd been chewing. "I'm sorry, did you say Grigoris?"

"Oh yes, historians have traced them back to the Middle Ages. They were . . ." She paused, searching for the words. "A sort of research cluster, to put it in modern layperson's terms. They specialized in a certain type of fallen-angel folklore."

She reached between the girls again and Luce marveled as her fingers raced across the keyboard. The search engine struggled to keep up, pulling up article after article, primary source after primary source, all on the Grigoris. Daniel's family name was everywhere, filling up the screen. Luce felt a bit light-headed.

The image from her dream came back to her: unfurling wings, her body heating up until she smoldered into ash.

"There are different kinds of angels to specialize in?" Penn asked.

"Oh, sure—it's a wide body of literature," Miss Sophia said while she typed. "There are those who became demons. And those who threw in with God. And there are even ones who consorted with mortal women." At last her fingers were still. "Very dangerous habit."

Penn said, "Are these Watcher dudes any relation to the Daniel Grigori here?"

Miss Sophia tapped her mauve lips. "Quite possible. I wondered that myself, but it is hardly our place to be digging into another student's business, wouldn't you agree?" Her pale face pinched into a frown as she looked down at her watch. "Well, I hope I've given you enough to get started on your project. I won't hog any more of your time." She pointed at a clock on the computer screen. "You've only got nine minutes left."

As she walked back toward the front of the library, Luce watched Miss Sophia's perfect posture. She could have balanced a book on her head. It did seem like it had cheered her up a little to help the girls with their research, but at the same time, Luce had no idea what to do with the information she'd just been given about Daniel.

Penn did. She'd already started scribbling furious notes.

"Eight and a half minutes," she informed Luce, handing her a pen and a piece of paper. "There's way too much here to make sense of in eight and a half minutes. Start writing."

Luce sighed and did as she was told. It was a boringly designed academic Web page with a thin blue border framing a plain beige background. At the top, a header in a severe blocky font read: THE GRIGORI CLAN.

Just reading the name, Luce felt her skin warm.

Penn tapped the monitor with her pen, snapping Luce's attention back to her task.

The Grigoris do not sleep. Seemed possible; Daniel always did look tired. *They are generally silent.* Check. Sometimes talking to him was like pulling teeth. *In an eighth-century decree*—

The screen went black. Their time was up.

"How much did you get?" Penn asked.

Luce held up her sheet of paper. Pathetic. What she had was something she didn't even remember doodling: the feathered edges of wings.

Penn gave her a sideways glance. "Yes, I can see you're going to be an excellent research assistant," she said, but she was laughing. "Maybe later we can theorize a game of MASH." She held up her own much more copious notes. "It's okay, I've got enough to lead us to a few other sources."

Luce stuffed the paper into her pocket right next to the crumpled master list she'd started of all her interactions with Daniel. She was beginning to turn into her father, who didn't like to be anywhere too far away from his paper shredder. She bent down to look for a recycling bin and spotted a pair of legs walking down the aisle toward them.

The gait was as familiar as her own. She sat back up—or attempted to sit back up—and smacked her head on the underside of the computer table.

"Ow," she moaned, rubbing the spot where she'd hit her head in the library fire.

Daniel stood still a few feet away. His expression said that the last thing in the world he'd wanted to do right now was run into her. At least he'd shown up after the computer had logged them off. He didn't need to think she was stalking him any more actively than he already did.

But Daniel seemed to be looking through her; his violet-gray eyes were fixed over her shoulder, on something—or someone else.

Penn tapped Luce on the shoulder, then jerked her thumb toward the person standing behind her. Cam was leaning over Luce's chair and grinning at her. A bolt of lightning outside sent Luce practically jumping into Penn's arms.

"Just a storm," Cam said, cocking his head. "It'll blow over soon. Shame, because you look pretty cute when you're scared."

Cam reached forward. He started at her shoulder, then traced the edge of her arm with his fingers all the way down to her hand. Her eyes fluttered, it felt so good, and when she opened them, there was a small ruby velvet box in her hand. Cam flipped it open, just for a second, and Luce saw a flash of gold.

"Open it later," he said. "When you're alone."

"Cam—"

"I went by your room."

"Can we—" Luce looked over at Penn, who was blatantly staring at them with a front-row moviegoer's captivation.

Finally snapping out of her trance, Penn waved her hands. "You want me to leave. I get it."

"No, stay," Cam said, sounding sweeter than Luce expected. He turned to Luce. "I'll go. But later—you promise?"

"Sure." She felt herself blush.

Cam took her hand and pushed it and the box down inside the front left pocket of her jeans. It was a tight fit, and it made her shiver to feel his fingers spread out on her hips. Then he winked and turned on his heel.

Before she'd even had a chance to catch her breath, he'd doubled back. "One last thing," he said, gliding his arm behind her head and stepping close to her.

Her head tilted back and his tilted forward, and his mouth was on hers. His lips were as plush as they'd seemed all the times Luce had stared at them.

It wasn't deep, just a peck, but Luce felt like it was much more. She couldn't breathe for the shock and the thrill and the public viewing potential of this very long, very unexpected—

"What the—!"

Cam's head had spun away, and then he was hunched over, clutching his jaw.

Daniel was standing behind him, rubbing his wrist. "Keep your hands off her."

"Didn't hear you," Cam said, drawing himself up slowly.

Oh. My. God. They were fighting. In the library. Over her.

Then, in one clean movement, Cam lunged toward Luce. She screamed as his arms began to close around her.

But Daniel's hands were quicker. He swatted Cam away hard, and shoved him against the computer table. Cam grunted as Daniel grabbed a fistful of his hair and pinned his head down flat.

"I said keep your filthy hands off her, you evil piece of shit."

Penn squealed, picked up her pencil bag, and tiptoed over to the wall. Luce watched as she tossed her dingy yellow pencil bag once, twice, three times in the air. The fourth time, it went high enough to nail the small black camera screwed into the wall. The hit sent the camera's lens swerving far to the left, toward a very still stack of nonfiction books.

By then, Cam had thrown Daniel off and they were circling each other, their feet squeaking on the polished floor.

Daniel started ducking before Luce even realized Cam was winding up. But Daniel still didn't duck quickly enough. Cam landed what looked like a knockout punch just below Daniel's eye. Daniel wheeled back from the force of it, jostling Luce and Penn against the computer table. He turned and muttered a woozy apology before careening back around.

"Oh my God, stop!" Luce cried, just before he leaped at Cam's head.

Daniel tackled Cam, throwing a messy flurry of punches at his shoulders and the sides of his face.

"That feels good," Cam grunted, popping his neck from side to side like a boxer. Still hanging on, Daniel moved his hands around Cam's neck. And squeezed.

Cam responded by throwing Daniel back against a tall shelf of books. The impact boomed out into the library, louder than the thunder outside.

Daniel grunted and let go. He dropped to the floor with a thud.

"What else you got, Grigori?"

Luce reeled, thinking he might not get up. But Daniel pulled himself up quickly.

"I'll show you," he hissed. "Outside." He stepped toward Luce, then away. "You stay here."

Then both boys thumped out of the library, through the back exit Luce had used the night of the fire. She and Penn stood frozen to their spots. They stared at each other, jaws dropped.

"Come on," Penn said, dragging Luce over to a window that looked out on the commons. They pressed their faces to the glass, rubbing away the fog of their breath.

The rain was coming down in sheets. The field outside was dark, except for the light that came through the library windows. It was so muddy and slick, it was hard to see anything at all.

Then two figures sprinted out to the center of the commons. Both of them were soaked instantly. They argued for a moment, then started circling each other. Their fists were raised again.

Luce gripped the windowsill and watched as Cam made the first move, running at Daniel and slamming into him with his shoulder. Then a quick spinning kick to his ribs.

Daniel keeled over, clutching his side. *Get up.* Luce willed him to move. She felt like she had been kicked herself. Every time Cam went at Daniel, she felt it in her bones.

She couldn't stand to watch.

"Daniel stumbled for a second there," Penn announced after Luce had turned away. "But he shot right up and totally clocked Cam in the face. *Nice!*"

"You're enjoying this?" Luce asked, horrified.

"My dad and I used to watch UFC," Penn said. "Looks like both of these guys have had some serious mixed martial art training. Perfect cross, Daniel!" She groaned. "Aw, man."

"What?" Luce peered out again. "Is he hurt?"

"Relax," Penn said. "Someone's coming to break up the fight. Just when Daniel was bouncing back."

Penn was right. It looked like Mr. Cole jogging across the campus. When he got to where the guys were fighting, he stood still and watched them for a moment, almost hypnotized by the way they were going at it.

"Do something," Luce whispered, feeling sick.

Finally, Mr. Cole grabbed each boy by the scruff of his neck. The three of them struggled for a moment until finally Daniel pulled away. He shook out his right hand, then paced in a circle and spat a few times into the mud.

"Very attractive, Daniel," Luce said sarcastically. Except it was.

Now for a talking-to from Mr. Cole. He waved his hands madly at them and they stood with heads hung. Cam was first to be dismissed. He jogged off the field toward the dorm and disappeared.

Mr. Cole placed a hand on Daniel's shoulder. Luce was dying to know what they were talking about, whether Daniel would be punished. She wanted to go to him, but Penn blocked her.

"All that over a piece of jewelry. What did Cam give you, anyway?"

Mr. Cole walked off and Daniel was alone, standing in the light from an overhead lamppost, looking up at the rain.

"I don't know," Luce told Penn, leaving the window. "Whatever it is, I don't want it. Especially not after this." She walked back to the computer table and pulled the box from her pocket.

"If you won't, I will," Penn said. She cracked the box open, then looked up at Luce, confused.

The flash of gold they'd seen had not been jewelry. There were only two things inside the box: another one of Cam's green guitar picks, and a golden slip of paper.

Meet me tomorrow after class. I'll be waiting at the gates.
—C

FIFTEEN

THE LIONS' DEN

It had been a long time since Luce had taken a good look in the mirror. She never used to mind her reflection— her clear hazel eyes; small, straight teeth; thick eye- lashes; and tumble of dense black hair. That was then. Before last summer.

After her mom had chopped off all her hair, Luce had started avoiding mirrors. It wasn't just because of her short cut; Luce didn't think she liked who she *was* any- more, so she didn't want to see any evidence. She started looking down at her hands when she washed them in the bathroom. She kept her head forward when walking past tinted windows and eschewed face powder in mirrored compacts.

But twenty minutes before she was supposed to meet Cam, Luce stood before the mirror in the empty girls' bathroom in Augustine. She guessed she looked all right. Her hair was finally growing out, and the weight was starting to loosen some of her curls. She checked her teeth, then squared her shoulders and stared into the mirror as if she were looking Cam in the eye. She had to tell him something, something important, and she wanted to make sure she could muster a look that demanded he take her seriously.

He hadn't been in class today. Neither had Daniel, so Luce assumed Mr. Cole had put them both on some sort of probation. Either that or they were nursing their wounds. But Luce had no doubt Cam would be waiting for her today.

She didn't want to see him. Not at all. Thinking about his fists slamming into Daniel made her stomach lurch. But it was her fault they'd fought in the first place. She'd led Cam on—and whether she'd done it because she'd been confused or flattered or the tiniest bit interested didn't matter anymore. What mattered was that she be direct with him today: There was nothing between them.

She took a deep breath, tugged her shirt down on her hips, and pushed open the bathroom door.

Approaching the gates, she couldn't see him. But then, it was hard to see anything beyond the construction zone in the parking lot. Luce hadn't been back to the school entrance since they'd started the renovations there, and she was surprised at how complicated it was to maneuver across the ripped-up parking lot. She sidestepped potholes and tried to duck under the radar of the construction crew, waving off the asphalt fumes that never seemed to dissipate.

There was no sign of Cam. For a second, she felt foolish, almost like she'd fallen for some kind of prank. The high metal gates were blistered with red rust. Luce looked through them at the dense grove of ancient elm trees across the road. She cracked her knuckles, thinking back to the time when Daniel had told her he hated it when she did that. But he wasn't here to see her do it; no one was. Then she noticed a folded piece of paper with her name on it. It was staked to the thick, gray-trunked magnolia tree next to the broken call box.

I'm saving you from Social tonight. While the rest of our fellow students stage a Civil War reenactment—sad but true—you and I will paint the town red. A black sedan with a gold license plate will bring you to me. Thought we could both use a dose of fresh air.
—C

Luce coughed from the fumes. Fresh air was one thing, but a black sedan picking her up from campus? To bring her to him, like he was some sort of monarch who could just arrange on a whim for women to be fetched? Where was he, anyway?

None of this was part of her plan. She'd agreed to meet Cam only to tell him that he was being too forward and she really couldn't see herself getting involved with him. Because—although she'd never tell him—every time his fist had struck Daniel the night before, something inside her had flinched and started to boil. Clearly, she needed to nip this little thing with Cam in the bud. She had the gold serpent necklace in her pocket. It was time to give it back.

Except now she felt stupid for assuming that Cam just wanted to talk. Of course he'd have something more up his sleeve. He was that kind of guy.

The sound of car wheels slowing made Luce turn her head. A black sedan rolled to a stop in front of the gates. The tinted driver's-side window rolled down and a hairy hand came out and picked up the receiver from the call box outside the gates. After a moment, the receiver was slammed back into its cradle and the driver just leaned on his horn.

At last, the great groaning metal gates parted and the car pulled forward, stopping in front of her. The doors softly unlocked. Was she really going to get into that car and drive who-knew-where to meet him?

The last time she'd stood at these gates had been to say goodbye to her parents. Missing them before they'd even pulled away, she'd waved from this very spot, next to the broken call box inside the gates—and, she remembered, she'd noticed one of the more high-tech security cameras. The kind with a motion detector, zooming in on her every move. Cam couldn't have picked a worse spot for the car to pick her up.

All of a sudden, she saw visions of a basement solitary confinement cell. Damp cement walls and cockroaches running up her legs. No real light. The rumors were still spreading through campus about that couple, Jules and Phillip, who hadn't been seen since they'd sneaked out. Did Cam think Luce wanted to see him so badly she'd risk just walking off campus in plain view of the reds?

The car was still humming on the driveway in front of her. After a moment, the driver—a sunglasses-sporting man with a thick neck and thinning hair—extended his hand. In it was a small white envelope. Luce hesitated a second before stepping forward to take it from his fingers.

Cam's stationery. A heavy, creamy ivory card with his name letterpressed in decadent gold at the bottom left-hand corner.

Should have mentioned before, the red's been duct. See for yourself. I took care of it, like I'll take care of you. See you soon, I hope.

Duct? Did he mean—? She dared a glance at the red. He did. A sharply cut black circle of duct tape had been placed cleanly over the lens of the camera. Luce didn't know how these things worked or how long it would take the faculty to find out, but in a weird way, she was relieved that Cam had thought to take care of it. She couldn't imagine Daniel thinking so far ahead.

Both Callie and her parents were expecting phone calls this evening. Luce had read Callie's ten-page letter three times, and she had all the funny details memorized from her friend's weekend trips to Nantucket, but she still wouldn't have known how to answer any of Callie's questions about her life at Sword & Cross. If she turned around and went inside to pick up the phone, she didn't know how she'd begin to catch Callie or her parents up on the strange, dark twist the past few days had taken. Easier not to tell them at all, or not until she'd wrapped things up one way or another.

She slid into the sedan's plush beige leather backseat and buckled up. The driver put the car in gear without a word.

"Where are we going?" she asked him.

"Little backwater place down the river. Mr. Briel likes the local color. Just sit back and relax, honey. You'll see."

Mr. Briel? Who was this guy? Luce never liked being told to relax, especially when it felt like a warning not to ask any more questions. Nonetheless, she crossed her arms over her chest, looked out the window, and tried to forget the driver's tone when he called her "honey."

Through the tinted windows, the trees outside and the gray paved road beneath them all looked brown. At the turning whose westward fork led to Thunderbolt, the black sedan turned east. They were following the river toward the shore. Every now and then, when their path and the river's converged, Luce could see the brackish brown water twisting beside them. Twenty minutes later, the car slowed to a stop in front of a beat-up riverside bar.

It was made of gray, rotting wood, and a swollen, waterlogged sign over the front door read STYX in jagged red hand-painted letters. A strand of plastic pennants advertising beer had been stapled to the wood beam underneath the tin roof, a mediocre attempt at festivity. Luce studied the images silk-screened onto the plastic triangles—palm trees and tanned, bikini-clad girls with beer bottles at their grinning lips—and wondered when the last time had been when a real live girl had actually set foot in this place.

Two older punk rock guys sat smoking on a bench facing the water. Tired Mohawks drooped over their middle-aged foreheads, and their leather jackets had the ugly, dirty look of something they'd been wearing since punk was new. The blank expressions on their tan, slack faces made the whole scene feel even more desolate.

The swamp edging the two-lane highway had begun to overwhelm the asphalt, and the road just sort of petered out into swamp grass and mud. Luce had never been out this far in the river marshes.

As she sat, unsure what she'd do once she left the car, or whether that was even a good idea, the front door of Styx banged open and Cam sauntered out. He leaned coolly against the screen door, one leg crossed over the other. She knew he couldn't see her through the tinted window of the car, but he raised his hand like he could and beckoned her toward him.

"Here goes nothing," Luce muttered before thanking the driver. She opened the door and was greeted by a blast of salty wind as she climbed the three steps to the bar's wooden porch.

Cam's shaggy hair was loose around his face and he had a calm look in his green eyes. One sleeve of his black T-shirt was pushed up over his shoulder, and Luce could see the smooth cut of his bicep. She fingered the gold chain in her pocket. *Remember why you're here.*

Cam's face showed no sign of the fight the night before, which made her wonder, immediately, whether Daniel's did.

Cam gave her an inquisitive look, running his tongue along his bottom lip. "I was just calculating how many consolation drinks I'd need if you stood me up today," he said, opening his arms for a hug. Luce stepped into them. Cam was a very hard person to say no to, even when she wasn't totally sure what he was asking.

"I wouldn't stand you up," she said, then immediately felt guilty, knowing that her words came from a sense of duty, not the romance Cam would have preferred. She was there only because she was going to tell him she didn't want to be involved with him. "So what is this place? And since when do you have a car service?"

"Stick with me, kid," he said, seeming to take her questions as compliments, as if she liked being whisked off to bars that smelled like the inside of a sink drain.

She was so bad at this kind of thing. Callie always said Luce was incapable of brutal honesty and that was why she got herself stuck in so many crappy situations with guys whom she should have just told no. Luce was trembling. She had to get this off her chest. She fished in her pocket and pulled out the pendant. "Cam."

"Oh good, you brought it." He took the necklace from her hands and spun her around. "Let me help you put it on."

"No, wait—"

"There," he said. "It really suits you. Take a look." He steered her along the creaking wooden floorboards to the window of the bar, where a number of bands had posted signs for shows. THE OLD BABIES. DRIPPING WITH HATE. HOUSE CRACKERS. Luce would rather have studied any of them than gaze at her reflection. "See?"

She couldn't really make out her features in the mud-flecked windowpane, but the gold pendant gleamed on her warm skin. She pressed her hand to it. It *was* lovely. And so distinctive, with its tiny hand-sculpted serpent snaking up the middle. It wasn't like anything you'd see at the boardwalk markets, where locals peddled over-priced crafts for tourists, state of Georgia souvenirs made in the Philippines. Behind her reflection in the window, the sky was a rich orange-Popsicle color, broken up by thin lines of pink cloud.

"About last night . . . ," Cam started to say. She could vaguely see his rosy lips moving in the glass over her shoulder.

"I wanted to talk to you about last night, too," Luce said, standing at his side. She could see the very tips of the sunburst tattoo on the back of his neck.

"Come inside," he said, guiding her back to the half-unhinged screen door. "We can talk in there."

The interior of the bar was wood-paneled, with a few dim orange lamps providing the only light. All sizes and shapes of antlers were mounted on the wall, and a taxidermied cheetah was poised over the bar, looking ready to lunge at any moment. A faded composite picture with the words PULASKI COUNTY MOOSE CLUB OFFICERS 1964–65 was the only other decoration on the wall, showcasing a hundred oval faces, smiling modestly above pastel bow ties. The jukebox was playing Ziggy Stardust, and an older guy with a shaved head and leather pants was humming, dancing alone in the middle of a small raised stage. Besides Luce and Cam, he was the only other person in the place.

Cam pointed to two stools. The worn green leather cushions had split down the middle, the beige foam bursting out like massive pieces of popcorn. There was already a half-empty glass at the seat Cam claimed. The drink in it was light brown and watered down with ice, beaded with sweat.

"What's that?" Luce asked.

"Georgia moonshine," he said, taking a gulp. "I don't recommend it to start." When she squinted at him, he said, "I've been here all day."

"Charming," Luce said, fingering the gold necklace. "What are you, seventy? Sitting in a bar by yourself all day?"

He didn't seem obviously drunk, but she didn't like the idea of coming all the way out here to break things off with him, only to have him be too trashed to understand it. She was also starting to wonder how she'd get back to school. She didn't even know where this place was.

"Ouch." Cam rubbed his heart. "The beauty of being suspended from class, Luce, is that no one *misses* you during class. I thought I deserved a little recovery time." He cocked his head. "What's really bothering you? Is it this place? Or the fight last night? Or the fact that we're getting *no service*?" He raised his voice to shout the last words, loud enough to cause a huge, burly bartender to swing in from the kitchen door behind the bar. The barman had long, layered hair with bangs, and tattoos that looked like braided human hair running up and down his arms. He was all muscle and must have weighed three hundred pounds.

Cam turned to her and smiled. "What's your poison?"

"I don't care," Luce said. "I don't really have my own poison."

"You were drinking champagne at my party," Cam said. "See who's paying attention?" He nudged her with his shoulder. "Your finest champagne over here," he told the bartender, who threw back his head and let out a snide hacking laugh.

Making no attempt to card her or even to glance at her long enough to guess at her age, the bartender bent down to a small refrigerator with a sliding glass door. The bottles clinked as he dug and dug. After what seemed like a long time, he reemerged with a tiny bottle of Freixenet. It looked like it had something orange growing around its base.

"I accept no responsibility for this," he said, handing it over.

Cam popped the cork and raised his eyebrows at

Luce. He poured the Freixenet ceremoniously into a wineglass.

"I wanted to apologize," he said. "I know I've been coming on a little strong. And last night, what happened with Daniel, I don't feel good about that." He waited for Luce to nod before he went on. "Instead of getting mad, I should have just listened to you. You're the one I care about, not him."

Luce watched the bubbles rise in her wine, thinking that if she were to be honest, she'd say it was Daniel she cared about, not Cam. She *had* to tell Cam. If he already regretted not having listened to her last night, maybe now he'd start to. She raised her glass to take a sip before she started in.

"Oh, wait." Cam put a hand on her arm. "You can't drink until we've toasted something." He raised his glass and held her eyes. "What should it be? You pick."

The screen door slammed and the guys who had been smoking on the porch came back in. The taller one, with oily black hair, a snub nose, and very dirty fingernails, took one look at Luce and started toward them.

"What are we celebrating?" He leered at her, nudging her raised glass with his tumbler. He leaned close, and she could feel the flesh of his hip pressing into hers through his flannel shirt. "Baby's first night out? What time's curfew?"

"We're celebrating you taking your ass back outside

right now," Cam said as pleasantly as if he'd just announced it was Luce's birthday. He fixed his green eyes on the man, who bared his small, pointed teeth and mouthful of gums.

"Outside, huh? Only if I take her with me."

He grabbed for Luce's hand. After the way the fight with Daniel had broken out, Luce expected Cam would need little excuse to fly off the handle again. Especially if he really had been drinking here all day. But Cam stayed remarkably cool.

All he did was swat the guy's hand away with the speed, grace, and brutal force of a lion swatting a mouse.

Cam watched the guy stumble back several steps. Cam shook out his hand with a bored look on his face, then stroked Luce's wrist where the guy had tried to grab it. "Sorry about that. You were saying, about last night?"

"I was saying . . ." Luce felt the blood drain from her face. Directly over Cam's head, an enormous piece of pitch-dark had yawned open, stretching forth and unfolding from itself until it had become the largest, blackest shadow she had ever seen. An arctic gush of air blasted from its core, and Luce felt the shadow's frost even on Cam's fingers, still tracing her skin.

"Oh. My. God," she whispered.

There was a crash of glass as the guy smashed his tumbler down on Cam's head.

Slowly, Cam stood from his chair and shook some of

the shards of glass from his hair. He turned to face the man, who was easily twice his age and several inches taller.

Luce cowered on her bar stool, rearing away from what she sensed was about to happen between Cam and this other guy. And what she feared *could* happen with the sprawling, dead-of-night black shadow overhead.

"Break it up," the huge bartender said flatly, not even bothering to look up from his *Fight* magazine.

Immediately, the guy started swinging blindly at Cam, who took the senseless punches as if they were smacks from a child.

Luce wasn't the only one stunned by Cam's composure: The leather-pants-wearing dancer was cowering against the jukebox. And after the oily-haired guy had socked Cam a few times, even he stepped back and hung there, confused.

Meanwhile, the shadow was pooling against the ceiling, dark tendrils growing like weeds and dropping closer and closer to their heads. Luce winced and ducked just as Cam fended off one last punch from the seedy guy.

And then decided to fight back.

It was just a simple flick of his fingers, as if Cam were brushing away a dead leaf. One minute, the guy was all up in Cam's face, but when Cam's fingers connected with his opponent's chest, the dude went flying— knocked off his feet and into the air, discarded beer bottles scattering in his wake, until his back slammed into the opposite wall near the jukebox.

He rubbed his head and, moaning, began to pull himself into a crouch.

"How did you do that?" Luce's eyes were wide.

Cam ignored her, turned toward the guy's shorter, stockier friend, and said, "You next?"

The second guy raised his palms. "Not my fight, man," he said, shrinking away.

Cam shrugged, stepped toward the first guy, and lifted him off the floor by the back of his T-shirt. His limbs dangled helplessly in the air, like a puppet's. Then, with an easy toss of his wrist, Cam threw the guy against the wall. He almost seemed to stick there while Cam cut loose, pounding the guy and saying again and again, "I *said* go outside!"

"Enough!" Luce shouted, but neither one of them heard her or cared. Luce felt sick. She wanted to tear her eyes away from the bloody nose and gums of the guy pinned against the wall, from Cam's almost superhuman strength. She wanted to tell him to forget it, that she'd find her own way back to school. She wanted, most of all, to get away from the gruesome shadow now coating the ceiling and dripping down the walls. She grabbed her bag and ran out into the night—

And right into someone's arms.

"Are you okay?"

It was Daniel.

"How did you find me here?" she asked, unabashedly burying her face in his shoulder. Tears she didn't want to deal with were welling up inside her.

"Come on," he said. "Let's get you out of here."

Without looking back, she slipped her hand into his. Warmth spread up her arm and through her body. And then the tears began to flow. It wasn't fair to feel so safe when the shadows were still so close.

Even Daniel seemed on edge. He was dragging her across the lot so quickly, she nearly had to sprint to keep up.

She didn't want to glance back when she sensed the shadows spilling out of the door of the bar and brewing in the air. But then, she didn't have to. They flowed in a steady stream over her head, sucking up all light in their path. It was as if the whole world were being torn to pieces right before her eyes. A rotting sulfur stench stuck in her nose, worse than anything she knew.

Daniel glanced up, too, and scowled, only he looked like he was merely trying to remember where he'd parked. But then the strangest thing happened. The shadows flinched backward, boiled away in black splatters that pooled and scattered.

Luce narrowed her eyes in disbelief. How had Daniel done that? *He* hadn't done that, had he?

"What?" Daniel asked, distracted. He unlocked the

passenger-side door of a white Taurus station wagon. "Something wrong?"

"We do not have time for me to list all of the many, many things that are wrong," Luce said, sinking into the car seat. "Look." She pointed toward the entrance to the bar. The screen door had just swung open on Cam. He must have knocked out the other guy, but he didn't look like he was done fighting. His fists were clenched.

Daniel smirked and shook his head. Luce was fruitlessly stabbing her seat belt again and again at the buckle until he reached over and pushed her hands away. She held her breath as his fingers grazed her stomach. "There's a trick," he whispered, fitting the clasp into the base.

He started the car, then backed out slowly, taking his time as they drove past the door to the bar. Luce couldn't think of a single thing to say to Cam, but it felt perfect when Daniel rolled down the window and simply said, "Good night, Cam."

"Luce," Cam said, walking toward the car. "Don't do this. Don't leave with him. It will end badly." She couldn't look at his eyes, which she knew were pleading for her to come back. "I'm *sorry*."

Daniel ignored Cam entirely and just drove. The swamp looked cloudy in the twilight, and the woods in front of them looked even cloudier.

"You still haven't told me how you found me here," Luce said. "Or how you knew I went to meet Cam. Or where you got this car."

"It's Miss Sophia's," Daniel explained, turning on the brights as the trees grew together overhead and threw the road into dense shadow.

"Miss Sophia let you borrow her car?"

"After years living on skid row in L.A.," he said, shrugging, "you might say I've got a magic touch when it comes to 'borrowing' cars."

"You *stole* Miss Sophia's car?" Luce scoffed, wondering how the librarian would note this development in her files.

"We'll bring it back," Daniel said. "Besides, she was pretty preoccupied by tonight's Civil War reenactment. Something tells me she won't even notice it's gone."

It was only then that Luce realized what Daniel was wearing. She took in the blue Union soldier's uniform with its ridiculous brown leather strap slung diagonally over his chest. She'd been so terrified of the shadows, of Cam, of the whole creepy scene, that she hadn't even paused to fully take Daniel in.

"Don't you laugh," Daniel said, trying not to laugh himself. "You got out of possibly the worst Social of the year tonight."

Luce couldn't help herself: She reached forward and flicked one of Daniel's buttons. "Shame," she said, putting on a southern drawl. "I just had my belle-of-the-ball gown pressed."

Daniel's lips crept up in a smile, but then he sighed. "Luce. What you did tonight—things could have gotten really bad. Do you know that?"

Luce stared out at the road, annoyed that the mood had shifted so suddenly back to grim. A hoot owl stared back from a tree.

"I didn't mean to come *here*," she said, which felt true. It was almost like Cam had tricked her. "I wish I hadn't," she added quietly, wondering where the shadow was now.

Daniel banged his fist on the steering wheel, making her jump. He was gritting his teeth, and Luce hated that she was the one who'd made him look so angry.

"I just can't believe you're involved with him," he said.

"I'm not," she insisted. "The only reason I showed up was to tell him . . ." It was pointless. Involved with Cam! If Daniel only knew that she and Penn spent most of their free time researching *his* family . . . well, he would probably be equally annoyed.

"You don't have to explain," Daniel said, waving her off. "It's my fault, anyway."

"Your fault?"

By then Daniel had turned off the road and brought the car to a stop at the end of a sandy path. He switched the headlights off and they stared out at the ocean. The dusky sky was a deep plum shade, and the crests of the waves looked almost silver, sparkling. The beach grass whipped in the wind, making a high, desolate whistling sound. A flock of ragged seagulls sat in a line along the boardwalk railing, grooming their feathers.

"Are we lost?" she asked.

Daniel ignored her. He got out of the car and shut the door, started walking toward the water. Luce waited ten agonizing seconds, watching his silhouette grow smaller in the purple twilight, before she hopped out of the car to follow him.

The wind whipped her hair against her face. Waves beat the shore, tugging lines of shells and seaweed back in their undertow. The air was cooler by the water. Everything had a fiercely briny scent.

"What's going on, Daniel?" she said, jogging along the dune. She felt heavier walking in the sand. "Where are we? And what do you mean, it's your fault?"

He turned to her. He looked so defeated, his costume uniform all bunched up, his gray eyes drooping. The roar of the waves almost overpowered his voice.

"I just need some time to think."

Luce felt a lump rising in her throat all over again. She'd finally stopped crying, but Daniel was making this all so hard. "Why rescue me, then? Why come all the way out here to pick me up, then yell at me, then ignore me?" She wiped her eyes on the hem of her black T-shirt, and the sea salt on her fingers made them sting. "Not that that's very different from the way you treat me most of the time, but—"

Daniel spun and smacked both his hands to his forehead. "You don't get it, Luce." He shook his head. "That's the thing—you never do."

There was nothing mean about his voice. In fact, it was almost *too* nice. Like she was too dim to grasp whatever was so obvious to him. Which made her absolutely furious.

"I don't get it?" she asked. "*I* don't get it? Let me tell you something about what I get. You think you're so smart? I spent three years on a full academic scholarship at the best college-prep school in the country. And when they kicked me out, I had to petition—petition!—to keep them from wiping out my four-point-oh transcript."

Daniel moved away, but Luce pursued him, taking a step forward for every wide-eyed step he took back. Probably freaking him out, but so what? He'd been asking for it every time he condescended to her.

"I know Latin and French, and in middle school, I won the science fair three years in a row."

She had backed him up against the railing of the boardwalk and was trying to restrain herself from poking him in the chest with her finger. She wasn't finished. "I also do the Sunday crossword puzzle, sometimes in under an hour. I have an unerringly good sense of direction . . . though not always when it comes to guys."

She swallowed and took a moment to catch her breath.

"And someday, I'm going to be a psychiatrist who actually listens to her patients and helps people. Okay? So *don't* keep talking to me like I'm stupid and *don't* tell me I don't understand just because *I* can't decode *your* erratic, flaky, hot-one-minute-cold-the-next, frankly"— she looked up at him, letting out her breath—"really hurtful behavior." She brushed a tear away, angry with herself for getting so worked up.

"Shut up," Daniel said, but he said it softly and so tenderly that Luce surprised both of them by obeying.

"I don't think you're stupid." He closed his eyes. "I think you're the smartest person I know. And the kindest. And"—he swallowed, opening his eyes to look directly at her—"the most beautiful."

"Excuse me?"

He looked out at the ocean. "I'm just . . . so tired of this," he said. He did sound exhausted.

"Of what?"

He looked over at her, with the saddest expression on his face, as if he had lost something precious. This was the Daniel she knew, though she couldn't explain how or from where. This was the Daniel she . . . loved.

"You can show me," she whispered.

He shook his head. But his lips were still so close to hers. And the look in his eyes was so alluring. It was almost as if he wanted *her* to show him first.

Her body quaked with nerves as she stood on her tiptoes and leaned toward him. She put her hand on his cheek and he blinked, but he didn't move. She moved slowly, so slowly, as if she were scared to startle him, every second feeling petrified herself. And then, when they were close enough that her eyes were almost crossing, she closed them and pressed her lips against his.

The softest, featherlight touch of their lips was all that connected them, but a fire Luce had never felt before coursed through her, and she knew she needed more of—all of—Daniel. It would be too much to ask of him to need her the same way, to fold her in his arms like he'd done so many times in her dreams, to return her wishful kiss with one more powerful.

But he did.

His muscled arms circled her waist. He drew her to him, and she could feel the clean line of their two bodies connecting—legs tangled up in legs, hips pressed into hips, chests heaving in time with each other. Daniel backed her up against the boardwalk's railing, pinning her closer to him until she couldn't move, until he had her exactly where she wanted to be. All of this without once breaking the passionate lock of their lips.

Then he started to really kiss her, softly at first,

making subtle, lovely pecking noises in her ear. Then long and sweet and tenderly, along her jawline and down her neck, making her moan and tilt back her head. He tugged lightly on her hair and she opened her eyes to glimpse, for a second, the first stars coming out in the night sky. She felt closer to Heaven than she ever had before.

At last, Daniel returned to her lips, kissing her with such intensity—sucking her bottom lip, then edging his soft tongue just past her teeth. She opened her mouth wider, desperate to let more of him in, finally unafraid to show how much she yearned for him. To match the force of his kisses with her own.

She had sand in her mouth and between her toes, the briny wind raising goose bumps on her skin, and the sweetest, spellbound feeling spilling from her heart.

She could, at that moment, have died for him.

He pulled away and stared down at her, as if he wanted her to say something. She smiled up at him and pecked him softly on the lips, letting hers linger on his. She knew no words, no better way to communicate what she was feeling, what she wanted.

"You're still here," he whispered.

"They couldn't drag me away." She laughed.

Daniel took a step back, and with a dark look at her, his smile was gone. He began pacing in front of her, rubbing his forehead with his hand.

"What's wrong?" she asked lightly, pulling his sleeve so he'd come back in for another kiss. He ran his fingers over her face, through her hair, around her neck. Like he was making sure she wasn't a dream.

Was this her first real kiss? She didn't think she was supposed to count Trevor, so technically it was. And everything felt so right, like she had been destined for Daniel, and he for her. He smelled . . . beautiful. His mouth tasted sweet and rich. He was tall and strong and . . .

Slipping from her embrace.

"Where are you going?" she asked.

His knees bent and he sank a few inches, leaning up against the wooden railing and looking at the sky. He looked like he was in pain.

"You said nothing could drag you away," he said in a hushed voice. "But they will. Maybe they're just running late."

"They? Who?" Luce asked, looking around at the deserted beach. "Cam? I think we lost him."

"No." Daniel started walking away down the boardwalk. He was shivering. "It's impossible."

"Daniel."

"It will come," he whispered.

"You're scaring me." Luce followed behind, trying to keep up. Because suddenly, even though she didn't want to, she had a feeling she knew what he meant. Not Cam, but something else, some other threat.

Luce's mind felt foggy. His words knocked on her

brain, ringing eerily true, but the reasoning behind them eluded her. Like the wisp of a dream she couldn't remember the whole of.

"Talk to me," she said. "Tell me what's going on."

He turned, his face pale as the bloom of a peony, his arms held out in surrender. "I don't know how to stop it," he whispered. "I don't know what to do."

SIXTEEN

HANGING IN THE BALANCE

Luce stood at the crossroads between the cemetery on the north side of campus and the path to the lake on the south. It was early evening and the construction workers had gone home. Light sifted down through the branches of the oaks behind the gym, casting dappled shadows on the lawn that led to the lake. Tempting Luce toward it. She wasn't sure which way to go. She held two letters in her hands.

The first, from Cam, was the apology she had

expected, and a plea for her to meet him after school to talk it out. The second, from Daniel, said nothing other than "Meet me at the lake." She couldn't wait to. Her lips still tingled from their kiss last night. She couldn't get the thought of his fingers in her hair, or his lips on her neck, out of her mind.

Other parts of the night were hazier, like what had happened after she sat down next to Daniel on the beach. Compared to the way his hands had ravished her body not ten minutes earlier, Daniel had seemed almost terrified to touch her.

Nothing could shake him from his daze. He kept murmuring the same thing over and over—"Something must have happened. Something changed"—and staring at her with pain in his eyes, as if she held the answer, as if she had any idea what his words meant. At last, she'd fallen asleep leaning on his shoulder, looking out at the ethereal sea.

When she woke up hours later, he was carrying her up the stairs back to her dorm room. She was startled to realize she'd slept through the whole ride back to school—and even more startled by the strange glow in the hallway. It was back. Daniel's light. Which she didn't even know if he could see.

Everything around them was bathed in that soft violet light. The white bumper-stickered doorways of the other students had taken on a neon hue. The dull linoleum tiles seemed to glow. The windowpane looking out on the cemetery cast a violet shine on the first hint of dull yellow morning light outside. All of it directly under the gaze of the reds.

"We're so busted," she whispered, nervous and still half asleep.

"I'm not worried about the reds," Daniel said calmly, following her eyes to the cameras. At first his words were soothing, but then she started to wonder about something uneasy in his tone: If Daniel wasn't worried about the reds, he was worried about something else.

When he laid her down in her bed, he kissed her lightly on the forehead, then took a deep breath. "Don't disappear on me," he said.

"No chance of that."

"I'm serious." He closed his eyes for a long time. "Get some rest now—but find me in the morning before class. I want to talk to you. Promise?"

She squeezed his hand to pull him to her for one last kiss. She held his face between her palms and melted into him. Every time her eyes flickered open, his were watching her. And she loved it.

At last, he backed away, and stood in the doorway gazing at her, his eyes still doing as much to make her heart race as his lips had done a moment before. When he slinked back into the hallway and closed the door behind him, Luce drifted off into the deepest sleep.

She'd slept through her morning classes and had awoken in the early afternoon feeling reborn and alive. Not caring at all that she had no excuse for missing school. Only worried that she'd slept through meeting Daniel. She would find him as soon as she could, and he would understand.

Around two o'clock, when it finally occurred to her to eat something or maybe pop in on Miss Sophia's religion class, she grudgingly crawled out of bed. That was when she saw the two envelopes that had been slipped underneath her door, which set her back severely in her goal of leaving her room.

She had to tell Cam off first. If she went to the lake before the cemetery, she knew she'd never be able to make herself leave Daniel. If she went first to the cemetery, her desire to see Daniel again would make her bold enough to say to Cam the things she'd been too nervous to say before. Before everything had gotten so scary and out of control last night.

Pushing through her fears about seeing him, Luce started across the commons toward the cemetery. The early evening was warm, and the air was sticky with humidity. It was going to be one of those sweltering nights when the breeze from the distant sea never got strong enough to cool things down. There was no one out on campus, and the leaves on all the trees were still. Luce could have been the only thing at Sword & Cross that was actually on the move. Everyone else would be released from class, herded into the dining hall for dinner, and Penn—and possibly others—would be wondering about Luce by now.

Cam was leaning up against the lichen-speckled gates of the cemetery when she got there. His elbows rested on the carved vine-shaped iron posts, his shoulders hunched forward. He was kicking up a dandelion with the steel tip of his thick black boot. Luce couldn't remember seeing him look so internally consumed—most of the time Cam seemed to have a keen interest in the world around him.

But this time, he didn't even look up at her until she was directly in front of him. And when he did, his face was ashen. His hair was flat against his head and she was surprised to notice that he could have used a shave. His eyes rolled over her face, as if focusing on each of her features required effort. He looked wrecked, not beaten up from the fight, but simply as if he hadn't slept in a few days.

"You came." His voice was hoarse, but his words ended with a small smile.

Luce cracked her knuckles, thinking he wouldn't be smiling much longer. She nodded and held up his letter.

He reached for her hand, but she pulled her arm away, pretending she needed the hand to brush the hair from her eyes.

"I figured you'd be mad about last night," he said, pushing himself away from the gate. He took a few steps into the cemetery, then sat cross-legged on a short gray marble bench among the first row of graves. He wiped the dirt and brittle leaves away, then patted the empty spot next to him.

"Mad?" she said.

"That's generally why people storm out of bars."

She sat down facing him, cross-legged too. From up here, she could see the top branches of the enormous old oak down in the center of the graveyard, where she and Cam had had their afternoon picnic what seemed like a very long time ago.

"I don't know," Luce said. "More like baffled. Confused, maybe. Disappointed." She shuddered at the memory of that seedy guy's eyes when he grabbed her, the sick flurry of Cam's fists, the deep black roof of shadow . . . "Why did you take me there? You know what happened when Jules and Phillip snuck out."

"Jules and Phillip were morons whose every move was monitored by tracking wristbands. Of course they were going to get busted." Cam smiled darkly, but not at her. "We're nothing like them, Luce. Believe me. And besides, I wasn't trying to get in another fight." He rubbed his temples, and the skin around them bunched up, looking leathery and too thin. "I just couldn't stand the way that guy talked to you, touched you. You deserve to be handled with the utmost care." His green eyes widened. "I want to be the one to do it. The only one."

She tucked her hair behind her ears and took a deep breath. "Cam, you seem like a really great guy—"

"Oh no." He covered his face with his hand. "Not the let-him-down-easy speech. I hope you're not going to say we should be friends."

"You don't want to be my friend?"

"You know I want to be much more than your friend," he said, spitting out "friend" as if it were a dirty word. "It's Grigori, isn't it?"

She felt her stomach constrict. She guessed it wasn't too hard to figure it out, but she'd been so wrapped up in her own feelings, she'd barely had time to consider what Cam thought about the two of them.

"You don't really know either of us," Cam said, standing and stepping away, "but you're prepared to choose right now, huh?"

It was presumptuous of him to assume he was even still in the running. Especially after last night. That he could think there was some contest between him and Daniel.

Then Cam crouched before her on the bench. His face was different—pleading, earnest—as he cupped her hands in his.

Luce was surprised to see him so wound up. "I'm sorry," she said, pulling back. "It just happened."

"Exactly! It *just* happened. What was it, let me guess—last night he *looked* at you some new romantic way. Luce, you're rushing into a decision before you even know what's at stake. There could be . . . a *lot* at stake." He sighed at the confused look on her face. "I could make you happy."

"Daniel makes me happy."

"How can you say that? He won't even touch you."

Luce closed her eyes, remembering the tangle of their lips last night on the beach. Daniel's arms encircling her. The whole world had felt so right, so harmonious, so safe. But when she opened her eyes now, Daniel was nowhere to be seen.

It was only Cam.

She cleared her throat. "Yes, he will. He does."

Her cheeks felt warm. Luce pressed a cool hand to them, but Cam didn't notice. His hands curled into fists.

"Elaborate."

"The way Daniel kisses me is none of your business." She bit her lip, furious. He was mocking her.

Cam chuckled. "Oh? I can do just as good as Grigori," he said, picking up her hand and kissing the back of it before abruptly letting it drop back at her side.

"It was nothing like that," Luce said, turning away.

"How about this, then?" His lips grazed her cheek before she could shrug him off.

"Wrong."

Cam licked his lips. "You're saying Daniel Grigori actually *kissed* you the way you deserve to be kissed?" Something in his charcoal eyes was beginning to look baleful.

"Yes," she said, "the best kiss I've ever had." And even though it had been her only real kiss, Luce knew that if you asked her again in sixty years, a hundred years, she would say the same thing.

"And yet here you are," Cam said, shaking his head in disbelief.

Luce didn't like what he was insinuating. "I'm only here to tell you the truth about me and Daniel. To let you know that you and I—"

Cam burst out laughing, a loud, hollow cackle that echoed across the empty cemetery. He laughed so long and hard, he gripped his sides and wiped a tear away from his eyes.

"What's so funny?" Luce said.

"You have no idea," he said, still laughing.

Cam's you-wouldn't-get-it tone wasn't far off from the one Daniel had used last night when, almost inconsolable, he kept repeating, "It's impossible." But Luce's reaction to Cam was entirely different. When Daniel walled her out, she felt even more of a pull toward him. Even when they argued, she yearned to be with Daniel more than she ever wanted to be with Cam. But when Cam made her feel like an outsider, she was relieved. She didn't want to be any closer to him.

In fact, right now she felt too close.

She'd had enough. Gritting her teeth, she rose and stalked toward the gates, angry at herself for wasting even this much time.

But Cam caught up to her, swinging around in front of her and blocking her exit. He was still laughing at her, biting his lip, trying not to. "Don't go," he chuckled.

"Leave me alone."

"Not yet."

Before she could stop him, Cam caught her up in his arms and bent her backward into a sweeping dip so that her feet came off the ground. Luce cried out, struggling for a moment, but he smiled.

"Let go of me!"

"Grigori and I have fought a pretty fair fight so far, don't you think?"

She glared at him, her hands pushing against his chest. "Go to Hell."

"You're misunderstanding," he said, drawing her face closer to his. His green eyes bored down at her and she hated that a part of her still felt swept away in his gaze.

"Look, I know things have gotten crazy the past couple of days," he said in a hushed voice, "but I care for you, Luce. Deeply. Don't pick him before you let me have one kiss."

She felt his arms tighten around her, and suddenly, she was scared. They were out of sight of the school, and no one knew where she was.

"It won't change anything," she told him, trying to sound calm.

"Humor me? Pretend I'm a soldier and you're granting my dying wish. I promise, just one kiss."

Luce's mind went to Daniel. She pictured him waiting at the lake, keeping his hands busy skipping stones over the water, when he should have had her in his arms. She didn't want to kiss Cam, but what if he really wouldn't let her go? The kiss could be the smallest, most insignificant thing. The easiest way to break loose. And then she'd be free to get back to Daniel. Cam had promised.

"Just one kiss—" she started, but then his lips were on hers.

Her second kiss in as many days. Where Daniel's kiss had been hungry and almost desperate, Cam's kiss was gentle and too perfect, as if he had been practicing on a hundred girls before her.

And yet she felt something in her rise up, wanting her to respond, taking hold of the anger she'd felt only seconds before and blowing it away into nothing. Cam still had her tilted back in his arms, balancing all her weight on his knee. She felt safe in his strong, capable hands. And she needed to feel safe. It was such a change from, well, every moment when she wasn't kissing Cam. She knew that she was forgetting something, someone—who? she couldn't remember. There was only the kiss, and his lips, and—

Suddenly, she felt herself falling. She slammed into

the ground so hard the wind was knocked out of her. Raising herself up on her arms, she watched as, a few inches away, Cam's face came into contact with the ground. She winced despite herself.

The early-evening sun cast a dusty light on two figures in the graveyard.

"How many times must you ruin this girl?" Luce heard the sad southern drawl.

Gabbe? She looked up, blinking into the setting sun.

Gabbe and Daniel.

Gabbe rushed over to help her to her feet, but Daniel wouldn't even look her in the eye.

Luce cursed herself under her breath. She couldn't figure out what was worse—that Daniel had just seen her kissing Cam, or that—she was sure—Daniel was going to fight Cam again.

Cam stood up and faced them, ignoring Luce completely. "All right, which one of you is it going to be this time?" he snarled.

This time?

"Me," Gabbe said, stepping forward with her hands on her hips. "That first little love tap was all me, Cam honey. What you going to do about it?"

Luce shook her head. Gabbe had to be joking. Surely this was some kind of game. But Cam didn't seem to think anything was funny. He bared his teeth and rolled up his sleeves, raising his fists and moving forward.

"Again, Cam?" Luce scolded him. "You haven't gotten in enough fights already this week?" As if that weren't enough, he was actually going to hit a girl.

He shot her a sideways smile. "Third time's the charm," he said, his voice dripping malice. He turned back just as Gabbe came at him with a high kick to the jaw.

Luce scurried backward as Cam fell. His eyes were pinched shut and he was clutching his face. Standing over him, Gabbe looked as unfazed as if she'd just pulled a perfectly baked peach cobbler from the oven. She glanced down at her nails and sighed.

"Gonna be a shame to have to beat up on you just when I touched up my manicure. Oh well," she said, proceeding to kick Cam repeatedly in the stomach, relishing each kick like a kid winning at an arcade game.

He staggered up into a crouch. Luce couldn't see his face anymore—it was buried between his knees—but he was moaning in pain and choking on his own breath.

Luce stood and looked from Gabbe to Cam and back again, unable to make sense of what she was seeing. Cam was twice the size of her, but Gabbe seemed to have the upper hand. Just yesterday, Luce had seen Cam beat up that huge guy at the bar. And the other night, outside the library, Daniel and Cam had seemed evenly matched. Luce marveled at Gabbe, with her rainbow ribbon holding her hair back in a high ponytail. Now she had Cam pinned to the ground and was twisting his arm back. "Uncle?" she taunted. "Just say the magic word, sugar. I'll let you go."

"Never," Cam spat into the ground.

"I was hoping you'd say that," she said, and shoved his head down into the dirt, hard.

Daniel put his hand on Luce's neck. She relaxed against him and looked back, terrified to see his expression. He must hate her right now.

"I'm so sorry," she whispered. "Cam, he—"

"Why would you come here to meet him?" Daniel sounded hurt and incensed at the same time. He grabbed her chin to make her look at him. His fingers were freezing against her skin. His eyes were all violet, no gray.

Luce's lip quivered. "I thought I could take care of it. Be up-front with Cam so that you and I could just be together and not have to worry about anything else."

Daniel snorted, and Luce realized how stupid she sounded.

"That kiss . . . ," she said, wringing her hands. She wanted to spit it from her mouth. "It was such a huge mistake."

Daniel closed his eyes and turned away. Twice he opened his mouth to say something, then thought better of it. He gripped his hair in his hands and swayed. Watching him, Luce feared he might cry. Finally, he took her in his arms.

"Are you mad at me?" She buried her face in his chest and breathed in the sweet smell of his skin.

"I'm just glad we got here in time."

The sound of Cam's whimpers made both of them glance over. Then grimace. Daniel took Luce's hand and tried to pull her away, but she couldn't take her eyes off Gabbe, who had Cam in a headlock and wasn't even winded. Cam looked battered and pathetic. It just didn't make any sense.

"What's going on, Daniel?" Luce whispered. "How can Gabbe kick the crap out of Cam? Why is he letting her?"

Daniel half sighed, half chuckled. "He's not letting her. What you're seeing is only a sample of what that girl can do."

She shook her head. "I don't understand. How—"

Daniel stroked her cheek. "Will you take a walk with me?" he asked. "I'm going to try to explain things, but I think you should probably sit down."

Luce had a few things of her own to come clean about to Daniel. Or, if not to come clean about, at least to throw out into the conversation, to see if he showed signs of thinking she was completely, verifiably deranged. That violet light, for one thing. And the dreams she couldn't—didn't want to—stop.

Daniel led her toward a part of the cemetery Luce had never seen before, a clear, flat space where two peach trees had grown together. Their trunks bowed toward each other, forming the outline of a heart in the air below them.

He led her under the strange, gnarled coupling of the branches and took her hands, tracing her fingers with his.

The evening was quiet except for the song of crickets. Luce imagined all the other students in the dining hall. Spooning mashed potatoes onto their trays, slurping thick room-temperature milk through a straw. It was as if, all of a sudden, she and Daniel were on a different plane of being from the rest of the school. Everything but his hand around hers, his hair shining in the light of the setting sun, his warm gray eyes—everything else felt so far away.

"I don't know where to start," he said, pressing harder as he massaged her fingers, like he could rub the answer out. "There's so much to tell you, and I have to get it right."

As much as she wanted Daniel's words to be a simple confession of love, Luce knew better. Daniel had something difficult to say, something that might explain a lot about him, but might also be hard for Luce to hear.

"Maybe do one of those I-have-good-news-and-bad-news kind of things?" she suggested.

"Good idea. Which do you want first?"

"Most people want the good news first."

"Maybe so," he said. "But you are worlds away from most people."

"Okay, I'll take the bad news first."

He bit his lip. "Then promise me you won't leave before I get to the good news?"

She had no plans to leave. Not now, now that he was no longer pushing her away. Not when he might be about to offer up some answers to the long list of questions she'd been obsessing over for the past few weeks.

He brought her hands to his chest and held them against his heart. "I'm going to tell you the truth," he said. "You won't believe me, but you deserve to know. Even if it kills you."

"Okay." A raw knot of pain took hold of Luce's insides, and she could feel her knees start to shake. She was glad when Daniel made her sit down.

He paced back and forth, then took a deep breath. "In the Bible . . ."

Luce groaned. She couldn't help it; she had a knee-jerk reaction to Sunday school talk. Besides, she wanted to discuss the two of them, not some moralistic parable. The Bible wasn't going to hold the answers to any of the questions she had about Daniel.

"Just listen," he said, shooting her a look. "In the Bible, you know how God makes a big deal about how everyone should love him with all their soul? How it has to be unconditional, and unrivaled?"

Luce shrugged. "I guess so."

"Well—" Daniel seemed to be searching for the right words. "That request doesn't only apply to people."

"What do you mean? Who else? Animals?"

"Sometimes, sure," Daniel said. "Like the serpent. He was damned after he tempted Eve. Cursed to slither on the ground forever."

Luce shivered, thinking back to Cam. The snake. Their picnic. That necklace. She rubbed at her clean, bare neck, glad to be rid of it.

He ran his fingers down her hair, along her jawline, and into the hollow of her neck. She sighed, in a state of bliss.

"I'm trying to say . . . I guess you could say I'm damned, too, Luce. I've been damned for a long, long time." He spoke as if the words tasted bitter. "I made a choice once, a choice that I believed in—that I still believe in, even though—"

"I don't understand," she said, shaking her head.

"Of course you don't," he said, dropping down onto the ground next to her. "And I don't have the best track record at explaining it to you." He scratched his head and lowered his voice, like he was speaking to himself. "But all I can do is try. Here goes nothing."

"Okay," she said. He was confusing her, and he'd barely even said anything yet. But she tried to act less lost than she felt.

"I fall in love," he explained, taking her hands and holding them tightly. "Over and over again. And each time, it ends catastrophically."

"Over and over again." The words made her ill. Luce closed her eyes and withdrew her hands. He'd already told her this. That day at the lake. He'd had breakups. He'd been burned. Why bring up those other girls now? It had hurt then and it hurt even more now, like a sharp pain in her ribs. He squeezed her fingers.

"Look at me," he pleaded. "Here's where it gets hard."

She opened her eyes.

"The person I fall in love with each time is you."

She'd been holding her breath, and meant to exhale, but it came out as a sharp, cutting laugh.

"Right, Daniel," she said, starting to stand up. "Wow, you really are damned. That sounds horrible."

"Listen." He pulled her back down with a force that made her shoulder throb. His eyes flashed violet and she could tell he was getting angry. Well, so was she.

Daniel looked up into the peach tree canopy, as if for help. "I'm begging you, let me explain." His voice quaked. "The problem isn't loving you."

She took a deep breath. "What is it?" She willed herself to listen, to be stronger and not to feel hurt. Daniel looked like he was broken up enough for both of them.

"I get to live forever," he said.

The trees rustled around them, and Luce noticed the faintest trickle of a shadow out of the corner of her eye. Not the sick, all-consuming swirl of blackness from the bar last night, but a warning. The shadow was keeping its distance, seething coldly around the corner, but it was waiting. For her. Luce felt a deep chill, down in her bones. She couldn't shake the sensation that something colossal, black as night, something *final* was on its way.

"I'm sorry," she said, dragging her eyes back to Daniel. "Could you, um, say that again?"

"I get to live forever," he repeated. Luce was still lost, but he kept talking, a stream of words pouring out of his mouth. "I get to live, and to watch babies being born, and grow up, and fall in love. I watch them have babies of their own and grow old. I watch them die. I am condemned, Luce, to watch it all over again and again. Everyone but you." His eyes were glassy. His voice dropped to a whisper. "You don't get to fall in love—"

"But . . . ," she whispered back. "I've . . . fallen in love."

"You don't get to have babies and grow old, Luce."

"Why not?"

"You come along every seventeen years."

"Please—"

"We meet. We *always* meet, somehow we're always thrown together, no matter where I go, no matter how I try to distance myself from you. It never matters. You always find me."

He was staring down at his clenched fists now, looking like he wanted to hit something, unable to raise his eyes.

"And every time we meet, you fall for me—"

"*Daniel*—"

"I can resist you or flee from you or try my hardest not to respond to you, but it makes no difference. You fall in love with me, and I with you."

"Is that so terrible?"

"And it kills you."

"Stop it!" she cried. "What are you trying to do? Scare me away?"

"No." He snorted. "It wouldn't work, anyway."

"If you don't want to be with me . . . ," she said, hoping that it was all an elaborate joke, a breakup speech to end all breakup speeches, and not the truth. It could not be the truth. ". . . there's probably a more believable story to tell."

"I know you can't believe me. This is why I couldn't tell you until now, when I *have* to tell you. Because I thought I understood the rules and . . . we kissed, and now I don't understand anything."

His words from the night before came back to her: *I don't know how to stop it. I don't know what to do.*

"Because you kissed me."

He nodded.

"You kissed me and when we were done, you were surprised."

He nodded again, having the grace to look a little sheepish.

"You kissed me," Luce continued, searching for a way to put it all together, "and you thought I wasn't going to *survive* it?"

"Based on previous experience," he said hoarsely. "Yes."

"That's just crazy," she said.

"It's not about the kiss this time, it's about what it means. In some lives we can kiss, but in most we can't." He stroked her cheek, and she wrestled with how good it felt. "I must say, I prefer the lives where we can kiss." He looked down. "Though it does make losing you that much harder."

She wanted to be mad at him. For making up such a bizarre story when they should have been locked in an embrace. But something was there, like an itch at the back of her mind, telling her not to run from Daniel now, but to stick around and listen as long as she could.

"When you *lose* me," she said, feeling out the shape of the word in her mouth. "How does it happen? Why?"

"It depends on you, on how much you can see about our past, on how well you've come to know me, who I am." He tossed his hands up in a shrug. "I know this sounds incredibly—"

"Crazy?"

He smiled. "I was going to say vague. But I'm trying not to hide anything from you. It's just a very, very delicate subject. Sometimes, in the past, just talking like this has . . ."

She watched for the shape of the words on his lips, but he wouldn't say anything.

"Killed me?"

"I was going to say 'broken my heart.'"

He was in obvious pain, and Luce wanted to comfort him. She could feel herself drawn, something in her breast tugging her forward. But she couldn't. That was when she felt certain that Daniel knew about the glowing violet light. That he had everything to do with it.

"What are you?" she asked. "Some kind of—"

"I wander the earth always knowing at the back of my mind that you're coming. I used to look for you. But then, when I started hiding from you—from the heartbreak I knew was inevitable—you started seeking me out. It didn't take long to realize that you came around every seventeen years."

Luce's seventeenth birthday had been in late August, two weeks before she enrolled at Sword & Cross. It had been a sad celebration, just Luce, her parents, and a store-bought cake. There were no candles, just in case. And what about her family? Did they come back every seventeen years, too?

"It's not long enough for me to ever have gotten over

the last time," he said. "Just long enough that I would let my guard down again."

"So you knew I was coming?" she asked dubiously. He looked serious, but she still couldn't believe him. She didn't want to.

Daniel shook his head. "Not the day you showed up. It's not like that. Don't you remember my reaction when I saw you?" He looked up, like he was thinking back on it himself. "For the first few seconds every time, I'm always so elated. I forget myself. Then I remember."

"Yes," she said slowly. "You smiled, and then . . . is *that* why you flipped me off?"

He frowned.

"But if this happens every seventeen years like you say," she said, "you still *knew* I was coming. In some sense, you knew."

"It's complicated, Luce."

"I saw you that day, before you saw me. You were laughing with Roland outside Augustine. You were laughing so hard I was jealous. If you know all this, Daniel, if you're so smart that you can predict when I'm going to come, and when I'm going to die, and how hard all of that is going to be for *you,* how could you laugh like that? I don't believe you," she said, feeling her voice tremble. "I don't believe any of this."

Daniel gently pressed his thumb to her eye to wipe away a tear. "It's such a beautiful question, Luce. I adore you for asking it, and I wish I could explain it better. All I can tell you is this: The only way to survive eternity is to be able to appreciate each moment. That's all I was doing."

"Eternity," Luce repeated. "Yet another thing I wouldn't understand."

"It doesn't matter. I can't laugh like that anymore. As soon as you show up, I'm overtaken."

"You're not making any sense," she said, wanting to leave before it got too dark. But Daniel's story was so much more than nonsensical. The whole time she'd been at Sword & Cross, she'd half believed she was crazy. Her madness paled in comparison to Daniel's.

"There's no manual for how to explain this . . . *thing* to the girl you love," he pleaded, brushing her hair with his fingers. "I'm doing the best I can. I want you to believe me, Luce. What do I need to do?"

"Tell a different story," she said bitterly. "Make up a saner excuse."

"You said yourself you felt as if you knew me. I tried to deny it as long as I could because I knew this would happen."

"I felt I knew you from somewhere, sure," she said. Now her voice was clotted with fear. "Like the mall or summer camp or something. Not some *former life*." She shook her head. "No . . . I can't."

She covered her ears. Daniel uncovered them.

"And yet you know in your heart it's true." He clasped her knees and looked her deeply in the eye. "You knew it when I followed you to the top of Corcovado in Rio, when you wanted to see the statue up close. You knew it when I carried you two sweaty miles to the River Jordan after you got sick outside Jerusalem. I told you not to eat all those dates. You knew it when you were my nurse in that Italian hospital during the first World War, and before that when I hid in your cellar during the tsar's purge of St. Petersburg. When I scaled the turret of your castle in Scotland during the Reformation, and danced you around and around at the king's coronation ball at Versailles. You were the only woman dressed in black. There was that artists' colony in Quintana Roo, and the protest march in Cape Town where we both spent the night in the pen. The opening of the Globe Theatre in London. We had the best seats in the house. And when my ship wrecked in Tahiti, you were there, as you were when I was a convict in Melbourne, and a pickpocket in eighteenth-century Nîmes, and a monk in Tibet. You turn up everywhere, always, and sooner or later you sense all the things I've just told you. But you won't let yourself accept what you feel might be the truth."

Daniel stopped to catch his breath and looked past her, unseeing. Then he reached over, pressing his hand to her knee and sending that fire through her again.

She closed her eyes, and when she'd opened them,

Daniel was holding the most perfect white peony. It practically glowed. She turned to see where he had plucked it from, how she hadn't noticed it before. There were only weeds and the rotting flesh of fallen fruit. They held the flower together.

"You knew it when you picked white peonies every day for a month that summer in Helston. Remember that?" he stared at her, like he was trying to see inside her. "No," he sighed after a moment. "Of course you don't. I envy you for that."

But even as he said it, Luce's skin began to feel warm, as if it were responding to the words her brain didn't know what to make of. Part of her wasn't sure of anything anymore.

"I do all of these things," Daniel said, leaning into her so that their foreheads touched, "because you're my love, Lucinda. For me, you're all there is."

Luce's lower lip was trembling. Her hands went slack in his. The flower's petals sifted through their fingers to the ground.

"Then why do you look so sad?"

It was all too much to even begin to think about. She leaned away from Daniel and stood up, wiping the leaves and grass from her jeans. Her head was spinning. She had lived . . . *before?*

"Luce."

She waved him off. "I think I need to go somewhere,

by myself, to lie down." She leaned her weight on the peach tree. She felt weak.

"You're not okay," he said, standing up and taking her hand.

"No."

"I'm so sorry." Daniel sighed. "I don't know what I expected to happen, telling you. I shouldn't have . . ."

She would never have thought a moment could come when she'd need a break from Daniel, but she had to get away. The way he was looking at her, she could tell he wanted her to say she would find him later, that they would talk about things more, but she was no longer sure that was a good idea. The more he said, the more she felt something waking up inside her—something she wasn't sure she was ready for. She didn't feel crazy anymore— and she wasn't sure Daniel was, either. To anyone else, his explanation would have made less and less sense as it went along. To Luce . . . she wasn't sure yet, but what if Daniel's words were *answers* that could make sense out of her whole life? She didn't know. She felt more afraid than she ever had before.

She shook his hand loose and started toward her dorm. A few strides away, she stopped and slowly turned.

Daniel hadn't moved. "What is it?" he asked, lifting his chin.

She stood where she was, at a distance from him. "I

promised you I'd stick around long enough to hear the good news."

Daniel's face relaxed into an almost-smile. But there was something vexed about his expression. "The good news is"—he paused, carefully choosing his words—"I kissed you, and you're still here."

SEVENTEEN

AN OPEN BOOK

Luce collapsed on her bed, giving the weary springs a jolt. After she'd fled the cemetery—and Daniel—she'd practically sprinted up to her room. She hadn't even bothered to turn on a light, so she'd tripped over her desk chair and stubbed her toe hard. She'd curled into a ball and gripped her throbbing foot. At least the pain was something real that she could cope with, something sane and of this world. She was so glad to finally be alone.

There was a knock on her door.

She could *not* catch a break.

Luce ignored the knock. She didn't want to see anyone, and whoever it was would get the hint. Another knock. Heavy breathing and a phlegmy, allergy-ridden throat-clearing sound.

Penn.

She couldn't see Penn right now. She'd either *sound* crazy if she tried to explain all that had happened to her in the last twenty-four hours, or she'd *go* crazy trying to put on a normal face and keep it to herself.

Finally, Luce heard Penn's footsteps treading away down the hallway. She breathed a sigh of relief, which turned into a long, lonely whimper.

She wanted to blame Daniel for unleashing this out-of-control feeling inside her, and for a second, she tried to imagine her life without him. Except that was impossible. Like trying to remember your first impression of a house after you've lived in it for years. That was how much he had gotten to her. And now she had to figure out a way to wade through all the strange things he'd told her tonight.

But at the edge of her mind, she kept spiraling back to what he'd said about the times they'd spent together in the past. Maybe Luce couldn't exactly remember the moments he'd described or the places he mentioned, but in a strange way, his words *weren't* shocking at all. It was all somehow familiar.

For example, she had always inexplicably hated dates. Even the sight of them made her feel queasy. She'd started claiming she was allergic so her mom would stop trying to sneak them into things she baked. And she'd been begging her parents to take her to Brazil practically her whole life, though she never could explain exactly why she wanted to go. The white peonies. Daniel had given her a bouquet after the fire in the library. There had always been something so unusual about them, yet so familiar.

The sky outside her window was a deep charcoal, with just a few puffs of white cloud. Her room was dark, but the pale full blooms of the flowers on her windowsill stood out in the dimness. They'd sat in their vase for a week now, and not a single petal had withered.

Luce sat up and inhaled their sweetness.

She couldn't blame him. Yes, he sounded crazy, but he was also right—she was the one who had come to him again and again suggesting that they had some sort of history. And it wasn't only that. She was also the one who saw the shadows, the one who kept finding herself involved in the deaths of innocent people. She'd been trying not to think about Trevor and Todd when Daniel started talking about her own *deaths*—how he had watched her die so many times. If there had been any way to fathom such a thing, Luce would have wanted to ask whether Daniel ever felt responsible. For the loss of her. Whether his reality was anything like the secret, ugly, overriding guilt she faced every day.

She sank onto the desk chair, which had somehow made its way to the middle of the room. Ouch. When she reached underneath her, hand groping for whatever hard object she'd just plopped down on, she found a thick book.

Luce moved to the wall and flicked on her light switch, then squinted in the ugly fluorescent light. The book in her hands was one she'd never seen before. It was bound in the palest gray cloth, with frayed corners and brown glue crumbling at the bottom of the spine.

The Watchers: Myth in Medieval Europe.

Daniel's ancestor's book.

It was heavy and smelled faintly of smoke. She tugged out the note that was tucked inside the front cover.

Yes, I found a spare key and entered your room unlawfully. I'm sorry. But this is URGENT!!! And I couldn't find you anywhere. Where are you? You need to look at this, and then we need to have a powwow. I'll swing by in an hour. Proceed with caution.
xoxo,
Penn

Luce laid the note next to the flowers and took the book back to her bed. She sat down with her legs dangling over the edge. Just holding the book gave her a strange, warm buzzing sensation just below her skin. The book felt almost alive in her hands.

She cracked it open, expecting to have to decode some stiff academic table of contents or dig through an index at the back before she'd find anything even remotely related to Daniel.

She never got beyond the title page.

Pasted inside the front cover of the book was a sepia-toned photograph. It was a very old *carte de visite*–style picture, printed on yellowing albumen paper. Someone had scrawled in ink at the bottom: *Helston, 1854.*

Heat flashed across her skin. She yanked her black sweater over her head but still felt hot in her tank top.

The memory of Daniel's voice sounded hollow in her mind. *I get to live forever,* he'd said. *You come along every seventeen years. You fall in love with me, and I with you. And it kills you.*

Her head throbbed.

You're my love, Lucinda. For me, you're all there is.

She fingered the outline of the picture glued inside the book. Luce's dad, the aspiring photography guru, would have marveled over how well-preserved the image was, how valuable it must be.

Luce, on the other hand, was hung up on the people in the image. Because, unless every word out of Daniel's mouth had been true, it made no sense at all.

A young man, with light cropped hair and lighter

eyes, posed elegantly in a trim black coat. His raised chin and well-defined cheekbones made his fine attire look even more distinguished, but it was his lips that gave Luce such a start. The exact shape of his smile, combined with the look in those eyes . . . it added up to an expression that Luce had seen in every one of her dreams these last few weeks. And, over the last couple of days, in person.

This man was the spitting image of Daniel. The Daniel who had just told her that he loved her—and that she had been reincarnated dozens of times. The Daniel who had said so many other things Luce didn't want to hear that she had run away. The Daniel whom she'd abandoned under the peach trees in the cemetery.

It could have been just a remarkable likeness. Some distant relative, the author of the book maybe, who'd funneled each one of his genes straight down the family tree right to Daniel.

Except that the young man in the picture was posed next to a young woman who also looked alarmingly familiar.

Luce held the book inches from her face and pored over the woman's image. She wore a ruffled black silk ball gown that hugged her body to her waist before billowing out in wide black tiers. Black lace-up wristlets encased her hands, leaving her white fingers bare. Her small teeth showed between her lips, which were parted in an easy smile. She had clear skin a few tones lighter than the man's. Deep-set eyes bordered by thick eyelashes. A black flood of hair that fell in thick waves to her waist.

It took a moment for Luce to remember how to breathe, and even then, she still couldn't tear her strained eyes away from the book. The woman in the photograph?

It was her.

Either Luce had been right, and her memory of Daniel had come from a forgotten trip to a Savannah mall, where they'd posed for cheesy dress-up shots at Ye Old Photo Booth that she also couldn't remember—or Daniel had been telling the truth.

Luce and Daniel did know one another.

From an altogether different time.

She could not catch her breath. Her whole life tossed in the roiling sea of her mind, everything came into question—the itchy dark shadows that haunted her, the gruesome death of Trevor, the dreams . . .

She had to find Penn. If anyone could come up with an explanation for such an impossible occurrence, it would be Penn. With the inscrutable old book tucked under her arm, Luce left her room and raced toward the library.

The library was warm and empty, but something about the high ceilings and endless rows of books made

Luce nervous. She walked quickly past the new call desk, which still looked sterile and unlived in. She passed the formidable unused card catalog and the endless reference section until she had reached the long tables in the group study section.

Instead of Penn, Luce found Arriane, playing a game of chess with Roland. She had her feet up on the table and was wearing a striped conductor's cap. Her hair was tucked under the hat, and Luce noticed again, for the first time since the morning she'd cut Arriane's hair, the glossy, marbled scar along her neck.

Arriane was fixated on the game. A chocolate cigar bobbed between her lips as she contemplated her next move. Roland had twisted his dreads into two meaty knots on the crown of his head. He was giving Arriane the hawk eye, tapping one of his pawns with his pinky.

"Checkmate, bitch," Arriane said triumphantly, knocking over Roland's king, just as Luce thudded to a stop in front of their table. "Lululucinda," she sang, looking up. "You've been hiding from me."

"No."

"I've been *hearing* things about you," Arriane said, causing Roland to tilt his head attentively. "Nudge nudge, wink wink. That means sit down and spill. Right now."

Luce hugged the book to her chest. She didn't want to sit down. She wanted to scour the library for Penn.

She couldn't make small talk with Arriane—especially not in front of Roland, who was clearing his things off the seat next to him.

"Join us," Roland said.

Luce lowered herself reluctantly onto the edge of the seat. She'd just stay a few minutes. It was true that she hadn't seen Arriane in a few days, and under normal circumstances, she would really have missed the girl's bizarre ways.

But these were far from normal circumstances, and Luce could think of nothing other than that photograph.

"Since I just wiped the chessboard with Roland's ass, let's play a new game. How about 'who saw an incriminating photo of Luce the other day?'" Arriane said, crossing her arms on the table.

"What?" Luce jumped back. She pressed her hand down firmly on the cover of the book, feeling certain that her tense expression was giving everything away. She should never have brought it here.

"I'll give you three guesses," Arriane said, rolling her eyes. "Molly snapped a picture of you ducking into a big black car yesterday after class."

"Oh." Luce sighed.

"She was going to turn you in to Randy," Arriane continued. "Until I gave her what for. Mmm-hmm." She snapped her fingers. "Now, to show your gratitude, tell me—are they sneaking you away to see an off-campus shrink?" She lowered her voice to a whisper and tapped her fingernails on the table. "Or have you taken a lover?"

Luce glanced at Roland, who was giving her a fixed stare.

"Neither," she said. "I just left for a little while to have a talk with Cam. It didn't go exactly—"

"Bam! Pay up, Arri," Roland said, grinning. "You owe me ten bucks."

Luce's jaw dropped.

Arriane patted her hand. "No big deal, we just made a little wager to keep things interesting. I assumed it was Daniel you'd gone off with. Roland here picked Cam. You're breaking my bank, Luce. I don't like it."

"I *was* with Daniel," Luce said, not really knowing why she felt the need to correct them. Didn't they have anything better to do with their lives than sit around wondering what she did on her own time?

"Oh," Roland said, sounding disappointed. "The plot thickens."

"Roland." Luce turned to him. "I need to ask you something."

"Talk to me." He pulled a notepad and a pen out of his black-and-white pinstriped blazer. He held the pen poised over the paper, like a waiter taking an order. "What do you want? Coffee? Booze? I only get the hard stuff on Fridays. Dirty magazines?"

"Thigars?" Arriane offered, lisping through the chocolate one in her mouth.

"No." Luce shook her head. "None of that."

"Okay, special order. I left the catalog up in the room." Roland shrugged. "You can come by later—"

"I don't need you to get me anything. I just want to know—" She swallowed dryly. "You're friends with Daniel, right?"

He shrugged. "I don't hate the guy."

"But do you trust him?" she asked. "I mean, if he told you something that sounded crazy, how likely would you be to believe him?"

Roland squinted at her, seeming momentarily stumped, but Arriane quickly hopped up on the table and swung her legs over to Luce's side. "What exactly are we talking about?"

Luce stood up. "Never mind." She should never have raised the subject. The whole mess of details came rushing back to her. She grabbed the book from the table. "I've got to go," she said. "I'm sorry."

She pushed her chair in and walked away. Her legs felt heavy and dull, her mind overloaded. A breath of wind lifted the hair at the back of her neck and her head darted around in search of shadows. Nothing. Just an open window high up near the library rafters. Just a tiny bird's nest tucked into the window's narrow open corner. Scanning the library again, Luce found it hard to believe her eyes. There really was no sign of them, no inky black tendrils or shuddering gray weather system roiling overhead—but Luce could feel their distinct closeness, could almost smell their salty sulfur in the air. Where were they, if not haunting her? She'd always thought of them as hers alone. She'd never considered that the shadows might go other places, do other things—torment other people. Did Daniel see them, too?

Rounding the corner toward the computer stations at the back of the library, where she thought she might find Penn, Luce ran smack into Miss Sophia. Both of them stumbled, and Miss Sophia caught Luce to steady herself. She was dressed in fashionable jeans and a long white blouse, with a beaded red cardigan tied around her shoulders. Her metallic green glasses hung from a multi-colored bead chain around her neck. Luce was surprised at how firm her grip was.

"Excuse me," Luce mumbled.

"Why, Lucinda, what's the matter?" Miss Sophia pressed a palm to Luce's forehead. The baby powder smell of her hands filled Luce's nose. "You don't look well."

Luce swallowed, willing herself not to burst into tears just because the nice librarian was taking pity on her. "I'm *not* well."

"I knew it," Miss Sophia said. "You missed class to-day and you weren't at the Social last night. Do you need to see a doctor? If my first-aid kit hadn't been burned up in the fire, I'd take your temperature right here."

"No, well, I don't know." Luce held the book out in front of her and contemplated telling Miss Sophia everything, starting from the beginning . . . which was when?

Only, she didn't have to. Miss Sophia took one glance at the book, sighed, and gave Luce a knowing look. "You finally found it, didn't you? Come, let's have a talk."

Even the librarian knew more than Luce did about her life. Lives? She couldn't figure out what any of it meant, or how any of it was possible.

She followed Miss Sophia to a table at the back corner of the study section. She could still see Arriane and Roland from the corner of her eye, but they seemed at least to be out of earshot.

"How did you come across this?" Miss Sophia patted Luce's hand and slipped her glasses on. Her small black-pearl eyes twinkled behind the bifocals' frames. "Don't worry. You're not in trouble, dear."

"I don't know. Penn and I had been looking for it. It was stupid. We thought maybe the author was related to Daniel, but we didn't know for sure. Whenever we went to look for it, it seemed like it had just been checked out. Then, when I came home tonight, Penn had left it in my room—"

"So Pennyweather knows about its contents as well?"

"I don't know," Luce said, shaking her head. She

could feel herself rambling, and yet she couldn't make herself shut up. Miss Sophia was like the cool, zany grandmother Luce had never had. Her own grandmother's idea of a big shopping trip was going to the grocery store. Besides, it felt so good just to talk to someone. "I haven't been able to find her yet, only because I was with Daniel, and usually he acts so weird, but last night he kissed me, and we stayed out until—"

"Excuse me, dear," Miss Sophia said, a little too loudly, "but did you just say Daniel Grigori kissed you?"

Luce covered her mouth with both hands. She could not believe she'd just spilled that to Miss Sophia. She must really be losing it. "I'm sorry, that's completely irrelevant. And embarrassing. I don't know why that slipped out." She fanned her burning cheeks.

Already it was too late. Across the study section, Arriane boomed at Luce, "Thanks for telling *me*!" Her face looked stunned.

But Miss Sophia snapped Luce's attention back when she shook the book from Luce's hands. "A kiss between you and Daniel is not only irrelevant, dear, it's usually impossible." She stroked her chin and looked up at the ceiling. "Which means . . . well, it *couldn't* mean . . ."

Miss Sophia's fingers started flying through the book, tracing down each page at a miraculously rapid pace.

"What do you mean, 'usually'?" Luce had never felt so left out of her own life.

"Forget the kiss." Miss Sophia waved her hand at Luce, taking her aback. "That's not half of it. The kiss doesn't mean anything unless . . ." She muttered under her breath and went back to flipping through the pages.

What did Miss Sophia know? Daniel's kiss meant everything. Luce watched Miss Sophia's flying fingers dubiously until something on one of the pages caught her eye.

"Go back," Luce said, laying her hand over Miss Sophia's to stop her.

Miss Sophia leaned slowly away as Luce turned back the thin, translucent pages. There. She pressed a hand to her heart. In the margin was a series of drawings sketched in blackest ink. Quickly done, but in an elegant, fine hand. By someone with a certain talent. Luce ran her fingers over the drawings, taking them in. The slope of a woman's shoulder, seen from the back, her hair knotted into a low bun. Soft bare knees crossed over each other, leading up to a shadowy waist. A long, thin wrist giving way to an open palm in which a large, full peony rested.

Luce's fingers started to tremble. A lump rose in her throat. She didn't know why this, out of everything she'd seen and heard today, was beautiful enough—tragic enough—to finally bring her to tears. The shoulder, the knees, the wrist . . . all were her own. And she knew—all of them had been drawn by Daniel's hand.

"Lucinda." Miss Sophia looked nervous, slowly

inching her chair away from the table. "Are you—are you feeling quite all right?"

"Oh, Daniel," Luce whispered, desperate to be near him again. She wiped away a tear.

"He's damned, Lucinda," Miss Sophia said in a surprisingly cold voice. "You both are."

Damned. Daniel had spoken of being damned. That was his word for all of this. But he'd been referring to himself. Not her.

"Damned?" Luce repeated. Only, she didn't want to hear any more. All she wanted was to find him.

Miss Sophia snapped her fingers in front of Luce's face. Luce met her eyes, slowly, languidly, smiling dopily.

"You're still not awake," Miss Sophia murmured. She closed the book with a smack, catching Luce's attention, and laid her hands down on the table. "Has he told you anything? After the kiss, maybe?"

"He told me . . . ," Luce started. "It sounds crazy."

"These things often do."

"He said the two of us . . . we're some kind of star-crossed lovers." Luce closed her eyes, remembering his long catalog of past lives. At first the idea had felt so foreign, but now that she was getting used to it, she thought it might just be the most romantic thing that had ever happened in the history of the world. "He talked about all the times we've fallen in love, in Rio, and Jerusalem, Tahiti—"

"That does sound rather crazy," Miss Sophia said. "So, of course, you don't believe him?"

"I didn't at first," Luce said, thinking back to their heated disagreement under the peach tree. "He started out by bringing up the Bible, which my instinct is to tune out—" She bit her tongue. "No offense. I mean, I think your class is really interesting."

"None taken. People often shy away from their religious upbringings around your age. You're nothing new, Lucinda."

"Oh." Luce cracked her knuckles. "But I didn't have a religious upbringing. My parents didn't believe in it, so—"

"Everyone believes in something. Surely you were baptized?"

"Not if you don't count the swimming pool built under the church pews over there," Luce said timidly, jerking her thumb toward Sword & Cross's gym.

Yeah, she celebrated Christmas, she'd been to church a handful of times, and even when her life made her and everyone around her miserable, she still had faith that there was someone or something up there worth believing in. That had always been enough for her.

Across the room, she heard a loud clatter. She looked up to see that Roland had fallen out of his chair. The last time she'd glanced at him, he'd been leaning back on two legs, and now it looked like gravity had finally won.

As he stumbled to his feet, Arriane went to help him. She glanced over and offered a hurried wave. "He's okay!" she called cheerily. "Get up!" she whispered loudly to Roland.

Miss Sophia was sitting very still, with her hands in her lap under the table. She cleared her throat a few times, flipped back to the front cover of the book and ran her fingers over the photograph, then said, "Did he reveal anything more? Do you know who Daniel is?"

Slowly, sitting up very straight in her chair, Luce asked, "Do you?"

The librarian stiffened. "I study these things. I'm an academic. I don't get tangled up in trivial matters of the heart."

Those were the words she used—but everything from the pulsing vein along her neck, to the almost un-noticeably light sheen of sweat dotting her brow told Luce that the answer to her question was *yes.*

Over their heads, the giant black antique clock struck eleven. The minute hand trembled with the effort of snapping into its place, and the whole contraption gonged for so long it interrupted their conversation. Luce had never noticed how loud the clock was. Now, each chime made her ache. She'd been away from Daniel for too long.

"Daniel thought . . . ," Luce started to say. "Last night, when we first kissed, he thought I was going to die." Miss Sophia didn't look as surprised as Luce would have liked her to look. Luce cracked her knuckles. "But that's crazy, isn't it? I'm not going anywhere."

Miss Sophia took off her bifocals and rubbed her tiny eyes. "For now."

"Oh God," Luce whispered, feeling the same wash of fear that had made her leave Daniel in the cemetery. But why? There was something he still wasn't telling her—something she knew had the power to make her either much more or much less afraid. Something she knew already on her own but couldn't believe. Not until she saw his face again.

The book was still open to the photograph. Upside down, Daniel's smile looked worried, like he knew—as he said he always did—what was coming around the next corner. She couldn't imagine what he must be going through right now. To have opened up about the uncanny history they shared—only to have her dismiss him so completely. She had to find him.

She shut the book and tucked it back under her elbow. Then she stood up and pushed in her chair.

"Where are you going?" Miss Sophia asked nervously.

"To find Daniel."

"I'll go with you."

"No." Luce shook her head, imagining showing up to throw her arms around Daniel with the school librarian in tow. "You don't have to come. Really."

Miss Sophia was all business when she bent down to double-knot the laces of her sensible shoes. She stood up and laid a hand on Luce's shoulder.

"Trust me," she said, "I do. Sword & Cross has a reputation to uphold. You don't think we just let students run around willy-nilly in the night, do you?"

Luce resisted filling Miss Sophia in on her recent escapade outside the school gates. She groaned inwardly. Why not bring along the whole student body so everyone could enjoy the drama? Molly could take pictures, Cam could pick another fight. Why not start right here, and pick up Arriane and Roland—who, she realized with a start, had already disappeared.

Miss Sophia, book in hand, had already taken off for the front entrance. Luce had to jog to catch up to her, speeding past the card catalog, the singed Persian carpet at the front desk, and the glass cases full of Civil War relics in the east wing special collections, where she'd seen Daniel sketching the cemetery the very first night she was here.

They stepped outside into the humid night. A cloud passed over the moon and the campus fell into inky blackness. Then, as if a compass had been placed in her hand, Luce felt guided toward the shadows. She knew exactly where they were. Not at the library, but not far away, either.

She couldn't see them yet, but she could feel them,

which was so much worse. An awful, consuming itch coated her skin, seeping into her bones and blood like acid. Pooling, clotting, making the cemetery—and beyond—reek with their sulfur stink. They were so much bigger now. It seemed like all the air on campus was foul with their wretched stench of decay.

"Where is Daniel?" Miss Sophia asked. Luce realized that though the librarian might know quite a bit about the past, she seemed oblivious to the shadows. It made Luce feel terrified and alone, responsible for whatever was about to happen.

"I don't know," she said, feeling as if she couldn't get enough oxygen in the thick, swampy night air. She didn't want to say the words she knew would bring them closer—far too close—to everything that was making her so afraid. But she had to go to Daniel. "I left him in the cemetery."

They hurried across campus, dodging patches of mud left over from the downpour the other day. Only a few lights were on in the dormitory to their right. Through one of the barred windows, Luce saw a girl she barely knew poring over a book. They were in the same morning block of classes. She was a tough-looking girl with a pierced septum and the tiniest sneeze—but Luce had never heard her speak. She had no idea if she was miserable or if she enjoyed her life. Luce wondered at that moment: If she could trade places with this girl—who never had to worry about past lives, or apocalyptic shadows, or the deaths of two innocent boys on her hands—would she do it?

Daniel's face—the way it had been bathed in violet light when he'd carried her home this morning—appeared before her eyes. His gleaming golden hair. His tender, knowing eyes. The way one touch of his lips transported her far away from any darkness. For him, she'd suffer all of this, and more.

If only she knew how much more there was.

She and Miss Sophia jogged forward, past the creaking bleachers framing the commons, then past the soccer field. Miss Sophia really kept in shape. Luce would have worried about their pace if the woman hadn't been a few steps ahead of her.

Luce was dragging. Her fear of facing the shadows was like a hurricane-force headwind slowing her down. And yet she pressed on. An overwhelming nausea told her that she'd barely glimpsed what the dark things could accomplish.

At the cemetery gates, they stopped. Luce was trembling, hugging herself in a failed attempt to hide it. A girl was standing with her back to them, gazing into the graveyard below.

"Penn!" Luce called, so glad to see her friend.

When Penn turned to them, her face was ashen. She wore a black Windbreaker, despite the heat, and her glasses were fogging up from the humidity. She was trembling just as much as Luce was.

Luce gasped. "What happened?"

"I was coming to look for you," Penn said, "and then a bunch of the other kids ran this way. They went down there." She pointed toward the gates. "But I c-c-couldn't."

"What is it?" Luce asked. "What's down there?"

But even as she asked, she knew one thing that was down there, one thing that Penn would never be able to see. The curdling black shadow was coaxing Luce toward it, Luce alone.

Penn was blinking rapidly. She looked terrified. "Dunno," she said finally. "At first I thought fireworks. But nothing ever made it to the sky." She shuddered. "Something bad's about to happen. I don't know what."

Luce breathed in and coughed on a deep whiff of sulfur. "How, Penn? How do you know?"

Penn's arm shook as she pointed into the deep bowl in the middle of the cemetery. "See that?" she said. "Something's flickering down there."

EIGHTEEN

THE BURIED WAR

Luce took one look at the shuddering light at the base of the cemetery and started racing toward it. She hurtled down past the broken headstones, leaving Penn and Miss Sophia far behind. She didn't care that the sharp, twisting limbs of the live oak trees scratched her arms and face as she ran, or that clumps of thick-rooted weeds tripped up her feet.

She had to get down there.

The waning sliver of moon offered little light, but

there was another source—coming from the bottom of the cemetery. Her destination. It looked like a monstrous, cloud-ridden lightning storm. Only it was happening on the ground.

The shadows had been warning her, she realized, for days. Now their dark show had turned into something even Penn could see. And the other students who'd run ahead must have noticed it, too. Luce didn't know what it could possibly mean. Only that if Daniel was down there with that sinister flickering . . . it was all her fault.

Her lungs burned, but she was driven forward by the image of him standing under the peach trees. She wouldn't stop until she found him—because she'd been coming to find him anyway, to shove the book under his nose and cry out that she believed him, that part of her had believed him all along, but she'd been too scared to accept their unfathomable history. She would tell him that she wasn't going to let fear drive her away, not this time, not anymore. Because she knew something, understood something that had taken her far too long to piece together. Something wild and strange that made their past experiences together both more and less believable. She knew who—no, *what* Daniel was. Part of her had come to this realization on her own—that she might have lived before and loved him before. Only, she hadn't understood what it meant, what it all added up to—the pull she felt toward him, her dreams—until now.

But none of that mattered if she couldn't get down there in time to find some way to fend off the shadows. None of it mattered if they got to Daniel before she could. She tore down the steep tiers of graves, but the basin at the center of the cemetery was still so far away.

Behind her, a thumping of footsteps. Then a shrill voice.

"Pennyweather!" It was Miss Sophia. She was gaining on Luce, calling back over her shoulder, where Luce could see Penn carefully working her way over a fallen tombstone. "You're slower than Christmas coming!"

"No!" Luce yelled. "Penn, Miss Sophia, don't come down here!" She wouldn't be responsible for putting anyone else in the shadows' path.

Miss Sophia froze on a toppled white tombstone and stared up at the sky like she hadn't heard Luce at all. She raised her thin arms up in the air, as if to shield herself. Luce squinted into the night and sucked in her breath. Something was moving toward them, blowing in with the chill wind.

At first she thought it was the shadows, but this was something different and scarier, like a jagged, irregular veil full of dark pockets, letting flecks of sky filter through. This shadow was made of a million tiny black pieces. A rioting, fluttering storm of darkness stretching out in all directions.

"Locusts?" Penn cried.

Luce shuddered. The thick swarm was still at a distance, but its deep percussion grew louder with every passing second. Like the beating of a thousand birds' wings. Like a hostile sweeping darkness scouring the earth. It was coming. It was going to lash out at her, maybe at all of them, tonight.

"This is not good!" Miss Sophia ranted at the sky. "There's supposed to be an order to things!"

Penn came to a panting stop next to Luce and the two of them exchanged a bewildered look. Sweat beaded Penn's upper lip, and her purple glasses kept slipping down in the moist heat.

"She's losing it," Penn whispered, jerking her thumb at Miss Sophia.

"No." Luce shook her head. "She knows things. And if Miss Sophia's scared, you shouldn't be here, Penn."

"Me?" Penn asked, bewildered, probably because ever since the first day of school, she had been the one guiding Luce. "I don't think *either* of us should be here."

Luce's chest stung with a pain similar to what she'd felt when she had to say goodbye to Callie. She looked away from Penn. There was a split between them now, a deep division cutting them apart, because of Luce's past. She hated to own up to it, to call Penn's attention to it, too, but she knew it would be better, safer, if they parted ways.

"I have to stay," she said, taking a deep breath. "I

have to find Daniel. You should go back to the dorm, Penn. Please."

"But you and me," Penn said hoarsely. "We were the only ones—"

Before Luce could hear the end of the sentence, she took off toward the cemetery's center. Toward the mausoleum where she'd seen Daniel brooding on the evening of Parents' Day. She bounded over the last of the tombstones, then skidded down a slope of dank, rotting mulch until the ground finally evened out. She came to a stop in front of the giant oak in the basin at the cemetery's center.

Hot and frustrated and terrified all at once, she leaned against the tree trunk.

Then, through the branches of the tree, she saw him.

Daniel.

She let out all the air in her lungs and felt weak in the knees. One look at his distant, dark profile, so beautiful and majestic, told her that everything Daniel had hinted at—even the one big thing she'd figured out on her own—everything was true.

He was standing atop the mausoleum, arms crossed, looking up where the roiling cloud of locusts had just passed overhead. The thin moonlight threw his shadow in a crescent of darkness that dipped off the crypt's wide, flat roof. She ran toward him, weaving through the dangling Spanish moss and the tilted old statues.

"Luce!" He spied her as she neared the base of the mausoleum. "What are you doing here?" His voice showed no happiness to see her—more like shock and horror.

It's my fault, she wanted to cry as she approached the base of the mausoleum. And *I believe it, I believe our story. Forgive me for ever leaving you, I never will again.* There was one more thing she wanted to tell him. But he was far above her, and the shadows' horrible din was too loud, and the air was too soupy to try to make him hear her from where she stood below him.

The tomb was solid marble. But there was a big chip in one of the bas-relief sculptures of a peacock, and Luce used it as a toehold. The usually cool stone was warm to the touch. Her sweaty palms slipped a few times as she strained to reach the top. To reach Daniel, who had to forgive her.

She'd only scaled a few feet of the wall when someone tapped her shoulder. She spun around and gasped when she saw that it was Daniel, and lost her grip. He caught her, his arms circling her waist, before she could slide to the ground. But he'd just been a full story overhead a second earlier.

She buried her face in his shoulder. And while the truth still scared her, being in his arms made her feel like the sea finding its shore, like a traveler returning after a long, hard, distant trip—finally returning home.

"You picked a fine time to come back," he said. He smiled, but his smile was weighed down with worry. His eyes kept looking beyond her, into the sky.

"You see it, too?" she asked.

Daniel just looked at her, unable to respond. His lip quivered.

"Of course you do," she whispered, because everything was coming together. The shadows, his story, their past. A choking cry welled up inside her. "How can you love me?" she sobbed. "How can you even stand me?"

He took her face in his hand. "What are you talking about? How can you say that?"

Her heart burned from racing so fast.

"Because . . ." She swallowed. "You're an angel."

His arms went slack. "What did you say?"

"You're an angel, Daniel, I know it," she said, feeling floodgates open within her, wider and wider until it all just tumbled out. "Don't tell me I'm crazy. I have dreams about you, dreams that are too real to forget, dreams that made me love you before you ever said one nice thing to me." Daniel's eyes didn't change at all. "Dreams where you have wings and you hold me high up in a sky I don't recognize, and yet I know I've been there, just like that, in your arms a thousand times before." She touched her forehead to his. "It explains so much—how graceful you are when you move, and the book your ancestor wrote. Why no one came to visit you on Parents' Day. The way your body seems to float when you swim. And why, when you kiss me, I feel like I've gone to Heaven." She stopped to catch her breath. "And why you can live forever. The only thing it doesn't explain is what on earth you're doing with me. Because I'm just . . . me." She looked up at the sky again, feeling the black spell of the shadows. "And I'm guilty of so much."

The color was gone from his face. And Luce could draw only one conclusion. "You don't understand why, either," she said.

"I don't understand what you're still doing here."

She blinked and nodded miserably, then began to turn away.

"No!" He pulled her back. "Don't leave. It's just that you've never—we've never . . . gotten this far." He closed his eyes. "Will you say it again?" he asked, almost shyly. "Will you tell me . . . what I am?"

"You're an angel," she repeated slowly, surprised to see Daniel close his eyes and moan in pleasure, almost as if they were kissing. "I'm in love with an angel." Now she was the one who wanted to close her eyes and moan. She tilted her head. "But in my dreams, your wings—"

A hot, howling wind swept sideways over them, practically swatting Luce out of Daniel's arms. He shielded her body with his. The cloud of shadow-locusts had settled in the canopy of a tree beyond the cemetery and had been making sizzling noises in the branches. Now they rose up in one great mass.

"Oh God," Luce whispered. "I have to do something. I have to stop it—"

"Luce." Daniel stroked her cheek. "Look at me. You have done nothing wrong. And there's nothing you can do about"—he pointed—"that." He shook his head. "Why would you ever think you were guilty?"

"Because," she said, "my whole life, I've been seeing these shadows—"

"I should have done something when I realized that, last week at the lake. It's the first lifetime when you've seen them—and it scared me."

"How can you know it's not my fault?" she asked, thinking of Todd and of Trevor. The shadows always came to her just before something awful happened.

He kissed her hair. "The shadows you see are called Announcers. They look bad, but they can't hurt you. All they do is scope out a situation and report back to someone else. Gossips. The demonic version of a clique of high school girls."

"But what about those?" She pointed at the trees that lined the perimeter of the cemetery. Their branches were waving, weighed down by the thick, oozing blackness.

Daniel looked out with a calm stare. "Those are the shadows the Announcers have summoned. To battle."

Luce's arms and legs went cold with fear. "What . . . um . . . what kind of battle is that?"

"The big one," he said simply, raising his chin. "But they're just showing off right now. We still have time."

Behind them a tiny cough made Luce jump. Daniel bowed in greeting to Miss Sophia, who was standing in the shadow of the mausoleum. Her hair had come loose from its pins and looked wild and unruly, like her eyes. Then someone else stepped forward from behind Miss Sophia. Penn. Her hands were stuffed into the pockets of her jacket. Her face was still red, and her hairline was damp with sweat. She shrugged at Luce as if to say *I don't know what the heck is going on, but I couldn't just abandon you.* Despite herself, Luce smiled.

Miss Sophia stepped forward and raised the book. "Our Lucinda has been doing her research."

Daniel rubbed his jaw. "You've been reading that old thing? Never should have written it." He sounded almost bashful—but Luce slid one more piece of their puzzle into place.

"*You* wrote that," she said. "And sketched in the margins. And pasted in that photograph of us."

"You found the photograph," Daniel said, smiling, holding her closer as if the mention of the picture brought back a rush of memories. "Of course."

"It took me a while to understand, but when I saw how happy we were, something opened up inside me. And I knew."

She wrapped a hand around his neck and pulled his face to hers, not even caring that Miss Sophia and Penn were right there. When Daniel's lips touched hers, the whole dark, horrid cemetery disappeared—the worn graves, too, and the pockets of shadows rooting around in the trees; even the moon and the stars above.

The first time she'd seen the Helston picture, it had scared her. The idea of all those past versions of herself existing—it was just too much to take in. But now, in Daniel's arms, she could feel all of them somehow working together, a vast consortium of Luces who'd loved the same Daniel over and over and over again. So much love—it spilled out of her heart and her soul, pouring off her body and filling the space between them.

And she at last heard what he had said when they were looking at the shadows: that she had done nothing wrong. That there was no reason to feel guilty. Could it be true? Was she innocent of Trevor's death, of Todd's, as she'd always believed? The moment she asked herself, she knew that Daniel had told her the truth. And she felt like she was waking from a long bad dream. She no longer felt like the girl with the shorn hair and the baggy black clothes, no longer the eternal screw-up, afraid of the putrid cemetery, and stuck in reform school for good reason.

"Daniel," she said, gently pushing his shoulders back so she could look at him. "Why didn't you tell me sooner that you were an angel? Why all that talk about being damned?"

Daniel eyed her nervously.

"I'm not mad." She reassured him. "Only wondering."

"I couldn't tell you," he said. "It's all wrapped up together. Until now, I didn't even know that you could discover it on your own. If I told you too quickly or at the wrong time, you'd be gone again and I would have to wait. I've already had to wait so long."

"How long?" Luce asked.

"Not so long that I've forgotten that you're worth everything. Every sacrifice. Every pain." Daniel closed his eyes for a moment. Then he looked over at Penn and Miss Sophia.

Penn was seated with her back against a mossy black tombstone. Her knees were curled up to her chin and she was chewing avidly on her fingernails. Miss Sophia had her hands on her hips. She looked like she had something to say.

Daniel stepped back, and Luce felt a rush of cool air waft between them. "I'm still afraid that any minute you could—"

"Daniel—" Miss Sophia called reprovingly.

He waved her off. "Our being together, it's not as simple as you're going to want it to be."

"Of course not," Luce said. "I mean, you're an angel, but now that I know it—"

"Lucinda Price." This time it was Luce who was the object of Miss Sophia's anger. "What he has to tell you,

you do not want to know," she warned. "And Daniel, you have no right. It will kill her—"

Luce shook her head, confused by Miss Sophia's request. "I think I could survive a little truth."

"It is not a *little* truth," Miss Sophia said, stepping forward to position herself between them. "And you will not survive it. As you have not survived it in the thousands of years since the Fall."

"Daniel, what is she talking about?" Luce reached around Miss Sophia for his wrist, but the librarian fended her off. "I can handle it," Luce said, feeling a dry pit of nerves in her stomach. "I don't want any more secrets. I love him."

It was the first time she had ever said the words aloud to anyone. Her only regret was that she'd directed the most important three words she knew at Miss Sophia instead of at Daniel. She turned to him. His eyes were shining. "I do," she said. "I love you."

Clap.

Clap. Clap.

Clap. Clap. Clap. Clap.

Slow, loud applause sounded from behind them in the trees. Daniel broke away and turned toward the woods, his posture stiffening, as Luce felt the old fear flood in, felt herself rooted by terror about what he was seeing in the shadows, frightened of what he saw before she did.

"Oh, bravo. Bravo! Really, I am touched to my very

soul—and not much touches me there these days, sad to say."

Cam stepped into the clearing. His eyes were rimmed with a thick, shimmering gold shadow, and it shone on his face in the moonlight, making him look like a wildcat.

"That is *so* incredibly sweet," he said. "And he just loves you, too—don't you, lover boy? Don't you, Daniel?"

"Cam," Daniel warned. "Do not do this."

"Do what?" Cam asked, raising his left arm in the air. He snapped his fingers once and a small flame, the size of a lit match, ignited in the air over his hand. "You mean that?"

The echo of his finger snap seemed to linger, to reflect off the tombs in the cemetery, to grow louder and multiply as it bounced back and forth. At first Luce thought the sound was more applause, as if a demonic auditorium full of darkness were clapping derisively at Luce and Daniel's love, the way Cam had done. But then she remembered the thundering wingbeats she'd heard earlier. She held her breath as the sound took the form of those thousand bits of flitting darkness. The swarm of locust-shaped shadows that had vanished into the forest reared up overhead once again.

Their drumming was so loud, Luce had to cover her ears. On the ground, Penn was crouched with her head between her knees. But Daniel and Miss Sophia stoically watched the sky as the cacophony grew and changed. It began to sound more like very loud sprinklers going off . . . or like the hiss of a thousand snakes.

"Or this?" Cam asked, shrugging as the hideous, formless darkness settled around him.

The insects each began to grow and unfold, becoming larger than any insect could ever be, dripping like glue and growing into black segmented bodies. Then, as if they were learning how to use their shadow limbs as they formed, they slowly hoisted themselves onto their numerous legs and came forward, like mantises grown to human height.

Cam welcomed them as they swarmed around him. Soon they had formed a massive army of embodied night behind Cam.

"I'm sorry," he said, smacking his forehead with his palm. "Did you tell me *not* to do that?"

"Daniel," Luce whispered. "What's happening?"

"Why did you call an end to the truce?" he called to Cam.

"Oh. Well. You know what they say about desperate times." Cam sneered. "And watching you plaster her body with those perfectly angelic kisses of yours . . . it made me feel *so* desperate."

"Shut up, Cam!" Luce shouted, hating that she'd ever let him touch her.

"In good time." Cam's eyes rolled over to her.

"Oh yes, we're going to brawl, baby. Over you. Again."
He stroked his chin and narrowed his green eyes.
"Bigger this time, I think. A few more casualties. Deal
with it."

Daniel gathered Luce in his arms. "Tell me why,
Cam. You owe me that much."

"You *know* why," Cam boomed, pointing at Luce.
"*She's* still here. Won't be for long, though."

He put his hands on his hips, and a series of dense
black shadows, now shaped like endless fat serpents,
slithered up along his body, encircling his arms like
bracelets. He petted the largest one's head dotingly.

"And this time, when your love blows into that tragic
little puff of ash, it's going to be *for good*. See, everything's different this time." Cam beamed, and Luce
thought she felt Daniel quake for just a second.

"Oh, except one thing is the same—and I do have a
soft spot for your predictability, Grigori." Cam took a
step forward. His shadow-legions inched up accordingly,
making Luce and Daniel, and Penn and Miss Sophia,
inch back. "You're afraid," he said, pointing dramatically
at Daniel. "And I'm not."

"That's because you have nothing to lose," Daniel
spat. "I would never trade places with you."

"Hmmm," Cam said, tapping his chin. "We'll see
about that." He looked around, grinning. "Must I spell it
out for you? Yes. I hear you may have something *bigger*

to lose this time. Something that's going to make annihilating her so much more enjoyable."

"What are you talking about?" Daniel asked.

To Luce's left, Miss Sophia opened her mouth and let out a howling string of feral noises. She waved her hands wildly over her head in a jerking dancelike motion, her eyes almost transparent, as if she were in some sort of trance. Her lips twitched, and Luce realized with a shock that she was speaking in tongues.

Daniel took Miss Sophia's arm and shook her. "No, you are absolutely right: It doesn't make sense," he whispered, and Luce realized he could understand Miss Sophia's strange language.

"You know what she's saying?" Luce asked.

"Allow us to translate," a familiar voice shouted from the roof of the mausoleum. Arriane. Next to her was Gabbe. Both seemed to be lit from behind and were enshrouded in a strange silver glow. They hopped down from the crypt, landing next to Luce without a sound.

"Cam's right, Daniel," Gabbe said quickly. "Something's different this time . . . something about Luce. The cycle could be broken—and not the way we want it to. I mean . . . it could end."

"Someone tell me what you're talking about," Luce said, butting in. "What's different? Broken how? What's at stake with this whole battle, anyway?"

Daniel, Arriane, and Gabbe all stared at her for a moment as if trying to place her, as if they knew her from somewhere but she'd changed so completely in an instant that they no longer recognized her face.

Finally Arriane spoke up. "At stake?" She rubbed at the scar on her neck. "If they win—it's Hell on earth. The end of the world as anyone knows it."

The black shapes screeched around Cam, wrestling with and chewing on each other, in some sort of sick, devilish warm-up.

"And if we win?" Luce struggled to get out the words.

Gabbe swallowed, then said gravely, "We don't know yet."

Suddenly Daniel stumbled back, away from Luce, and pointed at her. "Sh-she hasn't been . . . ," he stammered, covering his mouth. "The kiss," he said finally, stepping forward to grip Luce's arm. "The book. That's why you can—"

"Get to part B, Daniel," Arriane prompted. "Think fast. Patience is a virtue, and you know how Cam feels about those."

Daniel squeezed Luce's hand. "You have to go. You have to get out of here."

"What? Why?"

She looked at Arriane and Gabbe for help, then shrank away from them as a host of silver twinkles began to flow over the roof of the mausoleum. Like an endless stream of fireflies released from an enormous mason jar. They rained down on Arriane and Gabbe, making their eyes shine. It reminded Luce of fireworks—and of one Fourth of July, when the light had been just right and she'd looked into her mother's irises and seen the fireworks' reflection, a booming silvery flash of light, as if her mother's eyes were a mirror.

Only, these twinkles didn't peter into smoke like fireworks. When they hit the cemetery grass, they bloomed into graceful, shimmery iridescent beings. They weren't exactly human shapes, but they were vaguely recognizable. Gorgeous, glowing rays of light. Creatures so ravishing that Luce knew instantly they were an army of angelic power, equal in size and number to the great black force behind Cam. This was what true beauty and goodness looked like—a spectral, luminescent gathering of beings so pure it hurt to look directly at them, like the most glorious eclipse, or maybe Heaven itself. She should have felt comforted, standing on the side that *had* to prevail in this fight. But she was starting to feel sick.

Daniel pressed the back of his hand to her cheek. "She's feverish."

Gabbe patted Luce on the arm and beamed. "It's okay, sugar," she said, guiding Daniel's hand away. Her drawl was somehow reassuring. "We'll take it from here. But you have to go." She glanced over her shoulder at the horde of blackness behind Cam. "Now."

Daniel pulled Luce to him for one last embrace.

"I'll take her," Miss Sophia called loudly. The book was still tucked under her arm. "I know a safe place."

"Go," Daniel said. "I'll find you as soon as I can. Just promise me you'll run from here, and that you won't look back."

Luce had so many questions. "I don't want to leave you."

Arriane stepped between them and gave Luce a final, rough shove toward the gates. "Sorry, Luce," she said. "Time to leave this fight to us. We're kind of professionals."

Luce felt Penn's hand slide into hers, and soon they were running. Pounding up toward the gates of the cemetery as quickly as she'd bounded down on her way to find Daniel. Back up the slippery mulch slide. Back through the jagged live oak branches and the ramshackle stacks of broken headstones. They hurdled the stones and jogged up the slope, making for the distant ironwork arch of the gates. Hot wind blew her hair, and the swampy air still lay thick in her lungs. She couldn't find the moon to guide them, and the light in the cemetery's center was gone now. She didn't understand what was happening. At all. And she didn't like it at all that everyone else did.

A bolt of blackness struck the ground in front of her, cracking the earth and opening up a jagged gorge. Luce and Penn skidded to a halt just in time. The gash was as wide as Luce was tall, as deep as . . . well, she couldn't see down to the dark bottom. The edges of it sizzled and foamed.

Penn gasped. "Luce. I'm scared."

"Follow me, girls," Miss Sophia called.

She led them to the right, winding among the dark graves while blast after blast rang out behind them. "Just the sounds of battle," she huffed, like some sort of strange tour guide. "That will go on for some while, I fear."

Luce winced at every crash, but she kept pushing forward until her calves were burning, until behind her, Penn let out a wail. Luce turned and saw her friend stumble, her eyes rolling back in her head.

"Penn!" Luce screamed, reaching out to catch her just before she fell. Tenderly, Luce lowered her to the ground and rolled her over. She almost wished she hadn't. Penn's shoulder had been sliced through by something black and jagged. It had bit into her skin, leaving a charred line of flesh that smelled like burning meat.

"Is it bad?" Penn whispered hoarsely. She blinked rapidly, clearly frustrated at being unable to lift her head up to see for herself.

"No," Luce lied, shaking her head. "Just a cut." She gulped, trying to swallow the nausea rising in her as she tugged Penn's frayed black sleeve together. "Am I hurting you?"

"I don't know," Penn wheezed. "I can't feel anything."

"Girls, what *is* the holdup?" Miss Sophia had doubled back.

Luce looked up at Miss Sophia, willing her not to say how bad Penn's injury looked.

She didn't. She gave Luce a swift nod, then stretched her arms beneath Penn and lifted her up like a parent carrying a child to bed. "I've got you," she said. "It won't be long now."

"Hey." Luce followed Miss Sophia, who carried Penn's weight like she was a bag of feathers. "How did you—"

"No questions, not until we're far away from all of this," Miss Sophia said.

Far away. Luce wanted nothing less than to be far away from Daniel. And then, after they'd crossed the threshold of the cemetery and were standing on the flat ground of the school commons, she couldn't help herself. She looked back. And instantly understood why Daniel had told her not to.

A twisting silver-gold pillar of fire burst forth from the dark center of the cemetery. It was as wide as the cemetery itself, a braid of light rising hundreds of feet up into the air and boiling away the clouds. The black shadows picked at the light, occasionally tearing tendrils free and carrying them off, shrieking, into the night. As the coiling strands shifted, now more silver, now more gold, a single chord of sound began to fill the air, full and unending, loud as a mighty waterfall. Low notes thundered in the night. High notes chimed to fill the space around them. It was the grandest, most perfectly balanced celestial harmony ever heard on earth. It was beautiful, and horrifying, and everything stank of sulfur.

Everyone for miles around must have believed the world was ending. Luce didn't know what to think. Her heart seized up.

Daniel had told her not to look back because he knew the sight of it would make her want to go to him.

"Oh, no you don't," Miss Sophia said, grabbing Luce by the scruff of the neck and dragging her across campus. When they reached the gymnasium, Luce realized that Miss Sophia had been carrying Penn the whole time, using only one arm.

"What *are* you?" Luce asked as Miss Sophia pushed her through the double doors.

The librarian pulled a long key from the pocket of her beaded red cardigan and slipped it into a part of the brick wall at the front of the foyer that didn't even look like a door. An entrance to a long stairway opened silently, and Miss Sophia gestured for Luce to precede her up the stairs.

Penn's eyes were closed. She was either unconscious or in too much pain to keep them open. Either way, she was staying remarkably quiet.

"Where are we going?" Luce asked. "We need to get out of here. Where's your car?" She didn't want to scare Penn, but they needed to get to a doctor. Fast.

"Quiet, if you know what's good for you." Miss Sophia glanced at Penn's wound and sighed. "We're going to the only chamber in this place that hasn't been desecrated with athletic equipment. Where we can be alone."

By then, Penn had begun groaning in Miss Sophia's arms. The blood from her wound was a thick, dark stream on the marble floor.

Luce eyed the steep staircase. She couldn't even see its end. "I think for Penn's sake we should stay down here. We're going to need to get help pretty soon."

Miss Sophia sighed and laid Penn down on the stone, quickly popping back up to lock the front door they'd just come through. Luce fell to her knees in front of Penn. Her friend looked so small and fragile. In the dim light coming from the delicate wrought iron chandelier overhead, Luce could at last see how badly she'd been injured.

Penn was the only friend Luce had at Sword & Cross she could really relate to, the only one she wasn't intimidated by. After Luce had seen what Arriane and Gabbe and Cam were capable of, few things made sense. But one did: Penn was the only kid at Sword & Cross like her.

Except Penn was stronger than Luce. Smarter and happier and more easygoing. She was the reason Luce had made it through these first few weeks of reform school at all. Without Penn, who knew where Luce would be?

"Oh, Penn." Luce sighed. "You're going to be okay. We're going to get you all fixed up."

Penn murmured something incomprehensible, which made Luce nervous. Luce turned back to Miss Sophia, who was closing all the windows in the foyer one by one.

"She's fading fast," Luce said. "We *need* to call a doctor."

"Yes, yes," Miss Sophia said, but something in her tone sounded preoccupied. She seemed consumed with closing up the building, as if the shadows from the cemetery were on their way here right now.

"Luce?" Penn whispered. "I'm scared."

"Don't be." Luce squeezed her hand. "You're so brave. This whole time you've been such a pillar of strength."

"Give me a break," Miss Sophia said from behind her, in a rough voice Luce had never heard her use. "She's a pillar of salt."

"What?" Luce asked, confused. "What does that mean?"

Miss Sophia's beady eyes had narrowed into thin black slits. Her face pinched into wrinkles and she bitterly shook her head. Then, very slowly, from the sleeve of her cardigan, she produced a long silver dagger. "The girl is only slowing us down."

Luce's eyes widened as she watched Miss Sophia raise the dagger over her head. Dazed, Penn didn't register what was happening, but Luce certainly did.

"No!" she screamed, reaching up to stop Miss

Sophia's arm, to turn away the dagger. But Miss Sophia knew what she was doing and deftly blocked Luce's arm, pushing her aside with her free hand while she dragged the blade across Penn's throat.

Penn grunted and coughed, her breath turning ragged. Her eyes rolled backward in their sockets the way they did when she was thinking. Except she wasn't thinking, she was dying. At last her eyes met Luce's. Then they slowly dulled and Penn's breathing quieted.

"Messy but necessary," Miss Sophia said, wiping the blade clean on Penn's black sweater.

Luce stumbled backward, covering her mouth, unable to scream and unable to look away from her dying friend, unable to look at the woman who she'd thought was on their side. Suddenly, she realized why Miss Sophia had bolted all the doors and windows in the foyer. It wasn't to keep anyone out. It was to keep her in.

NINETEEN

OUT OF SIGHT

At the top of the stairs was a flat brick wall. Dead ends of any kind had always made Luce claustrophobic, and this one was even worse because of the knife poised at her throat. She dared a glance back at the steep flight they'd climbed. From here, it looked like a very long and painful fall.

Miss Sophia was speaking in tongues again, muttering under her breath as she skillfully eased open another hidden door. She shoved Luce into a tiny chapel and locked the door behind them. It was freezing inside and smelled overwhelmingly of chalky dust. Luce struggled to breathe, to swallow the bilious saliva in her mouth.

Penn could not be dead. That whole thing could not just have happened. Miss Sophia *could not be that evil.*

Daniel had said to trust Miss Sophia. He'd said to go with her until he could come for Luce. . . .

Miss Sophia paid Luce no attention, merely made her way around the room, lighting candle after candle, genuflecting at each one, and continuing to chant in a language Luce didn't know. The twinkling votives revealed that the chapel was clean and well maintained, which meant it must not have been too long since someone else had been up there. But surely Miss Sophia was the only one on campus who would have a key to the hidden door? Who else would even know this place existed?

The red tile ceiling was sloping and uneven. Broad, faded tapestries cloaked the walls, depicting images of creepy half-man, half-fish creatures battling on a roiling sea. There was a small white altar up at the front, and a few rows of simple wooden pews ranked along the gray stone floor. Luce looked around frantically for an exit, but there were no other doors and no windows.

Luce's legs were shaking with fury and fear. She was in agony over Penn, betrayed and lying alone at the foot of the stairs.

"Why are you doing this?" she asked, backing up against the arched chapel doors. "I trusted you."

"That's your own fault, dear," Miss Sophia said, roughly twisting Luce's arm. Then the dagger was back at her neck and she was being marched up the chapel's aisle. "Trust is a careless pursuit at best. At worst, it's a good way to get yourself killed."

Miss Sophia pushed Luce toward the altar. "Now be a dear and lie down, would you?"

Because the knife was still too close to her throat, Luce did as she was told. She felt a spot of coolness on her neck and reached up to touch it. When she took her fingers away, the tips were red with dots of blood where the knife had pricked her. Miss Sophia slapped her hand down.

"You think that's bad, you should see what you're missing outside," she said, making Luce shudder. Daniel was outside.

The altar was a square white platform, a single slab of stone no bigger than Luce herself. She felt cold and desperately exposed atop it, imagining the pews filled up with shadowy churchgoers waiting for her torture to take place.

Looking straight up, she saw that there was a window in this cavernous chapel, a large stained-glass rosette like a skylight in the ceiling. It had a complicated geometric floral pattern, with red and purple roses against a navy-blue background. It would have been a whole lot prettier to Luce if it had offered a view of the outside.

"Let's see, where did I . . . ah yes!" Miss Sophia reached below the altar and returned with a thick length of rope. "Don't wiggle, now," she said, waving the knife in Luce's direction. Then she set about securing Luce to four holes drilled into the altar's surface. First each ankle, then each wrist. Luce tried not to writhe as she was tied down like some sort of sacrifice. "Perfect," Miss Sophia said, giving her intricate knots a firm tug.

"You planned all this," Luce realized, aghast.

Miss Sophia grinned as sweetly as she had the very first day Luce had stumbled into the library. "I would say it's nothing personal, Lucinda, but actually, it is," she cackled. "I've been waiting a long time for this moment alone with you."

"Why?" Luce asked. "What do you want from me?"

"You, I just want eliminated," Miss Sophia said. "It's *Daniel* I want freed up."

She left Luce on the altar and moved to a lectern near Luce's feet. She hoisted the Grigori book onto the lectern and began rapidly flipping through the pages. Luce thought back to the moment she'd opened it and seen her face next to Daniel's for the first time. How it had finally hit her that he was an angel. She'd known next to nothing then, and yet she'd felt certain that the photograph meant she and Daniel could be together.

Now that felt impossible.

"You're just sitting there swooning over him, aren't you?" Miss Sophia asked. She smacked the book closed and banged her fist on its cover. "This is precisely the problem."

"What's wrong with you?" Luce strained against the ropes binding her to the altar. "What do you care about what Daniel and I feel for each other, or who either one of us dates in the first place?" This psycho had nothing to do with them.

"I should like to have a word with whoever thought putting the fate of all of our eternal souls in the hands of one lovesick pair of infants was so brilliant an idea." She raised a shaking fist high in the air. "They want the balance to be tipped? *I'll* show them tipping the balance." The point of her dagger gleamed in the candlelight.

Luce drew her eyes away from the blade. "You're crazy."

"If wanting to bring to a final head the longest, greatest battle ever fought means I'm crazy"—Miss Sophia's tone implied that Luce was dense for not knowing all this already—"so be it."

The idea that Miss Sophia could have any say in ending the battle didn't add up in Luce's mind. Daniel was fighting the battle outside. What was going on in here couldn't compare to that. Regardless of whether Miss Sophia had crossed over to the other side.

"They said it would be Hell on earth," Luce whispered. "The end of days."

Miss Sophia started laughing. "It would seem that way to you now. Is it such a surprise that I'm one of the good guys, Lucinda?"

"If you're on the good side," Luce spat, "it doesn't sound like a war worth fighting."

Miss Sophia smiled, as if she'd expected Luce to say those very words. "Your death may be just the push Daniel needs. A little push in the right direction."

Luce squirmed on the altar. "You—you wouldn't hurt me."

Miss Sophia crossed back toward her, and brought her face close. The artificial baby-powder old lady scent filled Luce's nose, making her gag.

"Of course I would," Miss Sophia said, bobbing the wild silver frizz of her unkempt hair. "You're the human equivalent of a migraine."

"But I'll just come back. Daniel told me." Luce gulped. *In seventeen years.*

"Oh, no you won't. Not this time," Miss Sophia said. "That first day you walked into my library, I saw something in your eyes, but I couldn't put my finger on it." She smiled down at Luce. "I've met you many times before, Lucinda, and most of the time, you're a downright bore."

Luce stiffened, feeling exposed, as if she were naked

on this altar. It was one thing for Daniel to have encountered her in other lives—but had others known her, too?

"This time," Miss Sophia continued, "you had something of an edge. A genuine spark. But it wasn't until tonight, that beautiful slipup about those agnostic parents of yours."

"What about my parents?" Luce hissed.

"Well, my dear, the reason you come back again and again is because all the other times you've been born, you were ushered into religious belief. This time, when your parents opted out of baptizing you, they effectively left your little soul up for grabs." She shrugged dramatically. "No ritual to welcome you into religion equals no reincarnation for Luce. A small but essential loophole in your cycle."

Could this have been what Arriane and Gabbe had been hinting at in the cemetery? Luce's head began to throb. A veil of red spots took over her vision and she heard a ringing in her ears. She blinked slowly, feeling even that tiny brush of her eyelids closing like a blast through her whole head. She was almost glad she was already lying down. Otherwise she might have fainted.

If this was really the end . . . well, it *couldn't* be.

Miss Sophia leaned close to Luce's face, sending spit flying with her words. "When you die tonight—you *die*. That's it. *Kaput*. In this lifetime you're nothing more than you appear to be: a stupid, selfish, ignorant, spoiled little girl who thinks the world lives or dies on whether she gets to go out with some good-looking boy at school. Even if your death wouldn't accomplish something so long-awaited, glorious, and grand, I'd still relish this moment, killing you."

Luce watched as Miss Sophia raised the knife and touched her finger to its blade.

Luce's mind reeled. All day, there had been so much she needed to process, so many people telling her so many different things. Now the dagger was poised over her heart and her eyes grew fuzzy once again. She felt the pressure of the blade's point against her chest, felt Miss Sophia probing along her breastbone for the space between her ribs, and she thought there was some truth in Miss Sophia's maddening speech. To place so much hope in the power of true love—which she felt she was only barely beginning to glimpse herself—*was* it naïve? After all, true love couldn't win that battle outside. It might not even be able to save her from dying right here on this altar.

But it had to. Her heart still beat for Daniel—and until that changed, something deep inside Luce believed in that love, in its power to turn her into a better version of herself, to turn her and Daniel into something glorious and good—

Luce cried out when the dagger pricked her skin—then in shock as the stained-glass window overhead seemed to shatter and the air around her filled with light and noise.

A hollow, gorgeous hum. A blinding brightness.

So she had died.

The dagger had gone deeper than it had felt. Luce was moving on to the next place. How else to explain the glowing, opalescent shapes hovering over her, descending from the sky, the cascade of twinkles, the heavenly glow? It was hard to see anything clearly in the warm silver light. Gliding over her skin, it felt like the softest velvet, like meringue frosting on a cake. The ropes binding her arms and legs were loosened, then released, and her body—or maybe this was her soul—was free to float up into the sky.

But then she heard Miss Sophia bleating, "Not yet! It's happening too soon!" The old woman had torn the dagger away from Luce's chest.

Luce blinked rapidly. Her wrists. Untied. Her ankles. Free. Tiny shards of blue and red and green and gold stained glass all over her skin, the altar, the floor beneath it. They stung as she brushed them away, leaving thin trails of blood on her arms. She squinted up toward the gaping hole in the ceiling.

Not dead, then, but saved. By angels.

Daniel had come for her.

Where was he? She could barely see. She wanted to wade through the light until her fingers found him, closed around the back of his neck, and never, never, never let him go.

There were just the living opalescent shapes drifting

toward and around Luce's body, like a roomful of glowing feathers. They flocked to her, tending to her body in the places where the shattered glass had cut her. Swaths of gauzy light that seemed to somehow wash away the blood on her arms, and on the small gash at her chest, until she was fully restored.

Miss Sophia had run to the far wall and was pawing frantically at the bricks, trying to find the secret door. Luce wanted to stop her—to make her answer for what she'd done, and what she'd almost done—but then part of the silver twinkling light took on the faintest violet hue and began to form the outline of a figure.

A bright pulsing shook the room. A light so glorious it could have outshone the sun made the walls rumble and the candles rock and flicker in their tall bronze holders. The eerie tapestries flapped against the stone wall. Miss Sophia cowered, but the shuddering glow felt like a deep massage, down to Luce's very bones. And when the light condensed, spreading warmth across the room, it settled into the form Luce recognized and adored.

Daniel stood before her, in front of the altar. He was shirtless, barefoot, clad only in white linen pants. He smiled at her, then closed his eyes and spread his arms out at his sides. Then, gingerly and very slowly, as if not to shock her, he exhaled deeply and his wings began to unfurl.

They came gradually, starting at the base of his shoulders, two white shoots extending from his back, growing higher, wider, thicker as they spread back and up and out. Luce eyed the scalloped edges, yearning to trace them with her hands, her cheeks, her lips. The inside of his wings began to glow with velvet iridescence. Just like in her dream. Only now, when it was finally coming true, she could look at his wings for the first time without feeling woozy, without straining her eyes. She could take in all of Daniel's glory.

He was still glowing, as if lit from within. She could still clearly see his violet-gray eyes and his full mouth. His strong hands and broad shoulders. She could reach out and fold herself into her love's light.

He reached for her. Luce closed her eyes at his touch, expecting something too otherworldly for her human body to withstand. But no. It was simply, reassuringly, Daniel.

She reached around his back to finger his wings. She reached for them nervously, as if they could burn her, but they flowed around her fingers, softer than the smoothest velvet, the plushest rug. The way she'd like to imagine that a fluffy, sun-drenched cloud would feel if she could cup it in her hands.

"You're so . . . *beautiful*," she whispered into his chest. "I mean, you've always been beautiful, but this—"

"Does it scare you?" he whispered. "Does it hurt to look?"

She shook her head. "I thought it might," she said, thinking back to her dreams. "But it hurts not to."

He sighed, relieved. "I want you to feel safe with me." The glittering light around them fell like confetti, and Daniel pulled her to him. "It's a lot for you to take in."

She bent her head back and parted her lips, eager to do just that.

The loud slam of a door interrupted them. Miss Sophia had found the stairs. Daniel gave a slight nod and a blazing figure of light darted through the secret door after the woman.

"What was that?" Luce asked, gaping at the trail of light fast fading through the open door.

"A helper." Daniel guided her chin back.

And then, even though Daniel was with her and she felt loved and protected and saved, she also felt a sharp stab of uncertainty, remembering all the dark things that had just happened, and Cam and his thundering black minions. There were still so many unanswerable questions running through her mind, so many awful events she felt she'd never understand. Like Penn's death, poor sweet innocent Penn, her violent, senseless end. It overwhelmed Luce, and her lip began to quiver.

"Penn's gone, Daniel," she said. "Miss Sophia killed her. And for a moment, I thought she'd killed me, too."

"I would never let that happen."

"How did you know to find me here? How do you always know how to save me?" She shook her head. "Oh my God," she whispered slowly as the truth slammed into her. "You're my guardian angel."

Daniel chuckled. "Not exactly. Though I think you were giving me a compliment."

Luce blushed. "Then what kind of angel are you?"

"I'm sort of in between gigs right now," Daniel said.

Behind him, the remaining silver light in the room pooled and split in half. Luce turned to watch it, her heart thumping, as the glow finally gathered, as it had around Daniel's figure, around two distinct shapes:

Arriane and Gabbe.

Gabbe's wings were already unfurled. They were broad and plush and three times the size of her body. Feathery, with softly scalloped edges, the way angels' wings looked on greeting cards and in movies, and with just a hint of the palest pink around the tips. Luce noticed them beating very lightly—and that Gabbe's feet were a few inches off the ground.

Arriane's wings were smoother, sleeker and with more pronounced edges, almost like a giant butterfly's. Partially translucent, they glowed and cast shifting opalescent prisms of light on the stone floor beneath them. Like Arriane herself, they were strange and alluring, and totally badass.

"I should have known," Luce said, a smile sweeping across her face.

Gabbe smiled back, and Arriane gave Luce a little curtsy.

"What's going on out there?" Daniel asked, registering the worried expression on Gabbe's face.

"We need to get Luce out of here."

The battle. Was it not over yet? If Daniel and Gabbe and Arriane were all here, they must have won—right? Luce's eyes flashed over to Daniel's. His expression gave nothing away.

"And someone needs to go after Sophia," Arriane said. "She could not have been working alone."

Luce swallowed. "Is she on Cam's side? Is she some kind of . . . devil? A fallen angel?" It was one of the few terms that had stuck with her from Miss Sophia's lecture.

Daniel's teeth were clenched. Even his wings looked stiff with fury. "No devil," he muttered, "but hardly an angel, either. We thought she was with us. We should never have let her get this close."

"She was one of the twenty-four elders," Gabbe added. She lowered her feet to the ground and tucked her pale pink wings behind her back so she could sit down on the altar. "A very respectable position. She kept this part of her well hidden."

"As soon as we got up here, it was like she just went crazy," Luce said. She rubbed her neck where the dagger had nicked her.

"They *are* crazy," Gabbe said. "But very ambitious. She's part of a secret sect. I should have realized it sooner, but the signs are very clear now. They call themselves the Zhsmaelim. They dress alike, and all have a certain . . . elegance. I always thought they were more show than anything else. No one took them too seriously in Heaven," she informed Luce, "but they will now. What she did tonight was grounds for exile. She might be seeing more of Cam and Molly than she bargained for."

"So Molly's a fallen angel, too," Luce said slowly. Out of everything she'd learned today, this made the most sense.

"Luce, we're *all* fallen angels," Daniel said. "It's just that some of us are on one side . . . and some of us are on the other."

"Is anyone else here on"—she swallowed—"the other side?"

"Roland," Gabbe said.

"Roland?" Luce was stunned. "But you were friends with him. He was always so charismatic and great."

Daniel only shrugged. It was Arriane who looked concerned. Her wings beat in a sad, agitated way and sent forth a brush of dusty wind. "We'll get him back someday," she said quietly.

"What about Penn?" Luce asked, feeling a knot of tears in the back of her throat.

But Daniel shook his head, squeezing her hand. "Penn was mortal. An innocent victim in a long, pointless war. I'm so sorry, Luce."

"So that whole fight out there . . . ?" Luce asked. Her voice choked. She couldn't bring herself to really talk about Penn yet.

"Just one of many battles we wage against the demons," Gabbe said.

"Well, who won?"

"Nobody," Daniel said bitterly. He picked up a large shard from the stained-glass ceiling and flung it across the chapel. It shattered into a hundred tiny fragments, but it didn't seem to have released any of his anger. "Nobody ever wins. It's close to impossible for one angel to extinguish another. It's just a lot of beating until everyone gets tired and calls it a night."

Luce jolted when a strange image flashed into her mind. It was Daniel being struck directly on the shoulder by one of the long black bolts that had hit Penn. She opened her eyes and looked at his right shoulder. There was blood on his chest.

"You're hurt," she whispered.

"No," Daniel said.

"He can't get hurt, he's—"

"What is that on your arm, Daniel?" Arriane asked, pointing at his chest. "Is that blood?"

"It's Penn's," Daniel said brusquely. "I found her at the foot of the stairs."

Luce's heart constricted. "We need to bury Penn," she said. "Next to her father."

"Luce, honey," Gabbe said, standing up. "I wish there were time for that, but right now, we've got to go."

"I won't abandon her. She doesn't have anyone else."

"Luce," Daniel said, rubbing his forehead.

"She died in my arms, Daniel. Because I didn't know any better than to follow Miss Sophia to this torture chamber." Luce looked at all three of them. "Because none of you told me anything."

"Okay," Daniel said. "We'll make things as right for Penn as we can. But then we need to get you far away from here."

A gust of wind filtered down from the gash in the ceiling, causing the candles to flicker and making the remaining shards of glass in the broken window sway. In the next moment, they fell in a rain of sharp splinters.

Just in time, Gabbe glided off the altar and came to stand at Luce's side. She seemed unfazed. "Daniel's right," she said. "The truce we called after the battle applies only to angels. And now that so many know about the"—she paused, clearing her throat—"um, *change* in your mortality status, there are a lot of bad ones out there who'll be interested in you."

Arriane's wings lifted her off the ground. "And a lot of good ones who will come out to help fend them off," she said, gliding toward Luce's other side as if to reassure her.

"I still don't get it," Luce said. "Why does it matter so much? Why do *I* matter so much? Is it just because Daniel loves me?"

Daniel sighed. "That's part of it, as innocent as it sounds."

"You know everyone loves to hate a happy pair of lovebirds," Arriane chimed in.

"Honey, this is a very long story," Gabbe told her, the voice of reason.

"We can only give it to you a chapter at a time."

"And like with my wings," Daniel added, "you'll have to awaken to a lot of it on your own."

"But why?" Luce asked. This conversation was so frustrating. She felt like a child being told she would get it when she was older. "Why can't you just help me understand?"

"We *can* help," Arriane said, "but we can't unload everything on you at once. Like how you're never supposed to shock a sleepwalker into wakefulness. It's too dangerous."

Luce wrapped her arms around herself. "It would kill me," she said, offering up the words the rest of them were circumventing.

Daniel put his arms around her. "It has before. And you've had enough close encounters with death for one night."

"So what? Now I just have to leave school?" She turned to Daniel. "Where will you take me?"

His brow furrowed, and he looked away from her. "*I* can't take you anywhere. It would draw too much attention. We're going to have to rely on someone else. There's one mortal here we can trust." He looked at Arriane.

"I'll get him," she said, rising.

"I won't leave you," Luce said to Daniel. Her lip quivered. "I've only just gotten you back."

Daniel kissed her forehead, igniting a warmth that spread through her body. "Luckily, we still have a little time."

TWENTY

DAYBREAK

Dawn. The break of the last day Luce would see at
Sword & Cross for—well, she didn't know how long. A
single wild dove's coo rang out in the saffron sky as she
stepped through the gym's kudzu-swathed doors.
Slowly, she set off toward the cemetery, hand in hand
with Daniel. They were quiet as they walked across the
still grass of the commons.

Just before they'd left the chapel, one at a time, the
others had retracted their wings. It was a sobering,

laborious process that left them lethargic once they were back in human form. Watching the transformation, Luce couldn't believe how the massive, brilliant wings could turn so small and feeble, finally vanishing into the angels' skin.

When it was over, she'd run her hand over Daniel's bare back. For the first time, he seemed modest, sensitive to her touch. But his skin was as smooth and unblemished as a baby's. And in his face, in all of their faces, Luce could still see the silver light manifested inside them, shining out in all directions.

In the end, they'd carried Penn's body back up the steep stone stairs to the chapel, wiped the altar clean of glass, and laid her body there. There was no way they could bury her this morning—not with the cemetery teeming with mortals, as Daniel promised it would be.

It was agonizing for Luce to accept that she would have to settle for whispering a few last words to her friend inside the chapel. All she could think to say was "You're with your father now. I know he's happy to have you back."

Daniel would bury Penn properly as soon as the school calmed down—and Luce would show him where Penn's father's grave was so Penn could be laid to rest at his side. It was the very least she could do.

Her heart was heavy as they crossed the campus. Her jeans and tank top felt stretched out and dingy. Her fingernails needed a good scrub, and she was glad there were no mirrors around so she could see what was up with her hair. She wished so much that she could take back the dark half of the night—could have saved Penn, most of all—while keeping the beautiful parts. The climactic thrill of piecing Daniel's true identity together. The moment he appeared before her in all his glory. Witnessing Arriane and Gabbe growing their wings. So much of it had been so lovely.

So much of it had resulted in utter, bleak destruction.

She could feel it in the atmosphere, like an epidemic. She could read it on the faces of the many students roaming the commons. It was way too early for any of them to be awake of their own accord, which meant they must all have heard or seen or felt some of the battle that had taken place last night. What would they know? Would anyone be looking for Penn yet? For Miss Sophia? What could any of them possibly think had happened? Everyone was paired up and speaking in hushed whispers. Luce longed to linger close to them and eavesdrop.

"Don't worry." Daniel squeezed her hand. "Just imitate any of the baffled looks on their faces. No one will give us a second thought."

Though Luce felt entirely conspicuous, he was right. None of the other students' eyes lingered on the two of them any longer than they did on anyone else.

At the gates of the cemetery, blue and white police

lights flashed, reflecting in the leaves of the oak trees overhead. The entrance had been marked off with yellow hazard tape.

Luce saw Randy's black silhouette outlined against the sunrise ahead of them. She was pacing before the cemetery's entrance and shouting into a Bluetooth clipped to the collar of her shapeless polo shirt.

"I think you *should* wake him up," she yelled into the device. "There's been an incident at the school. I keep telling you . . . I don't *know*."

"I should warn you," Daniel told her as he steered her away from Randy and the blinking lights of the cop cars, through the oak grove that bordered the cemetery on three sides. "It will look strange to you down there. Cam's style of warfare is messier than ours. It's not gory, it's just . . . different."

Luce didn't think much could alarm her at this point. A few toppled statues certainly weren't going to set her off. They picked their way through the forest, brittle fall leaves crunching beneath their feet. Luce thought about how, the night before, these trees had been consumed by the thundering locust-shadow cloud. There was no trace of them now.

Soon, Daniel gestured to a badly bent segment of the cemetery's wrought iron fence.

"We can enter there without being seen. We'll have to be quick about it."

Stepping out from the shelter of the trees, Luce slowly understood what Daniel meant about the cemetery looking different. They stood at the rim, not far from Penn's father's grave at the east corner, but it was impossible to see more than a few feet in front of them. The air above the grounds was so murky it might not even have qualified as air. It was thick and gray and gritty, and Luce had to fan her hands through it just to see in front of her face.

She rubbed her fingers together. "Is this—"

"Dust," Daniel said, taking her hand as they walked. He was able to see through it, didn't have to choke and cough it out of his lungs as Luce did. "In war, angels don't die. But their battles leave this thick carpet of dust in their wake."

"What happens to it?"

"Not much, besides the fact that it baffles mortals. It will settle eventually, and then they'll come out to study it by the carload. There's a crazy scientist in Pasadena who thinks it comes from UFOs."

Luce thought with a shudder about the unidentifiable flying black cloud of insectlike objects. That scientist might not be too far off.

"Penn's father was buried up here," she said, pointing as they neared his corner of the graveyard. As eerie as the dust was, she was relieved that the graves, statues, and trees within the cemetery all seemed to have been left standing. She got down on her knees and wiped away the pelt of dust from the grave she thought belonged to Penn's father. Her shaking fingers brushed clean the letters that nearly made her weep.

STANFORD LOCKWOOD
WORLD'S BEST FATHER

The space beside Mr. Lockwood's grave was bare. Luce stood up and stamped her foot woefully on the ground, hating that her friend would join him there. Hating that she couldn't even be present to give Penn a proper memorial.

People always talked about Heaven when someone died, how they were certain the deceased were there. Luce never felt like she'd known the rules, and now felt even less qualified to speak about what might or might not be.

She turned to Daniel, tears in her eyes. His face fell at the sight of her sorrow. "I'll take care of her, Luce," he said. "I know it's not the way you wanted, but we'll do the best we can."

The tears came harder. Luce was sniffling and sobbing and wanting Penn back so badly she thought she might collapse. "I can't leave her, Daniel. How can I?"

Daniel gently wiped her tears with the back of his hand. "What happened to Penn is terrible. A huge mistake. But when you walk away today, you won't be leaving her." He laid a hand over Luce's heart. "She's with you."

"Still, I can't—"

"You can, Luce." His voice was firm. "Believe me. You have no idea how many strong and impossible things you are capable of." He looked away from her, out at the trees. "If there's any good left in this world, you'll know soon."

A single blip of a police car's siren made both of them jump. A car door slammed, and not far from where they stood, they heard the crunch of boots on gravel. "What in the hell—Ronnie, call the central office. Tell the sheriff to get down here."

"Let's go," Daniel said, reaching for her hand. She slid it into his, giving the crest of Mr. Lockwood's headstone a somber pat, then started moving with Daniel back through the graves near the eastern side of the cemetery. They reached the bent part of the ornate wrought iron fence, then quickly ducked back into the grove of oak trees.

A cold wall of air slammed into Luce as they walked. In the branches ahead of them, she saw three small but seething shadows hanging upside down like bats.

"Hurry," Daniel commanded. As they passed, the shadows reared back, hissing, somehow knowing not to mess with Luce when Daniel was at her side.

"Now where?" Luce asked at the edge of the oak grove.

"Close your eyes," he said.

She did. Daniel's arms circled her waist from behind and she felt his strong chest press into her shoulders. He was lifting her off the ground. A foot maybe, then higher, until the soft leaves of the treetops skimmed her shoulders, tickling her neck as Daniel pushed through them. Higher still, until she could feel the two of them burst free of the woods and into the bright morning sun. She was tempted to open her eyes—yet she sensed intuitively that it would be too much. She wasn't sure that she was ready. And besides, the feeling of the clear air on her face and the rushing wind in her hair was enough. More than enough. Celestial. Like the feeling she'd had when she'd been rescued from the library, like riding a wave on the ocean. She knew for certain now that Daniel had been behind that, too.

"You can open your eyes now," he said quietly. Luce felt the ground under her feet again and saw they were at the only place she wanted to be. Under the magnolia tree near the lake's edge.

Daniel held her close. "I wanted to bring you here because this is one place—one of many places—where I've really wanted to kiss you these past few weeks. I almost lost it that day when you dove right into the water."

Luce stood on her toes, tilting her head back to kiss Daniel. She had wanted to kiss him badly that day, too—

and now she *needed* to kiss him. His kiss was the only thing that felt right, the only thing that comforted her, and reminded her that there was a reason to go on, even when Penn couldn't. The tender pressure of his lips soothed her, like a warm drink in the dead of winter, when every part of her felt so cold.

Too soon, he pulled back, looking down at her with the saddest eyes.

"There's another reason I brought you here. This rock leads to the path we'll need to take to move you somewhere safe."

Luce lowered her eyes. "Oh."

"This isn't goodbye for good, Luce. I hope it's not even goodbye for long. We'll just have to see how things . . . develop." He smoothed her hair. "Please don't worry. I will always come for you. I won't let you go until you understand that."

"Then I refuse to understand," she said.

Daniel laughed under his breath. "See that clearing over there?" He pointed across the lake about half a mile away where a small pocket of forest opened up to a flat, grassy knoll. Luce had never noticed it before, but now she saw a small white plane with red lights on its wings blinking in the distance.

"That's for me?" she asked. After all that had happened, the sight of an airplane barely fazed her. "Where am I going?"

She couldn't believe she was leaving a place she'd

hated but where she'd had so many intense experiences in just a few short weeks. What was Sword & Cross going to be anymore?

"What's going to happen to this place? And what am I going to tell my parents?"

"For now, try not to worry. As soon as you're safe, we'll tackle everything else we need to. Mr. Cole can call your parents."

"Mr. Cole?"

"He's on our side, Luce. You can trust him."

But she had trusted Miss Sophia. She hardly knew Mr. Cole. He seemed so teachery. And that mustache . . . She was supposed to leave Daniel and get on a plane with her history teacher? Her head throbbed.

"There's a path that follows the water," Daniel continued. "We can pick it up down there." He curved his arm around the small of her back. "Or," he proposed, "we could swim."

Holding hands, they stood at the edge of the red rock. They'd left their shoes under the magnolia tree, but this time, there'd be no going back. Luce didn't think it would feel so great to dive into the cold lake in her jeans and a tank top, but with Daniel smiling next to her, everything she did felt like the only thing there was to do.

They raised their arms overhead and Daniel counted to three. Their feet lifted off the ground at exactly the same time, their bodies arched in the air in exactly the same shape, but instead of going down, as Luce instinctively expected, Daniel pulled her higher, using only the tips of his fingers.

They were flying. Luce was hand in hand with an angel and she was flying. The crests of the trees seemed to bow to them. Her body felt lighter than air. The early-morning moon was still visible just over the tree line. It dipped nearer, as if Daniel and Luce were the tide. The water lapped below them, silver and inviting.

"Are you ready?" Daniel asked.

"I'm ready."

Luce and Daniel drifted down toward the deep, cool lake. They broke the surface fingers first, the longest swan dive anyone had ever pulled off. Luce gasped at the cold as they surfaced, then started laughing.

Daniel's hand took hers again, and he motioned for her to join him on the rock. He pulled himself up first, then reached down and lifted her. The moss made a fine, soft carpet for the two of them to spread out on. Water droplets clung to his chest. They lay on their sides facing each other, propping themselves up on their elbows.

Daniel put his hand on the hollow of her hip. "Mr. Cole will be waiting when we reach the plane," he said. "This is our last chance to be alone. I thought we might say our real goodbye here.

"I'm going to give you something," he added, reaching inside his pocket and pulling out the silver medallion she'd seen him wear around school. He pressed the chain into Luce's open palm and she realized it was a locket, a rose engraved on its face. "It used to belong to you," he said. "A very long time ago."

Luce clicked open the locket to find a tiny photograph inside, behind a glass plate. It was a picture of the two of them, looking not at the camera, but deep into each other's eyes, and laughing. Luce's hair was short, as it was now, and Daniel was wearing a bow tie.

"When was this taken?" she asked, holding up the locket. "Where are we?"

"I'll tell you the next time I see you," he said. He lifted the chain over her head and placed it around her neck. When the locket touched her collarbone, she could feel a deep heat pulsing through it, warming her cold, wet skin.

"I love it," she whispered, touching the chain.

"I know Cam gave you that gold necklace, too," Daniel said.

Luce hadn't thought about that since Cam had forced it onto her at the bar. She couldn't believe that was only yesterday. The thought of wearing it made her feel sick. She didn't even know where the necklace was—and she didn't want to.

"He put it on me," she said, feeling guilty. "I didn't—"

"I know," Daniel said. "Whatever happened between you and Cam, it wasn't your fault. Somehow he held on to a lot of his angelic charm when he fell. It's very deceptive."

"I hope I never see him again." She shuddered.

"I'm afraid you might. And there are more like Cam out there. You'll just have to trust your gut," Daniel said. "I don't know how long it will take to catch you up on everything that's happened in our past. But in the meantime, if you feel an instinct, even about something you think you don't know, you should trust it. You'll probably be right."

"So trust myself even when I can't trust those around me?" she asked, feeling like this was part of what Daniel meant.

"I'll try to be there to help you, and I'll send word as much as I can when I'm away," Daniel said. "Luce, you possess your past lives' memories . . . even if you can't unlock them yet. If something feels wrong to you, stay away."

"Where are you going?"

Daniel looked up at the sky. "To find Cam," he said. "We have a few more things to take care of."

The moroseness in his voice made Luce nervous. She thought back to the thick felt of dust Cam had left in the cemetery.

"But you'll come back to me," she said, "after that? Do you promise?"

"I—I can't live without you, Luce. I love you. It matters not just to me, but . . ." He hesitated, then shook his head. "Don't worry about any of that now. Only know that I will come for you."

Slowly, reluctantly, the two of them stood up. The sun had just peeked over the trees, and it shimmered in tiny star-shaped shards on the choppy water. There was only a short distance to swim from here to the muddy bank that would lead them to the plane. Luce wished it were miles away. She could have swum with Daniel until nightfall. And every sunrise and sunset after that.

They hopped back into the water and started swimming. Luce made sure to tuck the locket inside her tank top. If trusting her instincts was important, her instincts told her never to part with this necklace.

She watched, awestruck all over again, as Daniel began his slow, elegant stroke. This time, in the moonlight, she knew the iridescent wings she saw outlined in drops of water were not figments of her imagination. They were real.

She brought up the rear, cutting through the water with stroke after stroke. Too soon, her fingers touched the shore. She hated that she could hear the hum of the plane's engine further up in the clearing. They'd reached the place where they would have to part, and Daniel practically had to drag her out of the water. She'd gone from feeling damp and happy to being dripping wet and freezing. They walked toward the plane, his hand on her back.

To Luce's surprise, Mr. Cole was holding out a large white towel when he hopped down from the cockpit. "A little angel told me you might need this," he said, unfolding it for Luce, who took it gratefully.

"Who you calling little?" Arriane popped up from behind a tree, followed by Gabbe, who brought forward the Watchers book.

"We came to say *bon voyage*," Gabbe said, handing the book to Luce. "Take this," she said lightly, but her smile looked more like a frown.

"Give her the good stuff," Arriane said, nudging Gabbe.

Gabbe pulled a thermos out of her backpack, handing it to Luce. She lifted off the top. It was hot chocolate, and it smelled incredible. Luce nestled the book and the thermos in her towel-dried arms, feeling suddenly rich with possessions. But she knew as soon as she got on that plane that she'd feel empty and alone. She pressed against Daniel's shoulder, taking advantage of his nearness while she still could.

Gabbe's eyes were clear and strong. "We'll see you soon, okay?"

But Arriane's eyes darted away, as if she didn't want to look at Luce. "Don't do anything stupid, like turning into a pile of ash." She shuffled her feet. "We need you."

"*You* need *me*?" Luce asked. She'd needed Arriane to show her the ropes at Sword & Cross. She'd needed Gabbe that day in the infirmary. But why would they need her?

Both girls only answered with somber smiles before retreating into the forest. Luce turned to Daniel, trying to forget that Mr. Cole was still standing a few feet away.

"I'll give you two a moment alone," Mr. Cole said, taking the hint. "Luce, from the time I start the engine up, it's three minutes to takeoff. I'll meet you in the cockpit."

Daniel swept her up and pressed his forehead to hers. As their lips connected, Luce tried to hold on to every part of this moment. She would need the memory the way she needed air.

Because what if, when Daniel left her, the whole thing started to feel like just another dream? A partially nightmarish dream, but a dream nonetheless. How could it be that she felt what she thought she felt for someone who wasn't even human?

"This is it," Daniel said. "Be careful. Let Mr. Cole guide you until I come." A shrill whistle from the plane— Mr. Cole telling them to wrap it up. "Try to remember what I said."

"Which part?" Luce asked, slightly panicked.

"As much as you can—but mostly, that I love you."

Luce sniffed. Her voice would break if she tried to say a thing. It was time to go.

She jogged toward the open door of the cockpit, feeling the hot blasts from the propellers almost knock her down. There was a three-step ladder, and Mr. Cole reached out his hand to help her up. He pressed a button and the ladder withdrew into the plane. The door closed.

She looked at the complicated dashboard. She'd never been in such a small plane. Never been in a cockpit at all. There were flashing lights and buttons everywhere. She looked at Mr. Cole.

"You know how to fly this thing?" she asked, wiping her eyes on the towel.

"U.S. Air Force, Fifty-ninth Division, at your service," he said, saluting her.

Luce awkwardly saluted back.

"My wife always tells people not to get me started on my flying days in Nam," he said, easing back on a wide silver gearshift. The plane shuddered into motion. "But we've got a long flight, and I've got a captivated audience."

"You mean a captive audience," she let slip out.

"Good one." Mr. Cole elbowed her side. "I'm kidding," he said, laughing heartily. "I wouldn't subject you to that." The way he turned to her when he laughed reminded her of the way her dad always did when they were watching a funny movie, and it made her feel a little better.

The wheels were rolling quickly now and the "runway" before them looked short. They would need to lift off pretty soon or they'd end up flying straight into the lake.

"I know what you're thinking," he shouted over the roar of the engine. "Don't worry, I do this all the time!"

And just before the muddy bank below ended, he pulled hard on the lever between them, and the nose of the plane tilted up toward the sky. The horizon dropped out of view for a moment and Luce's stomach lurched along with it. But a moment later, the plane's motion settled down, and the view before them flattened out to just trees and a clear, starlit sky. Below them was the twinkling lake. Every second, it grew more distant. They had taken off to the west, but the plane was making a circle, and soon Luce's window was filled with the forest she and Daniel had just flown through. She gazed into it, pressing her face to the window to look for him, and before the plane straightened out again, she thought she saw the smallest flash of violet. She gripped the locket around her neck and brought it to her lips.

Now the rest of campus was beneath them, and the foggy cemetery just beyond it. The place where Penn would soon be buried. The higher they went, the more Luce could see of the school where her biggest secret had come out—though so differently than she ever could have imagined it would.

"They really did a number on that place," Mr. Cole said, shaking his head.

Luce had no idea how much he knew about the events that had taken place last night. He seemed so normal, and yet he was taking all of this in stride.

"Where are we going?"

"A little island off the coast," he said, pointing out in the distance toward the sea, where the horizon faded into black. "It's not too far."

"Mr. Cole," she said, "you've met my parents."

"Nice people."

"Will I be able to . . . I'd like to speak with them."

"Of course. We'll figure something out."

"They could never believe any of this."

"Can you?" he asked, giving her a wry smile as the plane rose higher, leveling itself in the air.

That was the thing. She *had* to believe it, all of it—from the first dark flicker of the shadows, to the moment when Daniel's lips found hers, to Penn lying dead on the marble altar of the chapel. It all had to be real.

How else could she hold out until she saw Daniel again? She gripped the locket around her neck, which held a lifetime of memories. Her memories, Daniel had reminded her, hers to unlock.

What they held, she didn't know, any more than she knew where Mr. Cole was taking her. But she'd felt like a part of *something* in the chapel this morning, standing next to Arriane and Gabbe and Daniel. Not lost and afraid and complacent . . . but like she might matter, not just to Daniel—but to all of them.

She looked through the windshield. They would have passed the salt marshes by now, and the road she'd driven on to get to that awful bar to meet Cam, and the long stretch of sandy beach where she'd first kissed Daniel. They were out over the open sea, which— somewhere out there—held Luce's next destination.

No one had come right out and told her that there were more battles to be fought, but Luce felt the truth inside her, that they were at the start of something long and significant and hard.

Together.

And whether the battles were gruesome or redemptive or both, Luce didn't want to be a pawn any longer. A strange feeling was working its way through her body— one steeped in all her past lives, all the love she'd felt for Daniel that had been extinguished too many times before.

It made Luce want to stand up next to him and fight. Fight to stay alive long enough to live out her life next to him. Fight for the only thing she knew that was good enough, noble enough, powerful enough to be worth risking everything.

Love.

EPILOGUE

TWO GREAT LIGHTS

All night long he watched her sleeping fitfully on the narrow canvas cot. A single army-green lantern hanging from one of the low wooden beams in the log cabin illuminated her frame. Its soft glow highlighted her glossy black hair splayed out on the pillow, her cheeks smooth and rosy from her bath.

Every time the sea roared up against the desolate beach outside, she tossed onto one side. Her tank top hugged her body so that when the thin blanket bunched up around her, he could just make out that tiny dimple marking her soft left shoulder. He had kissed it so many times before.

By turns she sighed in her sleep, then breathed evenly, then moaned from someplace deep inside a dream. But whether it was in pleasure or pain, he couldn't tell. Twice, she called out his name.

Daniel wanted to float down to her. To leave his perch atop the sandy old boxes of ammunition high in the raftered loft of the beachfront cabin. But she could not know he was there. She could not know he was anywhere nearby. Or what the next few days would bring for her.

Behind him, in the salt-stained storm window, he glimpsed a passing shadow from the corner of his eye. Then the faintest tapping on the glass pane. Wresting his eyes from her body, he moved toward the window, released the lock. A torrent of rain poured down outside, reuniting with the sea. A black cloud hid the moon and shone no light on the face of his visitor.

"May I come in?"

Cam was late.

Though Cam possessed the power to have simply appeared out of thin air at Daniel's side, Daniel pushed open the window further to allow him to climb through. So much was pomp and circumstance these days. It was important for them both to be clear that Daniel had welcomed Cam in.

Cam's face was still cast in shadow, but he showed no sign of having traveled thousands of miles in the rain. His dark hair and his skin were dry. His auric wings, compact and solid now, were the only part of him that gleamed. As if they were made of twenty-four-karat gold. Though he tucked them neatly behind him, when he sat down next to Daniel on a splintering wooden box, Cam's wings gravitated toward Daniel's iridescent silver ones. It was the natural state of things, an inexplicable reliance. Daniel couldn't inch away without giving up his unobstructed view of Luce.

"She is so lovely when she sleeps," Cam said softly.

"Is that why you wanted her to sleep for all eternity?"

"*Me?* Never. And *I* would have killed Sophia for what she attempted—not let her run free into the night as you did." Cam leaned forward, resting his elbows on the railing of the loft. Down below, Luce tightened the covers around her neck. "I just want her. You know why."

"Then I pity you. You will end up disappointed."

Cam held Daniel's eyes and rubbed his jaw, chuckling cruelly under his breath. "Oh, Daniel, your shortsightedness surprises me. You don't have her yet." He stole another long glance at Luce. "She may think you do. But we both know how very little she understands."

Daniel's wings pulled taut against his shoulder

blades, but the tips were reaching forward. Closer to Cam's. He couldn't stop it.

"The truce lasts eighteen days," Cam said. "Though I have a feeling we may need each other before then."

Then he stood, shoving the box back with his feet. The scraping along the ceiling over her head made Luce's eyes flicker, but both angels ducked back among the shadows before her gaze could settle anywhere.

They faced each other, each still weary from the battle, each knowing it was a mere taste of what was to come.

Slowly, Cam extended his pale right hand.

Daniel extended his.

And while Luce dreamed below of the most glorious wings unfurling—the likes of which she'd never seen before—two angels in the rafters shook hands.

CAN YOU BEAR THE . . .

TORMENT

THE SEQUEL TO
FALLEN
BY LAUREN KATE

IS COMING

30 SEPTEMBER 2010

TO READ AN EXCLUSIVE EXTRACT FROM
TORMENT
TURN THE PAGE NOW . . .

PROLOGUE: NEUTRAL WATERS

Daniel stared out at the bay. His eyes were as gray as the thick fog enveloping the Sausalito shoreline, as the choppy water lapping the pebble beach beneath his feet. There was no violet to them at all; he could feel it. She was too far away.

He braced himself against the biting gale off the water. But even as he tugged his thick black pea coat closer, he knew it was no use. Hunting always left him cold.

Only one thing could warm him today, and she was

out of reach. He missed the way the crown of her head made the perfect ledge for his lips. He imagined filling the circle of his arms with her body, leaning down to kiss her neck. But it was a good thing Luce couldn't be here now. What she'd see would horrify her.

Behind him, the bleat of sea lions flopping in heaps along the south shore of Angel Island sounded the way he felt: jaggedly lonely, with no one around to hear.

No one except Cam.

He was crouched in front of Daniel, tying a rusty anchor around the bulging wet figure at their feet. Even engaged in something so sinister, Cam looked good. His green eyes had a sparkle and his black hair was cut short. It was the truce; it always brought a brighter glow to the angels' cheeks, a shinier sheen to their hair, an even sharper cut to their flawless muscled bodies. Truce days were to angels what a beach vacation was to humans.

So even though Daniel ached inside each time he was forced to end a human life, to anyone else he looked like a guy coming back from a week in Hawaii: relaxed, rested, tan.

Tightening one of his intricate knots, Cam said, "Typical Daniel. Always stepping aside and leaving me to do the dirty work."

"What are you talking about? I'm the one who

finished him." Daniel looked down at the dead man, at the wiry gray hair matted to his pasty forehead, his gnarled hands and cheap rubber galoshes, at the dark red tear across his chest. It made him feel cold all over again. If the killing weren't necessary to insure Luce's safety, to save her, Daniel would never raise another weapon. Never fight another fight.

And something about killing this man did not feel quite right. In fact, Daniel had a vague, troubling sense that something was profoundly wrong.

"Finishing them is the fun part." Cam looped the rope around the man's chest and tightened it under his arms. "The dirty work is seeing them off to sea."

Daniel still gripped the tree branch in his hand. Cam had snickered at the choice, but it never mattered to Daniel what weapon he used. Tree branch, dagger, automatic rifle—it may as well have been a feather duster; Daniel could kill with anything.

"Hurry up," he growled, sickened by the obvious pleasure Cam took in human bloodshed. "You're wasting time. The tide's going out now anyway."

"And unless we do this my way, high tide tomorrow will wash Slayer here right back ashore. You're too impulsive, Daniel, always were. Do you ever think more than one step ahead?"

Daniel crossed his arms and looked back out at the white crests of the waves. A tourist catamaran from the San Francisco pier was gliding toward them. Once, the vision of that boat might have brought back a flood of memories. A thousand happy trips he'd taken with Luce across a thousand lifetimes' seas. But now—now that she could die and not come back, in this lifetime when everything was different and there would be no more reincarnations—Daniel was always too aware of how blank *her* memory was. This was the last shot. For both of them. For everyone, really. So it was Luce's memory, not Daniel's, that mattered, and so many shocking truths would have to be gently brought to the surface if she was going to survive. The thought of what she had to learn made his whole body tense up.

If Cam thought Daniel wasn't thinking of the next step, he was wrong.

"You know there's only one reason I'm still here," Daniel said. "We need to talk about her."

Cam laughed. "I *was* talking about Luce." With a grunt, he hoisted the sopping corpse up over his shoulder. The dead man's navy work-suit bunched up around the lines of rope Cam had tied. The heavy anchor rested on his bloody chest.

"This one's a little gristly, isn't he?" Cam asked. "I'm

almost insulted that the Elders didn't send a younger, more challenging hit man."

Then—as if he were an Olympic shot-put thrower—Cam bent his knees, spun around three times to wind up, and launched the dead man out across the water, a hundred feet clear into the air.

For a few long seconds, the corpse sailed over the bay. Then the weight of the anchor dragged it down . . . down . . . down. It splashed grandly into the deep aquamarine water. And instantly sank out of sight.

Cam wiped his hands. "I think I've just set a record."

"How you take human death so lightly," Daniel said, "it's a mystery to me."

"This guy deserved it," Cam said. "You really don't see the sport in all of this?"

That was when Daniel got in his face and spat, "She is not a game to me."

"And that is exactly why you will lose."

Daniel grabbed Cam by the collar of his steel-gray trench coat and considered tossing him into the water the same way he'd just tossed the predator. A cloud drifted past the sun, its shadow darkening their faces.

"Easy," Cam said, prying Daniel's hands away. "You have plenty of enemies, Daniel, but right now I'm not one of them. Remember the truce."

"Some truce," Daniel said. "Eighteen days of others trying to kill her."

"Eighteen days of you and me picking them off," Cam corrected.

It was a longstanding celestial tradition for a truce to last eighteen days. In Heaven, eighteen was the luckiest, most life-affirming number, the number by which all groups and categories were broken down. In some mortal languages, eighteen had come to mean life itself—though in this case, for Luce, it could just as easily mean death.

Cam was right. As the news of her mortality trickled down the celestial tiers, the ranks of her enemies would double and redouble each day. Miss Sophia and her cohorts, the Twenty Four Elders of Zhsmaelim, were still after Luce. Daniel had glimpsed the Elders in the shadows cast by the Announcers just that morning. He had glimpsed something else, too—another darkness, a deeper cunning, one he hadn't recognized at first.

A shaft of sunlight punctured the clouds, and something gleamed in the corner of Daniel's vision. He turned and knelt down to find a single silver arrow planted in the wet sand. It was slimmer than a normal arrow, a dull silver color, laced with swirling etched designs. It was warm to the touch.

Daniel's breath caught in his throat. It had been eons since he'd seen a starshot. His fingers quaked as he gently drew it from the sand, careful to avoid its deadly blunt end.

Now Daniel knew where that other darkness had come from in this morning's Announcers. The news was even darker than he'd feared. He turned to Cam, the feather-light arrow balanced in his hands. "That predator wasn't acting alone."

Cam stiffened at the sight of the arrow. He moved towards it almost reverently, reaching out to touch it the same way Daniel had. They both knew it was incredibly rare. "Such a valuable weapon to leave behind. The Outcast must have been in a great hurry to get away."

The Outcasts: A sect of spineless, waffling angels, shunned by both Heaven and Hell. Their one great strength was the reclusive angel Azazel, one of the few remaining starsmiths, who still knew how to produce starshots. When loosed from its silver bow, a starshot could do little more than bruise a mortal. But to angels and demons, it was the deadliest weapon of all.

Everyone wanted them, but none were willing to associate with Outcasts, so bartering for starshots was always done clandestinely, via messengers. Which meant the guy Daniel had killed was no hit man sent by the Elders. He was merely a barterer. The Outcast, the real enemy, had spirited away—probably at the first sight of Daniel and Cam. Daniel shivered. This was not good news.

"We killed the wrong guy."

"How 'wrong?'" Cam brushed him off. "Isn't the world better off with one less predator? Isn't Luce?" He stared at Daniel, then the sea. "The only problem is—"

"The Outcasts."

Cam nodded. "So now they want her, too."

Daniel could feel the tips of his wings bristling under his cashmere sweater and heavy black coat, a burning itch that made him flinch. He stood still, with his eyes closed and his arms at his sides, straining to subdue himself before his wings burst forth like the violently unfurling sails of a ship, and carried him up and off this island and over the bay and away. Straight towards her.

He closed his eyes and tried to picture Luce. He'd had to tear himself away from that cabin, from her peaceful sleep on the tiny island east of Tybee. It would be evening there by now. Would she be awake? Would she be hungry?

The battle at Sword & Cross, the revelations, and the death of her friend—it had taken quite a toll on Luce. The angels expected her to sleep all day and through the night. But by tomorrow morning, they would need a plan in place.

This was the first time Daniel had ever proposed a truce. To set the boundaries, make the rules, and draw up a system of consequences if either side transgressed—it was a huge responsibility to shoulder with Cam. Of course he would do it, he would do anything for her . . . he just wanted to make sure he did it *right*.

"We have to hide her somewhere safe," he said. "There's a school up north, near Fort Bragg—"

"The Shoreline School." Cam nodded. "My side has looked into it as well. She'll be happy there. And educated in a way that won't endanger her. And, most importantly, she'll be shielded."

Gabbe had already explained to Daniel the type of camouflage Shoreline could provide. Soon enough, word would spread that Luce was hidden away there, but for a time at least, within the school's perimeter, she would be nearly invisible. Inside, Francesca, the angel closest to Gabbe, would look after Luce. Outside, Daniel and Cam would hunt down and kill anyone who dared draw near the school's boundaries.

Who would have told Cam about Shoreline? Daniel didn't like the idea of their side knowing more than his.

He was already cursing himself for not visiting the school before they made this choice, but it had been hard enough to leave Luce when he did.

"She can start as early as tomorrow . . . Assuming"— Cam's eyes ran over Daniel's face—"assuming you say yes."

He pressed a hand to the breast pocket of his shirt where he held a recent photograph. Luce on the lake at Sword & Cross. Wet hair shining. A rare grin on her face. Usually, by the time he had a chance to get a picture of her in one lifetime, he had lost her again. This time, she was still here. It was he who wasn't with her.

"Come on, Daniel," Cam was saying. "We both know what she needs. We enroll her—and then let her be. We can do nothing to hasten this part but leave her alone."

"I can't leave her alone that long." He'd tossed out the words too quickly. He looked down at the arrow in his hands, feeling ill. He wanted to fling it into the ocean but he couldn't.

"So." Cam squinted. "You haven't told her."

Daniel froze. "I can't tell her anything. We could lose her."

"*You* could lose her," Cam sneered.

"You know what I mean." Daniel stiffened. "It's too risky to assume she could take it all in without . . . "

He closed his eyes to banish the image of the agonizing red-hot blaze. But it was always burning at the back of his mind, threatening to spread like wildfire. If he told her the truth and killed her, this time she would *really* be gone. And it would be all his fault. Daniel couldn't do anything—he could not exist—without her. His wings burned at the thought. Better to shelter her just a little longer.

"How convenient for you," Cam muttered. "I just hope she isn't disappointed."

Daniel ignored him. "Do you really believe she'll be able to learn at this school without distraction?"

"I do," Cam answered slowly. "Assuming we agree she'll have no . . . external distractions. That means no Daniel, and no Cam. That has to be the cardinal rule."

Not see her for eighteen days? Daniel couldn't fathom it. More than that, he couldn't fathom Luce ever agreeing to it. They had only just found each other in this lifetime and finally had a chance at being together. And, as usual, explaining the details could kill her. She couldn't hear about her past lives from the mouths of angels. Luce didn't know it yet, but very soon, she would be on her own to figure out . . . everything.

The buried truth, specifically what Luce would think of it, terrified Daniel. But Luce uncovering it by herself was the only way out of this horrible cycle. This was why her experience at Shoreline was so crucial. For eighteen days, Daniel could wreck as many Outcasts who came his way. But when the truce was over, everything would be in Luce's hands again. Luce's hands alone.

The sun was setting over Mount Tamalpais and the evening fog was rolling in.

"Let me take her to Shoreline," Daniel said. It would be his last chance to see her.

Cam looked at him strangely, wondering whether to concede. A second time, Daniel had to physically force his aching wings back into his skin.

"Fine," Cam said at last. "In exchange for the starshot."

Daniel handed over the weapon, which Cam slipped inside his coat.

"Take her as far as the school and then find me. Don't screw up; I'll be watching."

"And then?"

"You and I have hunting to do."

Daniel nodded and unfurled his wings, feeling the deep pleasure of their release all through his body.

He stood for a moment, gathering energy, sensing the wind's rough resistance against his armor. Time to flee this cursed, ugly scene with Cam, to let his wings carry him back to a place where he could be his true self.

Back to Luce.

And back to the lie he would have to live a little while longer.

"The truce begins at midnight tomorrow," Daniel called, kicking back a great spray of sand on the beach as he bent his knees, lifted off, and soared across the sky.

LAUREN KATE grew up in Dallas, went to school in Atlanta, and started writing in New York. She now lives in Los Angeles with her husband and their dog. Her first book was *The Betrayal of Natalie Hargrove*. *Fallen* is the first book in a proposed quartet about Luce and Daniel.

Rosemary Clement-Moore

the splendour falls

A heroine who will steal your heart.
A house that will haunt you.
A love story that will leave you breathless.

OUT NOW
978 0 552 56135 8